Tutankhamun's

By

Fiona Deal

Text copyright 2012 Fiona Deal
All Rights Reserved

This is a work of fiction.
Names, characters, places and incidents
either are the product of the author's imagination
or are used fictitiously.

Chapter 1

Early summertime 2012

I looked from the newly discovered ancient papyrus to the expressions on the faces of my boyfriend Dan and my new soul mate Adam and couldn't help but be struck by the contrast. Dan's countenance was one of such raging scepticism he looked as if he might be auditioning for the role of arch-cynic in a theatrical farce. His dark and rather unruly eyebrows beetled so high they were in danger of merging with his hairline. Adam, on the other hand, wore a look of such rapt wonder I was put forcibly in mind of a little kid on Christmas Eve coming face to face with Santa. His blue eyes shone like sapphires, or perhaps it was amethysts. I'd noticed they seemed to change colour from deep blue to a kind of intense violet when he was excited. And I'd never seen him more so than he was right now.

Such was the variation in the reaction of the two men in my life to the slice of Pharaonic history resting snugly inside the silken lining of the antique suitcase sitting open on the table in front of us in Adam's tiny flat near the Souk in Luxor.

'You seriously expect me to believe these crusty old scrolls are priceless relics from Tutankhamun's tomb?' Dan derided, not altogether rudely, but with just enough acerbity to suggest he wasn't daft enough to accept it, even if we were.

'There can be no doubt about it,' Adam said thrillingly. The incredulity in his voice was equal to Dan's. But it was the joyous amazement of the "I don't believe my eyes" type, not the "you must be joking" sentiment so eloquently expressed by my boyfriend. 'Howard Carter himself discovered them on the night he opened Tutankhamun's tomb.'

'Then what the hell were they doing walled up in that other tomb where you found them tonight, instead of being on display in the Cairo Museum with all the other stuff?'

I zoned out for a moment. All I could do was stare at the crumbling papyrus scrolls in a kind of awed astonishment of my own. Like Adam, I knew they were genuine. And I knew exactly how and why they'd come to be separated from the other tomb contents, so they were still unknown to the world. I knew all of this because, impossibly, I'd been the one to stumble across the trail of clues that led us to their discovery.

I should point out at this stage I'm not an archaeologist. Nor am I an Egyptologist, nor indeed a historian of any sort. I'd certainly own up to being an Egypt-freak, a label Dan attached to me many years ago. But it's of the strictly amateur variety; lived out as an enthusiastic tourist, avid reader of Egyptological books - fact and fiction - and subscriber to the Discovery and National Geographic channels. So, one might reasonably ask how I'd been the one to find ancient documents that might just rock the world.

Well, it started when I got locked inadvertently in Howard Carter's house, now a museum, on my post-redundancy trip to Luxor a few weeks back. I accidentally smashed one of his watercolour paintings trying to escape and discovered a coded hieroglyphic message from Carter himself hidden inside the broken frame. It set me off on a quest to solve the puzzle of a lifetime.

It's a strange thing, when you've led a wholly unremarkable life such as mine, to be thrust suddenly into the midst of an adventure worthy of Lara Croft or Indiana Jones. In the last few weeks, I'd met and teamed up with Adam Tennyson, a kindred spirit and self-proclaimed "thwarted" Egyptologist, and his buddy Ahmed Abd el-Rassul from the local tourist police. Considering Ahmed is descended from a notorious family of local tomb robbers, he wears his police badge with a fair amount of irony and a healthy dose of humour.

Courtesy of Adam's encyclopaedic knowledge of ancient Egyptian history and Ahmed's ability to help us break and enter locked tombs, we'd been on a madcap sort of treasure hunt. It had culminated, this very night, with us cracking the last of Carter's clues, leading us to one of the most thrilling archaeological discoveries of all time.

So now, here we were, in possession of arguably the most incredible artefact ever to emerge from ancient Egypt. I was still pinching myself, daring myself to wake up and find it wasn't true. If I was imagining it, my resistance to bruising was truly remarkable. Probably, this was the find of the century – coming almost exactly ninety years after Howard Carter's discovery of Tutankhamun's tomb.

I gave myself a little mental shake, and tuned back into the conversation, just in time to hear Adam say, 'For all that he's the most famous pharaoh of them all, our knowledge of Tutankhamun and his time is really just a load of unanswered questions and blank spaces. These papyri could change all that.'

Adam is a good-looking man. It's fair to say it was the first thing I noticed about him when I met him at Hatshepsut's temple a few weeks ago. Right now, with the flush of excitement staining his tanned skin and the thrill of possibility shining in his eyes, he transcended handsome to become spellbinding and a bit film-star-ish. His glossy dark brown hair was tousled and full of tomb dust. He was slightly unshaven, the suggestion of stubble casting a dark shadow along his jawline. His chinos and cotton shirt were sweat-stained, streaked with grime and torn in places. I found myself gazing at him with something akin to the same awed fascination I'd felt contemplating the papyri a moment ago. The air around him seemed to sparkle and fizz with the energy he was radiating. I had to force myself to look away from his face and back at the papyri so I could concentrate on what he was saying. Even so, the intensity in his voice sent a shiver up my spine.

'It's highly ironic that Tutankhamun, in his lifetime, was one of the most insignificant kings in all of ancient Egyptian history,' he went on. 'Nowadays his fame is celebrated worldwide. Tut-mania has swept the globe. In less than a hundred years since Howard Carter discovered his tomb in 1922, he's shot from being a centuries-dead minor king to a cultural phenomenon. Yet we know almost nothing about him.'

Dan was still looking unconvinced. 'And you reckon these desiccating bits of parchment are going to change all that?'

Adam grinned at him; his optimism undimmed. 'Put it this way: I'm daring to hope.'

I sneaked a look at Dan's frowning features and suppressed a small smile at his inability to take the gloss off Adam's excitement. Adam is almost boyish in his enthusiasm for all things Egyptological. I figured it would take more than Dan's scowl to dent his spirits.

The professor re-joined us at this point. He'd been scouring Adam's flat to see if there were any sheets of glass handily lying about that we could use to protect the papyri so we could unroll them. It was a preservation technique he'd learned as a professor of philology at the Oriental Institute, Oxford.

It occurred to me that we made a rather unlikely foursome, Adam, Dan, the professor, and me. The professor, Edward – Ted – Kincaid was Adam's old university lecturer. He'd retired out to Cairo a few years back and was now in his early seventies. Adam and I had enlisted his help to decipher Howard Carter's mysterious hieroglyphics. Adam and Dan had met for the first time tonight and were sizing each other up. I think there was an extent to which I was looking at them both and doing the same.

'There's a couple of poster frames we could use,' Ted said, pushing his narrow-rimmed glasses back up his nose and staring at us a bit myopically. 'But what was it you were saying about Tutankhamun?'

Adam rubbed at his stubble with the back of his hand. 'Just that he's spawned whole industries in murder plots, archaeological conspiracy theories and occultist claims of a pharaoh's curse. Yet we know next to nothing about him. It seems to me there can't be many individuals who can achieve such celebrity status, his particular brand of fascination, and yet remain such a complete enigma.'

Dan cocked one eyebrow. 'Hmm, well, the sheer quantity of gold buried with him might have something to do with the fascination.' He sounded almost as jaded and world-weary as he looked. Although, to be fair, the bags under his eyes might have something to do with the fact that he'd spent the best part of yesterday travelling from England to get here.

'You're right,' Ted said, taking his words at face value and overlooking the rather astringent tone. 'The exquisite beauty and craftsmanship of the artefacts found in his tomb is staggering. I think the passage of time, more than three thousand years, is another part of our enthrallment. To think of him lying there in his silent tomb, surrounded by his fantastical grave goods, while the Greek and Roman empires rose and fell, while Jesus walked the earth, while America was discovered and later fought for independence, and while the British colonised the earth, is mind-boggling.'

We all stared at the papyri for a long moment trying to equate them to such an unimaginable passage of time.

'And perhaps some of what has us all so transfixed stems also from the mystery surrounding his life and death,' Adam said at last. 'Tutankhamun's life – like the lives of so many ancient Egyptians – is more speculation than established fact. We know he became pharaoh as a child of eight or nine, was married to a royal princess who was possibly his half-sister and died at roughly nineteen years old. He came to the throne after the infamous Akhenaten, the great heretic pharaoh, who was responsible for dramatic religious and social upheavals that shook ancient Egypt to the core. Tutankhamun is credited with restoring the traditional religious customs and ways of life, but, after a relatively uneventful reign of about ten years, he died. The circumstances of his death are unknown, but it seems he suffered a badly broken leg a few days before he died.'

'That's about it,' Ted agreed. 'The core facts about a young man whose beautiful face rendered in a solid gold death mask evokes such wonderment.

We gazed at the papyri, nestling in their silken surrounds inside Howard Carter's suitcase. It was impossible not to imagine if Tutankhamun himself might have handled the yellowed scrolls. I could feel myself succumbing to a bad case of the chills. All the little hairs on my forearms and across the nape of my neck were standing on end.

'Can we have a go at unrolling one?' I asked breathlessly.

A single glance at Adam and Ted was enough to show they shared my passionate eagerness.

Dan looked pointedly at his watch. 'It's nearly four o'clock in the morning,' he remarked. 'Can't it wait so we can all get some shuteye?' He scanned our faces and I realised the power of three lots of non-verbal communication. 'Ok, obviously not. Forgive me then if I crash out on the sofa for a while. It's been a long and trying day.'

Nobody raised any objections.

Adam helped Ted take the pair of poster frames apart so we could extract the large sheets of glass from each one. The papyrus scrolls were brittle and unbearably fragile. Terrified of causing damage, Adam slowly and carefully lifted the largest and strongest looking one out of Howard Carter's suitcase. Between them, he and Ted took an age to painstakingly unroll the first section and secure it between the two panes of glass. Dan was snoring rhythmically by the time they'd finished.

Ted bent over the glass-protected scroll. He had the kind of radiant glow about him I imagine a humble pilgrim might have stumbling across the Holy Grail. He spent a long time studying it in silence, then straightened and peered short-sightedly at Adam and me, belatedly pushing his glasses back up onto the bridge of his nose. 'The body of the papyrus is written in hieratic script, he said, then added for my benefit, 'that's an abbreviated, cursive – joined up – form of hieroglyphs. It allowed scribes to write quickly with their reed brushes without resorting to the time-consuming hieroglyphics. In general, hieratic was more important than hieroglyphs throughout Egypt's history, being the script used in daily life. It's usually pretty easy to read. But the ink here is very faded. I think it may take me a while to translate it.'

11

'Can you make out anything?' Adam asked, his bubbling impatience mirroring my own. 'Just enough to give us some idea what we have here?'

Ted bent forward again, so close to the poster frame his breath misted the glass. I watched a slow smile of scholarly delight spread across his features as he recognised something in the ancient scratchings. 'Well, what we have here at the top is a litany of royal titles belonging to Tutankhamun as pharaoh.' He proceeded, very slowly, to read them aloud, sending chills down my spine, as if he were invoking the dead king himself.

' *"Strong bull, fitting-of-created-forms. Dynamic-of-laws, who calms the Two Lands. He who propitiates all the gods. Great of the palace of Amun; Lord of all. The one who brings together the cosmic order. King of Upper and Lower Egypt. Nebkheperure, the lordly manifestation of Re. Tutankhamun, living image of Amun. May you reign immortal"*.'

I shivered. Adam's gaze locked with mine over the top of the professor's stooped back and we shared a moment of wonderment.

'My God, this is truly unreal. I must be dreaming,' Adam murmured, raking his hand in a distracted gesture through his dark hair. 'Merry, even if this turns out to be nothing more than a funerary text, it will still rate as one of the finds of the century.'

'No, it's not from the Amduat,' Ted said slowly, naming the ancient book of the underworld. 'In fact, there's something rather strange and confusing about it. It appears there's another royal stamp and cartouche at the end of this section.'

His words brought Adam and me quickly leaning forward over the framed papyrus.

'See here,' Ted pointed at the faded ink, where hieroglyphic symbols were written within a thick black oval. 'This is the cartouche of a pharaoh. But it is not Tutankhamun's. It reads "*Kheperkheperure*", which means everlasting are the manifestations of Re. And this script beneath it, here see, says "*it-netjer*" which reads as Father of the God.'

Adam's breath quickened alongside me. 'Those are the *nomen* and *prenomen* of pharaoh Ay,' he said in a strangled voice. I recognised the words as another way of referring to the royal titles of the anointed pharaohs. 'But that makes no sense! Ay didn't come to the throne until after Tutankhamun was dead. There was no co-regency between them. He only became pharaoh after he performed the opening of the mouth ceremony at Tutankhamun's funeral. How can it be possible for both their royal names to be recorded on the same document, sealed up within Tutankhamun's tomb?'

'A very good question, my boy,' said the professor. 'I need to make sense of the next passage. But it may take me some time. The ink is badly faded.'

'I think I need some air,' Adam murmured, disbelief and awe in his voice.

We left the professor poring over the ancient manuscript with the rapt concentration of a holy man handed a text containing the word of God.

I followed Adam outside onto his tiny balcony overlooking a narrow alleyway behind the Souk. We both took a moment to breathe in the velvety night air. It wrapped us in its warm embrace the moment we stepped out into the pre-dawn shadows. His hand reached for mine. We stood in a hallowed kind of silence for a long time, contemplating the staggering nature of our find.

'If those papyri end up casting new light on the most fascinating period of Pharaonic history of them all,' he murmured, 'then we'll need to dream up a pretty convincing story to explain to the world how we've come into possession of them. Preferably one that doesn't get us arrested for tomb robbery or murder.'

His words brought the events from earlier tonight spinning to the forefront of my mind again. It was an unavoidable fact that we'd – in a manner of speaking at least – broken into the tomb where we found the papyri.

And there'd been a point back there when we'd thought we might not escape with our lives.

This, in turn, called another recollection starkly back to mind. It pushed all thoughts of the papyri and any explanation we might offer the world into the shade for a moment. 'You asked me to remind you to kiss me,' I said softly.

I've never seen myself as a romantic heroine in a grand adventure. But tonight, I'd come close. Adam's words were branded on my memory, or my heart, or soul, or somewhere that seemed to matter. He'd said, "Merry, if we get out of this tomb alive, will you please remind me to kiss you? It's something I've wanted to do very badly almost from the day I met you. Your boyfriend will just have to understand". '

Now he cast me a quick agonised look. 'Merry, there's nothing in the world I want more than to kiss you. But Dan...'

I cut across him, 'You said Dan would just have to understand.'

'Yes, but that was when I imagined him safely tucked up back at home in England. It feels a bit disrespectful now he's here in Egypt; fast asleep in the very next room.'

I had to concede this. Neither of us had expected Dan's precipitous arrival tonight. He'd materialised in the depths of that ancient tomb shaft just at the opportune moment like the proverbial genie from a bottle.

I'm sure Adam and I would have managed perfectly adequately to deal with the Arabic scoundrel holding us at knifepoint. But I daresay Dan's arrival brought matters to a head.

I reached up and pressed a soft, sweet kiss against Adam's lips. 'It'll keep,' I promised him.

His face reflected anguish and passion, but he held himself rigidly in check, and I adored him all the more for it. I'd known Adam for a few short weeks, whereas Dan and I had been together for ten whole years. But these last weeks had been the most adventuresome of my life. I don't think it's exaggerating the point to say I'd recognised Adam as a soul mate from the start. But to be truthful, I think at the beginning it was more to do with our shared passion for ancient Egypt than any suggestion of shared passion between the two of us. All that had changed tonight. I guess there's something about being held at knifepoint that focuses the mind somewhat.

Things had moved pretty quickly since we finally decoded the last of Howard Carter's mysterious clues yesterday. One minute Adam and I were staking out a spot in the cliffs behind the Valley of the Kings at dead of night, ready to explore an ancient tomb shaft – handily unlocked for us by our chum Ahmed. (He was willing to view our nocturnal excavations as archaeological rather than strictly illegal.) The next we were fighting for our lives against an unknown villainous Arab who'd followed us there, instinctively scenting buried treasure, and willing to murder us for it. His disappointment, faced with the ancient papyrus scrolls instead of the expected gleam of gold was one of the high points of the night.

I doubted the rest of the world would take quite such a prosaic view of it. Which brought me back to Adam's point about thinking up a convincing story to tell. It was only now beginning to dawn on me quite what a quandary we were in.

Before I could pursue our options, a sudden hammering on his front door interrupted us. We both started violently and cast panicky glances into each other's eyes. Adam darted back through the sliding doors, with me hot on his heels. I spied Dan jerking sleepily from his stupor on Adam's sofa as we sped past.

I'm not sure whom we feared might be standing on the doorstep outside Adam's flat, but my relief was heartfelt when Ahmed fell through the entrance as Adam swung back the door. He instantly filled the small room with his bulk, a rotund uniformed giant in a black-and-gold tourist police uniform.

'I fix'ed it,' he announced with pride, lurching upright. I'm thinking of re-naming Ahmed 'Mr Fix-It'. It's definitely his favourite expression. 'Dat man who broked his neck in de Valley, he is now at de mortuary. His death will be recorded as an accident. I said I catched him trying to break into a tomb.'

It brought another part of our night-time jaunts flooding back. The awful truth was a man was dead. That he was the double-dyed villain who'd so ruthlessly held us at knifepoint was perhaps the reason I was struggling to care about his sad demise. But the sight of his inert body, head twisted back at an improbable angle, where he'd fallen from the cliffs onto the Valley floor was one I felt might haunt my dreams from now on. Perhaps it accounted for my reluctance to go to sleep, despite the improbable hour. None of us was guilty of his sudden departure from this mortal coil. He'd bolted out of the tomb with both Adam and Dan in hot pursuit. Then, attempting to scale the shingly Valley slopes, his foot caught in the folds of his galabeya robe, and he'd plunged to his death. Dan, Adam and Ahmed, all witnessing the tragedy, were powerless to prevent it.

'No one suspects you were dere,' Ahmed announced with satisfaction. He advanced into the room and lowered his impressive bulk into Adam's single armchair. 'So, you must tell to me now. What did you find in de tomb? What did you carry away in dat suitcase?'

Adam and I followed him into the room and sank onto the floor. There was nowhere else to sit. Dan was sprawled across the sofa, emerging blearily from sleep. While not of

Ahmed's stature, Dan is a big bloke. So, between them, he and Ahmed did a pretty solid job of taking up all the available seating space.

All our gazes swung in the direction of the professor sitting wedged behind the small dining table in the corner of Adam's compact living room. He was intent on his labour of love, poring reverently over our find. Ted is a dapper little silver-haired gentleman, usually immaculately attired. It suddenly struck me how incongruous he looked sitting there in his neat white vest, with a set of narrow glasses perched on the end of his nose. His lack of a shirt over his underwear was a further testament to the night's misadventures. We'd torn it up earlier into makeshift bandages to stem the flow of blood oozing from Adam's upper arm where he'd flung himself bodily at the knife-wielding Arab.

The professor's arrival in the tomb shaft just at the moment of discovery was perhaps even more astonishing than Dan's a few minutes later. It had really started to feel quite crowded down there in the stifling blackness of the narrow stone tunnel for a while.

The unimaginable part of tonight's events was Ted being the one to lead the murderous Arab to us. Inconceivably, the dead man was Ted's Egyptian son-in-law. It seemed he'd charmed Ted's daughter into marrying him before showing his true colours. Scenting buried treasure; he'd taken his wife hostage, put her under a kind of house arrest in Cairo and bent the professor to his will with threats to her safety.

Ted's relief at his son-in-law's demise was palpable. Even so, I think it's fair to say he hadn't given it a second thought since he saw the evidence of the man's broken neck with his own eyes. His worshipful absorption in the papyri was absolute. While Ahmed stayed behind in the Valley to deal with the dead body and cover our tracks, the rest of us trooped back here to Adam's flat carrying the priceless cargo in Carter's dusty 1930s style suitcase. We'd agreed to foster a plan to rescue Ted's daughter once Ahmed re-joined us.

'Papyrus?' Ahmed asked in amazement. 'You finded papyrus?' His mouth fell inelegantly open, revealing a set of teeth any self-respecting dentist would kill to get his hands on. He snapped it shut again and stared.

Adam leaned forward on the floor alongside me, resting his bandaged arm across his drawn-up knees. 'Yup; from Tutankhamun's tomb, no less. It was the one thing Howard Carter famously said he longed to find.' The thread of excitement in his voice was unmistakeable. 'His tragedy was that - in truth - he did find it, on an unauthorised nocturnal visit he and Lord Carnarvon paid to the tomb on the night of its discovery in November 1922. They took the papyrus from the tomb, meaning to return it in due course, after they'd had a chance to have a good look at it.'

'Carnarvon took it home to England with him in secret,' I interjected, desperate to share in telling the tale. 'He wanted to study it over Christmas. He came back to Egypt in the New Year without it, thinking he had all the time in the world. He promptly succumbed to an infected mosquito bite and inconveniently died. Carnarvon's widow inexplicably refused to give the papyrus back to Carter until the last possible moment, ten years later, after he'd finished clearing Tutankhamun's tomb. Of course, by then, it was impossible for Carter to return it to the tomb or to account for it.'

Adam took up the tale. 'Not able to admit how he came into possession of the papyrus without owning up to the dead-of-night visit when he and Carnarvon misappropriated it, Carter bricked it up inside an abandoned tomb shaft in the Valley. He left his mysterious message inside the frame of one of his watercolour paintings. Merry stumbled across them when she got locked in Howard Carter's Museum. So, the papyri have remained hidden for eighty years ... until tonight.'

We all stared with a kind of rapt fixation at the semi-unrolled papyrus scroll on Adam's dining room table, under its protective sheet of glass.

'Have you been able to make any more sense of it?' I asked Ted. 'Is it a funerary text after all?'

'I think not,' Ted said slowly, looking up at us. His face shone with an almost religious fervour. 'I think it's a letter.'

We all gaped at him.

'From Tutankhamun?' Adam asked.

'No, I think it is a letter *to* Tutankhamun. Impossibly, it seems to be from the Pharaoh Ay, who succeeded Tutankhamun, coming to the throne after his death. Listen, I've made a start on translating this first passage.'

I shivered but found it impossible to tear my gaze away from the professor's face as he stared intently at the script before him, translating as he read.

' " *Nebkheperure Tutankhamun, I write to you as your humble servant Kheperkheperure Ay, having ascended to the throne of the Two Lands in your place.*" '

Adam jumped to his feet and went to peer over the professor's shoulder. I scrambled up off the floor and joined him. We stared in silent fascination while Ted bent over the faded text. His forefinger hovered slowly over the pane of glass as word-by-word he made sense of the ancient language.

' "*May the hot breath of the immortals burn my heart for disturbing the heavenly paradise of my everlasting lord.*"'

It was as if the voice of the long dead pharaoh reached across more than three thousand years of history to echo in the airwaves around us. Adam and I stared, awestruck, into each other's eyes. Forgetful of Dan sitting less than half a dozen paces away, his hand reached for mine.

'So, he's writing to Tutankhamun posthumously?' I croaked, groping towards the only possible conclusion.

'It seems so.' Ted leaned forward again, and slow minutes ticked past while he tried to make sense of the next passage. The rest of us were held fast in a kind of living freeze-frame, as if waiting for the professor's voice to release the pause button. It really was the most unnerving experience. But I don't believe any of us could have spoken during those long minutes had the sunrise depended on it. I think we all shared the same ghostly sense of the ancient pharaoh materialising spectrally in the room with us.

There was no room for Ahmed and Dan to squeeze into the cramped space around the table, but I could tell they were gripped. Even Dan was sitting forward, looking intently at the professor's finger moving slowly across the glass pane. We were collectively holding our breath, as if cast under some sacred spell only the professor's next words held the power to release.

' "Others have come before me to intrude upon my lord's pleasure in the field of reeds. Please know, immortal one, that I, your earthly successor, Ay, everlasting manifestation of Re, have severely punished these evil trespassers. Anubis has weighed their hearts and Ammit has devoured their souls."'

'My God,' Adam breathed alongside me on a note of enlightenment. 'I think he's referring to ancient tomb robbers. Howard Carter always believed tomb robbers broke into Tutankhamun's tomb shortly after his burial, possibly the self-same men who helped carve it. There was evidence in the way the entrance passageway was refilled, and the tomb re-sealed with the necropolis stamp. Ay would have been on the throne at the time. It doesn't sound like he showed them much mercy, does it?'

I knew enough about ancient Egyptian mythology to know about the weighing of the heart ceremony; where Anubis, the jackal-headed god of the afterlife weighed a dead man's heart on a set of scales against the feather of truth. If the scales balanced, the deceased was deemed worthy to enter the underworld. If not, his heart was tossed to Ammit, the devourer, whose body was a terrifying amalgam of the three largest man-eating animals known to the ancient Egyptians: lion, hippopotamus and crocodile. Tomb robbers, caught red handed, really didn't stand a chance.

The professor translated the next section. ' "*I take this opportunity, immortal king, to set your imperishable soul once more at rest.*"'

'That's nice,' I whispered. 'A kind of apology and benediction all rolled up together.'

But the professor had only paused for breath. Each word in the next passage emerged in a slow and steady intonation, seemingly weighed down with a mythical and ancient importance. ' *"And I write to re-swear to you, oh imperishable one, my everlasting oath. I tell you this. That which was hidden by us remains hidden. Ma'at, the goddess of truth and justice, preserves our secret, so none may know of it. No man may gaze upon the golden images. None may touch the sacred shrines. Our shared and precious jewels shall persevere throughout all eternity".'*

Chapter 2

It was Dan who broke the awesome sense of prophecy – or perhaps it was destiny – holding us all spellbound.

'Meredith, please don't tell me you're about to embark on another treasure hunt. I don't think my nerves could stand it.'

It effectively sliced through the infinity-laden atmosphere, bringing us all crashing back into the twenty-first century. The spectral presence of the ancient pharaoh vanished into thin air. We stared at each other.

Dawn was fingering its way between the slats of the Venetian blind at the window and pressing in through the glass door from Adam's tiny balcony. Nearby the muezzin started its tuneless droning chant, blaring out from the frilly minaret, calling faithful Muslims to prayer. The noise, heat and light of modern Egypt joined my boyfriend in sweeping away the last vestiges of eternity from the papyrus.

It was Adam who recovered himself first. 'I think this is treasure enough,' he said shakily. 'My God! Think of it! We've found papyrus from the tomb of Tutankhamun, including a letter from Ay. It's mind-blowing. And that's just the start! There are two more scrolls in that suitcase. It's the most earth-shattering find since Carter first lit a candle and peered through the hole he'd made in the sealed-up entrance to the tomb.'

I met his eyes, knowing we were both wondering how on earth we were going to concoct a story persuasive enough to satisfy the world about how we found it.

'Adam, what the hell are we going to do with it?' I breathed, daring to ask the question we were both thinking aloud.

'I should think that's perfectly obvious, isn't it?' Dan cut sharply across us. 'Surely you do what I begged you to do with the dratted hieroglyphics that started all this. You take that antique-looking suitcase and all its improbable contents to the authorities and...'

'No, no, no.' Ahmed leaned forward anxiously, the armchair creaking ominously beneath his weight. 'Dey must not do dat!'

'Why on earth not?' Dan turned his incredulous stare on our police chum, as if he couldn't believe his ears hearing the voice of dissent coming from a uniformed representative of said authorities.

'Dat man who broked his neck tonight in de Valley!' Ahmed explained urgently. 'Dere was not on his body any signs to identify him. But dere will be an investigation. You must not bring on yourselves attention!' He sent Adam a look of naked appeal, as if his English was frustratingly inadequate to the task of explaining the trouble we'd find ourselves in.

But I think we'd all grasped it. Adam spelled it out, just in case. 'If we turn up with a priceless relic from King Tut's tomb hard on the heels of a dead body turning up in the Valley of the Kings, all hell will break loose.'

'Even without the dead body, it was always going to be a bit touch and go,' I remarked. 'I mean, just what are we supposed to tell the authorities about how we come to be inside that locked tomb?'

Dan glared at me. 'Good God woman! You leave it until now to ask that question? I've been banging my head against a brick wall trying to get you to face it from the start. First you stole a scrap of paper from Howard Carter's house. Then you wilfully tampered with private property to misappropriate his next hidden message. And last night you coerced an officer of the law into unlocking a barred tomb for you. You're hardly innocent and blameless in all this, are you?'

I cast a guilt-tinged glance at Adam, my partner in all these crimes bar one. Drawing strength from the way his blue eyes locked with mine, I re-focused on Dan's frowning face and launched into an impassioned defence. 'No one was meant to get hurt! How was I supposed to know Ted's barbaric son-in-law would try to muscle in on the act, and wind up dead?' I darted a quick glance at the professor, realising my words lacked something in the way of sensitivity. But he was poring over the papyrus again, oblivious to everything and everyone. So, I turned back to Dan and continued my energetic objections, contradicting my earlier misgivings with aplomb. 'If he hadn't turned up wielding his flippin' great knife, there's a chance we could have come up with a convincing story to tell the world.'

'Where is de knife now?' Ahmed cut across me, as if struck by a vicious thought delivered on the end of a club. I could see in his expression he was having visions of fingerprints and other forensic police procedures; terrified he might not have fixed it for us after all.

'It's alright, mate,' Adam soothed. 'It's over there.' He pointed at a shelf near the door. 'We brought it back with us, together with Ted's little jack-knife, from the Valley.'

Ahmed's sigh of relief left him in a great whoosh of sucked in air. 'I will toss it into de Nile later,' he vowed. 'Just to be sure.'

I returned to my heated defence, as if he hadn't interrupted me. 'Up until the point Ahmed helped us break into the tomb, I don't think we did anything strictly illegal. All we were doing tonight was trying to discover what it was Carter hid in the tomb shaft, and whether it was still there. We never had any intention of making off with it; at least, not permanently. But we'd have looked a right pair of idiots if we'd notified the authorities in advance and then come away empty handed. Now we've discovered the papyri, of course we've got to hand them over to the Supreme Council for Antiquities or whoever it is controls such things these days.'

'But not yet,' Adam put in firmly. 'Not until we've let some dust settle on tonight's events. We need to ensure there's no way anyone can link us to the mysterious death in the Valley. It allows us time to come up with a plausible tale to tell the world.'

I glanced across at him, knowing him well enough by now to pick up on what he wasn't saying. Although I'm quite sure it didn't take a psychic to work it out. Adam's eyes blazed with an Egyptological fervour to rival the professor's. He was as committed as the rest of us to ensuring the papyri found their rightful place into the history books. But he wanted to know what was in the old scrolls first.

'Yes, yes,' Ahmed was nodding furiously.

'You're right,' I said, reassured by their arguments. And let's face it; my eagerness to buy us more translation time was no less fervent for my being an Egyptologist of the strictly amateur variety. Now we'd started to learn the intriguing contents of the scroll, I was like an addict desperate for the next fix. All that tantalising stuff about golden images, sacred shrines and precious jewels; I mean, it would take a saint not to wonder. Saintliness is not a conspicuous part of my personality, at least not that I've noticed. And we'd only heard the very first section of a much longer scroll. Who could say what revelations it might contain? Dan gibed about treasure hunts, but wasn't the thirst for knowledge exactly that? Having spent the last few weeks of my life on this quest and considering the papyri had been bricked up in a wall for eighty years, I failed to see how a few more days, or even weeks, could possibly matter. And the voice rising up from the scroll hadn't spoken for more than three thousand years. The world wasn't exactly clamouring to hear what he had to say. Admittedly this was the result of blissful ignorance rather than a lack of interest. But the fundamental point remained the same. The world could wait. I figured all our sleuthing deserved a little reward. We'd surely earned the right to a few days' exclusivity. Conscience quieted, I nodded to reaffirm my stance.

'So, we're all agreed?' Adam looked around for confirmation. 'We're not taking the papyri with us to Cairo? We're not handing them over to the Egyptian Ministry for Antiquities when we go to rescue Ted's daughter?'

'Hang on, hang on!' Dan interjected. 'Who said anything about going to Cairo? Surely rescuing Ted's daughter is a job for the police!' And he looked meaningfully at Ahmed.

'No, no! Yes, yes – no... I mean...' Poor old Ahmed; in his agitation he quite clearly didn't know what he meant. He gathered his wits and fixed Dan with a ferocious glare, black eyes snapping. 'I, de police; yes. But Cairo de police; no.'

31

Dan stared perplexedly at him for a moment, trying to make sense of this impenetrable and contradictory statement. Then his brows drew together in a fierce frown, and he opened his mouth to argue. Adam forestalled him.

'I think Ahmed's worried if we involve the Cairo police, they'll make the link between Jessica and the dead body found in the Valley of the Kings. He was her husband, after all. But perhaps if we can free her ourselves, all that can be avoided, and we can get back to normal.'

Dan rolled his eyes. 'I fail to see anything normal about any of this.'

'Dan!' I objected. "There's no need to be rude!'

He turned his rather forbidding gaze on me again. 'And you intend to be part of this rescue party, Meredith, do you?' I can always tell when I'm out of favour with Dan by his use of my full name. Usually he calls me Pinkie; a nickname he fondly imagines is cute. Evidently, I was in his bad books, but I was used to his bluster; so I ignored his acidic tone of voice and arctic facial expression in favour of answering his question at face value.

'Yes. It's my fault she's locked up in the first place. It's because Ted was helping us translate the hieroglyphics; and Youssef – that's Ted's son-in-law – got wind of it.'

Ted had looked up at Adam's mention of his daughter a moment ago; quietly following our debate. Now he spoke up. 'Adam, Merry,' he looked at us in turn, 'I sincerely thank you for your willingness to help me in this. But I've placed you in enough danger already. I'm sure if Ahmed here is prepared to accompany me back to Cairo, then, between the two of us, we can somehow secure Jessica's release. Youssef's brother is the one holding her captive. He's under instructions not to let her go until Youssef returns. Since Youssef is now in a place from which there *is* no return, I'll be extremely grateful for the police escort. But I really don't want to drag the rest of you into a hazardous and potentially violent situation.'

Dan's wholehearted approval of this speech was evident in the triumphant look he shot me. 'Good,' he said. 'That means I can see about booking us onto a flight home.'

'No deal!' I said emphatically. 'Ted, of course we're coming with you.' I'm not sure if it was the mention of violence that made up my mind or Dan's determination to bully and harangue, and in all other ways live my life for me. Don't get me wrong; I'm no lover of danger – the opposite, in fact - but I couldn't, in all conscience, let Ted and Ahmed run all the risks. After all, it was me who started all this by finding the 'dratted' – Dan's word – hieroglyphics. And, though I'm sure Dan's peremptory desire to remove me from the situation was well intentioned in the small matter of my wellbeing, it was also as annoying as hell. So I loaded some additional weight to my position, adding, 'Surely there's more chance of success if we go mob handed.'

'Agreed,' Adam said firmly. 'It's my fault you've been mixed up in it, Ted. It was me who suggested to Merry you could help us translate Carter's clues.'

'No, no, de blame it is mine,' Ahmed assured us earnestly. 'I should not have let you enter de tomb tonight without standing guard outside.'

Dan raised his eyes to the ceiling, 'Ok, you've made your point,' he muttered. 'You're all in it together, and you're all equally culpable.'

I could see Ted was wavering, touched by our solidarity and wanting to be persuaded. 'But what about the papyri?' he ventured. 'They're too fragile to make the journey with us. And too precious to leave unguarded. Someone needs to stay behind to protect them.'

'First it was the damned hieroglyphics! Now it's the cursed papyrus!' Dan's soft growl was addressed to no one in particular. 'Just what is it about this ancient stuff that has you all so transfixed? I mean; the pharaoh characters in that disintegrating scroll over there have been dead for thousands of years. All your devoted and obsessive concern isn't going to bring them back. So why do you care so much?'

Four incredulous sets of eyes swung towards him revealing varying degrees of the self-same incomprehension he'd just expressed.

Adam nearly choked out his words. 'For an Egyptologist, it's like finding the pot of gold at the end of the rainbow. It's a chance to illuminate a period of antiquity shrouded in mystery. It's … it's … well, it's like coming face to face with a slice of eternity. The ancient Egyptian civilisation was the most sophisticated on earth. But after ruling supreme for almost thirty centuries – a mind-numbing passage of time - it crumbled into the sand and was lost under successive layers of Greek, Roman and Arabic culture. A find like these papyri could bring to light new evidence about a chapter of history we thought vanished forever.'

Dan looked a bit discomfited by Adam's unabashed emotion. He cleared his throat. 'Ok, I guess I can see some merit in adding to the historical record, the thirst for knowledge, and all that. But guys, I think you need a reality check. Some Arabic ruffian is holding Ted's daughter hostage up in Cairo. Tonight, I arrived on the scene to find the ruffian's even more thuggish brother holding you all at knifepoint…' (This wasn't strictly true. Adam had successfully divested the Arabic thug of his knife before Dan metamorphosed in the tomb; but Dan was on a roll, so I didn't interrupt him to set the record straight.) '…So, the papyrus may be thrilling, but it seems to me those scrolls are also attracting the attention of as unsavoury a bunch of characters as you'd ever want to meet. So, while I can perhaps understand your reluctance to hand them over to the authorities at the risk of linking yourselves with the dead body in the Valley of the Kings, you've still got some way to go to convince me that the right thing to do is to hang on to them. People are clearly willing to kill for them. I simply can't see that it's worth it.'

'So, what would you have us do instead?' I asked.

He gave one of his maddening shrugs. 'There's a museum here in Luxor, isn't there? From what I remember it's packed to the rafters with ancient Egyptian artefacts. Surely you could make an anonymous donation of the scrolls; I don't know how – perhaps post them to the museum or something? There must be historians or Egyptologists working there who'd recognise them for what it are and treat them with the reverence you all seem to think they deserve!'

I don't think Dan is a Philistine. But sometimes he gets awfully close.

'But Dan, this is the find of the century,' I appealed. 'All we're suggesting is to hang onto it for long enough to know what it says.'

'Convince me,' he said implacably. 'Convince me there's something in those faded scratchings worth risking life and limb for.'

All of our gazes were fixed on his face, and I knew each of the four of us, Adam, Ahmed, Ted and myself, would willingly risk – well, not life exactly, but certainly a bit of physical jeopardy - to know what it contained. We were hell-bent on the dual purpose of rescuing Ted's daughter whilst also hanging onto the papyrus for dear life – temporarily, of course. To give Ted the chance to translate it was to give him the opportunity to fulfil the dream of a lifetime. Only Dan seemed to view our twin objectives as mutually exclusive.

Adam met Dan's eyes in an unblinking stare that was a gentle challenge. 'If you think any of us would willingly expose ourselves or each other to danger,' he said softly, 'you're wrong. Speaking for myself, I can honestly say the safety of the people in this room matters more to me than anything; certainly, more than all the treasure in Tutankhamun's tomb.'

I didn't dare look at Dan while Adam said this; couldn't, in fact. My gaze was glued to Adam's face, my insides oddly marshmallow-like in consistency. I recognised a gauntlet being thrown down when I saw one.

'But those Arabic rogues weren't after papyri,' Adam went on. 'They wanted gold. So, I don't think Jessica's captor will have much of an incentive to hang on to her once he learns there isn't any. At least, I hope not.'

It was a bit of a shame he added this qualification on the end. I'd been daring to believe him up until that point. I darted a glance at Dan's face and found him pressing his lips together.

'So, now, let me tell you what these faded scratchings might contain that sets the rest of us on fire...' Adam paused for a moment, as if marshalling his thoughts, trying to decide how best to get across to Dan the electrifying possibilities held out by the first papyrus. 'Any discovery from the ancient world is like a miracle,' he said at length, 'but there's something especially magical about this one. It has the potential to shed light on the most extraordinary period of ancient Egyptian history of all. The Amarna years.'

His words sent another chill down my spine. 'The pharaohs of the sun,' I breathed.

'Some might call it the Amarna heresy,' Ted put in.

'Heresy?' Dan queried sceptically, suffering none of my susceptibility to chills. He wasn't scoffing, exactly, but there was a definite tilt to one eyebrow.

'It describes a period of dramatic upheaval towards the end of the 18th Dynasty in the New Kingdom,' Adam explained. 'It was the most powerful Dynasty of all – the golden age of the pharaohs. Egypt was the mightiest nation on earth. Its pharaoh literally ruled the world. Then along came the most enigmatic pharaoh of them all. Some have described him as the first individual in history. He changed his name from Amenhotep IV to Akhenaten and proceeded to turn everything on its head.'

Ahmed sat forward in his chair; eyes fixed on Adam's face. Nobody loves a good story as much as Ahmed.

'First, he built a completely new capital city, a place called Akhet-Aten, the Horizon of the Sun. He uprooted the court and some of the populace from ancient Thebes, the religious capital of ancient Egypt, and relocated them to his new city – a barren wasteland of a place mid-way between modern Luxor and Cairo, now called Amarna. Then he transformed the artwork, ordering his sculptors and artisans to ditch the traditional, stiffly posed depictions of the pharaohs, which emphasised their strength, youth and masculinity. Instead, he had them carve or paint him with grotesque physical deformities, an elongated head, wide hips, a distended belly; huge rounded thighs. But, most controversial of all, he led a religious revolution. Some claim him as the first monotheist; a forerunner of Moses.'

'A few of the more radical historians believe he *was* Moses,' Ted added as an aside.

'Far-fetched, but intriguing,' Adam smiled, and continued with his narrative. 'He abandoned the pantheon of Egyptian gods, closed their temples and shrines, and banned their worship. Instead, he elevated a single god, the Aten or sun disc, to become the one true god. It seems he made himself a kind of high priest of the Aten cult. This meant he alone could commune with the god. He set himself up as the god's sole representative on earth, and demanded the people worship through him.'

'Some historians view him as a fanatical, intolerant egomaniac,' Ted said. 'Others see him as enlightened and inspired; but born before his time.'

'The truth is, we simply don't know.' Adam concluded. 'After his death, Akhenaten was known as the great heretic. Later pharaohs sought to obliterate all memory of him, tearing down his temples and statues, chiselling out his name from the monuments, and omitting him from the king-lists. But the true facts elude us. All we have are a very few historical records and a few tantalising clues. Egyptologists have taken these small shreds of evidence and woven enough theory and conjecture around them to fill volumes. It's the most intriguing period of all, precisely because so little is known about it. We have very few hard facts to go on. It's a period that includes some of the most famous names to emerge from antiquity: Nefertiti, Akhenaten; and Tutankhamun himself. Tutankhamun was the pharaoh who led the restoration, coming to the throne shortly after Akhenaten. Yet, despite the discovery of his virtually intact tomb by Howard Carter, still we know next to nothing about him. He's credited with re-opening the temples and restoring the worship of the traditional pantheon of gods. He even changed his name. He was originally called Tutankh-Aten, to reflect the worship of the solar disc. But that's about it. The rest is pure speculation.'

'But that could be all about to change,' I murmured; and the shiver snaked down my spine again as I glanced at the three-thousand-year-old papyrus sitting on Adam's small table.

'And Ay?' Ahmed asked. 'De one in de papyrus and who writed de letter. Who is he?'

'Again, no one knows for sure. Many Egyptologists believe him to be Nefertiti's father. Nefertiti was Akhenaten's great royal wife, famous as one of the most beautiful women in history. It's also possible she was Akhenaten's cousin. Ay's sister was most likely Queen Tiye, famous throughout history as being a commoner elevated to the status of great royal wife when she married the great pharaoh Amenhotep III. They were Akhenaten's parents. So, Ay would have been Akhenaten's uncle and father-in-law. What's certain is Ay was the principal vizier, a kind of prime minister, under Akhenaten. And many believe he was the power behind the throne during Tutankhamun's reign. Tutankhamun was only a child, after all. What's mysterious about Ay is whether or not he believed in Akhenaten's religious revolution. He certainly stayed loyal to his king while Akhenaten outlawed the Egyptian pantheon and instituted the monotheistic worship of the sun disc god, the Aten. But whether he went along with his nephew's monotheism out of genuine religious conviction, or whether it was simply political convenience is less clear. The fact that Ay helped lead Egypt's return to the old pantheon after Akhenaten's death might imply his religious convictions were more politically than spiritually motivated. In the opinion of some historians, Ay was simply a shrewd politician who knew how to follow the undercurrents of society and affairs of state in order to elevate his own status and power. And, of course, it worked. Ay came to the throne on Tutankhamun's death. But he was an old man by then, only ruling for about four years, before dying himself.'

'And during those four years, he found the time to sit down and compose that lengthy scroll; addressing himself to the boy pharaoh who pre-deceased him,' Dan said dubiously. 'It's rather eccentric behaviour, isn't it?'

'Eccentric, yes,' Ted agreed. 'But intriguing, don't you think? Especially since he seems to address Tutankhamun with such reverence. There's a mystery in these scrolls, don't you agree? It sounds like Ay and Tutankhamen shared a secret and colluded in hiding something. What it was, and who they were hiding it from may or may not be revealed to us as we read on.'

Adam's expression reflected the same sense of wonderment. 'Perhaps we'll find out for sure whether Tutankhamun died of natural causes or whether there was some villainy at play.'

I turned shining eyes on Dan's face. 'Now can you see why we're so excited? We have a chance to solve one of the most riveting mysteries of all time.'

Chapter 3

'I must be mad,' Dan grumbled a bit later on.

The two of us had returned to the Jolie Ville hotel, just outside Luxor. I'd been staying here for the duration of my adventures in Egypt. Dan had flown in last night, stashing his luggage in the storage room behind the reception desk while he came in search of me. We'd brought the papyrus back to the hotel with us, safely rolled up again with the others in the 1920s suitcase.

'You're the obvious person to look after it while the rest of us go to Cairo,' I assured him.

'Great;' he muttered, 'baby-sitter to some three-thousand-year-old giant toilet rolls. Lucky me! It might not be so bad if I could read that weird squiggly writing they're covered in. At least then I could steal a march on you and find out what comes next. But, as it is, all I can do is keep them locked up and away from the prying eyes of the housekeeping staff.'

'It won't be for long,' I cajoled him cheerfully. 'Adam's booking us onto a flight to Cairo this afternoon. All being well, we'll be back tomorrow – the next day at the very latest. All you've got to do between now and then is kick back, relax and enjoy the wall-to-wall sunshine.'

We were lounging on a pair of sunbeds in the shade on the small terrace outside my hotel room. Dan would be taking it over for tonight. Adam had promised to call on my mobile as soon as he'd made our flight reservations. In the meantime, we'd all gone our separate ways to shower and recover from the night's exertions.

Adam and I had shared a long look on parting, loaded with enough unspoken vocabulary to fill volumes. It was thoroughly disorientating being back here at the hotel with Dan. A scant month ago we'd arrived here together, as a couple on a tourist holiday. With everything that had happened since, being a simple tourist on holiday with my boyfriend was the furthest thing from the reality of my presence here now.

Somehow, I felt myself to be woven into the fabric of this magical and mystical Egypt; this fabled land of the Pharaohs. It's fair to say it got under my skin the very first time I visited, years ago; spawning my enduring fascination with its ancient history and the lost civilisation that literally disappeared into the sands of time, only to emerge again so tantalisingly. But now I felt myself to be inextricably linked to the very essence of the place. It was in my soul, and, in turn, it had welcomed me to its shimmering, scintillating, golden landscape as if I'd always belonged. My spiritual home was here in this dry, barren, rather inhospitable country with its pounding heat, vigorous blue sky and infuriating flies; not in the gentle, leafy landscape of the garden-of-England back home in Kent. Egypt's colours are dry and sun-bleached; the narrow strip of greenery bordering the Nile perpetually coated in a delicate layer of sand-blown dust that makes it appear like a landscape viewed through a filmy lens of the type favoured by romantic photographers. To me, it's the most beautiful landscape on earth; majestic, timeless, evocative, with the shifting, dark, seemingly endless waters of the Nile snaking through it as they've done for millennia.

It's fair to say every day for the last four weeks I'd woken with a sense of profound wellbeing, thinking to myself, 'here I am, where I am meant to be'. But I daresay my affinity with this place, in the last couple of weeks in particular, had at least as much to do with my cameo role in the drama of ancient Egyptian history, as in my love of the eternal landscape. Egypt was offering up its secrets to me: first with Howard Carter's tantalising hieroglyphics, and now with the discovery of the ancient papyri.

So perhaps this accounted for my inability to view myself any longer as a tourist. Which left hanging the bit about being here as part of a couple with Dan.

I glanced across at him, sprawled on his back on his sun-lounger, wearing baggy shorts and a cotton shirt with all the buttons undone, with one knee drawn up, and his sunglasses pushed up on top of his head. His stomach protruded ever so slightly from his open shirt. He likes his beer, does Dan. He was so achingly familiar, all long gangly limbs, unruly dark hair and crumpled clothes. So, why was I feeling so off-beam?

It dawned on me unhappily that my inability to revert back to being a simple tourist wasn't the only thing to have changed in the last few weeks. Only I didn't feel half so good about it.

'I still don't understand why you have to go haring up to Cairo to rescue some damsel in distress you've never even met,' he said grumpily. 'Here am I trying my damndest to make a grand gesture, and you're barely taking the trouble to notice!'

I felt a bit sick hearing this. It was true; further proof, as if I needed it, that Dan really can be awfully sweet. And, of course, the shame and guilt of this realisation made me snappy and defensive. 'I didn't ask you to come racing back to Egypt on some heroic mission to stop me falling into a tomb shaft and breaking my silly neck, or whatever the hell it was you thought I was about to do,' I pointed out testily.

'What else was I supposed to do when you slammed the phone down on me? Pinkie, we've been together ten years, and I've never known you behave like this. First there was your decision to chuck in a perfectly good job without the prospect of another one to go to…'

'That's because the enhanced voluntary redundancy package was too good an offer to pass up,' I objected, cutting across him.

'Yes, well, maybe I can understand that. You'd been there fifteen years, and I know you were getting itchy feet. So, I was happy to come out here on holiday to give you time out to decide what you wanted to do next. But finding those hieroglyphics seems to have sent your life spinning out of control. I was crazy to go home and leave you here. But I didn't realise you were going to start trekking around in snake-and-scorpion-infested hills and breaking into abandoned tombs.'

'You accused me of living out a Lara Croft fantasy,' I reminded him.

Dan sighed. 'Pinkie, why won't you see just how much trouble you're courting?'

It was my turn to sigh. 'You still don't get it, do you?' Dan, I'm enjoying myself. I feel as if my life has burst into Technicolor'. This was an expression I'd borrowed from Adam, but it put perfectly into words the feeling that suddenly, in these last few weeks, I'd come truly alive. This was a bit of an odd phenomenon, kind of like recognising the start of one's life thirty-five years into the living of it. But it was true; everything before this remarkable trip to Egypt was pictured in my memory in a kind of faded monochrome.

'Hmm,' he said, investing the small sound with oceans of meaning. 'I seem to recall you saying something similar on the phone; something about breaking out of your hamster cage, if my memory serves me correctly; and that I should dare to do the same and try to live a little.'

You see, I'm not as poetic as Adam.

'Is that what brought you rushing back out here?' I asked.

'When I begged you to give up the crazy treasure hunt and come home, you yelled down the phone that you'd be crashingly bored at home. Honestly, Pinkie, you made it sound like I'd signed us up for lifetime membership of the old timers' brigade.'

'You didn't beg,' I said mildly, feeling a little shamefaced at hearing my angry words played back to me, but covering it with a gently provocative offensive. 'You demanded, bullied and hectored, and made a load of smart Alec wisecracks about me getting locked in pyramids and bitten by snakes.'

'I didn't mean to get all oafish. But you scared the life out of me with all your wild talk about hunting for buried treasure.'

'So, you took emergency leave from work and dashed to the airport and onto the first flight out here to be all heroic and masterful.'

'Yes, well...' he shifted on the sun-lounger, looking a bit embarrassed. 'It seemed a grand gesture of some sort was in order. It appeared to be what you wanted. I seem to recall you demanding rather cuttingly if I was a man or a mouse.'

'Oh Dan, you really are awfully sweet,' I said, reaching for his hand, and feeling thoroughly put out with myself for being such a scolding old harridan.

'Humph,' he muttered. Dan's not a great one for outward displays of affection. 'Yes, well, there's something in that saying, "if you can't beat them, join them". It seems to me if I hadn't given chase to that Egyptian chappie last night, he might not have fallen off the cliff and broken his neck. So, suddenly I'm up to my eyeballs in all this as much as you are.'

'In which case, I reckon the grandest gesture you can make right now is to look after the papyri,' I said consolingly. 'It makes you guardian of the treasure.'

He turned his head on the cushioned lounger to look at me. 'While you go chasing off to Cairo for more daredevil adventures with Adam.'

Dan's not the jealous type, as I've had cause to remark before. But neither is he a fool. There was a rather heart-stopping moment back in the tomb last night when Dan saw Adam for the first time, comparing him against the stereotype he'd been carrying around in his head and recognising his mistake. Dan knew all about Adam and how we'd teamed up on our quest to solve Howard Carter's riddles; but until last night he'd never actually met him. When I described him as a would-be Egyptologist, Dan pictured a harmless boffin, covered in dust and cobwebs, with faded eyesight from years poring over ancient texts and creaking joints from a lifetime of climbing in and out of tomb shafts. The tanned, blue-eyed, boyish reality was rather different.

'Like I said, we should be back here tomorrow,' I said quickly, rushing into speech to mask my discomfort at being on the receiving end of Dan's probing stare. I was well aware I needed to sort through the jumble of my feelings for Adam and for Dan, but I didn't want to face up to doing it just yet.

He stared at me for a moment longer, but let it go. I guess he didn't feel ready to bring things to a head right now either. He'd done his bit by jumping on a flight and hotfooting it out here. As grand gestures went, it really was rather romantic; all the more so for being completely out of character.

'And who knows …?' I went on, feeling the need to keep talking to cover up the silent undercurrents shifting between us, '…maybe Ted will have translated some more of the first papyrus by then. The photos Adam took of the next section of the hieratic script on his iPad looked like they came out pretty well. So, while you're guarding the real thing, we might be able to decipher the copy and see if it sheds any light on our ancient mystery.'

* * *

'Ted's struggling with the section of papyrus we photographed,' Adam said over the sound of the forward thrust of the engines as our flight took off from Luxor airport and arced in a board sweep over the bronzed rock of the Valley of the Kings below us. The aeroplane turned northwards, following the flow of the Nile towards Cairo. 'Some of the language is totally impenetrable, and he's at a bit of a loss without his reference books.'

I glanced across the narrow aisle, to where the professor was strapped into his seat alongside Ahmed. Less than a minute into the air, and already he was nodding off. It had been a long, eventful, and emotionally charged night. Ted was no longer a young man. No wonder he was exhausted. Alongside him, Ahmed also had his eyes closed. But the look on his face convinced me he wasn't asleep. This was Ahmed's first time on an aeroplane. He clearly wasn't enjoying the experience. The movement of his lips suggested deep and fervent prayer for our deliverance.

I smiled fondly at the pair of them and turned back to Adam. The only visible ill effect on him of our overnight exploits was his bandaged arm. In all other appearances he was alert, bright-eyed and full of his usual spirit of adventure. I was quite sure he whole-heartedly relished our daring rescue mission to break Ted's daughter free. Adam was romantically inclined towards any situation that allowed him to cast himself in the Indiana Jones persona. It was part of his charm.

To be fair, I was feeling pretty bushy-tailed too. There was something about all this treasure hunting; tomb breaking and papyrus finding that seemed to agree with me. 'Has he been able to make any sense of it at all?' I asked, my thoughts back on the papyrus, impatient to hear the ancient pharaoh's voice echoing out of the distant past again.

Adam smiled at my eagerness, and I knew he felt the same feverish thirst as me for whatever revelations the papyrus might contain. That was another part of his charm. Adam and I shared a fascination with ancient Egypt that bordered on obsession. His smile widened into a grin as he looked at my avid face. 'Apparently Ay keeps going on about the precious jewels being safely hidden away where none will ever find them. Ted says he seems a bit fixated about them.'

'If he's referring to jewellery like the stuff found in Tutankhamun's tomb, I should say that's perfectly understandable,' I said staunchly. 'Heavens, Adam, the sheer quantity of gold and precious stones buried with King Tut was astounding. And that's before you consider the exquisite workmanship of the pieces. Some of those pectorals were superb works of art. It makes you wonder, doesn't it? How much more stupendous must these jewels Ay's referring to be if Ay and Tutankhamun felt the need to hide them somewhere apart from their tombs?'

Adam grinned at me. 'There you go again,' he teased, 'intoxicated by the thought of buried treasure. As if the papyri weren't treasure enough, your eyes are lighting up in a quite shockingly avaricious fashion at the thought of more! Shame on you, Merry; I thought it was the noble spirit of archaeology that drove you, not the baser instincts of a common pirate.'

'You may mock me all you like,' I retaliated lightly, 'but I'll bet you'd be laughing on the other side of your face if we found it!'

I saw the light flare in his eyes and knew I had him. He pretends to be a studious Egyptologist, but honestly; he was like an excited little kid at Christmastime while we were tracking down Howard Carter's clues to find the papyri.

'Touché,' he chuckled. 'Poor old Carter must be turning in his grave to realise he's entrusted his precious discovery to such a pair of nefarious gold-diggers.'

It wasn't the first time in our short acquaintance Adam had demonstrated his uncanny ability to pick up on my thoughts like this. There must be some wavelength we both tuned in to subconsciously. It was a bit unnerving to tell the truth.

'Do you think he translated the papyri?' I asked. 'I mean, I understand why he bricked them up in that wall. He couldn't admit he and Lord Carnarvon took them from Tutankhamun's tomb without calling the wrath of the Egyptian Antiquities Service down on top of him. He didn't want to sully Carnarvon's reputation, or his own. I believe him when he said he'd have returned them to the tomb if only Carnarvon's widow had given it back before the clearance was completed. But, as it was, he had no choice. So, he walled them up, laid his trail of clues, and left the rest to fate. But surely, he must have been tempted to read them.'

Adam shrugged. 'I guess we'll never know. There's no message from Carter in the suitcase containing the papyri, and I kind of hoped there might be, even if it was only to acknowledge our cleverness in solving his last riddle. Maybe he wanted to leave the scrolls as a kind of virgin-territory discovery for whoever found it. He's handed us the thrill of translating them with absolutely no clue to what we might reveal. Perhaps he felt it was only fair. But I find it hard to imagine he'd have had them in his possession for however many weeks or months it was without wanting to know what they said.'

I stared out of the window for a while. The endless sky, pale blue and cloudless, arced above and beyond us. Below all was barren, buff coloured rock, desolate and sun-baked. Off in the distance I could see the Nile, stretched across the arid landscape like a lazy grey snake basking in the afternoon sunshine.

Adam's voice cut into my drifting, unfocused reverie. 'Ted said he gets a sense of a deep sorrow welling up from the hieratic script, almost that of a dying man sitting down to write his last confession.'

I turned back from the hazy view to stare at him. 'I thought you said it was all elaborate assurances that the priceless jewels remained hidden and undisturbed.'

'Yes, it seems that's the bulk of what Ted's translated so far. But he said there's also some stuff about Ay feeling the irresistible clutches of old age drawing him in, and deadly enemies circling like vultures around carrion.'

My breathing stalled. 'But Ay doesn't name these enemies?'

'No, it doesn't seem so from anything Ted's been able to decipher so far.

But the text is full of lengthy and emotional exhortations imploring his immortal lord Tutankhamun, to forgive Ay for something. Ted said the last section he's been able to translate with any sort of accuracy said something like, "*our precious jewels remain undisturbed, but in all else, my king, I have failed you.*"

Chapter 4

The Cairo I experienced on our mission to rescue the damsel in distress I'd never met was a whole different ball game from the last time I was here. Back then, a scant and somewhat nostalgic couple of weeks ago, Adam and I booked into the Mena House Oberoi, a historic hotel near the pyramids - the epitome of luxury and indulgent style. That time around we'd been on a quest to decipher Howard Carter's enigmatic hieroglyphics. Right now, we didn't so much as pause to touch down at Ted's apartment in the suburbs behind the Giza plateau. Instead, after landing from our short, one-hour flight from Luxor, and racing through the airport security controls, we jumped into the nearest taxi and made straight for the flat where Ted's daughter, Jessica, was being held hostage. Ted knew the address, a rather depressing high-rise block about a twenty-minute drive from the airport, with a broken neon Coca-Cola sign flashing intermittently from its roof and a traffic-choked flyover snaking past it, casting a pall of pollution across the scene.

'So, how exactly are we planning to pull this thing off?' I asked, after we'd paid the taxi driver and spilled out onto the dusty, chipped pavement in front of the uninspiring apartment block. There was a rather stomach-turning smell of rotting fruit permeating the air, and flies buzzed in languid patrols in the limpid afternoon heat. Traffic crawled past us, a strange blend of modern cars, motorbikes, scooters, donkey carts and camels. The constant honking of car horns was deafening. There are no discernible rules of the road in Cairo; so man and beast survive by their wits and their ability to break through the sound barrier. Believe me, if Concorde were to come out of retirement, it would have nothing on your average Cairene, human or otherwise.

'Show me where to go, and I will break down de door,' Ahmed vowed.

'I don't want her hurt,' Ted said urgently. 'I dread to think how she's been feeling these last couple of days, shut up against her will; and how she'll react to the news of Youssef's death.'

I could feel my eyebrows inching into my hairline and struggled to bring them under control. How the damsel had ever seen fit to enter into a romantic attachment – hang that; a marriage, in fact – with the deadly Egyptian maniac who'd held us at knifepoint last night was completely beyond my imagining. I think it's fair to say there were a few question marks hanging in the air about the sound judgement of our hapless heroine.

'We know these Egyptian brothers are dangerous,' Adam warned. 'Our experience last night with Youssef can leave no doubt about that. So, we need to tread carefully.'

Ted looked pained. 'I'm hoping Ahmed's police badge will be the deciding factor in bringing this thing to a rapid conclusion.'

The trouble was, of course, that while Ahmed's tourist police badge might get us some of the way, it lacked the impact of his tourist police gun. And he didn't have his gun with him. It seems even here in Egypt, where things are, admittedly, a little different from what we might expect back at home, the carriage of a gun onto an aeroplane is not the done thing; certainly not by a low-ranking officer of the law who was not a member of the military which was so prominent in these post-revolutionary days. It made me wonder if we shouldn't perhaps have opted for the sleeper-train to Cairo, instead of the far more immediate flight, just to keep our firearm options open. But Ted, understandably, held fast to the opinion time was of the essence.

We had no problem accessing the ground floor of the apartment block and making for the lifts. Concierges appeared not to be in abundant supply, or indeed any sort of prerequisite in this sadly run-down dwelling.

The lift, predictably, was broken.

'It's ten flights,' Ted said apologetically. I didn't fear for Ahmed in this off-putting statement. He's built like a tank but is as fit as a mountain goat. I had first-hand experience of this, trailing him across the rocky outcrops behind the Valley of the Kings. But I did wonder about Ted's ability to tackle the climb. Silly of me. For a seventy-something he's amazingly sprightly. Although not being a parent myself, it's impossible to say how much of his dedicated energy stemmed from fatherly concern for his daughter's safety.

Whatever, all four of us reached the tenth floor a few minutes later, puffed for sure, but none the worse for wear.

We stepped from the stairwell into a corridor redolent with the smell of boiled cabbage and stale garlic. 'That's it,' Ted nodded towards a doorway with chipped lime green paint falling off it in great flakes. 'Number 109.'

We all stared at the rotting door. It was a 1970's throwback, with a couple of lengths of wired, chipped glass either side of a central panel with a peephole embedded in it.

Ahmed straightened his black beret, puffed out his chest and approached the door with the purposeful stride of a man for whom this wasn't just a mission, but a holy crusade. We stood to one side while he hammered on the door, ready to leap forward at the first sign of trouble. The sound of his fist pounding on the woodwork echoed down the corridor. I doubted much in the way of extra force would be necessary to have the thing hanging off its hinges in no time.

There was no answer. All fired up and ready to battle our way to the rescue, this was a distinct anti-climax. Ahmed hammered some more. A couple of doorways down, a lady swathed from head to foot in voluminous black robes stepped out into the corridor, squawked, and scuttled back inside again, slamming the door.

'Now what?' I asked. 'It's a bit difficult to pull off a rescue mission when neither the victim nor the captor is at home.'

'This is definitely the right place, Ted?' Adam queried, looking doubtful.

'Yes, yes, absolutely. I was here just the other day. They locked Jessica in a room at the back and forced me at knifepoint to leave her there.'

'Is it possible Youssef's brother left her locked in the room and went out?' I asked.

We all stared at each other. If Jessica was in there on her own, pulling off this rescue mission might prove a whole lot easier than we'd dared to hope. Ahmed could have the door off in two seconds flat.

'Does anyone else live here?' Adam asked. 'Or is it just Youssef's brother?'

'There are two brothers,' Ted replied. 'One's called Mahmoud; the other is Hussein. I think they share the place.'

'Well, unless they're hiding in there, it doesn't seem like they're at home.' I said, feeling hope swell within me.

Ted got down on his hands and knees and lifted the rusty letterbox positioned at shin height in the door.

'Jessica?' he called through the narrow gap. 'Can you hear me? Are you in there?'

There was a moment of silence. It was long enough for me to have a horrible vision of two murderous Arabs holding her at knifepoint to stop her crying out. I shivered and felt some of my bravery slip away.

'Dad?' It was faint and far off, as if she was indeed calling out from behind a closed doorway in a far-off room at the back of the apartment. 'Dad, is that you?'

The very fact the voice was female and speaking English was all the proof we needed that we'd found her. My vision of her being terrorised by her two captors melted away and I let out a long sigh of relief. 'Let's get her out of there.' I said thankfully.

'Jessica, sit tight darling, we're coming in to get you,' Ted shouted. He started to scramble back to his feet so Ahmed could pile in with the killer blow to the door. His daughter's voice stopped him, and he leaned forward again to lift the letterbox. 'What did you say? I didn't hear you.'

'Is Youssef with you?' came the distant call.

Ted glanced up at Adam; then put his mouth back to the letterbox. 'No, he's not here. I'm with friends. We're going to set you free.'

'No!' It was an urgent plea. 'Dad, you mustn't do that. They're dangerous. They'll come after you.'

'Have they hurt you?' Ted's voice cracked a little as he called out to her.

'No Dad; not at all.'

He sagged with relief.

'But, Dad, I know too much now. If you let me out of here, they'll hunt us down; and then I'm afraid we might both get hurt.'

For all that her voice was far off and faint, her desperate words sent a chill through me. Adam's gaze locked with mine and I knew he was thinking the same thing I was. What exactly had we stumbled into here?

'Where are they now?' Ted shouted through the letterbox.

'They've gone to join the riots around Tahrir Square about the outcome of Mubarak's trial.'

We stared at each other. With all the excitement going on in our own lives over the last few days, we'd forgotten completely about this momentous moment in modern Egypt's political history in the wake of last year's Arab Spring.

Adam pulled his iPhone from his pocket, swiped through a couple of websites, and started reading aloud, ' "Protests have continued overnight in Cairo's Tahrir Square, after ex-President Hosni Mubarak was jailed for life for his part in the killing of protesters during the 2011 revolution. The crowds are furious at the acquittal of key security officials who were

64

on trial alongside Mubarak. Four interior ministry officials and two local security chiefs were cleared of complicity in protesters' killings. Announcing the verdicts, Judge Ahmed Refaat said Mubarak and former Interior Minister Habib al-Adly had failed to stop security forces using deadly force against unarmed demonstrators. They were both given life terms. Mubarak and his two sons, Alaa and Gamal, were acquitted on separate charges of corruption. But his sons will remain in detention as they are to be charged with stock-market manipulation. After the verdict, scuffles erupted in court. Outside, sentencing was initially greeted by celebrations, but anger soon took over when news of the acquittals spread."'

'Dad? Are you still there?'

Ted leaned forward to the letterbox again. 'We're still here, Jess.'

'Ask her what it is she knows too much about?' I suggested urgently. 'We need to know what we're dealing with here.'

A little further along the corridor a door opened again, and the veiled face peeped out.

'Let's hope she doesn't speak English,' Adam murmured.

Ahmed started moving towards the woman, I guess to offer some sort of explanation in their native Arabic; but she slammed the door again before he got there.

'Jess? What did you mean when you said you know too much?' Ted called.

'They're a gang of thieves, Dad.' She was shouting at the top of her voice, poor thing, but we could only just hear her. I was reasonably reassured by this, hopeful the occupants of the surrounding flats had both a sound barrier as well as a language barrier to penetrate to understand what she was saying. This old apartment block might be seedy, but it was remarkably well soundproofed. 'Do you remember in last year's riots in Tahrir Square, the Cairo Museum was broken into?'

Adam's gaze locked with mine across Ted's crouching form. I think we'd both just guessed what was coming.

'Youssef, Mahmoud and Hussein were the main culprits. They stole a range of artefacts, and they've been slowly selling them on the black market ever since. But they've still got a stash of them here. I know, because I'm locked up with them!'

'Nice family your daughter married into, Ted,' Adam muttered archly.

'So, do we deduce from this they're back at Tahrir Square now trying for another break-in to the museum?' I asked.

'De museum, it will be well-guarded dis time,' Ahmed declared. 'Dey will not risk more robbery. De whole world was up in arms about de last one!'

'I've an idea,' I said, literally as the idea struck me. 'Ted, you don't happen to have any contacts inside the museum, do you?'

Ted stared up at me from his kneeling position in front of the doorway. His eyes looked a little misty for a moment. 'Yes, Dr Shukura al-Busir. She and I had a rather enchanting romantic dalliance many years ago on an archaeological dig in Syria after my wife died and before Shukura met her husband. She's a professor of Numismatics at the museum.'

I looked blankly at Adam.

'Ancient coins,' he supplied the translation. "The museum has an impressive collection from across the ancient world.'

'Come on then,' I urged. 'I have a sudden desperate need to meet Dr Shukura al-Busir. I have a feeling she may be able to help us.'

The others looked at me as if I'd taken leave of my senses.

'We need to find a way to break Jessica out of here without those villainous brothers coming after her, don't we?' I explained patiently.

Three heads nodded dumbly.

'Well, I think I've just thought of a way we might achieve it. Ted, let Jessica know to sit tight; we'll be back later.'

He stared at me in disbelief. 'But, Merry, there's no way I can go off and leave Jessica here...' His voice ground to a standstill. He gazed up at me in consternation; his mouth still working although no sound came out. It dawned on me he was struggling to think how to say what he wanted to without offending me. I realised I was approaching this like a bull in a china shop, as usual. Jessica had no choice but to sit tight unless we went in and got her out. And everyone but me was all for doing precisely that while the coast was clear.

I dropped down onto my knees alongside the professor and squeezed his shoulder. 'I totally understand your reluctance to leave her, Ted. But I think I may have hit on a way of getting her out of here and those damned brothers banged to rights at the same time.' I put my mouth as close to the letterbox as I dared without contaminating myself with the general grime and yelled through it. 'Jessica? This is Meredith Pink. I'm sorry to say it's thanks to me you're in your current predicament. Listen, how long do you think we've got before they return?'

There was a short silence, no doubt while she adjusted to the unfamiliar sound of my voice. 'I don't think they'll be back until tonight,' she called back.

'Do you think you're in imminent danger if we leave you here for another couple of hours?'

Her response was immediate this time. 'I'll be in danger – we'll all be in danger – if you let my Dad try anything heroic. You need to let Youssef come and get me out. It's the only way. They won't hurt me while they're waiting for him. Once he's back, they'll decide what to do with me. Where is he?'

I exchanged a pained look with the professor. Neither of us felt equal to the task of shouting the news of her husband's demise to her through the letterbox.

Ted leaned forward and took my place in front of the door. 'We left him in Luxor,' he called.

'They can't possibly have identified his body yet,' I whispered urgently. So, we've got some time. Please, Ted, trust me. I've got a plan.'

Reassuring Jessica we'd be back and that we promised not to try anything heroic, we left Ahmed staking out the joint from a sleazy looking coffee shop across the street. We needed to know if two Egyptian men fitting the description of Youssef's brothers returned – and it was a job Ahmed was trained for. It's fair to say Ahmed was bitterly disappointed at being denied the opportunity to bash the door down. He put up an impassioned objection, entreating us to see the sense in rescuing Jessica while the coast was clear, and she was alone. But I prevailed in the end; full of the zealous fire I get when a brilliant idea hits me. Ahmed reluctantly subsided into his role of stake-out scout and Ted was finally persuaded to leave when I explained we needed him to make the introductions to his one-time sweetheart. The fact Jessica virtually begged him to go helped to reassure him that the ends justified the means.

Adam, Ted and I piled into the back of a taxi and directed the driver to take us to the Egyptian Museum. He looked at us a bit askance. European tourists were well advised to stay away from the scenes of rioting; but we promised him a king's ransom in baksheesh, so he gave in with good grace and an avaricious gleam in his eyes.

On the way, I set Adam to work on his iPhone to find out all we could about last year's break-in at the museum during the revolution.

He found a news website, and started to read aloud, ' "30 January 2011. A group of men broke into the Egyptian Museum, which is on the edge of Tahrir Square, the epicentre of protests, searching for gold. The looters broke into ten cases to take figurines. When they discovered the figures did not contain gold, they dropped them, and the items broke. They then seized two skulls of 2,000-year-old mummies and fled. Dr Zahi Hawass, Director of the Museum, said: "Demonstrators in collaboration with security forces stopped the thieves and returned the relics to the museum – but they were already damaged." Egyptologists described the smashing of the irreplaceable artefacts as "devastating".'

Ted looked a bit sick. 'It's absolutely appalling,' he said sadly. 'I've always found the Egyptians a friendly and peace-loving people; but when a minority of Egyptians start looting their own heritage, it's truly terrible. And to think my daughter bears their name.' He shook his head with shame. 'What evil men they must be.'

Adam was reading on. 'It says here Zahi Hawass, the Minister of Antiquities and Director of the Museum announced to the media that nothing had been robbed and the thieves had been caught and were being detained. It goes on to say this was sadly untrue…'

'As we know for a fact,' I concurred. 'Ted, didn't you tell us Youssef got injured in the rioting last year and lost his job?'

'Yes, that's why he and Jessica came to live with me.'

Adam skimmed through the website, seeing what else he could find out. 'It says on 2 February last year the situation in Tahrir Square got more violent with raging fires close to the museum and firebombs being thrown at the crowd. A second attempt to raid the museum was made. As the chaos escalated, the military closed the pyramids to tourists, positioned armed personnel and erected barriers outside archaeological sites and museums throughout Egypt, including Luxor and Aswan.'

'Early February,' Ted mused. 'Yes, that's about the time Youssef got injured. I recall him saying men in balaclavas shot at protestors, and I remember the reports of gunfire being heard throughout the night. Youssef got trampled in the crowd and broke his leg.'

'Likely story,' I muttered sarcastically. 'I'd lay odds he was one of the men in the balaclavas.'

Adam frowned over his iPhone. 'It says on 4 February Hawass offered conflicting reports about what was or was not stolen from the Egyptian Museum. Apparently, Hawass threatened to resign in protest about the failure of the army and police to protect Egyptian archaeological sites.'

'It wasn't long after that Mubarak ceded presidential power, if I remember rightly,' Ted said.

'You're right,' Adam nodded, still reading. 'On 11 February 2011 under massive pressure Mubarak finally agreed to resign as President and transfer power to the armed forces of Egypt.'

'Yes,' Ted said. 'They promised free, open elections.'

'Listen to this!' Adam cut across him. 'It says after Mubarak resigned, Zahi Hawass became a target for protesters, who demanded his removal as Minister of Antiquities. Like Mubarak, Hawass was besieged by allegations about his business interests, and his close ties with Mubarak's regime. Some accused him of turning Egypt's archaeology into a one-man show, shutting out foreign missions, forbidding archaeologists to announce their own findings and claiming other's discoveries as his own.'

'They're rather damning claims, aren't they?' I said, rather shocked. 'I remember Zahi Hawass from a lot of the Discovery Channel documentaries I've watched. I've always thought he had a little bit of Hollywood about him, but you can't knock the man for this enthusiasm or willingness to go in front of the camera.'

Adam read on. 'It says here on 13 February, in an effort to save face, Hawass abruptly altered his story and announced that there were indeed eight pieces missing from the Cairo Museum. He reversed his previous decision forbidding the heads of departments to enter the museum, allowing them in to do an inventory. They discovered – not eight – but over 100 artefacts missing.'

We stared at each other as the taxi bumped and bounced its way through the pothole strewn suburban streets towards central Cairo. 'And we know exactly where at least some of them are,' I breathed.

Adam scrolled a bit further through the website. 'Later in the day, hundreds of unemployed archaeologists held a rally at the Ministry of Antiquities gates protesting the corruption and nepotism they claimed was rife in the Ministry. A couple of weeks later, in early March, Hawass announced his resignation. He said his Ministry was incapable of protecting Egypt's ancient sites and museums.'

'That sounds like a bit of an about-turn from his earlier statements which seemed to down-play the seriousness of the break-in,' I remarked.

Adam looked up. 'This article rounds off by saying on 15 March 2011 an official list was released by the Supreme Council for Antiquities of some of the stolen artefacts from the Egyptian Museum. There are literally dozens of items listed including gilded wooden figures of Tutankhamun, countless bronze statues of various gods, and busts and small statues of Nefertiti and an Amarna princess.'

'Some of that stuff must be priceless,' I breathed. 'And to think Jessica's locked up in a room with it. She's right when she says she knows too much. They can never let her walk out of there with that sort of knowledge.'

Ted looked ill. 'I had no idea about any of this. I knew things were bad when Youssef got wind of the trail you were on and forced me at knifepoint to follow you. But I had no idea it went as far as this. I just thought he was an opportunistic rogue with the gleam of gold in his eyes.'

'No Ted; sadly, it sounds as if your daughter married into a family of professional antiquities thieves.' Adam sympathised.

'We'll get her out,' I promised. 'And we'll get those damned brothers put behind bars where they belong.'

Chapter 5

The noise of the demonstrations reached us as we approached Tahrir Square. Huge crowds swarmed through the adjoining streets. We kept the taxi window wound up but, even so, I could hear chants of "illegitimate" resounding from the crowds, presumably in reference to the verdicts delivered on Mubarak and his officials.

The afternoon was wearing on. I could see knots of people gathered together as our taxi driver steered us cautiously down a side street, some banner waving, others in animated discussions about this critical moment in Egypt's democratic transition.

Our driver muttered away to himself in Arabic as we skirted the crowds.

'He's lamenting the fact there's been no reform to the interior ministry in the way protesters demanded last year,' Ted translated. Ted had lived in Cairo for years and spoke the language fluently. 'He's saying the first goal of the revolution was the removal of the regime, and he's questioning why they're still fighting it after more than a year.'

'That doesn't sound unreasonable,' I remarked, meeting the driver's dark eyes in his rear-view mirror and smiling at him.

As we turned into the street alongside the museum, we got a glimpse of Tahrir Square itself, and the sound of hammering rose above the general hubbub.

'What are they doing?' I asked, leaning forward to peer through the front window of the taxi.

'It looks like they're erecting tents at the centre of the roundabout,' Adam said, following my gaze.

Ted let out a sigh. 'It seems this could turn into a long demonstration, perhaps even heading into the second round of the presidential election later this month.'

The taxi driver brought the car to a stop at the back of the museum. 'You want I wait?' he asked, clearly not relishing the prospect.

Adam glanced at me.

'No, that's ok, thank you,' I decided. 'I think we can take things from here.'

'I hope you know what you're doing,' Adam murmured fervently. 'If I can claim to know Dan at all from such a short acquaintance, I'd say he'll have my guts for garters for letting you march straight into a riot.'

'I have no intention whatsoever of getting involved in any rioting,' I assured him. 'It's the museum I want to march into, not Tahrir Square.'

Adam paid the taxi driver the astronomical fee we'd agreed, and we watched him turn the taxi around and drive away.

Unsurprisingly, the museum was closed. We approached a side entrance where two armed guards stood with rifles unslung and at the ready. They looked decidedly perplexed at our approach. I don't imagine many English tourists were avid enough history buffs to ask for special admission to the museum in the middle of a potentially violent political demonstration.

Over the noise of the shouting, chanting and hammering behind us, Ted addressed them in steady Arabic. The only words I recognised were Dr Shukura al-Busir and his own name, Edward Kincaid.'

They looked even more perplexed when he finished and ran searching gazes over each of us in turn. I don't think we looked at all disreputable, but there was something about their minute scrutiny that made me feel like a grubby little street urchin.

Ted spoke again, repeating the name Dr Shukura al-Busir, and gesturing to the door behind them.

The guards held a short debate in rapid Arabic; then one of them shrugged and disappeared through the door, leaving his colleague to watch over us with his rifle clasped loosely in both hands.

Slow minutes ticked by, and I started to question whether my brilliantly conceived plan was quite so smart after all. In view of the rioting, there was every chance the staff of the museum had been told to go home.

Luckily, my belated fears proved unfounded. The guard returned to the door, bringing with him an attractively rounded Egyptian lady in her early fifties at a guess, wearing a navy suit, with flat black ballet pumps on her feet, and a brightly pattered scarf wound around her head and shoulders.

She peered at us with an expression in which curiosity and trepidation vied for supremacy; then her gaze latched onto Ted and her face broke into wreaths of smiles. 'Ted, Ted, this man here said it was you, and I didn't believe him. I said I had to come to see for myself. You're looking well. My dear, how many years has it been? More than I care to count. Come in, come in; and these must be your friends...' She turned and beamed at Adam and me in turn.

She certainly looked like an Egyptian lady, but her accent was pure English Home Counties. She saw my expression and correctly interpreted it. 'I was educated at Oxford, my dear. They were the happiest days of my life. Come in, come in.' And she turned and led the way back through the open doorway behind her.

When Ted said he'd had a romantic dalliance with a professor from the museum, I never in my wildest dreams imagined such a whirlwind of a woman. I think I'd pictured someone small and dainty, the way he was small and dapper. But Dr Shukura al-Busir was pleasantly plump, a little bit dusty as if we'd interrupted her digging up the coins she studied, and she never stopped talking.

'What on earth brings you here in such troubled times? This poor museum doesn't deserve to be sitting here in the middle of a political hotspot. You know, tourist numbers have been less than a quarter of the usual footfall since the revolution. I fear for this country, I really do. Let's hope we can get through the forthcoming elections in peace and return to some semblance of normality.'

As she said this, she was leading us through long corridors in the behind-the-scenes part of the museum. I looked about me in open fascination. I've always thought the public part of the museum has the feeling of a storage warehouse; just one in which the contents are visible and on display, rather than enclosed in packaging. Away from the public gaze, it was very much the same. We passed shelves piled high with talatat blocks; the small stone tablets used by Akhenaten in his building projects. They were covered in painted decorations depicting scenes from Akhet-Aten; but broken up, like a giant jigsaw puzzle awaiting assembly. There were granite statues lining the corridors, some immense in size; and boxes and boxes of ostraca and potsherd, covered in ancient, scratched writing.

Shukura led us into a tiny office, spent a few moments clearing papers and boxes of ancient coins off the wooden seats and swiping at the dust with her handkerchief; and then invited us to sit down. 'Now, tell me to what I owe this pleasure? What can I do for you?'

By the time I'd finished speaking a few minutes later, her dark eyes were alive and snapping with excitement. 'Some of the stolen artefacts are priceless,' she exclaimed. 'There was a gilded wooden figure of Tutankhamun on a skiff throwing a harpoon, an unfinished limestone statue of Nefertiti, a gold, stone and faience collar dating to the 18th Dynasty – the list goes on an on. Over a hundred precious objects were looted. And you think we can recover at least some of them for the museum? This is good news indeed.'

'But we need you to play your part,' I said. 'I thought if someone from inside the museum, someone respected and professional, a professor like yourself, notified the police, or the military, or whoever it is we need to contact, they're more likely to take it seriously and act on it. Ted has some professional standing, of course, but as he's retired it doesn't have quite the same clout.'

'What do I need to do?'

'Well, we need to organise a raid on the flat where the artefacts are stored. I know the armed forces have got their hands a bit full right now, what with the demonstrations and everything; but hopefully we can still convince them to mount enough of a force to secure the right outcome.'

'You expect violence?' Shukura asked, not sounding at all perturbed by the possibility.

'Well, we have it on pretty good authority that the two ring-leaders are outside in Tahrir Square right now, no doubt hoping for another shot at some antiquity looting. My feeling is if we can get the police inside the flat and recover the stolen artefacts, then they can ambush the thieves when they return and catch them in possession, so to speak. It seems to me the outcome we need to be aiming for is to get Jessica out of there safely, the stolen artefacts back on display here at the museum, and the two thugs responsible for it all behind bars.'

'My God, Merry,' Adam said in awe, 'You've got it all worked out.'

Of course, these things never go completely according to plan. The first little obstacle was convincing the military police, or whatever they were, to believe Shukura when she said she'd had an anonymous tip-off about the stolen artefacts. They said they were extremely busy and in no mood for crank calls; at least, I think that's the way it translated out of the native Arabic. Honestly! These demonstrations really were a damned nuisance.

I did wonder about producing Ted as the anonymous tipper-offer, but it seemed foolhardy to link him any more closely than was strictly necessary to the scene of the crime. At some point it was bound to come out that Youssef was Jessica's husband, that Youssef was one of the brotherhood of thieves, and that Youssef was the dead body found in the Valley of the Kings. I didn't think anyone could positively identify Ted as Youssef's companion on his illicit jaunt to Luxor, but it didn't seem worth taking the risk.

Shukura persisted, proving herself quite imaginative. The military police finally decided to take her seriously when she threatened to go to the press with her story and told them exactly what she planned on saying to the journalist about the lackadaisical attitude of the military police to the possible recovery of priceless relics from Tutankhamun's tomb. She promised them media coverage across the globe and foretold what she thought the western world would have to say about their single-issue approach to law and order.

Ted, Adam and I made ourselves scarce while a uniformed military sergeant – or whatever the Egyptian equivalent is – and his more junior sidekick came to check Shukura out. We hid in a store cupboard behind Shukura's office, sitting stock still and as quiet as mice.

We could hear Shukura giving the performance of her life. I don't know about Numismatics; in my view was she was a loss to the stage. Her personality seemed ideally suited to the dramatic arts. I couldn't tell what she was saying because she was playing her role in full-throttled Arabic. I envied Ted and Adam, sitting statue-like on boxes beside me, their ability to speak the language. Ted's Arabic was fluent; Adam's more pigeon than perfect, but it was enough to get by. Still, even without the benefit of understanding the voluble gush of words rising and falling in such theatrical style, I knew the basic plot. We'd kept the story simple enough: Shukura was minding her own business cataloguing Roman coins at the museum, a telephone rang, she answered it, and a querulous female voice informed her that she knew where the stolen artefacts were hidden. The voice went on to say she'd observed strange goings on at the apartment block where the Said brothers lived and overheard raised voices shouting about items stolen from the Egyptian museum during last year's riots. (I had in mind the veil-swathed face of the lady who'd peeped out of her doorway in the next-door flat earlier, while concocting this story. I hoped she wouldn't mind me weaving this fabrication around her. It was unquestionably true she'd heard raised voices; and they had indeed been discussing the stolen artefacts. I hoped the fact these discussions had been conducted in English not Arabic would render her ignorant and innocent should the police ever ask her to help them with their enquiries). She finished up giving the address and put the phone down.

Finally, the military police were persuaded to act. They set off in their police car, accompanied by a gleeful Shukura, clearly having the time of her life, and talking all the way. We followed at a safe distance in Shukura's car. She'd given Ted the keys and told him where it was parked before the sergeant and his sidekick arrived at the museum.

We managed to skirt the demonstrations without incident as the sun started to set over the Cairo skyline.

The second little glitch came when Adam's mobile phone rang, and he answered to find Ahmed's excitable voice beamed into his ear by satellite. The upshot of the call was that one of the brothers had returned home. Ahmed had been following the comings and goings to and from the apartment block since we left him there. He'd trailed the latest individual to broadly fit the description Ted gave him into the building and, lo and behold, saw him enter flat number 109 on the tenth floor; the one with the flaking lime green paint on the door.

There was no way of warning the military police up ahead that they were no longer approaching a benign situation. We just had to cross our fingers they'd keep their wits about them; especially if the other brother returned halfway through the operation.

Things moved pretty quickly after that. We were able to watch some of the events unfolding from our parking space across the street, where Ahmed joined us. But it was Shukura who filled in the details later, while we were reflecting on things over a much-needed glass of wine. Shukura saw it all.

First, the military police bashed the door in. This did not take much effort, as we'd predicted. The door came swinging off its hinges at the first shove. The police stormed into the apartment to find the brother who'd returned, Mahmoud, throwing packing cases out of a bedroom window into the small yard at the back of the building. On later inspection, the packing cases (thankfully stuffed with straw) contained bronze statues dating back to the time of the pharaohs. It seemed pretty much the whole pantheon was represented: seated statues of Anubis (the jackal headed god) and Bastet (the cat goddess); and striding statues of Sekhmet (lion), Sobek (crocodile) and Osiris (the god of the underworld). They were worth a fortune.

Jessica was found with her ankles tied together, helplessly watching this sacrilege from the chair she was bound to. She was thankfully unharmed, but it seemed she'd said something to put the wind up Mahmoud; hence the priceless artefacts being casually tossed out of the tenth floor window.

As the military police burst in on proceedings, Mahmoud, caught red-handed, faced down his options. It seemed the prospect of a lifetime in an Egyptian prison flashed before his eyes. The alternative choice must have seemed preferable; and before anyone could make a move to stop him, he followed the last packing case, hurling himself through the open tenth floor window. Suffice it to say, he was very dead within a moment of landing, cracking his skull open on the concrete paving.

Jessica was taken to the police station, accompanied by a clucking Shukura; all motherly concern and formidable vocabulary.

Jessica's story to the police was that she'd had a bitter argument with her Egyptian husband Youssef, and he'd walked out on her. She'd gone to his brothers' apartment, thinking to find him there, and hopeful of reconciliation. She'd interrupted the two other brothers packing the stolen artefacts from the Egyptian Museum for sale on the black market. Knowing she'd caught them in the act, the brothers held her captive. They hadn't decided what to do with her.

Asked if she knew where her husband, Youssef, was now, she said she had no idea. She hadn't seen him for a couple of days.

Let's face it: it was the truth.

'Two dead bodies in two days,' I said darkly, swirling my wine around in my glass. 'It's turning into a distressingly bad habit.'

We were recovering from the day's exertions at a small restaurant in a side street near where Ted lived, out at Giza. Adam, Ahmed and I had booked into Le Meridien Hotel near the pyramids; but we'd opted for a night out in a homely local brasserie over the glitz of a modern hotel. Shukura had come along for a drink and to fill us in volubly on the events we'd missed. Now she'd gone home to her husband and family, no doubt ready to regale them with it, too. Things had certainly quietened down a bit since her departure. The rest of us were still here, the four of us, plus Jessica.

Safely returned to the loving arms of her father, Jessica had taken the news of her husband's death with heartening equanimity. She'd restricted her grief to a small, rather Gaelic shrug and remarked that it saved her the trouble of filing for divorce. The charm with which Youssef once wooed her was self evidently lacking in more recent times.

I think I'd been prepared not to like Jessica. I'd cast her as a kind of ditsy damsel in distress and a bit of an inconvenience in our adventures. But it was impossible not to warm to her. She was a tiny elfin-like creature, as pretty as a picture, extremely delicate and fragile looking. I soon discovered the fragility was all surface appearances. She emerged from the undoubted trauma of her incarceration with a nicely turned quip about the off-putting smell of boiled cabbage.

I returned to the subject of the dead bodies. 'Still, at least it means they can't talk. Sorry to be heartless, but there's a rather reassuring permanence about the place they've gone to.'

'It still leaves one brother on the loose and potentially dangerous,' Adam said, a small frown knitting his brows together.

'I'm sure the police will round him up soon enough,' Ted reassured him. 'They're staking out the flat for his return; so, he'll walk straight into their net and on into police custody. I have to say; I'm feeling better than I have in days, and itching to get stuck into my reference books. It strikes me we have the small matter of some rather important papyri awaiting translation.'

Jessica turned her bright, sparkling gaze on each of us in turn. 'Now, I want you to tell me everything,' she invited excitedly. 'Merry, it started with you getting locked in Howard Carter's house, is that right? How thrilling! And Ahmed, you were the one who set her free? Then Adam, you came on board to help Merry decipher the hieroglyphics she found? So clever! Now you must tell me the whole story and leave nothing out; including the fight with Youssef that led to you getting wounded Adam. I saw the size of his knife. You must be very brave!'

When she looked at Adam like that, all pink-cheeked and breathlessly admiring, I decided perhaps I didn't like her quite so much after all.

Chapter 6

I slept like the dead in my enormous bed at Le Meridien Hotel. I think I'd been running on sheer adrenaline for days. But now the treasure hunt was over, the damsel was rescued, and the villains were taking their chances at the Muslim version of the pearly gates. I didn't much fancy their odds. The only thing still in store was the tantalising prospect of translating the papyrus. And we could take a long, leisurely time over that while we decided how best to introduce it to the world.

I woke long after breakfast service was over but wasn't in the least bit upset by this since we'd all agreed to meet for a late morning brunch before catching our flight back to Luxor this afternoon.

Jessica and Ted were spending the morning packing. They'd decided to come back to Luxor with us. In Ted's case, the agony of being parted from the papyrus was almost more than he could bear. Now Jessica was safe, he was positively panting with impatience to get back to it. There was nothing holding Jessica in Cairo now Youssef was gone. We'd all agreed it would be sensible for her to come south with us, just in case the unaccounted-for brother decided to take matters into his own hands. I didn't think it was likely he'd want to call attention on himself in view of the warrant out for his arrest, but better safe than sorry.

Ahmed had decided to eschew the opportunity of a night in a luxury five-star hotel in favour of spending it camped out on a sofa in Ted's flat. He took his role as police escort and protector very seriously. If there was any chance of trouble from the last man standing of the villainous triad of thieves, he planned to be on hand to deal with it. But - perhaps disappointingly for Ahmed - the night passed without incident. Jessica and Ted arrived at Le Meridien at the agreed time looking fresh, neatly attired and well rested. Ahmed trailed behind them like a giant bodyguard, slightly less buoyant than usual, and somewhat more crumpled and creased.

There hadn't been an opportunity for a moment alone with Adam. The hour was late when we returned to the hotel last night after dinner, and the after-effects of all the excitement combined with the lack of sleep and a couple of glasses of wine were catching up with us. The unfulfilled promise of a kiss still hung tantalisingly on the airwaves. In quiet moments I found myself quite distracted by it. But quiet moments were relatively few and far between. And I think we both recognised Dan's presence in Egypt put a somewhat different perspective on things. Reluctantly, I was compelled to accept the kiss might just have to wait until I'd sorted things out with my boyfriend.

We all met at the outside snack bar overlooking the swimming pool as morning started to drift towards mid-day. The sun climbed high in the cavernous blue sky above us. We sank gratefully into padded chairs around a circular table under the shade of a wide canvas canopy; ordered club sandwiches, juice and coffee all round; then settled back to enjoy the opportunity to relax before our flight back to Luxor.

'Rather nice here, isn't it?' Adam commented, looking around. 'If it wasn't for the papyrus, I might be tempted to stay another couple of days and chill out a bit.'

We spent a moment soaking in the vacation vibe. Tourists lounged on sunbeds under umbrellas around the swimming pool. It was actually a series of inter-connecting pools shaped a bit like an open flower, around a central sunken swim-up bar. But what gave the pool area wow factor was its view of the pyramids. They loomed from the sandbank behind the hotel, timeless and evocative. My gaze was drawn to them as if by a magnet. I found it almost impossible to pull it away again as superlatives tumbled through my mind. There was something imperious and effortlessly commanding about these immense wonders of the ancient world; a majesty and tangible presence that demanded awe and reverence.

Ted followed my line of sight. 'Their sheer age is logic defying, my dear, don't you think? It's a humbling thought to realise those monuments were already over a thousand years old when Tutankhamun was pharaoh. It makes one feel quite insignificant. Our lifetime is but a blink of an eye to the eternity they've watched over.'

I nodded dumbly. For all the superlatives, there really were no words adequate to describe the man-made mountains of stone rising from the desert plateau, silently standing sentinel over the rise and fall of civilisations past, present and, no doubt, future.

We all paid them a thoughtful homage for a few moments; then our food arrived, tearing our focus forward by a few millennia. The bread was soft and still warm from the bakery and for a short while I gave myself over to the simple pleasure of a freshly prepared sandwich.

'I've made some progress with the section of papyrus we photographed,' Ted announced as the last crumbs disappeared from the plates and we sat back with our coffee.

His words brought us all sitting bolt upright again.

'I'm starting to feel rather sorry for Pharaoh Ay,' he went on. 'I get a sense of a lonely old man who's lost everything he ever loved.'

I stared at him with my coffee cup suspended midway between the saucer and my mouth. 'Adam told me you got a sense of a dying man sitting down to write his last confession. There was something about the clutches of old age, and enemies circling like vultures around carrion.'

Adam leaned forward, his face as transfixed as mine surely was. 'You said the last words you'd been able to translate read, "*our precious jewels remain undisturbed, but in all else, my king, I have failed you.*"'

Adam has a quite remarkable ability to quote things word-for-word. It's really most impressive and brought the ancient hieratic script bursting back to life again. The long-dead pharaoh's voice echoed across the centuries. A quick glance showed Ahmed and Jessica silently agog. We were all hanging on Ted's next words like a bunch of disciples waiting for a prophecy.

'I think the next section relates to Tutankhamun's widow and great royal wife,' Ted said.

'Ankhesenamun,' Adam supplied her name in a breathless kind of sigh.

I felt the little hairs on my forearm stand on end as a shiver ran up my spine. I wondered if it was possible to call up the ancient spirit of the dead queen by the utterance of her name in that sanctified tone of voice. The modern surroundings of the luxury hotel seemed to fade to a dull blur.

Ted nodded. 'It's as if Ay has taken the opportunity of the robbery of Tutankhamun's tomb, and his need to reseal it, to write a lengthy testimonial addressed to the boy king setting out all his trials and tribulations, whilst re-swearing his oath to keep the "precious jewels" safely hidden.'

'Ankhesenamun was Tutankhamun's half sister, wasn't she?' I asked.

'If you believe Akhenaten was Tutankhamun's father, then yes,' Ted nodded. 'But scholars are still in fierce debate over Tut's paternity. I think an alternative is that Tutankhamun and Ankhesenamun may have been cousins. What's certain is Ankhesenamun was the third daughter of Akhenaten and Nefertiti. She was a few years older than Tutankhamun. When he died, aged about nineteen, she was probably in her early twenties.'

'So, de papyrus, what does it say?' Ahmed asked eagerly, slopping coffee over the rim of his cup as he shifted his bulk forward in his chair.

Ted took out a small notebook from the inside breast pocket of the light linen jacket he was wearing. He flipped a couple of pages, and I spied lines of pencilled text in densely packed tiny handwriting. 'Listen,' he said, 'this is as exact a translation as I've been able to achieve... *"Honoured lord, you are pure of the Thutmoside line of great kings. Your queen, the lady of the palace, beloved of the king her father, beloved of the king her husband, is pure of the Thutmoside line of great kings. I, Kheperkheperure Ay, though king now in your stead, remain your humble and devoted servant. While yet you lived, I was honoured to* have bestowed on me the titles *God's Father* and *Fan-Bearer on the Right Side of the King*. Now you reign immortal, and I carry the earthly crook and flail of Per-Ah, the royal house. Yet I am not pure of the Thutmoside line of great kings.'"

Ahmed was frowning with perplexity. 'But what does it mean?' Poor Ahmed: he had two language barriers to penetrate, the first from his native Arabic into English, and then this flowery Pharaonic Egyptian.

Adam sent him a sympathetic smile. 'It's a bit impenetrable, isn't it? I think it's just a long-winded expression of the royal family's lineage. Whether Akhenaten was Tutankhamun's father or not, it seems certain they were both descended from the unbroken line of 18th Dynasty kings, which started with the warrior pharaoh Ahmose. It's believed Ay was a commoner, coming to prominence because his sister Tiye married a pharaoh. She became great royal wife to Akhenaten's father Amenhotep III. So, it seems, in the papyrus text, Ay is acknowledging his inferior status and questionable right to rule.'

Ted turned a page in his notebook and continued to read from his minutely transcribed translation. ' "*I had the honour to protect you once, sacred lord. The power was mine to ensure your smooth passage to the throne of the Two Lands, though your enemies sought to deny you and your betrothed queen your divine birthright. Now you rule in the Kingdom of the Dead, I have sought again to protect your heritage from the unholy clutches of our enemies. I, Kheperkheperure Ay, stood father to a revered queen, Great of Praises, Mistress of Upper and Lower Egypt, Nefertiti. I, Kheperkheperure Ay, stood uncle to kings great of the Two Lands, descended from he who raised me up: the Mighty Bull, Nebmaatre Amenhotep. My blood flowed strong in the veins of kings and queens, though it was not the pure blood of the Thutmoside line. Was I to stand aside while our enemies sought to obliterate your Dynasty, and raise another in its place? No; old I may be, but I stand closer to the throne than any other save one."'*

'I thought you said this part of the papyrus was about Ankhesenamun,' Jessica queried, wrinkling her nose daintily. 'He's barely mentioned her so far. All he seems to be doing is justifying why he put himself on the throne after Tutankhamun's death in the absence of a pure blue-blooded alternative candidate.'

'Patience...' Ted chided gently. 'He's coming to Ankhesenamun. She's the "save one". In the meantime, we have proof scholars have searched for in vain. The papyrus confirms Ay's place in the Amarna period family tree. It's knowledge beyond price; evidence beyond riches.'

Looking at his intent face I was gripped with Egyptological fervour. The ancient scrolls we'd found were bringing ancient Egypt back to life. With every sentence

Ted translated, the fog cleared a bit more. Facts were slowly emerging from the swirling mists of time, revealing truths long buried, thought gone forever. It was the stuff that dreams are made of. My brain was on fire with the wonder of it and teeming with questions. Who were the enemies Ay stood firm against? What other king, besides Akhenaten, was his nephew? He said he stood uncle to kings – plural – not a single king. Did this imply brothers – or was it simply a reference to kinship with Tutankhamun?

A glance across at Adam suggested his brain was similarly buzzing. His gaze was fixed on Ted's face, and I'd swear he was holding his breath. There was no point mentally grappling with the possibilities. We just needed to let Ted read on uninterrupted.

I cast a quick frowning glance at Jessica, and she dimpled a smile back at me and mouthed the word 'sorry'. It really was impossible to be grumpy with Jessica. She was such a friendly little pixie-like creature. I'd learnt last night that Ted fathered her rather late on in life, not long before he lost his wife to cancer. He doted on her and she clearly returned the sentiment by the bucketful.

Ted took a sip of his coffee, cleared his throat, and continued to read from his notebook, taking up the ancient pharaoh's tale. ' "*Some may say, when my history comes to be told, that I ascended to the throne for reasons of power or personal glory. My revered lord, you alone among men know this is not true. As you slipped towards your rebirth in the field of reeds, you made me swear my oath. It was to protect she who was beloved to you, your most cherished treasure, the lady of the palace. In this I have failed you, immortal lord. I will follow you into the afterlife with this stain upon my everlasting ka. The gods of the underworld, if they prove to exist, will judge my heart too heavy and determine unfavourably my request for safe passage to Amenti. So, I must make my reckoning now, and lay all before you, as I may never join you in the field of reeds."'*

Ted drew a deep breath and read on. ' *"I brought the lady of the palace under my protection in the only way possible. I offered her sanctuary in Per-Ah, the great house of Kheperkheperure Ay as Tahemetnesu, the great wife."'*

Ted paused dramatically, and we all stared at him.

'Is he saying he married Ankhesenamun?' I asked.

Jessica wrinkled her brow. 'But she was his granddaughter, wasn't she? If she was Nefertiti's daughter, and Ay was Nefertiti's father, then she had to be. And wasn't Ankhesenamun related to Ay through her father Akhenaten too? Didn't you say Ay was Akhenaten's uncle by virtue of being Queen Tiye's brother?'

Adam's eyes moved from Ted's face, to mine, and onto Jessica's, where his gaze settled. 'Yes, yes and yes again,' he breathed. 'There's always been speculation Ay married Ankhesenamun – his supposed granddaughter and great-niece - after Tutankhamun's death. Early twentieth century excavators found a gold ring whose bezel bears the joined cartouches of Ay and Ankhesenamun, side by side, in the way names of royal consorts were written. Many historians interpret it as a cynical and calculated scheme of Ay's to consolidate his claim to the throne.'

'Egyptologists believe Per-Ah, meaning "great house" was the ancient Egyptian hieroglyph from which the word "pharaoh" derived,' Ted interjected. 'And Tahemetnesu translates literally as "great wife".'

'But Ay's papyrus suggests he didn't marry her to secure his own position, so much as to protect hers,' I said. 'But he seems to be saying he failed?'

'Ankhesenamun disappears from the historical record shortly after Ay's accession,' Adam said. 'Many scholars have interpreted it as more evidence of skulduggery on Ay's part. She'd served her purpose, secured his passage to the throne, so he did away with her. His tomb records only a woman called Tey as his senior wife, someone he was married to as a younger man. It makes no mention of Ankhesenamun.'

'But his papyrus suggests a deep sense of failure and bitter regret,' I said; 'So much so that he fears for the safe passage of his own ka, or soul, into the afterlife. He'd sworn an oath to Tutankhamun, on the boy king's deathbed, to protect her; and was clearly unable to do so. So, what are we to make of that?'

Ted's eyes were snapping with scholarly fever. 'What we are to make of that, my dear, is made clear in the next passage.'

Four avid gazes were pinned on his face again, and he read on from his tightly transcribed translation. My God, he must have been up half the night, poring over his reference books to make sense of the florid language of the ancient pharaoh. If ever I'd underestimated Ted's dedication to the school of Egyptology, I revised my opinion now.

' *"The lady of the palace, your most cherished treasure, accepted the protection of Per-Ah. But she knew it could not last. Kheperkheperure Ay's health steadily fails. She saw this. My day of judgement draws close. For me, it is the verdict at the weighing of the heart ceremony. For your esteemed lady it meant the death of her peace and security. Our enemies would seek to use her, as I did not need to use her (for the blood of kings and queens flowed from my veins): to gain access to the throne of the Two Lands. In terror for her fate on my death, she made a desperate appeal to our foreign enemies. Had I known of this, I could not have supported her in her strike against the very heart of Egypt. But her fear and misery pushed her beyond the limits of endurance. So, in my heart, I understood. Her despairing venture failed. In an agony of terror she begged*

Osiris, lord of the underworld, to take her to him before her time. He heard her plea. He has granted her access to his kingdom of the blessed dead. Even now, bathed in sacred natron, she awaits her final journey to the West."'

Ted looked up from his notebook and met our transfixed expressions.

'She's taken her own life?' Jessica squeaked.

'Yes,' Adam said slowly, 'It certainly sounds like suicide.'

'I think I know about this,' I said uncertainly. 'I'm sure I've read about it - no doubt in some romantic novel or suchlike! Wasn't Ankhesenamun supposed to have written a letter to a foreign king asking for a husband, or something like that?'

Adam's glowing gaze met mine. 'Yes. That's right. The story is known not from Egyptian archaeology, but from the excavation of the Hittite capital of Hattusa in modern Anatolia. In the royal archives was a cuneiform text of the Hittite king Shubilulliuma sent by an ancient Egyptian queen. Its extraordinary message said something along the lines of *"My husband is dead, and I have no son. People say that you have many sons. If you were to send me one of your sons, he might become my husband. I am loathe to take a subject of mine and make him my husband. I am afraid."'* Adam paused to collect his thoughts then went on, 'It's not known for sure who was the Egyptian queen who made this unprecedented plea to the Hittites who were historically Egypt's enemies. She is called Dakhamunzu in the Hittite annuals, a possible translation of the Egyptian title Tahemetnesu, or "great wife". Most scholars believe Ankhesenamun to be the most likely candidate.'

'That's correct, my boy,' Ted approved. 'And if Shubilulliuma had acted promptly, he might have changed the course of history. As it was, he dithered and sent a delegation to Egypt to see if the queen's plea was for real. By way of assurance, she sent a message both eloquent and heart-rending in its appeal. It read, "*Why do they say, 'they might try to deceive me'? If I had a son, would I write to a foreign country in a manner humiliating to me and to my country? He who was my husband died, and I have no sons. Shall I perhaps take a subject of mine and make him my husband? I have not written to any other country; I have written only to you. People say that you have many sons. Give me one of your sons, and he shall be my husband and king in the land of Egypt.*"' Ted looked around at us all. 'Assured this letter was, presumably, from the hand of the lady herself, Shubilulliuma sent a son to Egypt, a young man called Zannanza. But, according to the Hittite records, their young prince was intercepted, attacked and murdered on the way "by the men and horses of Egypt."'

'So, Ankhesenamun's conspiracy was discovered,' I said; 'but obviously not by her "protector", Grandfather Ay.

So, it must point the finger at the other enemies Ay cites in his papyrus scroll. Knowing Ay was ailing, she chose the only other way out of the certain fate that awaited her.'

'But she wasn't buried by Ay in Tutankhamun's tomb?' Jessica asked.

'No,' Adam responded. 'The tiny, mummified bodies of two foetuses were found in Tut's tomb. They're believed to be stillborn children of the royal couple. But Ankhesenamun wasn't there.'

'But she didn't die as Tutankhamun's wife,' I said. 'She died as Ay's wife. Maybe there was a protocol preventing her being buried with a former husband. Yet she wasn't buried with Ay either, albeit he must have died very shortly after her?'

'Archaeologists speculate they may have found Ankhesenamun's tomb as recently as 2005,' Adam said, 'when a small chamber was discovered in close proximity to Tutankhamun's tomb. Fragments of pottery bore the partial name "Paaten". Like Tutankhamun, Ankhesenamun changed her name when the court moved away from the Heretic's city of Akhet-Aten. She was originally called Ankhesenpaaten, meaning Living for Aten.'

'But no body was found in the chamber?' I queried.

'No, just a broken up wooden coffin; but the mummified remains of an 18th Dynasty queen were discovered by the nineteenth century explorer Giovanni Belzoni in 1817 in another small tomb nearby in the Valley. Recent DNA tests have proved this mummified queen to be the mother of the foetuses in Tutankhamun's tomb. And Tutankhamun is known to be their father. So, unless he had a second queen who is somehow absent from the historical record, it does seem very likely they've found Ankhesenamun.'

A shiver snaked up my spine again. 'Does the papyrus say anything about her burial?' I asked Ted.

He beamed at me. 'I was wondering when one of you was going to ask.' Once a university lecturer, always a university lecturer, I thought. 'There's only a small section left of the portion of papyrus we photographed. I haven't had time to translate all of it. But this next bit reads as follows, "*Great Lord, I have prayed for guidance on where to lay the lady of the palace to rest. I have chosen a small tomb in Ta-sekhet-ma'at, the great field, where she may pass into eternity in the loving embrace of her sister.*"'

'That's right!' Adam exclaimed. 'Belzoni found the mummified remains of two 18th Dynasty queens in that small tomb in the Valley of the Kings, which was known as the great field to the ancient Egyptians. Nobody's sure who the other one is, but some historians speculate she might be Meritaten, who was the eldest daughter of Akhenaten and Nefertiti. Some scholars believe she was given the status of great royal wife towards the end of the Amarna years. Does Ay name her in the papyrus?'

'Frustratingly, no;' Ted said, 'but listen to this... "*Our enemies seek out and destroy all that is holy in our heritage. They desecrate and they despoil and, as the hour of my passing draws near, I am powerless to stop them. I fear they will desecrate and despoil my final resting place: chisel out the name and image of Kheperkheperure Ay so I may know no lasting peace. They will know where I lie. But though this campaign of destruction has already begun – and in this I have failed you – I re-swear my oath. The lady of the palace, your cherished treasure, will rest where our enemies cannot find her; no one seeing, no one hearing. By my efforts the tombs of my immortal lord and lady will lie undisturbed in sepulchres of millions of years, for the eternal peace of your soaring spirits. I will cause the Valley floor to be moved. Tonnes of stone and sand will I cause to be shifted so none may ever find you. My own tomb I will cause to be built far away in a separate branch of the great field, so none may disturb my immortal lord and lady when they come to desecrate and despoil Kheperkheperure Ay. And when my work is done, I will cause the workers to be dispatched to the granite quarries of the south and the salt mines of the north, so none may learn of it.*"'

We stared at each other.

'Well, he was both remarkably successful in his endeavour and wholly accurate in his prophecy,' Adam said. 'Ankhesenamun wasn't found until the early nineteenth century, and Tutankhamun in the early twentieth. Howard Carter had to shift tonnes and tonnes of shale and dig right down to the bedrock. So, it sounds like old grandfather Ay did a damn good job of burying them deep enough for his enemies to have no idea where to start looking. And he was sadly right in predicting his own fate. Ay's burial was desecrated and most of the royal cartouches in his tomb wall paintings erased. His sarcophagus was smashed to bits. His mummy's never been found, but most believe it was destroyed in antiquity. Historians reckon it must have happened not long after his funeral and was part of a general campaign by his successors to destroy all traces of the Amarna legacy.'

I stared back at Ted, slowly absorbing everything we'd learnt. 'Is that it?' I asked. 'Is that as far as you've got with the translation?'

'There's just a tiny bit more,' Ted said and repositioned his narrow glasses on the end of his nose to read the final portion of the text he'd translated so far. ' *"I am determined all my precious jewels will lie undisturbed for all eternity."*'

I gaped at him and heard the indrawn breath of everyone else around the table. 'They're people?' I squeaked. 'The "precious jewels" are people?'

Adam's gaze caught on mine and locked there. 'Yes, of course, it makes sense...' We stared into each other's eyes as he went on, 'He describes Ankhesenamun as

Tutankhamun's "cherished treasure". We should have spotted it before! He's not talking about gold pectorals or faience beads. When he says his "precious jewels" remain hidden where none will ever find them, he's not talking about a cache of jewellery…'

'…He's talking about the kings and queens of ancient Egypt…' I breathed. 'My God Adam, there might be an undiscovered tomb out there…!'

Chapter 7

Slowly my vision cleared of the tantalising images dancing through my imagination, of lost tombs and the long dead personalities of the Amarna years. It seemed weird and out-of-place to see the holidaymakers cavorting in the pool and sunning themselves on their loungers. But a glance at the awesome pyramids was enough to know they bore witness to all and kept their own counsel. Time really was the most head-spinning concept. As the papyrus spilled light across the events of the most fascinating period of ancient Egypt, I felt like I was stepping backwards and forwards across thirty-two or three centuries. The pyramids had stood there throughout, immense, solid; eternal. Tutankhamun and Ay beheld them once as I did now. For all that in Pharaonic times the pyramids were coated in shining limestone, now sadly gone, they were essentially the same; a wonder of the ancient world whose true wonder may be in outlasting the modern one. They were a common link in the unbroken chain of history past, present and future. Quite frankly, it gave me the chills.

'We must go now,' Ahmed broke into the silent reverie we'd fallen into. 'We have to catch an aeroplane.' He shuddered to show exactly how he felt about the prospect.

We flew back to Luxor in a study of impatience to get back to the papyrus and translate the next section. The agony of suspense was only relieved by Shukura's face smiling gleefully out at us from the early evening edition of the newspapers handed out as we boarded the plane.

While the pages were mostly full of the political demonstrations, and angry scenes of protest from Tahrir Square, Shukura was given a small leader on the front page of the English language edition, with the full story inside. There she was, beaming out from a photograph taken among the display of Tutankhamun's treasures in the Egyptian Museum. She was holding aloft the gilded wooden figure of Tutankhamun on a skiff, throwing a harpoon. It was one of the most precious of the stolen artefacts we'd helped to recover.

The article described the museum's resident numismatist Shukura al-Busir as a modern-day heroine who'd received an anonymous call from a well-wisher and persuaded the military police to act. She'd been on the scene when armed police foiled the plot of a ruthless gang of antiquities thieves. They'd intended to use the disruption of the renewed political demonstrations as a cover to spirit the artefacts out of the country and onto the black market. Thanks to Mrs al-Busir and the anonymous caller, the darkest hour of the revolution – the theft by fellow Egyptians of treasures from the nation's shared heritage – could now be laid to rest.

I wasn't sure the plan of the villainous Said brothers was strictly as posited in the article. They seemed to me more opportunistic than well organised. But it made good copy. And with two of the villains dead, the other on the run, it seemed unlikely anyone was going to argue.

Shukura was praised for her decisive action in treating the call as genuine, not a hoax. All round, it was a very satisfying read. I allowed myself a nice little glow of pride for my part in returning the stolen items to their rightful place in the museum's display cabinets.

We were unable to sit together for the flight down to Luxor due to the short notice of our bookings. We were dotted about all over the aeroplane. I could see the back of Ahmed's head across the aisle three rows in front of me. From the way it was nodding I gathered he was once more fervently at prayer. Adam, Ted and Jessica were all strapped into their seats somewhere behind me. It was a short flight, so it didn't matter.

I leaned back against the headrest, closed my eyes and reflected on all the papyrus had revealed so far. I was struck by the tragic figure of the young Queen Ankhesenamun, barely into her twenties, and to have lived through such turmoil: two stillbirths, the loss of a young husband who clearly adored her; left as a pawn in the power struggles for the throne. Her desperate appeal to the Hittites may have amounted to treason, but it also struck me as rather headstrong, daring and brave. Here was a young woman making a last-ditch attempt to master her own destiny. It brought her alive somehow; made her curiously modern in her bid for emancipation. There was real poignancy to her words, acknowledging her lack of sons; the humiliation she felt, forced to beg for help outside her own country. Her loneliness and fear must have been crippling, but still she sought to act. She was the last in the pure line of the Thutmoside kings and queens of the glorious 18th Dynasty. She'd grown up in the glittering Amarna court and must once have believed herself semi-divine, part of the family of God-kings who ruled the earth. She must have known her death spelled the end of the golden era of the pharaohs. There was no one of royal birth left to inherit the empire. But still, faced with the failure of her mission, she chose to take her own life rather than submit to her enemies. A few tears leaked under my lashes as I contemplated her last moments, driven beyond all hope and endurance to place the passage of her immortal soul into the hands of the ailing grandfather who'd married her to protect her.

I had a fair idea who her enemies might be. I'd read enough ancient Egyptian fact and fiction to know the main protagonists on the stage of the Amarna period and its immediate aftermath. I knew the line of succession from Ay. But I didn't want to jump ahead of myself by speculating on anything else the papyrus might reveal. I used to be one of those sad creatures who read the last page of a novel to see how the story turned out before I was even halfway through it... but not anymore. History was unfolding with every section Ted managed to translate. I wanted to feel the thrill of each new revelation, without spoiling it with theories and conjectures of my own.

I opened my eyes to the sound of the undercarriage opening to let the wheels down in preparation for landing, and realised I'd been fast asleep for most of the flight.

The heat was physical, enfolding me in a stifling embrace as I stepped off the aircraft and onto the wheel-up steps leading down to the tarmac, where coaches awaited to whisk passengers to the terminal building a short distance away. Despite the shortness of the flight from Cairo, the sun was beginning to set. Airport procedures all took time.

Adam approached me as we entered the terminal. 'I'm coming back to the hotel with you before going home,' he said. 'I can't have the rest of you stealing a march on me with the papyrus. Ted and I have agreed we should photograph the rest of Ay's scroll for translation. It's the best way to preserve the original from too much handling.'

It was fine by me. As the original duo who'd sleuthed our way to the discovery of the hidden papyri, it went without saying we should both be present for any significant next steps. And let's be honest, it was never a hardship to have Adam's face within gazing distance.

We parted company with Ahmed at the airport as he was back on tourist police duty tonight. With hugs all round and much laughter at his exuberant relief at having his large feet firmly planted back on terra firma, we waved him off. The remaining four of us, plus Ted and Jessica's luggage, piled into a generously proportioned if rather beaten-up taxi for our trip to the Jolie Ville.

It was a pleasant drive through a dusty landscape bathed in a golden glow of fading light, as the fiery sun started its slow journey beyond the western horizon. Our conversation was desultory, each occupied with our own thoughts as we anticipated the prospect of an evening in the spine-tingling company of the ghosts brought to life by the ancient papyrus.

I stared out the window, absorbed by the view of semi-rural Egyptian life as the taxi jolted us towards our destination over and around sandy pot-holes big enough to play long-jump in. Raggedy children played in the dusty streets among roaming animals of the farmyard variety. I presumed all the chickens and goats must belong to someone despite the lack of any sort of tethering. Stray cats, mangy dogs and an occasional dejected-looking donkey added to the general melee of a typical Egyptian twilight. Generators hummed in the dark recesses of side streets as the agricultural fields near the airport gave way to the sprawling mud-brick suburbs of modern Luxor. The streets were lined with small one-room shops, selling knobbly looking fruit and vegetables, cheap toiletries and bottled water. There was a nod to the twenty-first century in the clunky-looking glass-fronted refrigerators standing by the roadside, filled with cans of soft drink and cartons of fruit juice; and in the old-fashioned freezers lining the pavement emblazoned with the branding of Walls ice-cream. But otherwise, these could have been street scenes from just about any time in the last hundred years. Men sat on the kerbside with their galabeyas hooked up to their knees, contentedly smoking their water pipes. Women, most of them dressed in the enveloping black robes of married Muslims, went about their business and paid no attention at all to the tourist traffic clattering along the streets. The unchanging scene gave me a profound sense of wellbeing. The demonstrations we'd witnessed in Cairo seemed a world away from this heartening slice of everyday life.

The sun had finished its descent by the time the taxi deposited us outside the reception building at the Jolie Ville. It's a beautiful oasis of a hotel, located on its own small island in the Nile a little way outside central Luxor.

While Ted and Jessica went about the business of checking in, I called through to Dan to let him know we'd returned and told him to come along and join us for a drink at the reception bar and to say hello.

He arrived a few minutes later as Ted and Jessica were handed their room cards, and small foldout maps of the island. We'd all gratefully downed the small glasses of hibiscus juice given to welcome our arrival, and now moved towards the bar on the far side of the palatial reception hall for something a little stronger.

'Dan, this is Jessica Said,' I performed the introduction to the one member of our party he hadn't met.

'Kincaid,' she corrected gently. 'It's Jessica Kincaid again now.'

I had to hand it to her; she really was a tough little cookie, determined to shake off the shackles of the past and move forward. Then I saw the look on Dan's face. He didn't appear to have registered Jessica, despite my introduction. His gaze was fixed on my face with an expression I didn't like the look of at all. 'Dan? What on earth is the matter?'

'It's the papyrus,' he croaked, 'God Pinkie, I don't know how to tell you...'

It brought all eyes swinging towards him, four gazes riveted to his face.

'What about the papyrus?' I demanded urgently.

'They... they're gone.'

'What do you mean, *they're gone*?'

'Stolen,' he choked. 'They've been stolen.'

We all stared at him in horror.

'I thought the safest place for them was locked up inside my own suitcase,' he jabbered, almost falling over himself to get the words out. His gaze didn't once leave my face, almost as if he didn't dare look at the others and could only just bring himself to give his accounting to me. 'That antique-looking case was too big to store in the safe deposit box, and I didn't want to just stash it under the bed. I thought the housekeeping staff might be curious about it. So, I hid it inside my own suitcase, and padlocked it.'

'But it's not there now?' Stupid question, I know; but he'd suddenly stalled in his telling of the story, as if he couldn't bear to say the next part. It was all I could think of to get him talking again in the paralysis of the moment.

'It was definitely there this morning. I shifted it out of the bottom of the wardrobe to get to my Birkenstocks and the padlock was intact. But when I got back half an hour or so ago after spending the afternoon by the pool and taking some snaps of the sunset, the door to my room was ajar. When I investigated, the lock had been forced. The wardrobe door was open. My suitcase was there, but the padlock was broken and the case with the scrolls in it was gone.'

All the oxygen seemed to seep from the air. Black dots swum before my eyes, and I felt my knees buckle. Adam's arm came around my waist and prevented me dropping to the floor. I sucked in a deep breath and tried to get my brain to function.

'It must be Hussein.' Jessica's breathless voice registered in some distant place in my consciousness. Struggling with a feeling akin to being under water, I swung my gaze to look at her. 'It's just hit me,' she exclaimed, 'Hussein never came back to the flat after Youssef left with Dad at knifepoint. It was always Mahmoud who checked on me. I presumed Hussein was involved in the protests in Tahrir Square. I know he was the one who led the break-in to the Egyptian Museum last year; I heard him say so on that first evening in the flat. But that was the last time I saw him. I felt sure he must be hoping to stage another robbery. But now I'm wondering if he trailed Youssef down here. There was never any love lost between Youssef and Hussein. Hussein and Mahmoud were the ones who were always in cahoots. I think they used Youssef as a kind of foil because he could charm the birds out of the trees when it suited him, and because of his association with a bona fide Egyptologist through me, i.e. my Dad. Youssef believed you guys were onto something because he caught the excitement when Dad and I talked about the hieroglyphics you'd found. Hussein must have decided to muscle in on the act. He'd have no qualms in relieving Youssef of whatever he discovered. Hussein was definitely the boss.'

'No honour among thieves,' Adam muttered against my hair.

'Oh God, if Hussein's got the papyri, all bets are off. We're in trouble,' Jessica whispered.

'I damn well hope he shows more respect for them than his brother did,' Adam ground out darkly. 'The *charming* Youssef...' – he invested the word with oceans of disdain – '...was all for putting a match to them!'

A sudden movement alongside us brought all gazes swinging towards Ted. He was clutching his chest, slowly sinking to the floor.

Jessica gave a yelp, and darted forward to break his fall.

It was the shock I needed to jolt me out of the previous one. I hammered on the bar for water while Adam, relieved of the need to prop me up, turned to help Jessica with Ted. Dan seemed frozen on the spot, his face an appalled mask as he contemplated the impact of his news.

I took the water to where Ted was propped on the floor in his daughter's arms. His face was ashen, but he was breathing, albeit in rasping gulps of air. I knelt alongside Adam and held the glass to his lips. Anxious bar and reception staff hovered around as Ted took a sip of the water.

'You may need to call an ambulance,' Adam advised them.

'No, no,' Ted murmured weakly. 'I'll be alright in a moment. Just a funny turn, that's all. Just need to catch my breath.'

'Let's get you somewhere more comfortable,' Adam suggested, and, between us, we moved him as gently as possible to one of the deeply cushioned sofas set around an ornamental fountain in the centre of the reception area. We all sat quietly while he recovered himself, assuring us a trip to the hospital or even to see the on-site doctor was unnecessary.

Finally, when his colour returned and his hands stopped shaking, Dan sat forward.

'I'm afraid I have a confession to make,' he said, with what can only be described as a hangdog expression on his face.

We all stared at him. I had a horrible premonition of what was coming next.

'I'm sorry to say; none of what I told you is true. Well, that is to say, I'm not sorry… because the papyrus scrolls aren't missing at all. They're still safely stowed away in the wardrobe in my room. But I am sorry, because I decided to play a practical joke on you… and I had no idea how disastrous the consequences would be.' He stared at Ted in abject misery, hanging his head like a shaggy puppy dog expecting a beating.

Only in Dan's case the beating was thoroughly deserved, and my fingers were itching to administer it. Dan's always had a disturbing penchant for practical jokes. I'm sure there must be some sinister reason for it buried deep down in his psyche; but if so, I've never been able to find it. He almost got fired from his job last year when he noticed his hated boss had popped out of the office without locking his computer. So, Dan sidled up to his desk and sent a message to the whole department from his boss's Inbox, inviting everyone to lunchtime drinks on his expense account. The only thing that prevented the precipitous – and wholly deserved – sacking was Dan's plea that he mistook the date for April Fool's Day, which was actually the following day.

It was one of those little freeze-frame moments; we all stared at Dan as if he'd switched to a foreign language and we couldn't quite make sense of what he'd said. This time he really did look truly sorry. I have to say, in the long and tortuous history of Dan's diabolical pranks, I don't think he's ever actually come close to killing anyone.

'I'm really dreadfully sorry,' he said.

'Sorry!' I thundered as my temper ignited, fired on all cylinders and achieved lift off. 'Sorry! Bloody hell, Dan; I'll give you sorry! Sorry doesn't even come close! Of all the despicable, scumbag tricks to play; what the hell did you hope to achieve?'

He looked quite wretched; not an expression I was used to seeing on his face. I took a moment to enjoy it, glaring at him. There are reasons why I've stayed with Dan for ten years, but quite frankly it's often a struggle to remember them. For instance, he's always been unfailingly polite to my mother – and she's not nicknamed Puff the Magic Dragon for nothing. She can be distinctly fiery. And his sense of humour can be quite engaging when it's directed at the occasional craziness of life in general. But right now, I was struggling to see any redeeming features whatsoever. His practical joke wasn't funny – and I was conscious of a sweeping embarrassment for having anything to do with him.

He attempted to justify himself. 'It's just, well, you were all so stirred up by the ancient bits of banana skin; and then you went rushing off to Cairo and left me here playing nursemaid to the damned stuff.'

I saw Ted's eyes nearly fall out of their sockets at Dan's disparagement of the precious scrolls as banana skin. I didn't think Dan and Ted were destined to hit it off all that successfully. It wasn't a promising start.

'I just thought I'd put the wind up you all a bit,' Dan finished lamely. 'It was just my little joke; I certainly never meant any harm by it. So, er, Ted... er, Mr Kincaid... I mean, er... Sir... I'm really most sincerely sorry. I didn't realise you had a weak heart.'

It was the last straw. 'He doesn't have a weak heart; you blunderbass!' I yelled. I don't quite know where that came from; I've never called anyone a blunderbass before in my life. 'Does he?' I looked urgently at Adam, relieved by the quick shake of his head. I did a quick, narrow-eyed double-take, suddenly quite sure my new soulmate was thoroughly enjoying the spectacle of me haranguing my boyfriend like a common fishwife. 'At least, he didn't have a weak heart until you started hurling bombshells about the place,' I modified as I fired back at Dan with rather less volume but equal heat. 'So, that's it! Stay in Egypt, by all means, if you wish to; it was, after all, your decision to come haring back here like some macho soldier with a score to settle. But don't expect me to share a room with you. After pulling a stunt like that, you can damn well stew in your own juices!' And, with that pithy little conclusion to my tirade, I stomped over to the reception desk, pulled out my credit card and booked another room.

Everything settled down after that. Ted declared himself quite recovered and willing to forgive the young man his sadly misplaced sense of humour. Jessica's eyes danced with devilment as she contemplated Dan's flushed face. Now her father was back to his old self, I think she saw the funny side in Dan's tragic little caper. I was glad someone did: I had a feeling it would take me a bit longer to see any comedic value in the drama he'd enacted.

We all shared a single thought – at least; those of us who went by anything other than the name Dan Fletcher did – which was to see the papyri; to stand in awe before the cracked and crumbling scrolls once more. And I think we wanted to prove to ourselves once and for all Dan's hoax was exactly that, so we could breathe easy again.

So, we trooped through the darkening hotel grounds to what had been my room up until yesterday, henceforth Dan's. I must confess I was quite grateful to have a reason to be angry with Dan. I'd been rather dreading the prospect of sharing a room with him in view of all that had happened over the last few weeks, but – coward that I am – I wanted to put off the awful moment of decision. Now I had a brilliant excuse to maintain my independence, and it was with a light step that I skirted the swimming pool and danced out of the way of the sprinklers.

The lock on the door was assuredly not broken. The wardrobe door was closed and, once Dan pulled it back, the big twenty-first century suitcase was very much in evidence as was the padlock when Dan lifted the case out onto the bed. We all breathed a hearty sigh of relief. The trouble was his practical joke had been all too horribly plausible. Still, Dan wasn't to know about the runaway Hussein, who'd added a horrible verisimilitude to his tale.

We didn't have handy sheets of glass to protect the papyri this time. I busied myself packing up my stuff for transfer to my new room in the next hexagonal bungalow block along where Ted and Jessica were also located. Adam and Ted painstakingly unrolled Ay's text and took iPad photographs of the last half. Everyone agreed we should handle the ancient scrolls as little as possible. We'd not looked at the other two yet and decided to savour this anticipation for later.

Job done, we glanced at our watches. 'How about dinner in town?' Adam asked.

'You youngsters go along,' Ted said, sounding a hundred years old; although it was great to see the colour back in his cheeks, the scholarly fever alight in his eyes. The ancient papyrus seemed to give him a rush of energy like wiring him up to the national grid. 'I'm for an early night tonight. I ate on the flight, so I'm not hungry. I'm sure room service can sort me out an omelette if I get peckish later.'

So, Adam, Jessica, Dan and I made up a rather uncomfortable foursome as we bundled into a taxi and headed back into Luxor. We ate at a wonderful restaurant tucked down a side street, called The Lantern. Owned by an English lady, who performed front-of-house duties, married to an Egyptian man, the chef. It was the first time I'd seen Jessica look really wistful as she contemplated what might have been if her cross-cultural marriage had been to a more civilised man. The food was delectable, an eclectic mix of traditional Egyptian and western fusion. As

Adam and Dan moved onto their second bottle of beer each, and Jessica and I shared a very palatable bottle of Omar Khayyyam red wine, we all started to relax.

Jessica's eyes were dancing again as she looked at Dan across the table. 'So, I gather these jokes are a bit of a habit of yours, are they?'

Dan grinned; back to his normal self now he knew Ted wasn't at imminent risk of popping his clogs. But he was still decidedly off beam with me since I'd taken the small matter of our sleeping arrangements into my own hands. 'The best one was on a cruise a year or so back,' he said.

I groaned. I knew exactly what was coming.

'Do you want to tell it, Pinkie, or shall I? he asked evilly; getting his own back on me in bundles.

'I'd hate to deny you the pleasure,' I muttered, and took a sip of wine followed by a mouthful of a rather tasty beef tagine.

'The purser came knocking at our cabin door early one morning,' Dan said. 'He said he'd received an email from a previous passenger who claimed to have lost a diamond ring. She'd attached a photograph of the ring, the gaudiest bit of bling you ever did see. Anyway, apparently it was worth a fortune; and as the previous occupant of our cabin, it didn't seem unreasonable to think she'd lost it there. So, we let him come in and search the place; pulling out all the drawers, looking behind the sofa, under the bed. It was only when he knocked Pinkie's handbag off the shelf the trouble really started. You've seen for yourself how she favours massive great canvas monstrosities. Anyway, in knocking it over, the concierge somehow managed to spill its contents right across the carpet. And, lo and behold, what should turn up among the general paraphernalia…? Yes, you guessed it… the blingsome diamond monstrosity.'

'It wasn't diamond, it was costume,' I said tetchily. 'And you'd know, because you planted it there.'

Dan's grin rivalled the Cheshire Cat's. 'Yes, but you didn't know that at the time. You should have heard her! Falling over herself with protestations of innocence!'

I sent him a fulminating glance from beneath my lashes. 'It was your guffaw – yes, there really is no other word for it; it was a definite guffaw – that gave the game away.'

He didn't look in the least put out. 'It was worth every cent of the twenty-dollar tip I had to pay him to see your face!'

Jessica giggled prettily; but I noticed Adam was sitting very still, his fork resting on his plate, watching me quietly from behind his beer bottle. I could have cheerfully throttled Dan right then.

The rest of the meal passed pleasantly enough with Jessica telling us how she'd finished university but come out to Cairo because she missed her Dad. She'd trained as a costume designer but found a job as a singer in one of the five-star Cairo hotels. That's where Youssef spotted her and began his courtship.

I found it hard to reconcile the murderous Arab I'd encountered in the tomb shaft with the urbane young man she described. She'd fallen for the romantic dream of an Egyptian idyll, but it seemed he'd shown his true colours soon enough; and their short marriage was not a happy one.

Dan paid the bill – it was the least he could do – and we said our goodbyes in the narrow street outside the restaurant. Adam was heading back to his flat near the Souk. Jessica, Dan and I clambered into another taxi and gave the driver the name of our hotel. Adam and I shared a glance before we went in our separate directions. I couldn't say exactly what I read into that momentary meeting of our eyes; only that I sensed a frustration that was possibly my own.

It was as I stepped out of the shower, having finished unpacking my stuff in my new room, a lovely carbon copy of the old one; that the telephone rang. I wound a towel turban-style around my head, wrapped another around my midriff and went to answer it, expecting a complaining Dan on the wire. But it was the night-duty receptionist. 'Miz Pink, there iz a man here who needz to speak wiz you urgently. Hiz name iz Mr Tennyson.'

'Oh,' I said, wondering what had happened to bring Adam back so quickly. 'Ok: I'm on my way.'

I pulled on cropped cotton trousers and a t-shirt and jogged along to the reception building with wet hair. Stars spangled the heavens above me, but I barely paused to notice them. One becomes frighteningly blasé about the wondrous beauty of an Egyptian night after a while.

Adam rose to meet me from the depths of a cushioned sofa as I burst into the reception area. I ran into his arms without thinking. He held me close a moment; then pulled back and looked into my eyes. 'Something's wrong, Merry.'

'What do you mean?'

'I got home to find my flat had been ransacked. There's literally stuff strewn all over.'

We stared into each others eyes a moment; then with a single thought turned and ran from the reception block. We retraced our steps from earlier at full pelt, and only came to a halt when the door to Dan's room stood before us. Adam banged on it loud enough to raise the dead. Dan came to the door clad only in his jockey shorts.

'Dan, was everything ok when you got back here tonight?' I asked urgently.

He frowned. 'Yes, I think so. The housekeeper was here changing the towels. Perhaps a bit later than usual; but all ship shape and Bristol fashion so far as I can tell.'

Adam strode into the room. 'We need to see the papyri.'

'But you saw them earlier,' Dan protested. 'Can't you leave the damn stuff alone for five minutes?'

'Now.' Adam said in a tone that brooked no refusal. I'd only heard him use that peremptory tone once before, seeing off the curio sellers at the pyramids, weeks ago. But it had me jumping to attention then; and it had a similar effect on Dan now. Adam had been a high-flier in the banking world once upon a time, and I supposed certain things stuck.

Dan loped across the room and slid back the wardrobe door. We all gaped at the empty space where his suitcase had been earlier.

'Where's the suitcase?' I said weakly.

Dan was in no position to answer. Raw and naked shock beaconed from his expression. 'But ...' he blustered and faltered into silence.

It was obvious he wasn't goofing around this time.

'Your practical joke was an unwitting prophecy,' Adam said grimly. 'Someone has stolen the papyri; and, if Jessica is to be believed, I think we can hazard a pretty shrewd guess about who it is.'

Chapter 8

We spent a troubled night, tossing it this way and that, but eventually conceded there was nothing we could do in the immediate wake of the awful discovery. We toyed briefly with the idea of calling Ahmed. But honestly, what could he do? We'd come into possession of the ancient papyri by rather circuitous means, not all of which were strictly on the right side of the law. And there was still the small matter of the so-far unidentified body in the Valley of the Kings. So, in the final analysis, it seemed better to sit tight rather than start running around like headless chickens.

'What I want to know is how the hell he got in,' Dan demanded. 'There's no sign of the door lock being forced. I thought it was a rather necessary part of the plot when I was the one devising it.'

'It wouldn't surprise me if he's been keeping watch for a couple of days,' Adam said. 'He must know Youssef's dead. I suppose we should be grateful he's not blown the whistle on us about that. But obviously he's been holding out for a bigger prize. He must have had you under surveillance, but maybe an opportunity never presented itself for him to make his move.'

'I was pretty much always in sight of the room,' Dan admitted. 'The pool's only across the grass there; so, I was never more than a few paces away. And I ordered breakfast and dinner from room service.'

'He may not even have been sure you had the object we removed from the tomb,' Adam conjectured. 'His first thought was clearly that we'd stored the suitcase in my flat; that's why he ransacked the place. It's possible he only realised it was in your room when he saw us all rush over here earlier this evening. He must have been staking out the hotel. It's even possible he was in reception when you were acting out your little drama, Dan. He might have learned about the suitcase within the suitcase that way, so knew what he was looking for.'

Dan looked a bit sick.

'And saw his chance when we all went out tonight,' I said.

'All he needed to do was to wait for the evening housekeeping service to do the rounds,' Adam concluded. 'Once the cleaner was inside the room, busily changing towels in the bathroom, it was a pretty simple matter for him to slip in and snatch the case. No one's going to raise an eyebrow at someone strolling through a hotel pulling a big, modern suitcase on wheels.'

'My God, we must just have missed him! We might even have walked past him!' Dan exclaimed.

'Well, however and whenever it happened; he's got the papyri now. And if Jessica's right, he's dangerous.'

We stared at each other as the stark horror of our situation washed over us. 'There's nothing we can do tonight,' Adam said flatly. 'Let's sleep on it and see if an idea occurs to one of us for how we can track him down. If he's read the newspapers, then he knows not to go back to his flat in Cairo. So, he may have the upper hand, but he's still a man on the run.'

We met early next morning for breakfast on the expansive terrace overlooking the dark shifting waters of the Nile. I'd begged Adam not to go back to his flat alone last night and, thank God, he heard my plea; so now we were all booked into rooms at the Jolie Ville. I don't mind admitting I slept a whole lot better knowing Adam was close by in another hotel room like mine, rather than out there alone in his flat.

I'm not sure any one of us had an appetite to speak of, but it seemed as good a place as any for a pow-wow; and the morning coffee was exceptionally good. So, over coffee and croissants, the three of us stared at each other; then across the Nile towards the distant Theban hills glowing deep pink in the soft early morning light; waiting for inspiration to strike.

We'd only been there a few minutes when Jessica appeared; all pink-cheeks, bright eyes and bouncing golden curls. I couldn't quite decide whether the best word to describe Jessica was jaunty or perky. There was definitely something a bit pixie-ish about her, in the cute, elfin way of pixies.

She said a cheery 'good morning', plopped herself down onto the spare seat, helped herself to coffee from the silver pot; then looked up. The bright smile froze on her face. 'What on earth's the matter?' she cried. 'You all look terrible.' I could see her taking in the dark circles under our eyes and the strained dejection coming off us in waves.

'Might as well tell her,' Dan said gloomily. 'She'll find out soon enough.'

Adam nodded and addressed himself to Jessica. 'As it turns out, the little bit of theatre Dan treated us to yesterday was just the warmup act. You might even go so far as to call it a dress rehearsal. Since then, the whole drama's been played out for real.'

'What?' she gaped around the table at us.

Adam has always enjoyed a poetic turn of phrase. 'What he's trying to tell you,' I said in plain and simple English, 'is the papyri have been stolen. The case was gone from Dan's room when we got back last night. We thought to check after Adam went home to find his flat had been ransacked.'

'Oh no!' she breathed, clutching at her throat, 'It can only be Hussein.'

'Yes, we reached the same conclusion,' Adam agreed.

'We mustn't tell my Dad,' she appealed urgently. 'You saw what it nearly did to him yesterday. He's a scholar, not a superhero. All this charging up and down the country, getting ordered about at knifepoint, rescuing me, rescuing the artefacts from the museum… it's putting too much of a strain on him. I'd never forgive myself if anything happened to him, all because I was dumb enough to marry into a family of criminals.'

If I'd been wavering about Jessica before; that was the moment I made up my mind to like her. It was heartfelt and impassioned, and I heartily approved every word. I smiled warmly at her, 'Have you seen Ted this morning?'

'Yes, I looked in on him just now. He's having breakfast in his room, looking forward to a day of translation. He told us to enjoy ourselves sight-seeing or chilling out by the pool.'

'Thank God we had time to photograph the last section of Ay's letter,' I said fervently. 'At least it gives him something to keep him absorbed for today.'

'But it still leaves two whole scrolls rolled up and in the hands of that villain.' Adam pointed out worriedly. 'We won't be able to keep it from Ted forever. He'll be itching to get to work on the remaining papyri. We need to think of a way of getting them back, and fast.'

'And not just to give Ted the chance to fulfil the dream of a lifetime,' I said. 'If the papyrus really does end up suggesting there's an undiscovered tomb in the Valley somewhere, that's knowledge we don't want to fall into the wrong hands.'

It was at that moment the ransom note arrived.

'Mizter Fletcher,' one of the reception staff came hurrying up to our table. 'Zis note haz been delivered. Ze man says very urgent… muzt be delivered to ze man in room H8 right now!'

'Thank you,' Dan said, reaching for the envelope with a frown.

'Is the man still there?' Adam asked quickly.

'No, no; he zaid he muzt go; but to bring zis right away.'

'I wondered if we might get something like this,' Adam said musingly, 'After all, the papyri aren't much good to him if he doesn't read hieratic script. And I doubt they're saleable on the black market in the way the museum artefacts were. They're too explosive; and he doesn't know their provenance. He needs us.'

I looked at him suspiciously. 'You thought no such thing!'

There was a shadow of his former boyish grin in the slight lift of his lips as he looked back at me. 'Makes sense though, doesn't it?'

Dan fumbled with the flap on the envelope, and pulled out a single sheet, which he unfolded. He looked at it blankly. 'It's written in Arabic.'

'It figures,' I said. 'I don't recall Youssef having much grasp of English. Jessica, do you read Arabic?'

'Passably well, if it's simple enough,' she said, reaching across the table for the note.

We all held our collective breath while she studied it.

'Yes, simple enough,' she said after a moment. 'He suggests a straight swap… the suitcase and its contents in return for a million Egyptian pounds.'

My eyes bulged, 'How much?'

Adam did a quick mental calculation. 'That's just over £100,000 on the current rate of exchange.'

'Where the hell are we supposed to get that sort of money?'

Unbelievably, Adam was smiling. 'It's a fraction of what the papyri are worth. So, it proves he's desperate. Or maybe he doesn't know the value of what he's got.'

'When does he want it?' Dan asked.

Jessica frowned at the note. 'He suggests 5 o'clock this afternoon, in the holy of holies at Luxor temple.'

'He has a funny sense of humour,' I muttered. 'I see very little holiness in theft and bribery.'

'It's a public place,' Adam remarked matter-of-factly, 'full of tourists. He can be pretty sure we won't try anything funny; and reassuringly, that works both ways. By 5 o'clock it should be busy after the lull in the early part of the afternoon when it's at its hottest. And it gives us all day to get the money together.'

'Now hang on just a damned minute,' Dan objected angrily. 'Are you seriously suggesting we buy back those disintegrating old tubes of paper with a hundred grand of our own money?'

'How else do you propose we raise it?' I asked archly. 'Rob a bank?'

He shot a poisonous look at me. 'Don't be bloody daft! But this has gone far enough. The most sensible thing, surely, would be to hand the whole sorry matter over to the police, and let them deal with him. You said yourself, he's on the run, wanted by the police as an antiquities thief. If they catch him in possession of those old scrolls, they'll have him banged to rights in no time.'

'You know we can't do that,' I said with exaggerated patience. I was really quite annoyed with him now but determined to keep it in check. Honestly, he was like a broken record, keep repeating the same thing over and over again. 'We'd have to admit to our part in everything, and that includes the dead body in the Valley of the Kings. Sorry Jessica,' I said as a small aside, 'I know he was your husband.'

She waved away my apology as an utter irrelevance.

Dan's eyes were snapping with anger, 'Well maybe that wouldn't be such a bad thing. It's not as if you actually killed him. He fell off that cliff all by himself. I know, because I was there when it happened; remember? It seems to me your only option is to make a clean fist of it to the authorities. Ok, so you have to admit to the hieroglyphics that started all this, and the fact you pinched them from Howard Carter's house. And you have to own up to getting your police chum to break you into a locked tomb. But I'm sure they'll turn a blind eye to these little peccadilloes if you're handing over a dangerous and wanted criminal; and making a gift of the papyrus scrolls at the same time. Who knows, you might even be lauded as a heroine, a bit like your friend from the Egyptian Museum in the article you showed me.'

There was a horrible sort of logic in all this. 'It's impossible,' I said flatly, before I could give my brain a moment more to consider it. 'We'll lose Ahmed his job. And that would be grossly unfair considering all the help he's given us; not to mention the abject terror he suffered flying for the first time.' I don't think I was trying to make sense; I was simply hurling out all the objections I could think of.

However far-fetched it may sound, the emotional attachment I felt to that papyrus – or perhaps to the story it was telling – was profound and deep-rooted. And I knew Adam felt the same way. I couldn't have been more determined to get it back had it been my own child the wretched Arab had kidnapped and was now holding for ransom. There was simply no way I could hand the whole thing over to someone else.

But Dan wasn't giving up. 'Ok, well, if not the authorities, what about the Egyptian Museum? Surely if you had a chat with your friend Suki, or whatever she was called…'

'Shukura,' I put in automatically.

'Yes, her, Shukura… surely she'd help you raise the ransom money if you told her what you were buying with it.'

'But then we'd have to hand the papyri over to the museum as soon as we got them back; and that doesn't seem fair on Ted. You've seen how all this has affected him. He's like a child whose Christmases have all come at once. It would be too cruel to snatch it away from him now and hand over the translations of the last two scrolls to the philologists at the museum.'

Dan was looking at me as if I was someone he'd never met before. 'You'd really hand over a hundred grand of your own money to keep your dodgy police buddy safe in a job he seems quite willing to play fast and loose with, and give your new friend Ted the chance to live out a dream?'

'Well, I don't actually have a hundred grand;' I qualified, 'but yes. And besides, I can't imagine the Egyptian museum wouldn't want to know how we came by the papyri. So, we're really no further forward.'

He rolled his eyes as if it was the final proof he needed that I'd gone over to the dark side. 'You're mad!' he said, just in case I hadn't quite grasped what he thought of me. 'I want no part in it. Well, put it this way, I'm willing to come along if an extra pair of fisticuffs are needed. I'm quite happy to get that desiccating parchment back in a fair fight. But I refuse to spend a single penny of my hard-earned money on it.' And he sat back and folded his arms making it quite clear that as far as he was concerned the subject was closed.

'Well maybe we can think about fight tactics later,' Adam said. 'But we mustn't do anything to put the papyri at risk. So, for now I suggest we stick with Plan A.'

Dan's expression revealed more eloquently than words what he thought of Adam's concern for the ancient scrolls, but he'd said all he intended to say on the matter and contented himself with a soft grunt.

'So, we need to set about raising a hundred grand,' I said. 'I've got a bit put by in premium bonds; and there's my redundancy money. If I clear out my savings account as well, I can probably get us some of the way there. But I doubt I can get my hands on it today.'

Adam's expression was soft and a bit misty-eyed as he gazed at me. 'Don't worry about the money,' he said quietly. 'I can cover that.'

We all stared at him. I knew he'd worked in the banking sector, and he'd mentioned bonuses, but I hadn't had him down as someone who could lay his hands on a hundred grand without blinking.

'I sold my house,' he said lightly. 'My ex-wife has already had her share of the profits. So, I've got a little nest egg we can use.'

'No way,' I said staunchly. 'It's not fair for you to shoulder all the cost, whether you can afford to or not; that's not the point. We should at least go halves. I could take out a loan. After all, I'm the one who got us into all this.'

'Oh God, let's not start all that again,' Dan groaned. 'We had all this the other night: who's to blame for what. I don't think I can bear it.'

A ghost of a smile played across Adam's face. 'Ok, so here's a suggestion. Let me sort the money out for now. We can agree how to divvy it up later if need be. For now, let's not argue about it; let's just concentrate on getting the papyri back. Right, I'm going to head back to my flat and clean things up a bit; then I'll pack some stuff, go to the bank, and meet you all back here later; say 3ish?'

I wished I could think of a good reason to go with him. I watched him thread his way between the breakfast tables, with the sunshine glinting on his dark hair and felt a bit bereft.

'I'm for a lazy day by the pool,' Dan said. 'Might as well try to treat this bizarre trip like a holiday when the opportunity presents itself. Coming Pinkie?'

'Maybe later,' I said; and watched him amble across the terrace and out of sight behind the hedge surrounding the adult-only swimming pool.

I looked at Jessica's downcast little face and a deep sense of foreboding came over me. She'd been very quiet while the argument was batting back and forth over the ransom of the papyrus scrolls.

'Are you alright, Jessica?' I asked.

'Hm, what? Sorry, Merry, I mean, pardon? Did you say something?'

The foreboding crystallised into a hard knot of premonition. She was planning something. 'I asked if you were alright. You look a bit peaky.' It was in stark contrast to the jaunty perkiness of earlier.

'I think it must be the shock of learning about the papyri being stolen and then receiving Hussein's ransom note like that. If you'll excuse me Merry, I think I might just go for a lie down.'

I didn't believe her for a second.

I watched her out of sight; then trailed her as she went back to her room. I hid in the conveniently located pergola in the grounds across from our bungalow block. It dripped with bright pink bougainvillea and provided great cover, so she didn't see me when she emerged again a few minutes later. I congratulated myself on my excellent female intuition and moved out of my hidey-hole. I had no need to return to my room before following her. I'd taken my huge canvas holdall with me to breakfast, as I always do – it accompanies me everywhere - so I was prepared for pretty much any eventuality.

She called up a taxi from the little hut outside the reception building. So, I did likewise from reception itself; stepping into my cab as hers swung in an arc around the courtyard outside the hotel. I've never in my life given the instruction to 'follow that cab'. It really did sound quite thrillingly melodramatic. I could quite easily imagine myself in a Hollywood movie for a moment. The taxi driver, Mohammed according to the little badge dangling from the wing mirror, looked at me askance and started jabbering about needing to fix a price. I told him I didn't have a clue where we were going but promised to make it worth his while. I waved some bank notes under his nose just to be sure. His eyes lit up, and he stamped on the throttle with a quite reassuring enthusiasm.

We followed Jessica's cab along the broken-up road into Luxor, swerving around pot-holes and abandoned chunks of concrete – presumably intended to be a central reservation – strewn in the middle of the road. There was a hairy moment when a donkey strayed into our path; and we barely missed a mangy dog when he pelted across the road in front of us; but all things considered the driver did a pretty good job.

I was unsurprised when Jessica's cab pulled up in the Corniche, the embankment running alongside the east bank of the Nile in Luxor. She darted into the building of the National Bank of Egypt near the Winter Palace Hotel. I think I had a pretty shrewd idea what she was up to. But I was very surprised indeed when the taxi turned around, headed back out of town towards the Jolie Ville, but then veered off down the little side street where the Sheraton Hotel was located. I knew where it was because Dan and I had enjoyed a meal in the Indian restaurant there back in the days when we were here as simple holidaymakers.

It flashed through my mind to wonder if Jessica could possibly be in cahoots with the villainous Hussein Said. As my imagination ran wild, I pictured her rushing up to him and urgently advising him to revise the ransom. The papyri were worth a fortune, and Adam was clearly loaded; so, he could probably at least double his demand and get away with it.

As my flight of fancy really took off, I even asked myself if Ted could possibly be in on the act. I shook my head to dismiss such rampant stupidity. I should have restricted my coffee intake at breakfast. The caffeine hit was sending me into cloud cuckoo land.

Jessica's cab dropped her at the gates of the Sheraton. I flung a fistful of notes at my driver – way too much for the fare he'd clocked up. But I didn't have time to waste counting it out and haggling – and jumped out to follow her. But she didn't turn in through the gates of the hotel. Instead, she struck out along a side street on foot. She didn't glance back. Why should she? She had no idea she was being followed. I trailed her at a safe distance feeling increasingly alarmed. At least there was relative safety in the cosmopolitan surroundings of a five-star hotel. This maze of alleyways and back streets, littered with rotting fruit, horse dung and refuse, and buzzing with swarms of small black flies, was more than intimidating. It was downright scary. There were very few people about. A few old ladies sat nodding toothlessly in doorways, and a couple of scruffy children were playing with a scrawny kitten in a yard as we passed. I could feel sweat breaking out along my hairline and starting to trickle down my back. Parts of this country of Egypt are truly wonderful; magical and inspiring, and parts of it are not. That's probably about the fairest thing I can say. This backwater of stinking mud-baked slums was definitely in the 'not' category. It made me feel depressed and a bit angry on behalf of the people who still had to live like this in the twenty-first century. We were in the far outskirts of the town, away from the buzz of downtown Luxor with its more modern flats, and life was basic; and that was putting it kindly. Still, this, in good part, was what all the rioting was about up in Cairo. If there was any chance of a less poverty-stricken way of life for these people, then I was full square behind it. I don't think people go hungry in Egypt – there's plenty of food – but some of the poorest people live in squalor, without even the bare essentials for health and hygiene.

Fired up with these semi-political musings, I followed Jessica through the refuse-strewn alleyways. How the hell did she know where she was? And, perhaps more importantly, how the hell did she know where she was going? We were starting to move out into the open fields. If she turned now there was no way she could fail to spot me, for all that I trailed her at as much distance as I dared.

The mud-brick dwellings we'd passed gave way to tumbledown shacks bordering the railway line on one side and fields of sugarcane and banana plantations on the other. I started to worry about snakes as my feet left the mud-baked streets and stepped onto the soft soil of agricultural land. I was only wearing little slip-on sandals, and cropped cotton trousers, with a loose t-shirt on top.

A few hundred yards in front of me Jessica stopped and shielded her eyes against the glare of the omnipresent sun. I ducked down behind a convenient stack of roughly chopped wood and peered around it to watch what she did next.

She seemed to be studying a shack located on the edge of the field. It was about the size of a single garage; with a base made of mud bricks, walls of lashed together cane, and a roof that might be corrugated iron or straw, it was hard to tell from this distance.

As she peered at it, a man stepped out through the doorway. My heart jumped into my throat and beat there unsteadily. He was wearing a dark galabeya, with a cloth wound into a turban around his head. He started waving his fist at her and shouting. Unbelievably, she moved towards him. Ok, so this must be Hussein. But what the hell was she doing, so far from the safety of civilisation, and how the hell did she know he was here? All sorts of suspicions started whispering in my brain again.

Jessica shouted back in Arabic. Both Ted and Jessica spoke fluent Arabic. Was that fact suggestive? My whirling brain struggled helplessly to make sense of what I was seeing.

The tiny English girl and the menacing Arab moved closer together. I saw her take something from her shoulder bag and wave it at him; money, I guessed. They were still shouting at each other nineteen to the dozen. They stopped a couple of paces apart. The shouting match continued for a minute or so. Then I saw him pull his fist back. There was no time to cry out to warn her. But I did cry out and leap up from behind my hiding place when his fist slammed into her face.

Stupid of me; I don't think Jessica had even hit the ground before he was after me. I turned and ran; the single thought in my head to get back to civilisation to get her some help. I had a head start on him, but I was wearing flimsy sandals poorly designed for running, and he was fast.

'Lady; stop!' It was a command barked from just behind me before I'd even reached the edge of the field.

I had no choice but to stop and turn. He loomed in front of me, grinning evilly. But what really caught my attention was the long-bladed jack-knife he was waving in my face. What was it with this family and knives? They seemed to make a discouraging habit of carrying them around, producing them from the pockets of their galabeya robes much in the same way a magician might pull a rabbit from a hat.

His English wasn't up to the task of telling me what to do. But a few waves of the knife and a bit of pointing and head jerking made it clear enough. With a heavy heart, and a healthy dose of fear, I turned and stumbled my way towards the shack.

Chapter 9

I insisted we stopped to scoop up Jessica as we approached the shack. She was starting to come round from the dizzying effects of the blow he'd landed on her, and her nose was bleeding. I glared at him and muttered a few well-chosen phrases to express exactly what I thought of men who hit women; especially great big hulking oafs who used violence on tiny little creatures like Jessica. I don't think he understood a word I said, but I'm sure he caught my meaning. He stood there, calmly pointing the knife at me, while I crouched down and eased her up off of the dirt.

Jessica groaned and looked dazedly up at me. 'Merry?'

'Shush, don't try to speak just yet. This black-hearted villain might decide to use his fists again. Just take it easy and give yourself some time to come to.'

Hussein jerked his head towards the door, making it clear he wanted us inside. I helped Jessica awkwardly to her feet, and we stumbled into the shack. It was stifling hot, filthy and smelled of sheep. It took no great leap of imagination to realise it was used as a farmyard pen. That is, when animals of the human variety weren't occupying it – one particular animal, I should say. It was furnished with a table, a chair and a camp bed; that's it. Over in the corner there was a holdall, which I imagined contained Hussein's essential staying-away-from-home items. It was small, so I assumed he travelled light. And there, alongside it, stood Dan's suitcase. If any doubt remained about whose company we were in, the sight of that suitcase removed it. The padlock was gone, so it was clear he'd checked out what was inside. I could only hope and pray he hadn't done any damage to the precious scrolls.

Hussein used the knife to wave us towards the bed. Reluctant as I was to sit on it, we had no choice, and it was infinitely preferable to the floor, which felt disturbingly sticky underfoot. I perched there with Jessica propped in my arms and glared mutinously at him. 'I'm going to try to clean her up a bit,' I told him, and reached into my canvas bag for a pack of tissues.

He kicked the bag away from me and growled ominously.

'Give me my bag back, you… heathen,' I stormed. 'I can't let her sit here with blood dripping down her face.' I mimed out my intentions, pointing at my bag, then Jessica's face, and making washing motions with my hands.

He grunted and kicked the bag back towards me; but hovered with the knife pointed at my left ear while I rummaged for tissues. He stood back when I brought them out with a little flourish and waved them at him. 'See?

Tissues! I'm hardly going to attack you with them, much as I'd like to!'

I did the best job I could of wiping Jessica's face clean with tissues dipped into the little bottle of water I also had in my bag. She stared at me a bit blearily, but I could see she was slowly coming back to her senses.

There was a long, tense stand off for a while. I could almost see the cogs of Hussein's brain turning while he tried to decide what to do next. It hadn't been part of his plan for us to fall into his lap, so to speak. But now he had us in his lair he just needed to figure out how to make the best use of us. I could only hope killing us wasn't high on the list of his most advantageous options.

Finally, he seemed to reach a decision. 'You... stay,' he said; then added something in Arabic.

'He said he's going out,' Jessica said. 'But he'll be back soon.'

He waved the knife under my nose to emphasise his instruction, then turned and strode from the shack. The door slammed and I heard a wooden bar come down across it, locking us in. It was rather dark with the door shut. There was no window to speak of; just a narrow air vent about six inches wide running around the top of the room, just above head height.

'You do seem to have formed a rather nasty habit of getting locked up by this family,' I remarked conversationally. 'What on earth did you think you were doing coming out here alone?'

Jessica put her head in her hands and started to cry. 'I just felt so wretched, and kind of guilty,' she gulped. 'I've brought everyone nothing but trouble. There's all the stuff my poor Dad's had to endure. And, if that wasn't enough, now you and Dan are falling out, and Adam's about to shell out a small fortune. And it's all because of me.'

'How do you figure that out?' I asked, genuinely baffled. 'You didn't put the gruesome Said brothers up to their villainous ways... Or did you?' I added suspiciously, suddenly remembering she'd known exactly where to come.

'No of course not! But if I hadn't been dumb enough to marry Youssef, none of this would have happened.'

'But you weren't to know he was a scoundrel.'

'Oh, I don't know,' she said miserably. 'I think some of the warning signs were there. But I chose to ignore them. And after we were married, he stopped being quite so careful to cover his tracks. But I still wasn't sure he and his brothers were actually criminals of any sort. It was really only when Dad guessed you and Adam might be onto something that things turned nasty.'

'But that's not your fault,' I said gently.

'I just keep thinking if Youssef hadn't tried to muscle in on the act, then you and Adam could have discovered those papyri in peace, and my Dad could be happily translating them now without any of this other stuff going on.'

I'd more or less reconciled myself to this unhappy truism days ago. 'But then Youssef and Mahmoud would still be alive, you'd still be married to a criminal, and we wouldn't have been able to return the stolen artefacts to the Egyptian Museum,' I reminded her.

She sniffed and dried her eyes with the back of her hand. 'That's true,' she acknowledged. 'But it's my fault we're both locked in here now.'

This simple reality I could not refute. 'What on earth were you hoping to achieve? You know Hussein's dangerous; you told us so yourself. And, perhaps more to the point, how did you know where to find him?'

She sat back and blew her nose. I was pleased to see it had stopped bleeding, and this didn't start it up again. 'Youssef brought me here once. I know it might seem a bit strange as a sightseeing destination. But believe it or not, this hovel is where his Dad grew up. Youssef wanted me to see how far his family had risen from these humble beginnings to the heady heights of modern suburbia in Cairo.'

'On the proceeds of a life of crime, no doubt,' I said archly.

'Yes, probably,' she admitted, 'He wasn't too specific about it. Anyway, sitting there at breakfast this morning, when you told me Hussein had stolen the papyri, it suddenly occurred to me he might be here. If he'd heard about Mahmoud's death, then he'd know he was a wanted man. So, I figured he wouldn't risk a hotel. This seemed like the logical place to lay low.'

I glanced around, wrinkling my nose at the squalor and the prospect of spending a night in it, as Hussein must have done, at least once. 'But, Jessica, why come out here on your own? Perhaps if you'd told us, we could have all come and sort of stormed the place. We could have brought Ahmed with us, and had the whole thing wrapped up quite nicely – including getting the papyri back and putting Hussein behind bars where he belongs.'

'I wasn't thinking straight,' she said with a small helpless shake of her head. 'Of course that would have been the obvious thing to do. But I just wanted to make him go away and leave you all alone.'

'So, you decided to play heroine,' I said. 'But Jessica, how the hell did you hope to persuade him?'

'I thought I could buy him off so Adam wouldn't have to. My Mum left me some money when she died. It's quite a tidy sum. I phoned my bank from the hotel this morning and asked them to arrange a cash transfer for me to sign for in Luxor. I thought if I could offer Hussein a bit more than he was asking for in the ransom note, he might take the money and run. I told him with Youssef and Mahmoud both dead his days were probably numbered. And if he thought he could get away with daylight robbery at Luxor temple this afternoon he had another think coming. My friends would never let him get away with it. They'd fight him to the bitter end. So why didn't he just hand the suitcase over to me now and I could save him the trouble of getting caught.'

'Was that what all the shouting was about before he hit you?'

'Yes. He didn't believe me. He thought it was a trick. He accused me of being a curse on him and his family.'

'So, he thumped you one just to vent his spleen – charming!'

'But Merry, what are you doing here?'

'I thought you might be up to something of the sort, so I followed you. But I didn't have the sense to keep quiet when he hit you. Sorry about that. If I'd kept my wits about me, I might have been able to go for help. As it is, we've both offered ourselves up like lambs to the slaughter.'

She shuddered, and I realised I could perhaps have chosen a slightly less graphic expression.

'I wonder where he's gone,' she said, 'and how long he's going to be.'

I took this to be a rhetorical question, so didn't bother to speculate an answer. 'I don't suppose you've got your mobile phone on you?' I asked instead. 'It's just I left mine charging while we went to breakfast; but it occurs to me we might be able to call for help.'

She stared at me, then started rummaging frantically in her shoulder bag. She pulled out her phone with a little squeal of delight and flipped it open. Then her face fell. 'No signal,' she said bitterly.

'Oh well, it was worth a try. I guess modern technology isn't the answer to everything.' I got up and started doing a slow circuit of the room, looking for possible weak spots in the threaded cane walls. They were dispiritingly sturdy, tightly lashed together. I kicked at the mud bricks a few times. This raised dust, but no prospect of shifting them. Which left only the roof. Close inspection revealed it to be made of straw coated in some claylike substance. I was just starting to scramble up on top of the table for a closer inspection when I heard the sound of the wooden bar being lifted from the door. I jumped down, and hastily returned to my spot on the edge of the bed next to Jessica.

Hussein strode back into the room carrying a satchel. The knife was no longer in evidence, but I had no doubt it was within reaching distance in the pocket of his roomy galabeya. He pointed me towards the table and chair. So, I got up again and moved across the room, seating myself at the table. He put a sheet of paper and a pen in front of me. 'You write,' he said.

I looked at him in confusion. 'Write what?'

He turned to Jessica and uttered a string of guttural Arabic.

'He said he'll dictate what he wants you to write to me so I can translate it for you,' she said.

I shrugged, and held the pen poised above the sheet of paper.

Hussein growled away in Arabic for a few moments. When he stopped, I looked at Jessica. 'Basically, it's another ransom note,' she said. 'He's using us to strengthen his position and to ensure Adam and Dan don't try any funny business when they hand over the money.'

I nodded, 'Makes sense I suppose. So, we're to be a kind of insurance policy. What does he want me to write?'

'That one man is to come alone to do the exchange. Hussein will post a note to the Jolie Ville saying where we are only after he's got away with the money.'

'Likely story,' I scoffed. 'It's far more likely he'll leave us here to rot.'

She looked pained. 'I don't see we have any choice Merry.'

'How will he know that I've written what he's said and not a message of my own if he doesn't read English? I could simply put, "We're locked in a shack in the fields behind the Sheraton Hotel. Please come and get us."'

Hussein growled again and took a menacing step towards me. He drew the knife out of his pocket and pricked my upper arm with it.

'Ouch! That hurt!

'You write,' he barked.

'Merry, you're scaring me. Please will you just write what he said! I don't want to sit and watch while he plays noughts and crosses on your arm with his knife.'

Fear drove all thoughts of subterfuge from my mind. I had no doubt he could prove quite adept at torture, and I had no desire to put him to the test. So, I wrote the short, simple essentials as dictated and signed it with a rather shaky hand.

He snatched the paper back from me when I'd finished. 'You stay,' he snarled, and strode back out through the door, dropping the bar firmly in place behind him.

I searched through my bag and found a single antiseptic wipe in its little foil sachet. I cleaned the small wound on my upper arm thoroughly. God knows what deadly germs lurked on the blade of his knife. I had no desire to go down with a killer virus just to round things off.

We heard the sound of a scooter firing up a short distance away, presumably Hussein setting off on his mission to deliver the letter. I glanced at my watch; amazed to see it was already lunchtime. Time really does fly when you're having fun. Adam wasn't due back to the Jolie Ville until 3ish; so Dan was the one who'd open the note. I tried to imagine his reaction. It did rather vindicate his view that we should have put the whole thing in the hands of the police. Oh well, it was too late for that now. Hussein would have no qualms in sending Jessica and me to meet our maker if he felt he was cornered. We really had played straight into his hands.

'I don't suppose you've got any water?' I asked.

Jessica shook her head. There was a tiny dribble left in the bottle I'd brought with me. We shared it between us. 'This isn't looking too promising,' I said; and scrambled up on top of the table again. 'So, we can either sit here tamely waiting to see what he does next and hope he doesn't take it into his head to murder us; or we can try to escape.' I used the empty water bottle to start prodding at the wattle and daub-type roof, testing for a weak spot.

I was rewarded when a large chunk of clay came loose, showering me in a cloud of crumbling powder. It landed with a thump on the tabletop and broke into little pieces. Breathing shallowly through the dust lingering in the air, I looked up to see a small patch of brilliant blue sky. Beautiful cloudless blue sky…

Jessica was watching me uncertainly, 'What good will a hole in the roof do us?'

'That will become clear when it's big enough to climb through,' I said with a grim sort of confidence.

Jessica jumped up. 'No! Stop! There's not time before he gets back. He won't be gone long; and if he comes back and catches us trying to escape who knows what he'll do?'

'Who knows what he'll do anyway?' I challenged. 'Speaking for myself, I'm really not prepared to spend any more time in this pigsty than I absolutely have to.'

'But surely, it's better to wait until he goes out to get the ransom money later on. Then we'll know we've got longer. If we rush it there's a chance one of us will fall and break our necks. I don't think he's likely to add murder to his list of crimes. He may be a thief, but I don't think he's a killer.'

I looked at her panicky face and reluctantly conceded she was probably talking sense. 'Ok, then we'd better find something to plug this hole with. We don't want him to see it when he gets back.'

We fashioned a serviceable plug from the bloodied tissues, the antiseptic wipe and a few other odds and ends we found in our bags and wedged it into the hole. If Hussein happened to look up, he probably couldn't fail to spot it; but hopefully he wouldn't feel the need to study the ceiling.

I brushed the crumbled clay from the table onto the floor. The dust had only just settled when the sound of the scooter returning reached our ears.

'Blimey, that was quick!' I said. 'You were right to make us wait.'

'He'll have gone cross-country,' she said. 'It's much quicker than using the roads.'

Hussein joined us in the cramped, odorous gloom of the shack once more. He hurled a bottle of water into each of our laps. I was oddly reassured by this gesture. I found it hard to believe he planned to kill us if he'd spared a thought for our thirst. Maybe there was a human being somewhere inside that voluminous galabeya after all.

Hussein sat in the shade of the open doorway smoking. A tortuous hour dragged by; then another. Jessica and I slowly sipped our water, making it last, and drifted in a kind of stupor. My eyes kept straying to Dan's suitcase, and I wondered how the professor was getting on with his translation. Perhaps Dan had felt obliged to tell him about Jessica's kidnap. It was approaching three o'clock and soon Adam would be arriving back at the Jolie Ville. I tried to imagine them all discussing this latest distressing turn of events. I was quite sure Dan would be haranguing the others with prophecies of doom. He'd basically been predicting it would all end in tears from the moment I found the hieroglyphics that started all this. I was quite sure Dan had no wish to attend my funeral; but if that did happen to be the sorry outcome of this whole affair, I was sure he'd suffer it with a glimmer of smug satisfaction for having been proved right.

Poor old Ted was back to square one, with his daughter once more held hostage. I sincerely hoped the signs of emotional exhaustion we'd seen yesterday were a one-off. I didn't think I'd forgive myself if anything happened to the professor because I'd thoughtlessly blundered into this situation. Adam's cool head and quick wits were definitely needed right now.

At the thought of Adam my blood seemed to slow in my veins. I wasn't happy at the thought of him being the one to complete the rendezvous with our villainous Egyptian friend. But there was nothing I could do about it, and if anyone could pull it off without a hitch it was Adam. I just wished I could be with him. When we were sleuthing our way through Carter's conundrums, we'd faced everything together. Somehow our twosome had more than doubled in the last few days. I was still trying to acclimatise to it, to be honest. But it still left him facing this alone. I didn't like it; not at all.

Finally, Hussein squashed out his umpteenth cigarette, pushed himself up from the doorway and stretched. He approached Jessica, said something in Arabic and held out his hand.

Jessica looked a bit crushed and reached for her handbag.

'What does he want?' I asked.

'He's remembered about the money I offered him. He wants it now.'

'But that's not fair!' I objected. 'That means he gets double: your money and Adam's.'

'It's my stupid fault for offering it to him.'

I glared at Hussein, and he grinned cruelly at me.

Jessica handed over several thick wedges of bank notes, each one held together with a large elastic band. Hussein put them in his satchel and gave her a small ironic bow. Then he collected up his holdall from the corner of the room; and took Howard Carter's small suitcase out from inside Dan's larger one. It was little more than the size of a briefcase, though antique-looking in design. I figured he'd decided it wouldn't attract as much attention as a big modern suitcase on wheels.

He turned and issued a volley of Arabic.

'What did he say?'

'He's going to take his leave of us now. He wants to stake out his spot at Luxor temple early to prevent any funny business. He wishes us well. If all goes according to plan, he will inform our friends of our whereabouts tomorrow. But he makes no promises.'

Hussein treated us to another evil grin and left. Once again, the door bolt fell into place behind him. Moments later we heard the scooter zip away.

I was on my feet before the sound of the engine died out in the distance. I climbed up onto the table, reached up for our makeshift plug and gave it a tug. It came loose in a shower of powdery clay and musty, sun-baked straw. Coughing, I stood for a moment spitting crumbs of clay out of my mouth. Then, ducking my head under the relative cover of one upraised arm, I reached up and started punching at the roof with my water bottle. The clay-like substance and straw came down easily, and the beams of what I presumed were some kind of cane weren't too much of a problem, though I had to pull and twist to break some pieces. In one way I was quite reassured by this, as it made my demolition of the roof relatively simple. But in another it was the cause of some alarm; suggesting it might not be strong enough to hold us once we were up there. My plan was to jump off the roof, not fall back through it.

I gave it another whack and encountered something big and hard. With relief, I realised this was a proper beam, running across the whole width of the ceiling. Good, that would give us something to hang onto while we hauled ourselves up.

Finally, I judged the hole big enough. 'Right, I suggest we collapse the camp bed to give us a bit more height. Can you do that, Jessica?'

She fiddled with it a bit, swearing quite colourfully. 'No, it won't budge,' she said. 'Why don't we just stand on the chair?'

'Oh, of course, I hadn't thought of that. Yes, hand it up.'

She passed the chair up to me and held its legs while I clambered up onto it and stuck my head through the roof. Bits of clay and straw brushed against my shoulders, but I was pretty sure we could squeeze through. I felt for the beam to support me and, with a bit of a struggle, wobbling on the precariously positioned chair, I managed to raise my arms through the hole, then get my elbows on top of it.

'Can you give me a shove?' I asked.

I felt Jessica's arms come around my thighs. She jerked me upwards. I put all my strength into it and heaved myself onto the roof, careful to keep my weight over the beam.

'Pass me up our bags,' I suggested, and tossed them to the ground as she did so. 'Leave Dan's suitcase; he'll just have to buy a new one. Ok, your turn; come on.'

Hauling Jessica out was no mean feat; for all that she was just about as small and dainty as a fairy on top of a Christmas tree. I slipped twice and thought I was going to send us both crashing back through the roof. But finally, I had her out next to me on the beam.

'Ok, so long as we stay over this solid part, we should be able to crawl our way to the edge and drop down. It's not too big a drop to the ground. Just remember to bend your legs when you land.'

We fitted the action to the words, and moments later we were climbing to our feet in the sugarcane field and swiping clouds of dust off our clothes.

'We're free!' I grinned. 'See? That wasn't too difficult, was it?'

'Now what?' Jessica asked, as we finished brushing ourselves down.

'Now I think a visit to our friend Ahmed Abd el-Rassul of the local tourist police might be in order.'

We trudged back across the field and into the network of litter-strewn alleyways leading back towards civilisation and our best chance of finding a taxi. Hussein hadn't thought to relieve me of my purse. I guess with the bundles of cash Jessica had given him and those he eagerly anticipated receiving from Adam he had no need to. All things considered, it was thoroughly decent of him - his being a thief and all that. It meant paying for a taxi posed no problem.

Jessica hung her head as we walked, no doubt regretting the eye-popping amount of money she'd shelled out for no purpose whatsoever. 'I'm sorry, Merry; you must think I'm horribly naïve.'

I looked at her, taking in the bruised swelling on her pretty face, and felt myself soften. She'd have a real shiner of a black eye by tomorrow. 'No; actually, I think you're incredibly brave; if a bit reckless. It was a very bold strike you attempted to pull off back there. I admire you for it.'

She brightened up a bit after this. We attracted a few interested glances as we trudged through the limpid afternoon heat. If a competition were to be had between the quantities of dust on the streets versus the amount on us – in our hair, on our clothes and streaked down our faces – we'd win hands down. And, believe me, the backstreets were dusty. Still, I don't suppose it's possible to demolish a roof from a position standing underneath it without a bit of collateral damage. All things considered; I decided things could be worse. I didn't mind the curious stares of the donkeys, mangy dogs and toothless old ladies we passed. But the disbelief and dismay in the look of the taxi driver we approached outside the Sheraton was a bit of a dent in my self-confidence. His taxi was by no means a pristine example of its type, but his howl of protest as we moved to get inside it spoke volumes about our dirty and dishevelled appearance. As usual the offer of baksheesh – of an amount wholly disproportionate to the task at hand – did the trick. But it didn't wipe the scowl off his face or quieten his incessant muttering as he drove us into Luxor.

The look on Ahmed's face when we were deposited unceremoniously at the police station was even more of a picture. If it's possible for someone's eyes to come out on stalks in a manner reminiscent of old Tom and Jerry cartoons, then his did so. He was behind the front desk when we arrived, midway through his shift. 'Mereditd, Djessica; is it you?'

'Hello Ahmed,' I said. 'How do you fancy the opportunity to arrest the last Said brother and put him behind bars where he belongs?'

Chapter 10

We knew the fiendish Hussein was already staking out his spot in the holy of holies at Luxor temple to prevent any "funny business". Ahmed was easily persuaded to make our stakeout spot a bit closer to the entrance, by the obelisk and small plinth displaying the head and shoulders statue of Ramses II, so beloved in tourist photographs. I hoped Hussein had miscalculated by making the location for the ransom exchange so deep inside the temple. By my reckoning, it meant he had to retrace his steps from the holy and holies and hypostyle hall of the inner sanctuary across the open courtyard and through the colonnade of Amenhotep III, then through the outer court of the temple lined with striding statues of Ramses II, and right past where we were laying in wait outside the huge stone pylon in the forecourt.

Ahmed was all fired up to make the arrest of his life. I think he had visions of being hailed as a hero, in the same way Shukura had been cited a heroine for her part in foiling the antiquities thefts. Taking the last member of the gang into police custody would be the coup of his career. Ahmed's deep brown eyes were positively snapping at the prospect.

We'd filled him in on the events since we'd parted company at the airport yesterday. It seemed so much longer ago than that. He stared agog while we described the theft of the papyri by the third member of the unholy triad of Said brothers, the ransom demand, and Jessica's courageous attempt to fly solo and buy it back so Adam didn't have to. He growled like an angry bear when I described the punch Hussein landed on her. The swollen bruising was plain to see beneath the sweat-streaked dust on her face. 'Dis bad man; I will put him in prison, and I will throw away de key,' he vowed.

Jessica and I were somewhat cleaner now. We'd put the police facilities to good use. We'd both ducked our heads under a wall-mounted shower hose. I'd waited in the washroom in just my underwear while Jessica took my clothes outside and shook billowing clouds of dust from them. Then I returned the favour. I didn't think we'd be allowed into Luxor temple looking like we'd just emerged from a volcanic ash fall.

We arrived at the temple at half past four. It wasn't busy exactly. Tourist numbers were down in these post-revolutionary days. I wasn't aware if the British Foreign Office, or those of other nations, had warned people away from visiting Egypt, considering the latest round of demonstrations in Cairo over the Mubarak trial verdict, but it wasn't hard to see why tourists were being circumspect, what with the democratic elections, and all. But there were enough people around to give it a sense of a popular public place, where Egyptians and Europeans could mingle without attracting undue attention.

If Hussein was here already - and we had no choice but to presume he was - then he'd passed through the security procedures of the ticket office and entrance in possession of papyri dating back more than three-thousand years. Still, I don't suppose modern security probes are wired to pick up ancient papyrus when you're asked to pass your bag through the sensor. I wondered if the museum piece of a suitcase, once having belonged to Howard Carter approximately a century ago, raised any eyebrows from the guards on entry-duty. If Hussein was safely inside the temple, we could only assume not. My experience of the security guards in the tourist attractions on this trip was that they were so delighted to have visitors of any nationality or creed; they simply waved them through the bag check. Hard to blame them, I guess. I daresay I'd have done the same in their shoes. I could only hope Hussein had been circumspect enough to leave his knife behind. I doubted he'd risk an encounter with the security systems with it still in his pocket. I felt much more comfortable about Adam going to meet him if Hussein was unarmed. Adam's arm was still bandaged up from his fight with Hussein's knife-wielding brother the other night. We were all sporting battle scars of one sort or another: Adam the gash in his arm, Jessica her swelling black eye, and me the little knife-wound near my shoulder where he'd jabbed his blade at me. Enough was enough. Dan's disgust at our willingness to risk life and limb for the papyri was turning out to be uncomfortably prophetic.

I toyed with the idea of sending Ahmed on a reconnaissance mission to see if our target was indeed in the inner sanctuary of the temple. But Ahmed – though unknown to Hussein – wearing his tourist police uniform and built like a small mountain, could be certain to put the wind up him. It was best to just wait and see. One thing could be said for sure: if we couldn't see Hussein from here, then neither could he see us. I told myself this was a good thing. It meant we had the element of surprise.

We'd been in our spot near the Ramses II statue for about fifteen minutes when we saw Adam arrive. We'd been standing as if chatting to Ahmed as a tourist adviser, trying not to draw attention to ourselves. We'd even asked him to take a couple of photographs of us posing by the statue.

As promised, Adam was alone. My heart gave a little lurch at the sight of him. He was dressed in his favourite outfit of sand-coloured chinos and a loose, white, brushed cotton shirt, open at the collar. Sunglasses shaded his eyes; and he was carrying a rucksack. Presumably this contained the ransom money. It was yet another example of the thankfully lackadaisical security procedures. I could only presume the bag sensors weren't designed to pick up bundles of cash any more than they raised the alarm for centuries-old papyrus scrolls.

Adam came down the wide stone steps leading from the ticket office on the Corniche onto the temple forecourt. He walked with a purposeful step, glancing once or twice at his wristwatch. I tried to imagine how he was feeling. He'd be grimly determined to see this thing through as quickly and simply as possible. He knew he was in no position, before or after the exchange, to risk a confrontation. As far as he was aware, Jessica and I were still holed up somewhere under lock and key. The only chance he had of discovering where was to play by the villainous Arab's rules. No, the interception and arrest of Hussein was down to us.

Part of me longed to run forward from our position behind the statue and let Adam know we were safe. But all the time Hussein had the papyri he had the upper hand. So, I could only let the scenario play itself out and put my faith in our ability to bring it all to a satisfactory conclusion once the ransom was paid and the papyri were safely back in our possession.

But it was with my heart in my mouth that I watched Adam turn in through the great pylon onto the aisle running through the centre of the temple. The sun beat down from the stretching blue sky, but the temple walls cast deep shadows. I watched him out of sight as he strode through patches of sunlight and shade into the open courtyard of Ramses II. I lost sight of him as he passed below the colossal, seated statue of the king to enter the colonnade beyond, where the central axis of the temple forked slightly to the left. Hussein was waiting for him in the deepest, darkest part of the temple. In my head I followed Adam's footsteps across the square, open sun-court, surrounded on all sides by tall stone columns, and up the shallow steps leading to the hypostyle hall. Built on nothing like the scale of the one at Karnak, it was just four rows of towering columns either side of the central aisle. This brought Adam into the Roman sanctuary, the last place he could look up and see the blue sky. From there he had to step inside the inner sanctums of the ancient temple, a series of dark, intimately secluded chambers leading to the holy of holies.

I was starting to feel a bit sick. To distract myself from the thought of Adam in the darkest recesses of the temple, alone with the barbarous Hussein, I turned back to Ahmed and Jessica and started to talk brightly. It occurred to me they might appreciate my attempt to keep our thoughts occupied. 'There were once two obelisks standing here, you know, one on either side of the central aisle through the temple. The other one was given to the French and now stands in the Place de la Concorde in Paris. In ancient times, this temple was known as the southern shrine, to differentiate it from Karnak, or the northern house of the god Amun. The two temples used to be joined by a two-and-a-half-kilometre avenue of sphinxes. You know, they're trying to excavate the whole avenue out again as part of their project to make Luxor a massive open-air museum. They've had to clear away whole swathes of modern buildings, most of them residential, but also businesses, churches; even your old police station, as I understand it, Ahmed. Luxor temple was once the centre of a great annual festival, known as the Opet festival. The statue of the god Amun was escorted in a joyous procession from Karnak to Luxor.' I broke off as I noticed Jessica staring at me strangely.

'Merry,' she said tentatively, 'why on earth are you giving us a history lesson at a time like this?'

I missed Adam in that moment with a pure longing, more than I thought it possible to miss another human being. He'd have understood perfectly. 'Oh, sorry,' I said. 'I didn't mean to get carried away. I was just trying to keep my mind off things.' I glanced at my watch, 'I wonder what's happening. Surely, they've had time to make the exchange by now?'

Ahmed was pacing nervously. 'It is five minutes since Adam went into de temple. Two minutes more and I will go in after him.'

Another five minutes dragged by while we dithered by the entrance pylon unsure what to do. If we lost our nerve, rushed it, and made our move too soon there was a chance we'd blow our carefully laid plan sky high.

'Adam's not going to give him the money until he's satisfied all the papyrus is there, and that the scrolls are intact and undamaged,' I said. 'There's no way he'll risk handing over more than a hundred grand for an empty suitcase or a load of desiccated fragments.'

'Maybe it's busy in the inner part of the temple,' Jessica suggested. 'At least it's shady in the sanctuary, out of the sun. There are quite often turbaned touts milling about in these places, hoping to lure unsuspecting tourists into a photo opportunity in return for some baksheesh. Neither Adam nor Hussein can risk showing the papyri or the money if there's a chance of being seen.'

'And Adam will be demanding to know our whereabouts,' I said. 'He'll know he can't trust Hussein to do the honourable thing and fulfil his promise of a note to the Jolie Ville tomorrow. He'll want to know where we are now. Perhaps he's making it another condition of handing over the money.'

'I don't like it,' Ahmed said. 'I don'td like itd atd all.' His accent became thicker when he was agitated.

Another couple of minutes crawled by.

'Something must have gone wrong,' I said in a strange, high voice that didn't sound like mine. My throat was constricted with fear, as if someone had sewn my vocal cords together with chicken wire. I suddenly realised I didn't care two hoots for the damned papyri. I just wanted Adam out of there in one piece.

'I'm going in after him,' I decided, and set off at a jog. The three of us ran through the huge stone gateway with the Mosque of Abu el-Haggag perched on top of it. It was built there back in the days when the temple was still buried under centuries' worth of sand. We were highly conspicuous as we darted across the open courtyard of Ramses II under the watchful eyes of the immense statues of the king striding forward from between the pillars around the perimeter. A few of the tourists and Egyptian tour guides and touts cast us strange looks as we passed but we spared barely a glance for them. There was no sign of Hussein or, more importantly, Adam.

We took the precaution of darting behind the huge row of columns lining the central colonnade rather than make our way along the central aisle. And we skirted the edge of the sun-court at the other end, weaving between the double rows of columns around the edge rather than dashing across the central open space. Still no sign of either of them.

It was as we emerged from the narrow hypostyle hall into the Roman sanctuary that we almost collided with Adam coming in the opposite direction through the doorway from the temple's inner chambers.

I went weak with relief at the sight of him, walking upright on his two feet, with all his precious limbs intact and no sign of blood marring his cherished features. My imagination had painted all sorts of grisly alternatives. A small cry escaped me. He looked up at the sound. Paralysed shock held him rigid for a split second. Then blazing joy swept away the wretched defeat in his features.

'Merry!' He closed the gap between us in two long strides and I flung myself into his arms.

He squeezed me close. 'Oh Merry; thank God! Are you alright? Did he hurt you? It was all I could do to stop myself murdering the bastard with my bare hands back there. But I was terrified I might never see you again. I realised I didn't give a damn about the papyri. I just wanted you back, safe, with me. If he's hurt you, so help me, I'll hunt him down and make him regret the sorry day he was born.'

I laughed, and gulped, and cried a bit, hugging him, and reassuring myself with the warm, solid feel of him. Speaking was beyond me for a moment, but I let him know I was unharmed with a few fierce squeezes.

'I begged him to tell me where you were,' Adam went on. 'My Arabic's not up to much but I did my best to make him understand he could keep the papyri as well as the money if he'd just tell me how to find you. But he just laughed in my face. He said you were somewhere I could never reach you, without food, without water, and with no means of escape. I've been torturing myself with images of you locked up and frightened and dying a long agonising death before I could get to you.'

'He never thought to check out the solidity of the roof of the damned cow shed he had us locked in,' I sniffed, drying my eyes and grinning up at him.

He gave a small shout of laughter and hugged me even harder. 'I should have known better than to think you'd sit there helplessly waiting to be rescued. Merry, I know I've had cause to say so before, but you are a wonder! Thank God you're safe.'

Ahmed and Jessica were watching this little display of emotion a little awkwardly, as if unsure where to look.

'And Jessica, you're ok too?' Adam suddenly remembered them. He took one look at Jessica's face, and the anger swept back across his features again. 'My God, the bastard hit you!' He translated the evidence of his eyes. 'I'm going to find him, and I'm going to kill him.'

'You have de scrolls,' Ahmed said urgently, looking at the old, battered suitcase Adam had dropped unceremoniously at his feet. 'But where is dis Hussein? He did not pass us in de temple.'

Thank God for Ahmed, calmly cutting through all the drama of reunion to ask the essential question.

'I never expected him to make his escape by walking back through the centre of the temple,' Adam said. 'Dan and I made a study of the temple layout on the Internet this afternoon. There's a little side exit from the inner sanctuary out to the open-air museum behind the temple. It's where they're restoring the piles of talatat blocks excavated from here and from Karnak. They were used as in-fill in later building works after the kings who came after Akhenaten smashed up his temples.'

Jessica was staring at him. Now she said rudely, 'What is It about you pair that you have to embellish every sentence you say with a damned historical masterclass? Just tell us where Hussein went.'

Adam looked a bit taken aback. 'Oh yes, of course, sorry,' he said quickly. 'He'll have skirted the edge of the temple through the open-air museum, but he has to re-enter the temple precinct just before the open courtyard of Ramses II to leave via the main pylon.'

'We should have stayed where we were,' Ahmed growled. 'He would have come past us.'

'Dan's staking out the exit in order to follow him,' Adam said.

'Dan's here?' I squeaked.

'Yes, of course. We knew Hussein would never tell us where you were. And we knew I had to play it straight not to put you in even more jeopardy. So, Dan's tasked with trailing him when he leaves the temple in the hope he'd lead us to you. Dan will be able to spot him by the bright red rucksack. I deliberately chose the most conspicuous bag I could find to put the ransom money in.'

'But Hussein's got a scooter,' I pointed out hurriedly. 'Dan won't be able to follow him on that...' Before I'd finished getting the words out, we were legging it back through the temple, choosing the wide open spaces this time over the shadowed cover of the pillars. Speed was of the essence. We tore across the sun court, down the colonnade and across the open courtyard beneath the mosque of Abu el-Haggag; bursting out into the forecourt between the towering pylons fronted by the immense seated statues of Ramses II.

'There!' I cried, spotting Hussein approaching the exit, on the slope by the refreshments kiosk above the avenue of sphinxes. I pointed frantically. Hussein was beating a hasty if circumspect retreat, not wanting to call the attention of the security guards to him. He had the satchel with Jessica's money in it slung over one shoulder; the bright red rucksack with Adam's ransom money strapped over the other.

As he exited through the side gate and turned left towards Luxor town centre, I saw Dan's tall frame peel away from the shade of a clutch of palm trees to follow him.

'Dan!' we yelled, pelting up the slope after them.

He half turned and stumbled with disbelief at the sight of the four of us sprinting towards him.

'Don't let him get away!'

Something in the urgency of our quadruple command cut through his shock at our sudden unexpected appearance. After only a second's hesitation as he registered that we were alive and well, no longer incarcerated, and patently ordering him to give chase, he turned and started to run.

His pursuit of our villainous kidnapper might have been easier if in shouting to Dan we hadn't also alerted Hussein to our presence. He shot a look back over his shoulder, spied us leaping onto the kerbstone outside the exit gate, and fled.

Hussein was fast; I knew that already from the scant few moments it took him to run me down in the field this morning. But Dan was fast too, with the long lanky legs and loping gait of a sportsman. Dan had the advantage of being unencumbered by the weight of two bags full of wads of cash. But Hussein had desperation on his side.

He tore along the pavement bordering the temple precinct, dodged between the curio sellers touting their concertina postcards and replica artefacts, and ducked out of sight behind the caleche drivers lined up at the kerbside with their horse and carriages hoping to entice tourists for a ride.

Dan leapt over a steaming pile of horse dung and plunged into the network of streets leading away from the temple in pursuit. The rest of us brought up the rear, panting with exertion but determined not to give up the chase.

Hussein wove his way through the alleyways lined with shops and market stalls. He pulled over sacks of spices, swept piled vegetables off their trestle tables, yanked hanging bunches of chillies and garlic off their awnings, even sent a bicycle spinning from its place propped against a wall into Dan's path; anything to form an obstacle course and slow Dan down.

Dan negotiated these hazards like an Olympic hurdler; leaping over each new obstruction in his path almost as if it wasn't there.

I could see Ahmed had unslung his gun alongside me. But he didn't dare raise it to shoot with Dan long-jumping and sprinting his way between our quarry and us. Dan can seem a bit gangly and awkward at times, all long limbs and big feet. But his frame was ideally suited to the purpose he was putting it to now, and I could see he was closing on the Arab, despite the objects Hussein kept hurling in his path.

Our progress through the narrow streets was accompanied by shouts of anger, cries of alarm and savage Arabic curses. Shopkeepers waved their fists at us. Young mothers snatched their children out of our way. But mostly people simply stood and gaped open-mouthed as we tore past them at full tilt. It was obvious we had a policeman with us, so no one dared intervene.

Finally, Hussein burst out of the side streets into the relative open space of the Corniche. Once upon a time it was possible to travel the length of this wide embankment bordering the Nile. But recently the Supreme Council of Luxor had taken it into their heads to pedestrianise the whole length of it from the roundabout near the Winter Palace at one end, through to Karnak at the other, and had started digging huge chunks of it up. We emerged from the back streets to find ourselves near the Luxor Museum. The whole stretch of the Corniche in front of it looked like a building site. Huge chunks of bulldozed concrete shot through with thick, twisted veins of rusted masonry poles littered what was once a street. But it wasn't this that made me catch what was left of my breath with dismay.

Hussein charged across the rubble-strewn wasteland and ploughed straight into a knot of about twenty small children playing an energetic game of football in the dust. Dan plunged in after him. He knew it was now or never. Dan launched himself at Hussein's feet in the most spectacular rugby tackle I've ever seen. It brought the Arab crashing to the ground. The children swarmed round, shouting and gesticulating, and generally getting in the way.

Spying us, some of them separated themselves from the main group and ran towards us with joyous cries of 'Baksheesh!'

Dan had Hussein on the ground. But surrounded by eager little faces there was no way he could beat the dark stuff out of him in the way I'm sure he was itching to.

'Grab the satchel,' I yelled. 'You need to get the satchel as well as the rucksack.'

We could see Dan and Hussein rolling around in the dust grunting. The children were dancing around them as if this was the best entertainment they'd had all year.

Ahmed had his gun in both hands, but there was no way he dared use it.

Adam managed to break free of the knot of children pressing us in, and leapt across the uprooted concrete paving slabs to lend a hand as Dan hauled the Arab to his feet.

'I need to arrest dat man,' Ahmed wailed urgently. But it was too late. Dan staggered back under the force of the vicious kick Hussein managed to land on him. Losing his balance, he knocked Adam, running up behind him, off his feet; so they both went crashing down together. It was the chance Hussein had been waiting for. The Arab leapt to his feet and sprinted away, disappearing down the street at the far corner of the museum.

Ahmed gave chase and promptly fell headlong over the top of the grubby little beggar standing in front of him.

All three men picked themselves up from the dust, testing for bruises. But as Dan got to his feet, he held his arms aloft. There, dangling from his outstretched left hand was Hussein's satchel; and hanging heavily from his right was Adam's rucksack.

'You did it!' I cheered, jumping up and down in my excitement.

'Oh well done!' Jessica chimed.

At the sound of our voices, Dan turned towards us and roared. 'There you are! Just what the hell do you think you've been playing at today? Of all the stupid, thoughtless, downright suicidal pranks to pull! What in God's name did you hope to achieve sneaking off like that? You women really are a menace to yourselves as well as to the rest of normal society. It doesn't seem you can be left alone for more than two minutes without getting yourselves locked in, locked up or kidnapped! Well, I'll tell you this for nothing; you damn well need locking up, the pair of you! In the bloody nuthouse!'

The contrast between Dan's apoplexy and Adam's rapture on finding Jessica and me safe and well couldn't have been starker. But before I could open my mouth to tell him exactly what I thought of the comparison, I was distracted by the small sensation of Jessica tugging on my t-shirt. I glanced at her in consternation.

'You *are* lucky, Merry,' she whispered, looking at me with bright, excited eyes. 'He's truly magnificent, isn't he?'

Chapter 11

We gathered back at the Jolie Ville, on the open terrace overlooking the Nile, to take stock and count bruises.

'It's not so bad,' I said optimistically. 'We have the papyri, and we got all the money back. Quite a good outcome, all things considered.'

'But Hussein is still on the loose and potentially dangerous,' Jessica put in uncertainly.

'I don't know so much about dangerous,' Adam mused. 'He's a wanted man with no money and without his lair to go back to, since we know where it is. I'd say his options are pretty few and far between right now.' He sent me a glowing smile, still in awe of my achievement in smashing Jessica and myself free through the roof of the shack.

'We should still stick together,' Dan said gruffly. 'No more wandering off in ones or twos until we know it's safe.' The warning look he shot me was a further demonstration of the difference between the two men in my life. 'Got that, Pinkie?'

'I will not sleep sound in my bed until I arrest dat man,' Ahmed declared; furious at being denied the chance of this feather in his cap.

A waiter arrived and dispensed stiff drinks all around, with a strong coffee for Ahmed. The sun was sinking across the Nile and over the western hills in a huge glowing ball of flame. Classical music played from the speakers set unobtrusively into the shrubberies. We swiped casually at mosquitoes, a mild irritant as dusk swept in to claim the day. It was only the subject matter of our conversation that marked us out as any different from a group of holidaymakers enjoying a sundowner. Well, that and the battle scars.

Ted had taken one look at his daughter's swollen face and let out a cry of horror. Dan and Adam had decided not to tell him about the kidnap in hope of being able to persuade Hussein to release us before the professor need be worried with it. As things turned out, this was a good judgement call. Ted was spared the anxious afternoon Dan and Adam had spent. Jessica's patent high spirits quickly assuaged his concern. 'Well, one thing's for sure,' he said now as he looked around at our faces bathed in the radiant glow of sunset. 'The papyri should be taken by Ahmed into police custody. Ahmed, I assume you have a locker or something you could keep the case safe in, do you?'

Ahmed nodded proudly. 'I will guard it witd my life.'

'I sincerely hope that won't be necessary, my fine fellow. But I know I'll sleep easier if it's stored somewhere our Arabic friend can't get to it. I know they say lightning doesn't strike twice, but it seems to me we can't be too careful.' He cast a loving look at the antique suitcase resting alongside Adam's chair. 'I think our plan for the evening should be to photograph the other two scrolls, and let Ahmed take the whole lot away with him. We shouldn't keep unrolling them, whatever happens. They're too susceptible to damage. And we need to start to think about how we can turn them over to the correct authorities so they can be properly preserved.'

I knew he was right, but part of me was fiercely reluctant to let the papyri go. Now Adam was safe, and we had the ancient scrolls back again, I couldn't help but revert to seeing them as my special prize. After all, if I hadn't sleuthed my way to their discovery following Howard Carter's trail of clues, they'd still be languishing bricked up inside a tomb wall. I convinced myself it entitled me to stake a claim, however temporarily. 'Have you made any more progress with the translation?' I asked. Now the petty distractions of theft, kidnap, and ransom demands had been swept aside, there was nothing I wanted more than to pick up the threads of the ancient story unfolding from the crumbling scrolls.

The professor turned a luminous gaze on me. It was hard to tell how much of this was down to the sunset glowing full on his face, and how much was lit from within; but I felt a thrill go through me none the less. 'Yes. I've translated the next section of Ay's testimonial. It makes fascinating reading. I didn't get quite as far as I'd hoped. I confess I fell asleep for most of the afternoon. The adventures of the last few days caught up with me. But I should think I'll be able to finish it tomorrow. I can share the portion I worked through today if you're ready to hear it?'

It was a silly question. Of course we wanted to hear it. There was a curious breathless moment while we mentally shifted gear, ready to be transported back into the past. The dark waters of the Nile drifted past, silent and eternal as time itself. The sun descended over the western horizon, slipping behind the Theban hills as it must have done in ancient times when the Egyptians believed it was the god Ra departing to travel through the twelve hours of the night in the underworld; leaving the moon to light the world above. The ancient pharaoh was about to speak to us once more, his voice echoing across thirty-two centuries. Goose bumps prickled across my skin, and the little hairs stood up on my forearms.

Adam leaned forward. 'If I remember rightly, Ay was saying how he buried Tutankhamun and Ankhesenamun in tombs so deep their enemies would never find them. He was determined they, and his other "precious jewels", would remain undisturbed through all eternity.'

'"Precious jewels" being people,' I breathed. 'Other members of the royal family.'

'He was talking about a campaign of destruction,' Adam said. 'He predicted, rightly, that his own tomb would be broken into and vandalised. He said this campaign had already begun, during his lifetime, and, in this, he'd somehow failed in his promise to Tutankhamun. That's about where we were up to, isn't it?'

Ted's eyes gleamed. 'That's right. And that's exactly where his narrative picks up. Listen...' He took out his small notebook from the breast pocket of his shirt and flipped through the pages to find the point in the translation where we'd left off in Cairo. We all pulled closer.

'"*Immortal lord, my most esteemed king Nebkheperure Tutankhamun, I, Kheperkheperure Ay, must complete this painful task and write these bitter words. It is my self-appointed duty to lay before you events that bring me to my knees and break my heart. I humbly pray your forgiveness and bow to the judgement you may, in your infinite wisdom, bestow upon me. My lord, I have failed you. My custody of your throne has been inadequate to protect all our precious jewels from desecration. The malicious hands of our enemies strike to obliterate your sacred line and re-write your history. They wait not upon the hour of my death, though it draws near. The mighty are fallen, and those who seek power rise up to claim it. As once these evil men murdered divinely anointed rulers, so now they seek to pull their souls from the imperishable stars.*"'

Dan snorted. 'Good old Ay,' he muttered, 'never one to tell it like it is, if he can equivocate and beat about the bush instead. Do any of you have the foggiest idea what he's wittering on about? Because I, for one, might as well be listening to Martian for all the sense it's making.'

'Murder,' Jessica said, a bit breathlessly. 'That was the word I latched onto among all the flowery stuff. Their enemies murdered someone.'

'Someone plural,' Dan replied, making it quite clear he'd understood far more than he was prepared to admit. He really was annoyingly contradictory. I suspect he made a great show of disparaging the Pharaonic tale just to spite me. But Jessica's evident enthusiasm was a bit different. I had a deep, dark suspicion Dan might have heard what she said to me earlier; and I wasn't at all sure how I felt about it. ' "Divinely appointed rulers" implies kings,' Dan explained to her. 'Or perhaps a king and queen.'

'So, who got murdered back then?' Jessica asked, wrinkling her nose. The effect wasn't quite as pretty as before, in among the swelling, but she still managed to look cute and appealing. 'Lots of people believe Tutankhamun met a grisly end, don't they? But Ay can't mean Tutankhamun, since he's the one he's addressing in the papyrus.'

I could have banged their heads together quite cheerfully. 'Perhaps if we just let Ted read on...' I suggested testily.

Adam, I noticed, hadn't once taken his gaze from Ted's face. I could almost see the cogs in his brain whirring. I'm not sure he'd even registered the idiotic drivel being exchanged between Dan and Jessica. He was mesmerised by the story and trying to figure out what it all meant.

Ahmed, trying to penetrate the language barrier, sat still and immovable as a giant rock, but his dark eyes were equally intent on Ted's face as he concentrated on understanding what he was hearing.

Ted smiled around at us in the gathering darkness and read on. ' *"In one thing alone can I be content. Our plan to bring our treasure south from Akhet-Aten to Ta-sekhet-ma'at, all seeing, all hearing, succeeded in being a cloak for the hiding of our most precious jewels. While we reburied our treasures in the Great Field, the Great and Majestic Necropolis of the Millions of Years of the Pharaoh, life, strength, health in The West of Thebes; our other, clandestine, hiding place was secure, no one hearing, no one seeing."'*

Ted paused and looked up to see what we made of this even more opaque passage.

'Ta-sekhet-ma'at, or the Great Field was what ancient Egyptians called the Valley of the Kings,' Adam said slowly. 'So, he's saying they brought their "precious jewels" from Akhenaten's city at Amarna, where they'd presumably been buried originally, here to ancient Thebes for reburial in the

Valley of the Kings. But they used the public reburial of their "treasure" as a cover for the secret reburial, presumably somewhere else, of their "most precious jewels".'

Ted smiled approvingly. 'My interpretation exactly, my boy. Now, listen to this… *"Our enemies swooped on Ta-sekhet-ma'at. They broke through the necropolis seals of Nebkheperure Tutankhamun and desecrated the Sepulchre of Millions of Years. If they thought to find our most precious jewels, in this they were disappointed. To this day our priceless ones enjoy the grace of the fields of Amenti. But forgive me, immortal king, our enemies reached into the imperishable stars and brought the souls of our other departed treasures crashing earthwards. Those who were dear to the Mighty Bull, Majesty of Horus: appearing in truth; Nebmaatre Amenhotep, have been despoiled. I have been powerless to prevent this sacrilege."'*

'He's talking about KV55,' Adam breathed on a note of wonderment.

All gazes swivelled towards him.

'I need another drink,' Dan said baldly; and detained a passing waiter to give an order for the same again all round.

The distraction was infinitesimal. While Adam explained his bewildering statement the waiter replaced our drinks with fresh ones. I regret to say I'm not sure any of us noticed sufficiently to thank him.

'The tomb known as KV55 was discovered in the Valley about fifteen years before Howard Carter found Tutankhamun. It's commonly believed the tomb was built to hold the mummy of Queen Tiye. She was the great royal wife of Amenhotep III, the mother of the heretic Akhenaten, grandmother of Tutankhamun, and sister of Ay. It's believed she was originally buried in Akhenaten's royal tomb in Akhet-Aten because a piece of smashed up sarcophagus found there had her name inscribed on it. The sealed door of the tomb in the Valley of the Kings actually had Tutankhamun's stamp on it. Early excavators took this as evidence they'd discovered the boy-king's tomb. But more recent archaeologists take this as proof that Tutankhamun was the one to perform the reburial. From what Ay's just told us, it would seem they're right.'

'Was anything found in the tomb?' Jessica asked, wide-eyed.

'There was a badly damaged gilded coffin and some canopic jars,' Adam said. 'The tomb was in chaos. Historians believe the damage was done in antiquity. All personal names inscribed on the coffin and the canopic jars had been hacked out. The ancient Egyptians believed this meant the soul of the deceased would be denied everlasting life. The damage made identification of the human remains inside the coffin almost impossible.'

'They found a body?' I asked excitedly.

'There's evidence to suggest several mummies may once have been interred there,' Adam said, turning his gaze on me. 'Most researchers believe Queen Tiye was one of them, although her body was no longer there and eventually turned up in one of the known mummy caches. The body they found in KV55, a skeleton rather than a wrapped mummy, was a man.'

'Do they know who he was?'

Adam smiled that soft smile of his. 'Merry, to answer your question we enter one of the hottest debates of Egyptology.'

I felt a thrill go through me.

'The big question is whether or not it's Akhenaten himself.'

The thrill magnified tenfold. I positively shivered, despite the blanket-like heat of the Egyptian dusk. My love affair with this ancient land intensified by the minute. Nowhere else on earth could cast the same spell; or weave its magic in quite the same way.

'There was certainly inscriptional evidence to suggest Akhenaten might have been moved to KV55 after his original interment in his tomb in Akhet-Aten. Zahi Hawass, when he was still the Minister for Antiquities, seemed to settle matters once and for all when he commissioned some DNA testing on the KV55 skeleton.'

'I remember this!' I exclaimed. 'I'm sure I saw a Discovery Channel documentary a year or so ago. It proved through DNA testing that Akhenaten was Tutankhamun's father.'

Adam grinned at me. 'Or so we all thought…'

'What do you mean…?'

'Hawass published his DNA findings in something called the JAMA paper in February 2010. JAMA stands for the Journal of the American Medical Association. These were the findings dramatised in the Discovery Channel documentary. I saw it too. The DNA testing proved the KV55 mummy was Tutankhamun's father. I don't think anyone has disputed that.'

'I'm not following you,' I said. 'What did you mean by "or so we all thought"?'

'Well, while it may be an established fact that the skeleton found in KV55 is Tutankhamun's father, debate rages on about whether the skeleton is, in fact, Akhenaten.'

'Who else would he be?' Jessica put in confusedly.

'Smenkhkare,' I breathed, remembering the novels I'd read.

Adam smiled at me with a slightly raised eyebrow. I loved that I could surprise and delight him by coming out with these little Egyptological nuggets from time to time. 'The problem historians have,' he said, 'is the conflicting and contradictory evidence of the textual and the anthropological evidence of KV55.'

'What do you mean?' Jessica sat forward.

Adam met her gaze. 'Well, while the name was hacked out, the inscriptions on the coffin point to Akhenaten. But DNA testing on the skeleton suggests it belonged to a male of not more than twenty-five years of age. That would seem to rule out our heretic king. We know he had a reign of around 17 years, and that he was already married to Nefertiti and had fathered at least one of his six daughters by the time he came to the throne. So, it stands to reason that he must have been older than twenty-five.'

Ted was nodding as Adan spoke. 'It is, indeed, problematic to positively identify the KV55 skeleton as Akhenaten,' he agreed. 'There is also the contradictory evidence of the two mummies they believe they've positively identified. Remember we talked about Ankhesenamun back in Cairo? She was Tutankhamun's great royal wife. DNA testing has proved conclusively that the mummy they believe to be Ankhesenamun was the mother of the mummified foetuses found in Tutankhamun's tomb. Similar testing has proved Tutankhamun was their father. The fly in the ointment is this: Ankhesenamun is known, unequivocally, from the historical record to be Akhenaten's third daughter. But the DNA evidence doesn't stack up. The DNA of the mummy researchers believe to be

Ankhesenamun and the DNA of the KV55 skeleton believed to be Akhenaten, don't equate to a father and daughter relationship. So, either we must posit that Tutankhamun had an unknown wife who may be the mother of the foetuses, which seems unlikely, or again, the skeleton in KV55 is not Akhenaten.'

I shifted my gaze from Ted's to Adam's face in the shadows of the gathering darkness. Lights were coming on in the gardens of the Jolie Ville, but Adam was facing the river, so they were behind him. I was concentrating hard, trying to follow their explanations. 'But the DNA testing proved the skeleton in KV55 was a son of Amenhotep III and Queen Tiye, didn't it?' I queried.

'It did,' Adam confirmed.

'So, if it's not Akhenaten, then Smenkhkare is the only other possible candidate.'

'Who the hell is Smenkhkare?' Dan asked, with a frown so deep it looked as if his face had caved in.

'That, young man, is a very good question,' said Ted from the sidelines.

'He's a shadowy, ephemeral character who never quite steps forward to make his presence felt,' Adam said. 'Let me try and sketch out for you the best representation of a family tree I can.' He reached for the paper napkin sitting alongside the untouched bowl of peanuts on the table in front of us. Smoothing it out, he accepted the pen Ted offered him and started to draw. 'Ok, on this side there's the royal lineage through the Thutmoside kings of the 18th Dynasty to Amenhotep III. You'll remember Ay had a lot to say about the pure royal line earlier in his missive. On the other side there's the 'commoner' line of Queen Tiye. It seems she and her brother Ay were the offspring of a couple called Yuya and Thuya. Their intact joint tomb was discovered in the Valley of the Kings in 1905. Their DNA has been extracted, so there's a clear line of descent to later mummies. Nobody has ever found Nefertiti's remains. But now we have Ay's own written testimony that he's her father; so we can draw a straight line from Ay to Nefertiti.' He matched action to his words drawing a line and writing the name of this most enigmatic of Egyptian queens. I watched the ancient family tree taking form on the napkin and felt myself go all shivery again.

Adam paused and looked up, the pen hovering enticingly over the blank space beneath his last entry. 'Zahi Hawass and his team believe they proved a few things conclusively through their DNA analysis. First, the skeleton in KV55 was a son of Amenhotep III and Queen Tiye. Second, the skeleton in KV55 was the father of Tutankhamun. Then the Hawass team turned to a mummy cache found in the tomb of Amenhotep II, KV35. This was discovered in the late nineteenth century. It's believed ancient priests moved the remains of past dynasty's kings and queens there when law and order broke down towards the end of the Pharaonic period. KV35 contained the unwrapped remains of a mummy tagged as the "elder lady", and another called the "younger lady".'

In my excitement I interrupted him again. 'The DNA testing proved the "elder lady" was Queen Tiye,' I said.

'That's right,' he approved. 'She was clearly descended from Yuya and Thuya. Equally clearly, she was the mother of the skeleton in KV55, and the grandmother of Tutankhamun. The interesting bit is this ...'

All eyes, even Dan's, were fixed on his face.

'...The DNA from the mummy of the "younger lady" proves she was the daughter of Queen Tiye and Amenhotep III, the mother of Tutankhamun, but also the full sister of the KV55 skeleton.'

We all went silent.

'So, Tutankhamun was the product of a full brother-sister incestuous relationship,' Jessica breathed.

'So it would seem,' Adam nodded. 'No wonder he was such a sickly kid.'

Dan shuddered. 'They were an immoral bunch, weren't they?'

'They didn't see it that way,' Adam replied. 'There's no evidence to suggest ordinary people indulged in incest. But the royal family saw it as a way of keeping their lineage strong. Brothers were married to sisters to prevent other minor royals doing so, and then staking a claim to the throne. The unfortunate part was that rather than making the royal line strong and pure, all the in-breeding weakened it.'

'You said Tutankhamun was sickly,' Jessica said. 'What was wrong with him?'

'You name it, he had it,' Adam said with a small shrug. 'It seems he was suffering from malaria when he died. Recent studies on his mummy also suggest he suffered from avascular bone necrosis in his foot – a disease in which the bone is unable to get sufficient blood flow. So, he had a deformed foot and also a mild form of scoliosis, which is curvature of the spine. Taken together, this evidence explains why Howard Carter found so many walking canes in Tutankhamun's tomb. There were hundreds of them.'

'Poor kid,' Jessica sympathised. 'And yet his face in all the carvings and paintings in his tomb, not to mention the death mask, looks so serene and beautiful.'

We all took a moment to ponder the misfortunes of Tutankhamun's life and health. But I wanted to get back to the central point of the discussion and understand who it was Tutankhamun and Ay buried in tomb KV55 only to have the tomb ransacked by their enemies during Ay's reign.

'There's no record of Akhenaten ever being married to one of his sisters,' I said, pretty sure of my ground on this one. 'Akhenaten's known wives were Nefertiti, and someone called Kiya. While it seems Nefertiti was his cousin, Kiya was supposed to be a foreign princess, wasn't she?' Adam's nod encouraged me to go on. 'So, if Zahi Hawass was right in stating the KV55 mummy is Akhenaten then we must believe that both Akhenaten and Tutankhamun had royal wives who somehow escaped the historical record. That seems a bit far-fetched to me. So, the only other conclusion we can reach, that seems to fit all the DNA evidence, is that the mummy in KV55 is not Akhenaten, but a brother of Akhenaten.'

'So, we're back to the mythical Smenkhkare,' Adam said. He continued sketching his family tree on the paper napkin. It showed Akhenaten descended from Amenhotep III and Queen Tiye, married to Nefertiti, descended from Ay and an unknown wife. Underneath he drew six lines to represent the six known daughters of Akhenaten and Nefertiti; of whom Ankhesenamun was the third.

'We know Smenkhkare existed from the historical record,' Adam went on, looking up from his scribbled genealogy. 'Someone called Ankhkepurure Smenkhkare succeeded Akhenaten to the throne, albeit briefly. But almost nothing is known about him. If he was a son of Amenhotep III and Queen Tiye, then it's likely his full sister, and mother to Tutankhamun, was either princess Nebetah or princess Beketaten. They were Amenhotep and Tiye's two youngest daughters. Again, almost nothing is known about them.'

'So, if Tutankhamun was the son of Smenkhkare and one of his sisters, that would have made him Akhenaten's nephew, and Ankesenamun's cousin.'

'Exactly,' Adam nodded, drawing this line of descent onto the napkin. 'And you know what? I think the most compelling reason for believing Tutankhamun was not Akhenaten's son is that it appears he didn't immediately come to the throne on Akhenaten's death. Smenkhkare did. There's evidence to suggest Smenkhkare was married to Meritaten, Akhenaten and Nefertiti's eldest daughter, and she became his great royal wife. There's nothing to stop him having two or more wives. So, my theory is he was married to his sister, either Nebetah or Beketaten, as a youngster and they produced Tutankhamun. Then, when Akhenaten died, he married Meritaten – either to further strengthen his own claim or to stop anyone else marrying her - and ascended to the throne. I watched a YouTube video of a lecture from the Metropolitan Museum in New York a while back. It seems they're adding three years between the reigns of Akhenaten and Tutankhamun. That would account for Smenkhkare's time on the throne.'

'So, it all fits,' I said excitedly. 'I've always thought if Tutankhamun was Akhenaten's son we'd have known about it from the artwork. Akhenaten plastered images of himself,

Nefertiti and their six daughters all over Akhet-Aten. But there's no sign of Smenkhkare or Tutankhamun. If they were only his brother and nephew, that might explain why.'

'Although we have to acknowledge that royal princes were never included in royal imagery – at least, not until the early 19th Dynasty,' Ted put in. 'So, that in itself was not unusual.'

But Adam was nodding at me. 'I have to agree, though, if Tutankhamun was Akhenaten's son, he'd have come straight to the throne without the three-year gap, despite being a small child of possibly only five or six when Akhenaten died,' he corroborated. 'Even if he were Akhenaten's son by a harem wife rather than one of the 'official' wives, Nefertiti or Kiya, it would still give him the right of ascent over Smenkhkare. There are plenty of examples of pharaohs who were born of harem wives coming to the throne as young children. Tutankhamun's grandfather Amenhotep III was one of them, as were Thutmosis II and III. I don't believe Akhenaten had any sons, which is why his younger brother Smenkhkare took the throne. It was only when Smenkhkare died that *his* son, Tutankhamun came to the throne as the legitimate son of the previous king.'

'So, we think that Ay's "treasures", whose reburial was desecrated by his enemies were Queen Tiye, and

Tutankhamun's parents: Smenkhkare and the "younger lady" who was either Nebetah or Beketaten,' I surmised.

'I'd put money on it,' Adam agreed.

'Well, I can understand why Ay felt the need to write his confession,' I said. 'He married Ankhesenamun to protect her, only to have her write off to Egypt's enemies the Hittites and then commit suicide. And he was unable to prevent the desecration of the tomb of Tutankhamun's parents despite all the effort they went to bringing them for reburial from Akhet-Aten. His failure must have been a pretty heavy burden to bear.'

'Yes, but in one key matter he's at pains to stress they've had a spectacular success, not a failure,' Adam pointed out.

'Their "most precious jewels" remain hidden and undisturbed,' I breathed.

'Exactly,' he nodded. 'And I, for one, don't know of any other late 18th Dynasty tombs ever to be discovered.'

'Which suggests the "precious jewels" might still be buried wherever Ay and Tutankhamun put them.'

'It does,' Adam murmured. 'And, if we accept the KV55 body is Smenkhkare, I think we can hazard a pretty shrewd guess about the identity of those "precious jewels".'

Chapter 12

We didn't have time to pursue this thrilling line of conjecture. Ahmed heaved himself out of his chair and said sadly that he had to get back to work.

'Before you go, we need to photograph the other two papyrus scrolls,' Ted said urgently. 'I'm not prepared to risk any more mishaps. The papyri are too precious and we're only their temporary custodians. Ahmed, I want you to take Carter's case back to the police station with you and lock it up tonight.'

Jessica giggled, presumably at a mental image of Ahmed flinging the antique suitcase into a police cell.

'It will be my honour to keep it safe,' Ahmed declared.

'But no one must know it's there,' Ted qualified.

'I will keep it as my most deepest secret.' Ahmed said stoutly.

So, we all trooped back to Adam's hotel room, set in its hexagonal bungalow in the grounds near the infinity pool. Dan and Jessica agreed to stand guard outside, just in case an unsuspecting member of housekeeping staff should come by to change the towels and see us poring over the ancient texts. We still needed to come up with a plausible way of introducing them to the world, hopefully one that wouldn't land us in a shedload of trouble.

I was glad Adam had decided to check into the hotel, rather than stay alone in his flat by the Souk. While there wasn't much Dan and I were in accord about right now, his point about the sense in sticking together was one I agreed with wholeheartedly.

Still, it felt a bit odd to step inside Adam's hotel room. For all that his room was exactly the same as mine, in the next block along, it still felt like entering a curiously personal space.

He'd had the presence of mind to bring with him the two sheets of glass from the poster frames in his flat. I wondered if they'd caused raised eyebrows at check-in. His decision to bring them spoke volumes about his determination to pay the ransom and get the papyri back.

'I know the papyri are intact,' he said. 'I made Hussein open the suitcase and show me before I handed over the money.'

'Thank God for that,' Ted said with feeling. 'I don't think I'd have forgiven myself otherwise. I'm sure Howard Carter didn't go to all the trouble of hiding them inside that tomb only for them to fall into the wrong hands and be destroyed within a couple of days of discovery.'

We all knew how close we'd come to this catastrophic outcome. 'We need to get them all photographed, so Ahmed can lock them away safely,' I agreed.

Adam lifted the antique suitcase onto the bed and fiddled with the spring-loaded locks. We gathered around as they popped open, and he lifted the lid. It was a silk-lined suitcase. The papyrus scrolls were protected under a further pillowcase-sized sheet of silk. As Adam drew it aside, we all sucked in a breath of pure wonderment. The three yellowed and cracked scrolls nestled snugly inside. Impossible to put into words the magical awe of gazing on these relics of the ancient world, touched by the hands of pharaohs, and entombed alongside Tutankhamun for time beyond imagining.

'I don't know about you,' Adam whispered shakily. 'But I don't think I could ever grow tired of looking at these things. The whole idea that we can reach out and touch something from Tutankhamun's time sets my brain on fire.'

We allowed ourselves the indulgence of standing in worshipful silence for a few moments more; then Ted reached carefully into the case and pulled out one of the smaller scrolls.

'Lay out a sheet of glass on the table over there, would you please Adam?' he asked.

Adam placed the glass on the tabletop as instructed. Ted leaned over it and started painstakingly to unroll the papyrus. We all held our breath. It was a precision operation, performed with infinite slowness. We all knew a sudden move could cause the ancient paper to disintegrate altogether. It was cracked and brittle. It wouldn't take much to reduce it to a pile of flakes and dust.

As Ted straightened the first section Adam stepped forward to hold the corners down on top of the glass. Finally, after long breathless moments, Ted had the whole thing flattened out on the glass frame. 'Ok, Ahmed, could you please – very carefully – lower the other sheet of glass on top. That's it... left a little. Now, just lower it. Yes, like that. Wonderful. We're done.' And he stepped back with a heartfelt sigh of relief.

This scroll was smaller than the one on which Ay's epistle was written. It fitted quite neatly sandwiched between its two sheets of poster glass. We all stood back and stared at it. It contained thirteen columns of closely and exquisitely drawn hieroglyphics.

Adam and Ted both sucked in a breath of stunned recognition at the same moment.

'It's the Great Hymn to the Aten!' Adam exclaimed.

'Akhenaten's Great Hymn,' Ted murmured simultaneously.

Their overlapping voices speaking holy words of reverence seemed to call up some ancient spirit. My scalp prickled as if a hot wind had blown through.

'Look...' Ted said excitedly. 'Look at the inscription at the top...' He brushed beads of perspiration from his brow with the back of his hand and leaned forward; his narrow-rimmed glasses slipping forward to perch precariously on the end of his nose. He started to read the hieroglyphs…

'"*Praise of Ra Harakhti, Rejoicing on the Horizon, in His name as Shu who Is in the Aten-disc, living forever and ever; the living great Aten who is in jubilee, lord of all that the Aten encircles, lord of heaven, lord of earth, lord of the House of Aten in Akhet-Aten. And praise of the King of Upper and Lower Egypt, who lives in truth, the Lord of the Two Lands: Neferkheperure Waenre; the Son of Re, the Lord of Diadems: Akhenaten, long in his lifetime. And praise of the Chief Wife of the King, his beloved, the Lady of the Two Lands: Neferneferuaten Nefertiti, living, healthy, and youthful forever and ever; by the Fan-Bearer on the Right Hand of the King … Ay.*"'

Ted stood back and looked across the table at Adam. For a transfixed moment they stared at each other.

'The whole hymn is transcribed in the columns underneath,' Adam said wonderingly. His gaze found my face and he stared into my eyes. 'Merry, this is incredible, but I don't pretend to understand it. The Great Hymn to Aten is attributed to Pharaoh Akhenaten. It's believed he wrote it as part of his attempt to convert ancient Egypt from its centuries of polytheism to monotheistic Atenism, with Aten as the only God of the universe. From the inscription at the top, it seems Ay transcribed this copy for Akhenaten when he was still a senior official in Akhenaten's court in

Amarna. What doesn't make sense is what it's doing here... I mean what it's doing as part of a store of papyri secreted by Ay inside Tutankhamun's tomb.'

'Tutankhamun and Ay are credited with returning ancient Egypt to the old religious beliefs,' Ted explained. 'They restored the Egyptian pantheon of gods and re-opened all the temples that were closed for worship during Akhenaten's reign. Tutankhamun even changed his name to reinforce his abandonment of Akhenaten's new religion. He was born Tutankh-Aten. One of the first acts of his reign, presumably under Ay's guidance, was to raise a restoration stela granting the people permission to go back to the old ways. In it, he waxed lyrical about the ruin Akhenaten had brought on the Two Lands of Egypt.'

Adam's gaze was unwavering on my face. 'So, what on earth is the Great Hymn to the Aten doing enshrined in Tutankhamun's tomb?'

There was no answer I could offer him. But I burned with an Egyptological fire every bit as intense as the one glowing in his eyes. We stood for a few moments pondering the imponderable. Then Adam got busy with his iPad, photographing the ancient scroll from every conceivable angle.

I could see Ahmed glancing at his watch and starting to twitch. 'We need to get the other scroll photographed so

Ahmed can get back to the police station,' I said. 'We don't want to get him fired.'

While Adam, Ted and Ahmed went through the nerve-jangling procedure of removing the papyrus from its glass protection and rolling it up again, I poked my head outside the door to let Dan and Jessica know how we were getting on. They were sitting at the little patio table, pooled in the soft light from the outside lamp. As I opened the door, she let out a delighted tinkling laugh at something he said. My instinctive reaction to this did me no credit so I quashed it. 'We've photographed one of the scrolls,' I said brightly. 'We're about to do the other one. We shouldn't be too much longer.'

'Take your time,' Dan said without looking up. 'There's no tearing hurry.'

I closed the door again with an odd little feeling of displacement.

'We're just about to unroll the last papyrus,' Adam said, with a thrill of excitement threading his words. I promptly forgot about everything else and hurried over to join him by the table.

The heart-in-the-mouth process of unrolling and securing the ancient parchment between the two sheets of glass was repeated. Once again, we all stood back and stared at it with a collective intake of breath.

'I don't understand what I'm seeing,' I said, staring at the series of intersecting lines drawn in faded black ink on the yellowed parchment. Towards the bottom of the sheet was a rectangle. Above it were two square boxes separated by a narrow band. Then rows of tiny squares and small circles before a final square box in the middle of the sheet at the top with two rows of tiny circles around its whole perimeter. 'Is it a drawing of some sort?'

Adam seemed to have stopped breathing. He was very still alongside me. I could almost hear his brain whirring.

'It looks like an architect's drawing,' Ted said.

'It *is* an architect's drawing,' Adam choked, as the breath he'd been holding caught in his throat. 'Look... Doesn't that sign there read "High Steward of the King, Senenmut"?'

Ted leaned forward, 'Good grief; you're right! Senenmut was the great architect of Hatshepsut, the queen who had herself declared pharaoh.'

'And this is... this is...'

'This is a drawing of Hatshepsut's mortuary temple,' I exclaimed, cutting across him as I put two and two together and started to see a shape that I recognised emerging from the intersecting lines on the sheet. The plan was drawn as if the artist were looking down on it from above. The rectangle was the courtyard in front of the temple. The two boxes were the north and south colonnades, separated by the narrow band, which was actually the central ramp, linking the lower and upper terraces. The small squares and circles were meant to depict the columns and statues lining the colonnades and circling the upper terrace. I had a particular fondness for Hatshepsut's temple. It was, after all, where I met Adam.

'Yes… look… "Djeser-Djeseru",' Ted said, pointing to some faded text at the bottom of the square of papyrus. 'It means "the holiest of holy places". It's what Hatshepsut called her temple.'

'But this makes even less sense than the Great Hymn to the Aten,' Adam frowned, his face a study in perplexity. 'For a start, Hatshepsut pre-dated Tutankhamun by something like a-hundred-and-fifty years. Her reign was towards the beginning of the 18th Dynasty, whereas his was right at the end. And second, Hatshepsut was the pharaoh who elevated the god Amun to prominence. She claimed divine birth from him. How are we supposed to square up one papyrus being all about the Aten, and the other being the plan of a temple dedicated ostentatiously to the opposing god Amun? What on earth is the link to Tutankhamun? Why did Ay bury these two papyri with him? They must have some special meaning attached to them.'

I tilted my head to one side, trying to puzzle it out. 'Well, as Ted said before, he had both "Aten" and "Amun" in his name at one time or another. Tutankh-Aten then

Tutankh-Amun. Maybe this is just Ay's way of making sure both gods helped him achieve a safe passage to the afterlife, since they were both his namesakes.'

'You might be right. Maybe they're supposed to represent the blessing of the gods or something.' But I could see Adam wasn't satisfied with this explanation. He leaned forward to minutely inspect the drawing beneath its protective sheet of glass. 'What does that say?' he asked, looking up at Ted and pointing to a square, which was drawn off to the left-hand side of the south-side lower colonnade. I recognised it from my visits to Hatshepsut's temple as the small shrine to the goddess Hathor. On the plan it was crammed with six rows of densely packed circles, meant to depict the stone columns each topped with a Hathor-headed capital. It was drawn in darker ink than the other parts of the plan and had a faded line of text written in hieratic script above it.

Ted leaned forward and pushed his glasses back up onto the bridge of his nose, squinting through them. His breath misted the glass while he concentrated on the almost invisible text. When he straightened again there was an odd expression on his face. 'How peculiar,' he said. 'If I'm reading it correctly, and I'm pretty sure I am, that text reads, "Aten is key".'

Adam and I stared at him.

'Aten..." Adam frowned. 'You're sure it's Aten, not Amun?'

'Positive,' Ted nodded. 'Look, that symbol there, while not the hieroglyphic sun-disc is unquestionably the word "Aten".'

'This is making less and less sense,' Adam said with a small shake of his head. 'Why would Aten be key in a temple dedicated to Amun?'

'There's something else,' Ted said. 'While I wouldn't stake my life on it, I'd hazard a pretty shrewd guess that what we have here is an original plan of the temple. But I think Ay has annotated it. See this darker line around this section? I think it was added to the drawing later, at the same time as the line of text. I think the same hand penned this as wrote Ay's testimonial; so that would mean Ay himself. I agree with you; it must have some special meaning.'

I looked into Adam's eyes and felt a thrill go through me. 'It's starting to seem to me that we've got another puzzle to solve,' I said. 'If we can figure out what links the sun god Aten to Hatshepsut's temple, we might be a step closer to understanding why Ay added that line of text.'

His eyes deepened from intense blue to violet as he looked back at me. I'd noticed they did that when he was excited. Adam's eyes had the power to hold me mesmerised at the best of times. But darkly violet and dilated like that, they were positively hypnotic. 'I can feel a visit to Hatshepsut's temple coming on,' he grinned.

'And I need to get on with translating the last section of Ay's testimonial,' Ted said. 'Then we'll know everything and can start trying to make some sense of how – *if*, I should say – if and how - the three papyrus scrolls are supposed to fit together.'

Chapter 13

A deep thrill ran through me as I gazed at the façade of Hatshepsut's temple next morning. The taxi deposited Adam, Dan, Jessica and myself in the car park slap bang in front of it, and my gaze was drawn like a magnate, ignoring the curio sellers and hawkers who immediately clustered around us. I felt a profound affinity with this place. For a start, it's beautiful. The temple rises on terraces from the shimmering desert plane to connect with the bay of craggy, mellow gold cliffs towering behind it. The cliffs act as a kind of gilded frame; a natural amphitheatre of vertical rock dramatically showcasing the temple. Among the monstrous grandeur of the other monuments of ancient Egypt, with their towering columns, massive stone pylons and colossal, egotistical statues, Hatshepsut's is a masterpiece of grace, style and feminine simplicity.

But I think the thrill had as much to do with a hefty dose of nostalgia as with the wondrous awe of gazing at the symmetrical perfection of this gem of a three-and-a-half thousand-year-old temple. This was where I'd first met Adam those scant few weeks ago, on the forecourt in front of the lower ramp. My life had changed immeasurably since.

And really, thinking about it, this was where the whole epic adventure had begun. A faint relief carving on the northern colonnade of Queen Ahmes, Hatshepsut's mother, had been Howard Carter's inspiration for a watercolour painting where he secreted his coded hieroglyphics. These had led us to the discovery of Tutankhamun's papyri. It was impossible not to feel a special affection for this most beautiful of ancient monuments.

I wasn't quite sure what we were here in search of, or exactly what we hoped to find. I couldn't fathom the significance of that single line of ancient hieratic script carefully penned in Ay's hand. But Adam seemed to think there must be a link to Akhenaten's sun god, Aten, here in Hatshepsut's temple, for all that it was dedicated to the worship of the rival god Amun. Specifically, we were looking for a reason why Aten should be a key deity within a small sanctuary of the temple dedicated to the goddess Hathor. Having no alternative to offer, I was very happy to go along with Adam's line of enquiry. It gave us something to do while Ted translated the last portion of Ay's testimonial.

I was breathless with impatience to know how he was getting on. We'd left him behind at the hotel while we made this trip to the west bank. He said he didn't feel up to scrambling over the uneven surfaces of the temple in the fearsome morning heat of early summertime. He preferred the cool shade of the Jolie Ville gardens where he could sip a cold drink and concentrate on his labour of love. He had Adam's iPad and his reference books for company now the papyri were locked up safely in police custody.

Ahmed had reluctantly left us last night to return to the police station after we finished photographing the scrolls. He took the papyri with him, once again secured inside Howard Carter's suitcase. Watching him go, with it pinioned safely under his arm, I'd felt strangely bereft. The papyri were passing out of our care, and I had a feeling next time I saw them we'd be handing them over to the authorities. I wondered how long we could reasonably put this off. The papyri weren't mine to keep. I knew that and I accepted it. But the thought of returning to my dull little life filled me with dread. These last few weeks in Egypt had been the most adventuresome of my life. I knew my redundancy money couldn't last forever. But somehow, all the time the scrolls were in our custody – even if it was police custody – I could delay the evil day of decision-making about my future and concentrate on the simple joy of straddling thirty-two centuries' worth of Egyptian history.

We bought our tickets at the ticket office sited at the end of a corridor of gaudy souvenir kiosks. We were accosted from start to finish as we ran this gauntlet of shopkeepers desperate to ply some trade. It was hard to blame them with tourist numbers so far down. I stopped and bought a wide-brimmed straw sunhat and enough bottles of ice-cold water to go around. But I really didn't have any need for the six-inch tall obelisk being waved in my face, or the concertina string of postcards trailing in the dust from the hands of a small boy which nearly tripped me up. I shook my head with an apologetic smile, and hurried to catch up with the others, where they were waiting for me by the low stone wall at the temple entrance.

Dan accepted the bottle of water I handed him with a muttered grunt that might have been a 'thank-you' if he wasn't in such high dudgeon with me, thanks to our unsatisfactory little exchange last night.

We'd all been sitting outside on the terrace in the darkness, sharing a companionable nightcap before we all turned in. He'd leaned across to my chair and whispered, 'Pinkie, how about we share a room tonight? Isn't it time we kissed and made up?'

I could understand his romantic inclination. We'd all been staring up at the stars spangling the inky sky. Not a breath of wind disturbed the sultry heat of the Egyptian night. A strong, tropical scent hung heavy in the air and the hotel lights played on the endlessly shifting waters of the Nile as they drifted languorously past. It was enough to stir the most frigid of temperaments.

I didn't know how to answer, but my traitorous gaze darted across to where Adam was sitting in the shadows, lost in some reverie of his own. Dan caught the quick glance, and I felt his body stiffen in the chair alongside me. 'No, of course not,' he muttered tightly. 'Silly of me to suggest it.'

'Dan...' I appealed. But it was too late. He rose and stalked off with a terse 'good night' directed at the others. I instinctively jerked forward to follow him, but subsided back into my chair with a small, muffled sigh. It was another part of my future I wasn't ready to face yet. It's not that I didn't appreciate Dan's grand gesture in hot footing it back out to Luxor when he thought I was diving headlong into a hornet's nest. It's just I'd been enjoying the freedom of living in the here-and-now, taking each madcap day as it came with no great thought for how it might turn out. Dan's presence reminded me I had choices to make, and responsibilities. Probably unfairly, I didn't want the pinprick to my conscience every time I looked at him. Strictly speaking, I hadn't done anything I needed to feel too guilty about. But it's possible Dan's sudden arrival was the only thing stopping me. It all just boiled down to lucky timing – or unlucky timing, depending on your point of view – certainly no great purity of thought or deed on my part.

I'd avoided eye contact with Adam after that, and we'd all headed off to our rooms shortly thereafter. I felt Jessica's gaze come to settle on my face a bit quizzically after Dan's departure but I was in no mood to engage in any exchange of non-verbals so I just concentrated on finishing my drink without looking up.

All this perhaps accounted for the rather awkward foursome we made up for our visit this morning to Hatshepsut's temple. The atmosphere between us thrummed with a dull tension that jangled the nerves and disinclined us towards idle conversation.

We didn't make directly for the electric trolley buses that snaked up and down the causeway leading to the temple, ferrying visitors back and forth to save them the lengthy stroll in the blistering heat and unrelenting sunlight. Instead, we walked across to the small Ministry building tucked alongside the ticket office. We'd been told to ask for someone by the name of Mustafa Mushhawrar.

This contact was courtesy of Ted's impeccable academic credentials and his links to the current darling of the Egyptian Museum in Cairo, a certain Shukura al-Busir. We knew from previous visits to the temple that the Hathor chapel cut into the mountainside beyond the pillared open hall of her shrine was closed to the public. So before dinner last night, Ted called Shukura and asked if she could pull any strings. She'd called back early this morning with confirmation that permission had been granted for a private, accompanied visit to the chapel. This was a rare privilege, and we were duly grateful. It was always worth having friends in high places. And one good turn deserved another after all.

Mustafa Mushhawrar was a crisply attired Egyptian of early middle age, with a thin moustache, a wiry frame, and closely cropped hair that shone blue-black in the sunshine. He wore tailored trousers, a gleaming white shirt with knife-edge creases in its short sleeves and shiny black shoes that had miraculously managed to avoid the dust. I sensed a fastidiousness about him, which perhaps manifested itself in the painfully brief handshake he offered each of us, after he'd inspected our passports and confirmed our identities against the list he'd been emailed. One eyebrow lifted before he could prevent it, catching sight of Jessica's black eye when she removed her sunglasses. But he was polite enough, or well enough trained, to refrain from comment.

'You are lucky to see the chapel,' he said, in clipped English overlaid with a soft Egyptian accent. He lifted a key off a hook on the wall behind him. 'It has been closed now for many years.'

'We're fortunate to be students of Professor Edward Kincaid,' Adam said, stretching the truth somewhat. Adam had once been a student of Ted's, many years ago before dropping out of university. The rest of us, I guess, might be classed students at a pinch, if Ted's translation of the ancient papyri could be called a masterclass in philology. I'm not sure Mustafa had heard of Edward Kincaid, once a senior lecturer at the Oriental Institute at Oxford University; now retired. But he'd heard of Shukura al-Busir and waxed lyrical about her amazing recovery of the stolen artefacts for the Cairo Museum while we stepped back out into the oppressive sunlight and waited for the next trolley bus.

'In these difficult days of our nation's emergence from tyranny,' he said, 'it is heart-warming to know there are good, solid citizens who will do their duty and return our nation's heritage to its rightful place. It is such a shame they chose to remain anonymous. The nation owes them a debt of gratitude.'

I smothered the warm glow his words spread though me. It was enough that our rather unorthodox connection with the gang of antiquities thieves enabled us to be in the right place at the right time; so, we could take advantage of Shukura's celebrity to be here now.

The trolley bus deposited us at the temple forecourt. 'I will take you to see the Hathor Chapel first, yes?' Mustafa asked. 'Then you can spend as long as you wish touring the rest of the temple.'

We all nodded and followed him up the central ramp to the middle terrace of Hatshepsut's temple. Mustafa turned tour guide as we reached the top and headed southwards towards the Hathor shrine. 'You will have seen the Punt reliefs carved on these walls, yes?' he asked, not stopping to show them to us. 'They are among the most interesting series of reliefs from ancient Egypt; depicting Hatshepsut's expedition to the fabled land of Punt.'

'Modern Somalia,' I interpreted, mainly for Dan's benefit. I had no idea how much of this stuff Jessica knew, growing up with an Egyptologist for a father.

'The reliefs can be divided into several sections, each illustrating a different stage of the expedition,' Mustafa said as we passed them by. The lower registers on the left end wall show the landscape of Punt, complete with wild animals including a giraffe, a panther, primates and what may be a rhinoceros. In the upper registers Egyptian sailors load their ships with incense and other exotic goods, ready for the long journey home.'

'Fascinating,' Dan murmured in a neutral tone of voice it was impossible to interpret as either rudely sarcastic or strictly sincere.

'We come now to the shrine you wish to see today. It is dedicated to Hathor, perhaps the most important goddess worshipped in the Deir el Bahri area.'

I knew Deir el Bahri was the Arabic name for Hatshepsut's temple, meaning "the Northern Monastery". It was derived from the Coptic monastery built into part of the upper terrace long after the ancient temple fell into disuse.

'Hathor was one of the most popular and revered of the ancient Egyptian pantheon,' Mustafa said, warming to his theme. 'She personified the principles of joy, feminine love and motherhood; worshipped by royalty and common people alike. In tombs she is depicted as "Mistress of the West" welcoming the dead into the next life. In other roles she was a goddess of music, dance and fertility. A hymn to Hathor says: "*Thou art the Mistress of Jubilation, the Queen of the Dance, the Mistress of Music, the Queen of the Harp Playing, the Lady of the Choral Dance, the Queen of Wreath Weaving, the Mistress of Inebriety Without End.*"'

I was impressed. Up until now the only person of my acquaintance who seemed able to quote from ancient texts almost at will was Adam. Perhaps it came with the territory, and an ability to learn ancient poetry parrot-fashion was a prerequisite of the study of Egyptology. It was just as well I'd never taken it up seriously. It was all I could do to hold a nursery rhyme in my head.

We followed Mustafa across a stepped stone threshold into a pillared hallway set against the far southern side of the temple. It was open to the sky, filled with columns about eight foot high, each topped with a Hathor-headed capital showing the goddess with a human head, and bovine ears, with a sistrum on her head.

'As I'm sure you know,' Mustafa said, careful not to patronise us in any way but clearly relishing the opportunity to showcase his knowledge, 'Hathor's cult developed from prehistoric cow cults based on the fertility associated with the cow's milk.' It made me wonder about his job. I got a sense of a man who loved his nation's ancient history and was clearly knowledgeable about it but spent most of his days chained to the boring bureaucracy of officialdom.

Adam stepped across the threshold and came to stand alongside me, joining me in peering up at the goddess capitals silhouetted against the dense blue of the sky.

'Hathor, along with the goddess Nut, was associated with the Milky Way,' Mustafa went on. 'The four legs of the celestial cow could, in one account, be seen as the pillars on which the sky was supported, with the stars on their bellies constituting the Milky Way. The Milky Way was seen as a waterway in the heavens, leading the ancient Egyptians to describe it as The Nile in the Sky, on which the solar barque of Ra, representing the sun, sailed. Hathor is commonly depicted as a cow goddess with wide apart horns on her head between which a sun disc is set.'

I felt rather than heard Adam's sharp intake of breath, and the sudden, familiar stillness that came over him.

'See, here...' Mustafa said, coaxing us forward to show us a particularly finely carved and painted figure of Hathor as a cow on the right-hand wall of the shrine. The sun disc on her head was plain to see between the curving horns.

'Now, you want to see inside the chapel, yes?'

Mustafa led us to the back of the small, pillared sanctuary. A stable door was fitted across the base of the opening, allowing visitors to peer into the rock-cut hallway through the open top half to see the brightly painted and well-preserved scenes of Hatshepsut before various deities.

Adam's gaze came to meet mine in a shared look loaded with meaning. But we didn't say anything; just preceded Mustafa inside the dimly lit chapel as he unlocked the door and held it open for us to enter.

Inside was a small, three-roomed chamber, carved into the cliffside. We stood and stared about us in awe. The walls seemed to be covered with images of Hatshepsut being suckled by the cow-headed goddess, with the sun disc set between her curved horns. Or maybe I was just to sensitised to those particular images that my eyes were magnetised by them and ignored everything else.

'See here...' Mustafa led us to a lower portion of the wall in one corner of the room. He took a small torch out of his pocket and shone it at the wall. 'See the small sketch of the man?'

We all peered at the wall and saw the rather crude line drawing of a man's face in profile.

'This is believed to be an image of Senenmut, Hatshepsut's great architect. Many believe he was also the queen's lover. It is said he carved his image behind this doorway to forever have a place close to his great love. Some people see it as a great declaration of enduring passion. Others view it as a vile stroke of egotism and conceit. I will leave you to make up your own minds.'

I stared at the small drawing and tried in vain to imagine what was in the brilliant architect's mind when he etched his own image behind the doorway.

'Over here in this archway,' Mustafa said, leading us to another part of the chapel, 'was found a perfect almost life-sized statue of the Hathor cow-head. It resides now in the Cairo Museum.'

I was reminded of a similar bust – the gilded head and shoulders of a cow – on display in the Luxor Museum and taken from Tutankhamun's tomb. There must be a link…

'I will leave you alone now for a short time, yes?' Mustafa said. 'You may take photographs, but I ask please that you refrain from using a flash. I will wait for you by the entrance way in the Hathor shrine.'

It didn't take long to make a minute inspection of the place. Adam got busy with his iPhone, and I did likewise with my camera, taking shots of every image of Hathor with the sun disc between her horns.

I noticed Adam tapping the walls, and felt a chill go through me, despite the stifling heat in the chapel. Mustafa had said Hathor was known as Mistress of the West – welcoming the dead to the afterlife. Could it possibly be suggestive?

'Deceptively simple,' Adam said a few minutes later after we'd emerged into the sunlight, watched Mustafa lock up behind us; thanked him and bid him farewell. He said he was honoured to have given us the opportunity to view the chapel and asked us to remember him to Shukura al-Busir, should we happen to see her anytime soon. Left to our own devices once more, we wandered out through the Hathor shrine and back onto the middle terrace. Sinking down to rest on a low stone wall in the shade, we sipped our tepid water, gazed at the azure sky unfurling across the barren landscape in front of the temple and contemplated all we'd seen. 'I nearly drove myself nuts last night,' Adam went on, 'tossing and turning, unable to sleep, trying to figure out what possible significance the Aten could have in this magnificent temple to Amun. But I was trying to be too clever, looking for some deep dark meaning historians had overlooked. How ridiculous! I should have seen it at once. There are images of the sun disc plastered all over the place in there. Hathor is almost always depicted with it on top of her head between her cow horns.'

'But what does it mean?' Jessica asked, wrinkling her nose; then wincing. The shiner the devilish Hussein had given her was obviously at the painful, fully developed stage.

Adam gazed up at a hawk riding the airwaves far above us. 'I don't know,' he admitted. 'Except to say it might to link it, however obliquely, to the Amarna period.' He shrugged. 'But archaeologists have been crawling all over this temple for at least a century. If there's anything to be discovered here, my guess is they'd have found it.'

'So now what?' Dan asked. To do him credit, there was only the merest touch of acerbity in his tone. 'We've come and we've seen; but it seems to me we haven't quite conquered. We've figured out this Aten so-and-so - a god didn't you say? – may have some relevance here; but we don't seem any closer to understanding it.'

Adam shrugged unperturbed. 'I reckon we should see it as a piece of the jigsaw and wait for the last section of Ted's translation of Ay's scroll before we attach any particular meaning to it.'

There was nothing else for it. But I still felt a profound sense of achievement and satisfaction, knowing that there was a sense in which Aten was indeed a key deity in his rival god's temple.

We'd all visited the temple before, even Dan; although, in his case, not recently. He'd submitted to a guided tour on a previous holiday we'd had a few years back.

'You know what?' he said unexpectedly. 'I wouldn't mind taking a look at the view from up there.' He pointed at the clifftop rising on vertical fissures above the temple. 'It's a clear day. I'll bet you can see for miles.'

I gaped at him. I'd have put money on him voting for a speedy return to the hotel and a few lazy hours by the pool. But it seemed he'd been surprisingly taken with my description of the clifftop pathway rising from the foothills on the northern side of Hatshepsut's temple. I'd waxed lyrical about it on the telephone to him when he was still back in England, after Ahmed took Adam and me for a hike up there not so long ago.

'Ahmed said it's possible to see the far hills before the Red Sea on a good day,' I enthused, immediately up for it.

So, we left the temple behind us and made our way back towards the car park. Just before reaching it, we branched left and joined the pathway leading up the northern side of the temple towards the clifftop.

The path was busier today than on the day Ahmed had led Adam and me up this same scree-covered slope recently. There weren't too many tour companies who offered the arduous trek as part of their excursion itinerary, but there were a few. Some of the high-end Nile cruise companies offered it to their well-heeled clients, if the evident social standing of the tourists we joined for the climb was anything to judge by. Designer labels abounded, little motifs on cotton shirts, baseball caps and hand-held bags. I didn't mind the company particularly. It was good to see the tourist industry hadn't completely turned up its toes in these post-revolutionary days since the Arab Spring.

The four of us were younger and, presumably, fitter than a goodly proportion of the tourists we passed on the path to the clifftop. We arrived at the summit first and had the view to ourselves. As before, it was spectacular.

The whole of the western Nile plain was laid out like a muted yellow and green striped carpet at our feet. In the foreground the ruins of centuries old temples rose from the sand and rock. Beyond Hatshepsut's temple directly below us, we only had to lift our eyes into the middle distance to see the great mortuary temple of Ramses II, the Ramesseum; and off to its right the active excavation behind the Colossi of Memnon, once the mortuary temple of Amenhotep III.

Beyond them, the cultivated land bordering the Nile seemed like a hand-painted strip of pastel green, the mighty river a brushstroke in dark blue beyond it. The modern suburbs of New Gurna this side of the river were of toy-town proportions, softened by heat haze to neutral beige tones. Luxor sprawled on the other side of the river, blurred through distance and sunlight into a chalky, buff coloured smudge from which the narrow minarets of mosques and the occasional crane rose like charcoaled-in details to touch the soft blue sky. In the far distance a deep band in mellow gold was the eastern desert between the Nile and the Red Sea, rising to a craggy line of mountains before the sea. It was beautiful.

Even Dan was impressed. He stood with his hand shading his eyes staring out to the far horizon. I wandered away from the edge to find a rock to sit on for a moment to catch my breath and drink some water. I could see Adam and Jessica a few feet away. He was pointing along the clifftop path branching southwards, no doubt telling her this was the pathway connecting with the Valley of the Kings and, further off, Deir el Medina, better known as the Village of the workers. These hills were criss-crossed with pathways, used by the ancients to traverse the barren, inhospitable landscape while they were tomb and temple building.

The tourist party joined us after a few minutes. For a while it was quite crowded up on the clifftop plateau overlooking the temple far below. I drifted in a pleasurable languor, sipping from my water bottle and letting my mind flit this way and that without actually settling on anything.

Then I saw something that made me jerk fully alert. I suddenly recognised a face in the small crowd milling around and taking photographs. He was in western dress, but I caught my breath, and my heart lurched as the horribly familiar figure of Hussein stepped towards the cliff edge.

It happened so fast it was over before I could take it in. Hussein sidled up behind Dan and gave him a hefty shove. Dan's body flailed and jerked, his arms windmilling wildly as he lost his balance. I was on my feet, my voice ringing out in a scream that echoed across the hills. But it was too late to serve as a warning. As Hussein turned and darted back from the cliff edge, running towards the track leading back down the temple forecourt as if the hounds of hell were in hot pursuit, Dan plunged off the clifftop. I took three running steps, as if I could somehow reach out for him in mid-air and yank him back from the fall. I skidded to a standstill, knowing it was hopeless. I could only watch in the ultimate agony of helplessness as he disappeared over the edge.

In the few heartbeats it took me, whimpering, to reach the edge of the cliff so I could peer down; the whole of my ten-year relationship with Dan flashed before my eyes.

Just as I reached the edge, I felt strong arms close around me and jerk me backwards. 'No, Merry – don't look!' It was Adam, drawn by my scream.

'Let go!' I wrestled out of his arms. 'I've got to...'

His face was a mask of horror. He reached out and pinned me back against him, but he knew he couldn't hold me back from the clifftop. We moved forward together, slipping slightly on the loose rock at the edge. My heartbeat was thundering in my chest. All sound seemed distorted to a slow, muted roar that was the blood rushing deafeningly through my body.

Terrified of the sight about to greet my eyes, I clutched at Adam's arm and peered down the cliff face.

Chapter 14

I don't know what I feared to see, but I don't think it was the heart-wrenching sight of Dan dangling from a ledge about thirty feet below me. His right hand was locked around a craggy outcropping of rock; his body hanging freely and at full stretch over the sheer drop below him. The sweat that soaked my body seemed to freeze on my skin. He wasn't dead, but it seemed but a temporary reprieve. His left hand moved frantically over the surface of the rock, searching for a handhold that wasn't there. The only thing keeping him from a fall that would smash half the bones in his body was his right hand clinging to that miraculously positioned ledge.

I couldn't breathe; almost didn't dare to. It seemed to me the slightest whisper of a breath might splinter the frozen tension and send him hurtling to his death. I could see the northern terrace edge of the temple far below us, people scurrying around on it like ants. And rocks, the fearsome, jagged, upward thrusting, deadly pikes of rock directly below! I didn't know how long he could hold on one-handed, but the ultimate horrific fall must surely be inevitable. I was frozen in horror – rooted to the spot, unable to tear my eyes away – knowing I'd have no choice but to watch when the awful moment came.

Adam sucked in a deep breath alongside me. And then all of a sudden, he wasn't alongside me anymore. In one smooth motion, he slipped over the edge of the cliff. My knees buckled at the realisation of what he planned to do. I had sickening visions of two bodies crashing hundreds of feet onto the rocky foothills below. As he scrambled down the craggy, treacherous surface of the cliff, clinging to the vertical fissures and finding footholds in the cracks and crevices, loose scree and chippings of rock crumbled away and tumbled down the cliff face. I closed my eyes in an agony of dread. Surely, he'd lose his footing at any moment. But it was impossible not to watch. My heart seemed to jump from my chest into my throat. It thumped there painfully, almost choking me. I couldn't swallow; could hardly even give voice to the desperate prayers tumbling through my mind. I could only look on helplessly as Adam scaled the sheer cliff face parallel to where Dan was swinging above the treacherous drop below him.

Jessica moved to stand alongside me and let out a horrified little squeak. After a moment her small hand came to clasp mine. It was an oddly comforting gesture. I could hear her softly whispered prayers, and they gave mine a frantic kind of focus. A knot of people gathered around Jessica and me at the clifftop. Their voices blended together like the irritating drone of some large insect asking, 'What happened? Oh my God! Did he fall? He must have been standing too close to the edge. The rock is dangerously soft and crumbly. Oh, my lord, the poor man!'

It seemed I was the only one to witness Hussein's deliberate attempt on Dan's life. Everyone else had been too occupied with his or her own enjoyment of the view to notice the murderous treachery going on closer at hand. When they saw Adam scrambling down the cliff face, the droning rose to a crescendo of buzzing, 'My God, that man's going to try to rescue him. It's suicidal. How the hell can he hope to reach him? He'll send them both over the edge,'

I hung onto my sanity with an effort of determined willpower and turned towards the voices. 'Do any of you people have anything you can tie together to make a rope?' I demanded a bit hysterically.

Thankfully, one of them had more presence of mind than the rest. 'Here, can we tie our shirts together, or use the straps of the ladies' handbags? Anyone else have anything we can use?' And he started organising the gawping onlookers to do something useful, rather than just stand there buzzing like a load of stirred up bees.

Blessing him, I tore my gaze back to Adam's gritty rescue attempt. Dan's right arm must surely be growing numb by now. He kept himself reasonably fit, but he was a big bloke, and his full weight dropping from his clamped hand must be tearing every muscle.

Adam levered himself parallel with Dan and edged forward on his stomach onto the ledge. I stopped breathing. If the rock gave way, they'd both tumble headlong into oblivion. The most dangerous part of his mission was upon him: how to get enough purchase on the rock to reach out and latch onto Dan's left hand without Dan pulling him off the cliff face. I didn't see how on earth he could achieve it. I could see him working his right foot deep into a vertical crack in the rock, the product of centuries of erosion, and testing the surface for a hand hold secure enough to take his weight. More chippings broke free and bounced down the cliff face, narrowly missing Dan's head.

I muttered a desperate plea to all the gods of all the ages and all the religions in the world to join forces and help us now. I clung tight to Jessica's hand and bit down hard on my bottom lip as Adam made his move.

He yelled Dan's name and lunged for his frantically waving left hand. A strangled cry tore from my throat as he missed, and a portion of the rock gave way beneath him. He didn't wait to re-secure his hold on the rock but lunged again. Just as Dan's right hand started to slip from around the outcrop of rock, Adam clamped hold of his left wrist.

Adam was half-lying across the narrow ledge. He brought his other hand to clasp Dan's elbow. For a long moment they were both frozen in that position and I thought my lungs would explode with the breath I was holding. Then slowly Adam started hauling him upwards. I was sure they must both fall; couldn't see how Adam could possibly take all the weight of the heavier man without being wrenched from his precarious perch. He must be straining every muscle and sinew in his body, his whole frame taut and focused on feeding every ounce of his strength into pulling Dan up onto the ledge. I could hardly bear to watch but was equally powerless to look away. I stood tense, rigid and terrified, the breath rasping in my throat as my lungs forced it up through my strangled windpipe. I clung to Jessica as if to a lifeline, as inch-by-inch Adam achieved the impossible.

Finally, it was done. I sank to my knees as I saw Dan collapse onto the narrow rim of rock jutting from the cliff face below us, his limbs entwined with Adam's in a tangle of arms and legs as they clutched each other. My chest was heaving, and I thought I might be sick as dark blotches blurred my vision. The nausea passed as I sucked in huge lungfuls of air. But I was too weak to get up. I could only kneel there panting.

Jessica, the angel, sprang into action. 'We've got to help them up from there,' she muttered. 'It's not over yet. Hey, you! Any luck with that rope?'

It was makeshift at best. Under any other circumstances I might have appreciated the sight of half a dozen men standing around bare-chested, with their shirts tightly knotted together. But I was too traumatised to do anything but watch mutely as they edged forward and the one who'd organised them called down to Adam and Dan. 'Guys, we're going to try to help you up. You need to come up one at a time.' He stepped forward. 'I'm going to come down as far as I dare…'

He crawled on all fours over the edge of the cliff and descended the first few feet, where the hand and footholds were reasonably secure. Then he swung the tightly lashed shirts over the edge and shouted out encouragement to the two men below.

Dan came up first. I noticed he favoured his left hand and made painstakingly slow process. Our new friend grabbed hold of him as soon as he dared and helped him negotiate his way up the last creases in the rock.

Jessica darted forward as he scrambled up onto the plateau. She whipped her water bottle out of her shoulder bag, sank onto the floor alongside him and held the bottle to his lips. Dan's chest was rising and falling with unhealthy speed, and his face was ashen; but the water helped. He choked, retched, then tumbled sideways and lay flat on the dusty ground, closing his eyes and shaking. He was alive.

'Oh, thank God!' I breathed. I crawled forward until I was close enough to reach out and touch him. My fingers connected with his foot. That was all, a ridiculous gesture probably. But I needed to feel him, to reassure myself that my eyes and my heart hadn't deceived me.

I didn't dare move closer, or else I'd be too far away from the cliff edge to see Adam make the treacherous ascent. Still breathless with fear, I had to watch.

He came clambering gingerly up the sheer cliff-face, using the shirt-rope to steady him when hand-and-foot holds weren't within easy reach. I choked out the breath I'd been holding, pushed myself up and staggered across to meet him as he hauled himself onto the flat surface of rock at the cliff edge.

'Of all the crazy, reckless …' I started, but ground to a standstill as emotion stitched my throat together and tears sprang in my eyes. I collapsed onto the ground alongside him, fumbled for my water bottle, and tried hard to follow Jessica's shining example of how to behave in the extremity of the moment.

Adam grinned a bit shakily at me, knowing the crisis was averted, the disaster over. 'It's no more or less than Indiana Jones would have done,' he murmured weakly, and he too rolled backwards and lay flat out on the hard rock.

I guess the feel of terra firma beneath you must be pretty wonderful after long moments dicing with death in mid-air. I sat there torn between hysterical laughter and great wracking sobs, which actually manifested as a kind of strangled wheezing.

The shirtless ones and their motif-clad companions clustered round. 'Are they ok? Any broken bones? No?

Thank goodness! What a miracle! I didn't think he could possibly survive that fall. What an amazing rescue!'

The shirt-rope was untied, and the crumpled garments buttoned back on again. Adam's shirt was torn, and I could see patches of grazed and bloodied skin across his chest and stomach where the rock scraped him as he hauled Dan over the ledge. The knife wound on his arm had obviously opened up again, because blood was seeping through the bandage. It was a miracle he hadn't cracked or broken his ribs, but I didn't doubt the bruising he'd suffer or the pain of strained muscles in his arms.

Dan was in worse shape. He'd sprained his right wrist and was pretty sure he'd torn a muscle in his right arm. Like Adam, he had lacerations across his chest and stomach where he'd been dragged across the rock onto the ledge.

But, all things considered, to have escaped with their lives, and with such minor injuries was little short of miraculous. I offered up a heartfelt thank you to all the gods, past, present and future, and counted a few lucky stars at the same time.

Dan pushed himself up into a sitting position and reached across to lay his hand on Adam's shoulder. 'Thanks mate; I owe you one.'

Something about this simple gesture really got to me. I had to turn away to bring my face under control.

'Are you guys going to be ok getting back down the track?' our new friend asked. 'It's just, we have to go because we need to get back to our cruise boat...'

'We'll be fine,' Adam assured him. 'I think we can both walk – right Dan?'

Dan got slowly to his feet. 'The old pins are a bit wobbly,' he said, 'but I think they'll hold me up. No serious harm done. Yes, you head off. We'll be fine. The girls can hold our hands to keep us steady. And thanks for all your help. That rope thingy was a great idea.'

We watched them head off towards the track leading back down the cliff side, leaving just the four of us on the rocky plateau. 'Well, that's given them a story to take home with them,' Adam commented, levering himself a bit tentatively to his feet. 'What the hell happened? I heard you scream Merry, but I didn't see Dan fall.'

'He was pushed,' I said with a shudder, running a mental action replay and feeling the horror all over again.

'What?' Adam and Jessica spoke in unison, doubling the shock.

'Yes, and a damned hard shove it was, too,' Dan muttered. 'If it hadn't been for that little ledge that you bodysurfed along to rescue me, Adam, I'd be a goner. I think I kind of bounced off it. It broke my fall and slowed me down just enough to grab hold of that outcrop of rock. That's what's known as a lucky break!'

This appalling wordplay elicited the groans it deserved.

'But who shoved you?' Adam asked. 'Or is that a stupid question?'

'You guessed it in one,' I said. 'That bloody menace Hussein managed to hide himself in among the tourists. He followed us up here unnoticed in the crowd and grabbed his chance the moment it presented itself. I saw the whole thing, but not in time to shout a warning. It all happened so quickly. He struck literally the moment I recognised him, then scarpered. He must have been watching us all morning; probably followed us here from the hotel.'

'But why?' Jessica asked with a bewildered toss of her curls. 'What on earth does he hope to achieve by killing one of us?'

'Well, look at it from his point of view,' Adam said. 'Both his brothers are dead, and we were on the scene each time. He thought he'd made a mint in ransom money, only to have us snatch it out of his hands again. Oh, and he's on the run from the law because we found and returned the antiquities he stole from the Cairo museum before he could flog them on the black market. I imagine he feels some deep grievance against us, which has morphed into a personal vendetta.'

Dan groaned. 'And I was too stupid to follow my own advice and make sure we stuck together. I was a sitting duck over there on the ledge.' He shuddered violently, no doubt reliving the jolt from behind that sent him hurtling over the edge the way I'd just done. 'When I said those cursed scrolls would be the death of someone, I didn't imagine it would be me! Next time I take it into my head to go sightseeing, stop me one of you, would you please? My time from now on is going to be spent strictly by the pool.'

'We're onto his game now,' I said, 'so we know to be extra vigilant. And we can tell Ahmed he's following us. So hopefully he can trail him and slap some handcuffs on him. Now, do you two feel up to making the trek back down to ground level? Because I, for one, am starting to fry! And I don't want to add a bad case of sunstroke to your other injuries.'

It was a slow trudge back down to the car park. I'm not sure Adam and Dan had any muscles they hadn't strained, and the lesions on their skin were oozing blood, and caked in grit. For once the hawkers who clustered around us made no attempt to sell us anything. I guess bandages weren't part of their stock in trade. We collapsed into the back of a taxi and, as we tore off in a cloud of dust, I didn't so much as glance back at the temple.

The afternoon was spent at the hotel's onsite medical centre getting Dan and Adam patched up. It took ages to pick tiny chips of rock out of the bloody abrasions on their fronts, then clean and dress the wounds. Dan emerged with his right arm in a sling and carrying a packet of strong painkillers in his left hand. He had bandages wound around his chest and stomach, with his shirt hanging undone over the top. 'No good for the suntan,' he moaned. 'I'm going to look like I've been wearing a tankini, or a boob tube, or something!'

I was glad to see his brush with death hadn't dented his sense of humour.

Adam was similarly bandaged, but without the sling or the painkillers. His knife wound had also been re-dressed.

Poor old Ted nearly had a fit when he saw our wounded soldiers. 'Yesterday it was Jessica coming back battered and bruised; today it's the two of you. Honestly, I don't think I should let you out of my sight. Dan, my boy, when you talked about risking life and limb for the papyri, I don't think you had it mind that you'd be the one to do so. Thank God you're back safe.'

The hotel staff didn't know quite what to make of things, and fussed over us to a quite excessive degree, plying us with free drinks, cold flannels and ice cream. Mostly I think it was because they were all agog to hear what had happened and were looking for any excuse to approach us. The freebies worked a treat. Our official story was that Dan went too close to the edge, lost his footing on some loose scree, and fell. After admitting that, the Jolie Ville staff practically queued up to hear about the fall and the daring rescue. By the time we'd told the story to the medical staff, the reception team, pool attendants, housekeeping staff, bar attendants, waiters, the girls from the spa and the keeper of Ramses, the hotel's resident camel, I think we were growing a bit fractious with all the unaccustomed attention. The only one who didn't have something to say about it was Ramses. He chewed on the flowers in the nearby garden border, making the most of his unexpected opportunity to indulge in a forbidden snack. Everyone else ooh'd and aah'd over Dan and Adam's injuries to a quite ridiculous extent and spoke volubly and excessively about the miracle of Dan breaking his fall by clutching hold of that rocky outcrop and Adam's bravery in leaping over the edge of a sheer precipice to rescue him.

I wouldn't have minded, except it meant I had to keep re-living the whole nauseating experience. And observing the rapidly inflating egos of the two heroes of the piece was a bit sickening, too. But I declined Dan's offer to go back to my room for a lie down to get over the shock. It might sound stupid, but, putting all the ooh's and aah's to one side, I was quite happy really just to sit there in the shade of a wide canopy drinking in the sight of these two bruised and battered men and counting my blessings. It struck me that my day – no, hang that; my *life* – might be very different right now if Hussein had shoved a bit harder. In such split seconds can the world be turned upon its head. My world, thankfully, was standing upright and ready to fight another day. I could look forward to the evening ahead safe in the knowledge that a few well-deserved glasses of wine were in order; and relish the prospect of hearing the last instalment of Ay's testimonial.

Chapter 15

'The whole sanctuary is plastered with images of the sun disc,' Adam said. Having exhausted the subject of Hussein's attempt to push Dan off the cliff above Hatshepsut's temple, it hadn't taken us long to get back to our favourite subject of the papyri. 'Of course, it should have struck me at once. Hathor is pretty much always depicted with cow horns and the sun disc on her head. But I didn't think we were looking for the obvious. Still, I guess they always say the best place to hide something is in plain sight. It's a clear link to the Aten; deceptively simple really.'

Ted tilted his head to one side and subjected Adam to a penetrating gaze through his narrow-rimmed glasses. As usual they'd slipped right to the end of his nose. He pushed them back up again. 'So, your theory is that Tutankhamun and Ay struck on the idea of hiding their "precious jewels" in Hatshepsut's temple?'

Adam shrugged, 'I'm not sure I'd go so far as to put money on it, but it's the best lead we've got. And let's face it; it's the one place their enemies could be pretty much guaranteed not to look. The temple is flagrant in its worship of Amun. Considering the persecution Akhenaten subjected Amun and his priests to, I'd class it as a masterstroke in subterfuge.'

I'm not sure I'd dared go quite so far in my conjecture. But I'd seen Adam tapping the walls, and I'd wondered.

We were mid-way through dinner in the Zigolini Italian restaurant on site. It had been quite a night so far. Even before we could conduct the important business of food-and-drink ordering, we'd had to submit gracefully to another bout of fuss. This time it included Jessica. There was no excuse for sunglasses inside the ambiently lit restaurant, so her black eye was on prominent display. I think Ted and I felt a bit left out amid all the clucking and flapping of hands as the waiters expressed their concern and exclaimed over the various injuries sported by our little party. Perhaps if I hadn't been quite so adept at smashing through the pigpen roof with my water bottle yesterday, I could've shown off a few cuts and bruises of my own and joined in. It might have been nice to have some of the ooh-ing and aah-ing turned in my direction. To be fair, I did have a few bruises – just not anywhere I was willing to expose. For the record, we told the waiters Jessica walked into a door. There's a reason why clichés are clichés. In my opinion, more often than not, it's because they're true. So, I saw no need to look for a more creative explanation for her shiner. Anyway, Dan, Adam and Jessica had a fine old time of it, while Ted and I looked on with as much patient indulgence as we remained capable of after so many re-tellings of the tale.

Luckily, the wonderful Jolie Ville staff remembered we were there to eat, not just provide the evening's entertainment. To give them absolute credit, they couldn't have done more to make us feel special. We had the best table in the house, the most impeccable service imaginable, extra-large portions, and an attentive drinks service. All in all, it was pretty fair compensation for the whole falling-off-a-cliff experience; albeit it didn't take away from our secret knowledge that Dan was pushed.

We spent a few minutes, while the drinks were served and the food was cooked, debating the nature and extent of the threat Hussein posed. We wanted to believe his attempt on Dan's life was the desperate action of a cornered man. But we couldn't be sure. Ahmed was on the case. Beyond that, all we could do was stay vigilant – and away from the edge of cliffs.

But the lure of the papyrus couldn't be denied for long. I'll qualify that by saying I'm sure Dan could have held out indefinitely. But the rest of us were keen as mustard to know how Ted had fared with his translation of the last section of Ay's scroll.

'So, we've made a link between Aten and the Hathor Sanctuary in Hatshepsut's temple,' Adam said, picking up the thread of our conversation after our main courses were served. 'But we don't really know what it means. Why should Aten be "key"? Why did Ay bury the Hymn to the

Aten alongside his missive to Tutankhamun? I think we need to hear the last part of Ay's testimonial.'

All eyes turned expectantly towards Ted.

'Where were we up to?' he asked, although I suspected he knew full well. Good university lecturer that he was, I'll bet he was just testing us to see how much attention we'd been paying. Either that or, like me, he felt a need to hold centre stage a moment, after all the fuss our companions had been treated to.

'Ay had just confessed to the desecration by their enemies of a tomb' I said eagerly. I wasn't much of a swat at school, and never came close to achieving the distinction of teacher's pet; but then my school didn't have Egyptology on the curriculum. The Industrial Revolution never held quite the same appeal for some reason. 'We think it's where they reburied some of the mummies they brought from Akhet-Aten.'

'He was probably referring to the tomb now known as KV55,' Adam put in with just as much eager enthusiasm. 'So, it's likely it was the remains of Smenkhkare, Queen Tiye and possibly the mummy now known as the "younger lady" they despoiled; although it's possible it was Akhenaten's body they were after.'

Ted nodded, and his glasses slipped to the end of his nose again. He peered at the four of us over the top of them. 'Good,' he approved. 'Ay said he'd been powerless to prevent this sacrilege. But he was still at pains to point out that their "most precious jewels" remained undisturbed.'

'Come on then Dad; don't keep us all in suspense,' Jessica coaxed him. 'How does it end?'

Ted smiled fondly at her and pulled his tiny notebook from his breast pocket. He looked around at us in the furtive way of someone about to impart a secret. A young couple with two small children occupied the table closest to us. They were way too distracted trying to force-feed pasta to their offspring to have any interest in eavesdropping on our conversation. Ted could finish reading us his translation without fear of being overheard. He flipped open his notebook, cleared his throat, and started to read.

"'Great one, the hour of our final parting draws near. I must complete this, my reckoning and atonement, and trespass no more on your everlasting peace. I will fulfil my promise. I will cause the landscape of Ta-sekhet-ma'at, the Great Field, to be altered, so our enemies may never find and profane your Sepulchre of Millions of Years. You and the lady of the palace will rejoice forever in the field of reeds, eternal life, eternal health, eternal prosperity.'"

I took a deep breath. 'Well, he achieved his promise to Tutankhamun for nearly 3,250 years from something like 1323 BCE to 1922 AD or CE, or whatever it's called nowadays, when Howard Carter found him. It's not quite forever, but it's probably as close as any of us can hope to come. And Ankhesenamun was found only a century or so earlier by Giovanni Belzoni. Not a bad slice of eternity.'

Nobody responded. Nobody even looked at me. Not even Adam.

'Sorry,' I said quickly. 'I didn't mean to interrupt.' Honestly, I was as bad as the rest of them, needing to comment on every section as Ted revealed it!

Ted waved away my apology and took a small sip of beer. He let his pause hang heavy in the air a moment, then went on,

' *"The Aten of the Day, Great of Majesty, will bathe you in his protective and life-giving rays. I, Kheperkheperure Ay, pray daily to receive His blessing when my hour comes. I, too, am a Son of Re, who lives by Ma'at. The weighing of my heart would be futile for my heart is heavy."'*

I opened my mouth to comment. There was so much I wanted to say. Luckily, I had the presence of mind to snap it shut again.

' *"The hold our enemies have over me remains vice-like in its grip. The daughter of my body lives still, hostage throughout these last twelve floods of your noble reign and my own by forced marriage to our enemy. Through her, and on my passing, the evil one can legitimise his claim to Per-Ah and sit on the throne of the Mighty Bull. I curse him daily and pray no issue will come of their union. All these summers my prayers have been answered. No dynasty will spring from his loins - none that has my blood in its veins. His last hope in claiming the glorious Thutmoside line of kings as his own lay in the lady of the palace on my death. But she has denied him, as she did once before when it was my honour to protect you. She joins you amid the imperishable stars.'"*

I knew better than to even attempt to interrupt this time. I couldn't, in fact. I was transfixed.

' *"My days grow short. The evil one can afford to wait for my time of passing. He has held two anointed kings in his strangle hold of treachery. I was once a powerful man. And you were destined to be a great king. But through threats and fear he has overturned the way to enlightenment. What is a father to do?*

"I will not write the evil one's name. Not through my hand will he prosper in the afterlife. His hands drip with blood; the blood of the pure Thutmoside line of kings who bore you. I pray he will face the judgement of a higher council than Per-Ah and answer for his crimes.

"Immortal lord, you are forced no longer to wear the false colours of false gods. The yoke of secrecy and subterfuge slipped from around your neck as you reached out to grasp eternity. I pray I may know the same freedom, and the Great Aten of Majesty will look kindly on my tarnished soul.

"I denied Him only to protect you, your lady, and the sole remaining daughter of my body, whom I love. I sought to preserve the pure Thutmoside line of great kings. It was not to be. I fear the kinship between my lord and great-nephew and my lady and granddaughter was too close. Your issue was not strong enough to survive. And you, sacred lord, were snatched from the throne of Per-Ah, the Great House, at the hour of your maturity. Your glorious line has perished. It plagues me that I have been unable to prove the evil one's hand at play in the accident that cut short your divine rule. You were denied your vow to return us to The One.

"But know this, oh sacred son of the Aten; my heart remains pure. I follow the path of enlightenment as taught to us by our most precious jewels. Though false deities may ascend to the pantheon of the Two Lands once more, one day the light of truth will shine again on men's souls. Aten will rule supreme. Until then, the golden images and sacred shrines of our most precious jewels will preserve His name.

"I will cause to be buried with you our private, triumphant knowledge. Our jewels rest still, no one seeing, no one hearing; and you, my immortal lord, are the only one to know the secret; for you devised it. This knowledge you will keep and protect through millions of years. For none will find your sacred shrine or know that Aten is key.

"I remain your devoted servant in truth through all eternity.

"Kheperkheperure Ay; he who was proud to say his blood flowed in your kingly veins."

* * *

I've always loved Italian food. But tonight, you'd have been forgiven for believing the opposite. I wasn't doing the freshly prepared food on my plate any justice at all. The only one of us eating with an undiminished appetite was Dan. But even he was moved enough by the significance of what we'd heard to refrain from smart-Alec comments between the mouthfuls that represented the demolition of his pizza. Perhaps it was the painkillers working.

My head was buzzing with a kind of weird electric static as I absorbed the pharaoh's words and tried to relate them to the bits and pieces I knew about Tutankhamun's life and death. The professor sat back in his chair, his glasses still perched precariously on the end of his nose and moved ravioli around on his plate with the aura of one on a higher than terrestrial plane, for whom food was an unnecessary distraction. The impression he gave was of a man whose sustenance came from the words he'd just read, not what was on his plate. Jessica looked a bit dreamy; or as dreamy as it's possible to look with one eye closing to a slit between the bruised swelling above and below it. Occasionally she raised her fork to her mouth, but it seemed it was more of a reflex action than because she was particularly mindful of the meal in front of her. But it was Adam who showed the most profound lack of appetite. His knife and fork rested untouched alongside his cooling plate of bolognaise; and his very stillness, the fixed way his eyes stared unfocused into the middle distance, made it clear that while he was with us in body, mentally he was somewhere else. To my knowledge they didn't have spaghetti bolognaise on the royal menu of ancient Egypt three thousand years ago. So, I guess his imperviousness to the aromatic dish before him was understandable.

Finally, his focus cleared, and he looked across the table at Ted. 'You read us a passage in Cairo,' he said. 'Something about when Ay protected Tutankhamun's passage to the throne…?'

Ted flipped back a few pages in his notebook. ' *"I had the honour to protect you once, sacred lord. The power was mine to ensure your smooth passage to the throne of the Two Lands, though your enemies sought to deny you and your betrothed queen your divine birthright."*'

'Yes, that's it,' Adam said in an odd, detached kind of voice, as if he was building a giant puzzle in his mind, fitting the pieces in one at a time. 'And there was something about murder. Jessica commented on it last night.'

Ted flipped forward a few pages, while I revised my earlier assessment and realised that Adam had been paying attention to yesterday's little interplay between Jessica and Dan after all. ' *"As once these evil men murdered divinely anointed rulers, so now they seek to pull their souls from the imperishable stars"'*

Adam stared off into space again and took an absent-minded sip of his beer. His thoughtful, inward-focused expression was achingly familiar. I'd seen it on his face often enough when we were sleuthing our way through Carter's Conundrums. Observing it now actually caused a strange but not wholly unwelcome tightening in my chest. This was Adam back on his favourite turf. I'd come to recognise and love the stillness that settled over him when something significant struck him; the way his darkly lashed eyes softened and seemed to change colour from blue to violet. I didn't take my eyes off him; just set my fork down and waited for him to speak. I knew he was about to.

'Ay didn't need to tell Tutankhamun's life story in his testimonial,' he said at last; his knife and fork still languishing unused either side of his plate. 'Why would he? Tutankhamun already knew it, so it was unnecessary. But I think he's told us enough that we can piece it together.'

Across the table, Ted's eyes gleamed. 'Go on then,' he said, 'because I've had a go at doing so, too.'

Adam took another small sip of his beer, met the professor's eyes, and gave a small half-smile. 'Ok, I think it goes something like this... For all that a child of nine or ten changed his name from Tutankhaten to Tutankhamun and re-opened all the temples to the old pantheon of ancient Egyptian gods and goddesses, I think it's pretty clear he and his protector – great uncle Ay – were Atenists. They subscribed to the new religion of Akhenaten: worship of the sun-disc as the one true god. Remember, Akhenaten was Ay's nephew and son-in-law, and Nefertiti was his daughter. The pharaoh and his great royal wife led a religious revolution. I think Ay subscribed to it, and Tutankhamun was born to it. So, they were monotheists. Ay tells us nothing about how Akhenaten or Nefertiti died. So, I think we can reasonably assume it was naturally. I think it's pretty clear Smenkhkare came to the throne on his brother's death. Smenkhkare probably had two wives. One was his sister, Tutankhamun's mother – the mummy we know now as "the younger lady" from the mummy cache in KV35. The other was Meritaten, oldest daughter of Akhenaten and Nefertiti. He possibly married her to secure his passage to the throne, or to stop anyone else staking a claim by doing so.

'From the passage about having blood on his hands, I think Ay's telling us their enemy lead a violent coup to overthrow Smenkhkare. Maybe he feared Atenism was gaining a real foothold, and his mission was to return Egypt to the old ways. Anyway, I think he murdered the new pharaoh and his wives and planned to take the throne. I don't think the studies on the skeleton found in KV55 have ever been able to establish a cause of death. But, as we said earlier, they suggest he was a young man. Analysis of the mummy of the "younger lady" shows a large wound in the left side of her mouth and cheek, which also destroyed part of the jaw. I read about it online. Originally it was thought the injuries were inflicted postmortem, probably the result of tomb robber's actions. But a more recent re-examination of the mummy while it was undergoing genetic tests determined the wound happened prior to death and that the injury was lethal.'

This was a bit too graphic for me. This wasn't just an ancient mummy being subjected to laboratory tests. This was a young woman – Tutankhamun's mother – being murdered and having her face smashed in. My eyes filled with tears, and I had to blink rapidly to dispel them.

Adam, setting out his exposition, was able to remain somewhat more dispassionate. 'And we know Meritaten was dead because Ay chose to bury Ankhesenamun with her older sister when she took her own life.'

He paused a moment to collect his thoughts and sip his beer before continuing. 'The one Ay calls "the evil one" possibly intended to legitimise his claim after murdering

Smenkhkare through marriage to Ankhesenamun; Ay's narrative suggests so. But somehow Ay out-foxed him and spirited the eight-or-nine-year-old Tutankhaten and the thirteen-or-so year old Ankhesenpaaten out of the new capital of Akhet-Aten. I think Ay was powerful enough, as the senior vizier of the Amarnan court, to ensure they were married, and to set them on the throne. But I think their enemy had one last trick up his sleeve.

'Ay had failed to account for his one remaining daughter. The historical record suggests Nefertiti had a sister, a second daughter of Ay. Her name was Mutnodjmet. The archaeology tells us a woman called Mutnodjmet was married to the pharaoh who succeeded Ay. His name was Horemheb. Before coming to the throne, he was general of all of Egypt's armies - a hugely powerful man.

'So, there, I've named him – and perhaps secured his everlasting life; the one thing Ay was loathe to do.

'As general of all the armies, he was probably powerful enough to lead a military coup to overthrow Smenkhkare. Ay outwitted him and put the boy Tutankhaten on the throne. But Horemheb retaliated by forcing Mutnodjmet into marriage. I think this was the hold he had over Ay, who must have been the power behind Tutankhamun's throne. I think Horemheb threatened to harm Ay's daughter if Ay didn't do his bidding.

'Through these threats I think Ay and Tutankhamun submitted to the appearance of converting back to Amunism and the old ancient Egyptian pantheon. They were possibly coerced into changing the names of the king and queen from the "aten" suffix to the "amun" one. But I think its pretty clear Tutankhamun was planning to take back the reins of religion on reaching manhood. He suffered a fatal accident just at the crucial time. He was already a sickly young man, so death was pretty much assured. Perhaps Horemheb had a hand in this, perhaps not. Ay seems not to have been able to prove it; much as I'm sure he'd have liked to.

'Ay married Tutankhamun's widow, Ankhesenamun, to protect her from Horemheb's suit. But she knew her grandfather was old, frail and dying. So, she sent her desperate and treasonous plea to the Hittites. When that failed, she saw suicide as her only way out.

'I believe Horemheb was cunning enough to let Ay mount the throne of Egypt because it meant he, Horemheb, was married to the daughter of a divinely anointed pharaoh. Through her, he could legitimise his claim to the throne on Ay's death. And that's exactly what I believe happened. When Ay died, Horemheb came to the throne and ruled for something like fourteen years. But he died without children – so Ay's prayers were answered on that score. Horemheb passed the throne to his old army pal Paramessu, another hard-bitten general. Paramessu became Ramses I and founded the 19th Dynasty. Scholars believe Horemheb and Paramessu were responsible for breaking into Ay's tomb and hacking it to bits. And they sought to re-write history, obliterating the Amarnan kings from the historical record through a campaign of destruction of their temples, statues, carvings and artwork. I think Horemheb and Paramessu were the ones Ay described as his "enemies".'

Silence descended on our table. Adam had spoken all this, the longest speech I'd ever heard him make, in a kind of hushed undertone. He wasn't a qualified Egyptologist. But that was due to circumstances beyond his control. He'd studied his subject academically but independently. I sensed he was sticking his neck out propounding his theory so confidently in front of his old mentor. I, for one, was with him every step of the way. I couldn't claim an academic knowledge of ancient Egypt, but I'd read up on it too. And everything he'd said fitted my understanding of what was known historically, as well as the tantalising but often oblique statements in Ay's testimonial. But the final verdict would be the professor's. He'd studied Egyptology his whole life. He was renowned in his own field of philology and knew more than the rest of us could ever hope to learn about this ancient civilisation. Adam sipped his beer and stared down at his untouched plate as if waiting for the sword of judgement to fall.

'I think you're right in everything you've said,' Ted said quietly. 'I'd reached exactly the same conclusions.'

I nearly cheered. There was a kind of gentle pride in the way he said this as if Adam was a much-loved protégée who'd proved worthy of his faith. I sensed an Egyptological baton being passed from one generation to the next and felt a small surge of elation.

The amazing thrill of ancient history coming to life almost before our eyes was unimaginable. Most archaeologists had to scrabble around in the dust and heat for years to find a tiny clue like the bezel ring linking pharaoh Ay in marriage to his posited granddaughter, Ankhesenamun. Our ancient scroll was as good as handing it to us on a plate. It proved the relationship, and it proved the marriage. It gave us the reasons. And it seemed to prove a whole lot more besides. My brain lit up with Egyptological fire.

'But, if Ay's testimonial is to be believed,' I piped up, feeling ridiculously privileged to be part of this voyage of discovery; 'then there's a sacred shrine his enemies weren't able to obliterate. It's possible it remains undisturbed to this day – hidden somewhere Horemheb and his henchmen would never find it; possibly near the Hathor sanctuary in Hatshepsut's temple.'

Adam lifted his gaze to my face. 'Ay said the knowledge was buried with Tutankhamun.'

'I wonder if he meant literally or metaphorically,' I mused, daring to hope.

He smiled at me; the first wholly twenty-first century expression I'd seen on his face in the last half-hour. 'Are you treasure hunting again, Merry?'

'Possibly,' I admitted, with a wry shrug.

He grinned broadly. 'Excellent. Well, I think we know enough to deduce that the "precious jewels" were probably Akhenaten and Nefertiti.'

My excitement was mounting to an earth shaking enough level to register on the Richter scale. 'And, if we accept the KV55 mummy is Smenkhkare – which Ay's narrative would seem to suggest – then we know their mummies have never been found,' I breathed.

Adam's eyes didn't move from my face. 'We have a plan of Hatshepsut's temple, showing a heavily drawn line around the Hathor shrine and an annotation telling us Aten is key,' he smiled. 'And we know the sun disc is plastered all over the place in there. We have the photos to prove it.'

I grinned back at him, and I knew we were reading each other's minds again, oblivious to everyone else sitting at the table. 'It does make you wonder if Aten might be literally the key,' I said. 'You know, of the turn in the lock variety. I wonder if there's a keyhole in that Hathor chapel, and whether something Aten-related from Tutankhamun's tomb is the key to unlock it.'

He picked up his fork, but it's fair to say it never came close to making contact with his dinner. He just waved it at me, a bit melodramatically. 'So, you're suggesting we need to minutely study all the artefacts discovered in Tutankhamun's tomb, to see if a key turns up among them?'

'Yes,' I nodded. 'It would seem like a logical next step. Don't you think?'

* * *

We nearly drove ourselves nuts with it. The others gave up and went to bed when we were only just making a start. But Adam and I were used to this stuff. This was the two of us back on familiar turf; presented with a challenge and pitting our wits to try to solve it.

We took Adam's iPad and my laptop out onto the terrace and sank into the deep cushioned sofas arranged around a low table with our after-dinner drinks on it. The Nile flowed past on its epic journey from Ethiopia to the Mediterranean. Stars spangled the heavens, and fruit bats flitted silently through the hot stillness of the night air. The Egyptian night-time worked its magic. A deep contentment settled over me.

We Googled Tutankhamun's treasure, and hit the images tab. It wasn't quite as effective as taking a stroll around the Egyptian Museum of Antiquities, but it wasn't far off: images to dazzle the eyes and stir the soul. Everybody loves the thrill of buried treasure. Tutankhamun was buried with vast quantities of it.

We surfed through pages and pages of gold. The famous death mask was a prominent feature, shown from every conceivable angle. There were pictures of glittering ceremonial daggers deeply inlaid with semi-precious stones; lavish pectorals set with turquoise and lapis lazuli; and ornately designed diadems from the royal regalia, breathtaking in their workmanship.

We hesitated for a long time over an image of the sumptuously inlaid back-panel of Tutankhamun's golden throne. It showed the royal couple within a floral pavilion open to the life-giving rays of the sun. There was something touching and informal about the scene, depicting Tutankhamun and his queen in the relaxed Amarna style, with Ankhesenamun, dressed in a pleated sheer linen robe, leaning forward to anoint her young husband with perfume. Tutankhamun was shown seated on a gilded chair, wearing a long kilt, wide beaded pectoral and an ornate headdress. It really was the most exquisite work of art. A few clicks on the mouse told us it was an armchair made of wood overlaid with sheet gold and silver and inlaid with the usual blend of coloured glass, faience and semi-precious stones. Prominent at the top of the panel was the round sun disc, reaching out with long rays to bathe the young couple in its protective warmth. Each golden ray ended in a tiny hand carved in gold, some of them holding the Egyptian Ankh, the sign of life.

But it wasn't this that made my eyes mist over. The deep affection between the royal couple seemed to glow from the image. I felt a moment of profound sadness, almost grief, thinking what a tragic pair the young pharaoh and his queen posed.

'See here,' Adam said, reading from Wikipedia. 'It says the inscriptions were altered to refer to the couple by the – Amun forms of their names. It suggests certain details of the panel have been changed since it was first made – most noticeably the head-ornaments worn by the king and queen, which in their final form cut through the life-giving rays of the sun disc. It seems like a deliberate attempt to reduce the power of the Aten, clearly shown above them.'

It was at this point that Dan and the others gave up the quest and went to bed. There was no suggestion of me sharing a room with Dan tonight. I could see he was in pain, but manfully trying not to let it show. After the day he'd had, a good night's sleep seemed the best possible tonic. Adam and I waved goodnight and turned back to our task.

Adam was sitting a bit stiffly, with his iPad on the table in front of him. It was the only indication his injuries might be similarly painful. I suppose a bandaged ribcage must rather inhibit the ability to slouch.

We flicked through image after image, and the wonder of Howard Carter's find came spectacularly to life. But there was nothing that seemed remotely to resemble a key, and nothing else we could see with the Aten sun disc on such prominent display.

After a while I sat back and let the Egyptian night envelop me in its deep, velvety cloak. I was tired. It had been a traumatic day – one of a series of rather traumatic days, truth to tell. But I was reluctant to call time on our research. My gaze was drawn irresistibly to Adam's face, intent on its scrutiny of the images he was slowly scrolling through on his computer screen. I let it rest there, conscious of the familiar tug of attraction. But it went deeper than that. I had a sneaking suspicion Adam was becoming as necessary to my life and wellbeing as the air I breathed, and to my happiness, too.

'You saved Dan's life today,' I said softly. I'm not sure I meant to say it aloud. But the thought was there, burgeoning through my mind. Of all the moments I'd been re-living all afternoon, the one when he dropped over the cliffside alongside me, and I realised what he planned to do, was the starkest. It sent a shudder through me every time.

He looked up and his eyes came to meet mine. He held my gaze for a long time, and it didn't seem we needed to say much. It was all there in that look.

'How do things stand between you?' he asked at last.

I let out a long sigh. 'I don't know.' It was a wholly unsatisfactory answer, for us both. But it was the truth. 'Dan and I go back a long way. When I saw Hussein push him off that cliff today I...' I couldn't finish. I remembered how the whole of my relationship with Dan had flashed before my eyes in that single moment. I'd re-lived our first date; seen his goofy smile when I fell for one of his diabolical practical jokes; heard him singing his favourite Rolling Stones songs tunelessly in the shower; seen snapshots of all the holidays and Christmases and birthdays; recalled our bitterest arguments as well as our most tender moments. Emotion clogged my throat, and sudden tears pooled my eyes. 'Sorry ... I ...' I stumbled to a halt again, struggling to bring my wobbling face under control.

Adam reached across and brushed the tears from my cheeks with his fingertips. It was such a tender gesture, far more poignant and resonant with feeling than pulling me into his arms. I stared at him through the sheen of tears and tried again. 'It's just, I ...' But I didn't know how to put it into words. For all that Dan meant to me, I wasn't sure it was enough. I felt guilty and dishonourable to be sitting here even thinking it. Especially so, looking into Adam's darkly lashed eyes and fighting the instinct to lean forward and kiss him.

'Oh Merry,' he said. That was it - just my name – but there was no need for him to say more. He understood, and he wouldn't press me, and the small, soft smile that lifted the corners of his mouth was like a peace offering. It was a smile that said simply: let's wait and see.

Chapter 16

Ahmed turned up unexpectedly while we were finishing a leisurely breakfast on the terrace overlooking the Nile under the spreading shade of a huge patio umbrella. We'd been lingering over our coffee, with nothing much planned for the day. Adam and I intended to apply ourselves to another online survey of the treasures from Tutankhamun's tomb, although I wasn't holding out too much hope of getting anywhere with it. But other than that, the prospect of the day ahead was unusually quiet. It was probably just as well after all the recent excitement. I figured it wouldn't hurt to take it easy for a change.

My heart leapt on first sight of Ahmed, hoping he'd come to tell us he'd arrested the despicable Hussein. But he was wearing a dark grey galabeya instead of his police uniform, so I guessed this wasn't a visit in his official capacity.

I proved sadly correct regarding our Arabic nemesis.

Ahmed shook his head after we'd pulled up a chair for him, found another cup and saucer, and poured him some coffee. He added vast quantities of sugar, stirred it enthusiastically, and then looked up. 'What is de English expression? De man has gone into de ground?'

'Gone to ground,' Adam supplied. 'It's a hunting term, I think. It means the quarry is hiding from the pack.'

'Yes, dis man he hides from de long arm of de law. But he cannot run forever. You must stay on your guard until den. We don't want any more injuries.'

Both Dan and Adam were moving stiffly this morning. I guessed their overworked muscles had tightened overnight, protesting the extreme and unaccustomed action demanded yesterday. Jessica, despite the purple swelling around her eye, was all sunshine again; constantly hopping up to fetch more croissants for the men, or charmingly entreating the waiters to bring fresh coffee and hot milk. I wish I could be that jaunty first thing in the morning.

I wasn't feeling quite so animated. It had taken me a long time to get to sleep last night. For one thing my inner movie-screen kept showing me action-replays of the clifftop scene at Deir el Bahri every time I closed my eyes. We'd done nothing but talk about it all yesterday afternoon, but it seemed my brain was still processing the shock. And second, I knew Adam had taken a long time to shift from his position overlooking the Nile. I knew this because, unable to sleep, I'd wrapped myself in a hotel bathrobe and gone outside to breathe in the night-time air and try to still my senses. From the end of the pathway, I'd been able to see him, pooled in the soft light of the terrace lamps. He was sitting where I'd left him, staring out across the dark waters, lost in some reverie of his own. I watched him for a while, but in the end my eyelids started to droop, and I headed back inside my room before the urge to sleep passed. So, what with one thing and another, I was feeling a trifle jaded this morning.

Ahmed sipped his coffee for a moment. His dark eyes flashed with life, and I narrowed my eyes on his face. He had an air of suppressed excitement about him that was highly suspicious.

'What is it Ahmed?' I said after watching him for a moment. 'You're clearly dying to tell us something.'

He grinned at me and puffed out his chest. I tried not to be too distracted by his teeth. Ahmed is quite a good-looking man, if you happen to like them large. He has very dark brown eyes that seem to snap with humour and mischief, and a cap of seal-like black hair. But his teeth do tend to detract from his overall appearance. It's a shame, because he has a beaming megawatt smile, so they're quite often on display. I made a mental note to hunt out a good dentist for him. Surely, they must have them in Egypt.

'I finded somedhing,' he said proudly.

We all stared at him, but he seemed determined to make us work for it. It was Adam who buckled first. 'What do you mean, you found something?'

'In de suitcase wid de papyrus scrolls inside.'

This time we positively gaped.

'But you can't have done,' Adam spluttered. 'I checked it inside and out. The three rolls of papyrus were all it contained.'

Ahmed's smile widened further. I forced myself to focus on his eyes not his teeth. 'You do not have de training of a police officer in how to search,' he said with a touch of puffed-up superiority I found quite engaging.

'No, nor the instincts of a tomb robber,' Adam muttered with an equally mild touch of irony. Ahmed was descended from one of the most notorious tomb robbing families Luxor had ever known and was fiercely proud of it. I daresay his professional training and his inherited faculties must combine to provide him with a powerful skillset to draw on.

Ahmed let out a shout of laughter. 'Dis is true. I am a lucky man, no?'

'Can we just cut to the chase?' Dan said testily. 'What did you find?'

Ahmed looked a bit injured. He loves a good story, and he'd spin this one out all morning if he could.

'We're all breathless with anticipation,' I soothed him.

Mollified, his eyes snapped excitedly again. 'I tested all de stitching on de outside of de leather case,' he told us. 'On one side, dere was a small section missing. It looked like it had been snipped away. I felt between de small flap wid some tweezers, and I finded dis…!' He withdrew a small scrap of paper from the pocket of his galabeya with a theatrical flourish.

Adam's eyes nearly fell out of his head. Ted sucked in a sharp breath. The rest of us stared. There was something enticingly familiar about that scrap of paper. It was remarkably reminiscent of a couple of others I had stored securely inside the safe in my room.

'It's from Howard Carter,' I breathed.

Ahmed unfolded it and handed it across the table to Adam. He stared at it unblinking for a moment, then handed it on to me, but not before I noticed the tell-tale stillness come over him.

There were only two words on the sheet, each scribbled in Howard Carter's distinctive but largely indecipherable handwriting. But what held me utterly spellbound was the small drawing of a key in the bottom left-hand corner. I stared at it a moment, then lifted my gaze to frown at the writing. 'What does it say?' I asked in frustration. 'The first word might be "try". But I can't make out the last word at all.'

I handed the scrap of paper to Ted. 'Mehet-Weret,' he said, after a fractional pause. 'It reads, "Try Mehet-Weret".'

'I'm none the wiser,' Dan said drily. He was duly passed the scrap of paper, frowned at it, shrugged, and passed it on to Jessica. She mimicked his frown-and-shrug combination to perfection; I think unconsciously, and handed the notepaper back to Adam.

'What's Mehet-Weret?' I asked.

'Not "what" but "who",' Adam corrected me. 'She was another cow-goddess, a bit like Hathor.'

'Mehet-Weret was a goddess of the sky in ancient Egyptian religion,' Ted said. 'In Egyptian creation myths she gave birth to the sun at the beginning of time, and in art she's portrayed as a cow with a sun disk between her horns. She's associated with the goddesses Neith, Hathor and Isis, all of whom have similar characteristics. The difference is, they were often depicted in human form, but with bovine ears and horns. Mehet-Weret was always depicted as a cow.'

'So, she gave birth to the sun, and she's shown with the sun disk on her head, between her horns,' I said. 'That sounds to me like a pretty strong link to the Aten.'

'Aten is key,' Adam breathed.

'And look...' I went on. 'Howard Carter has drawn a key. Doesn't that rather suggest to you that he was thinking along similar lines to us? That it's literally a key we're looking for?'

'Wait there!' Adam demanded. 'I'm going to get my iPad.' He leapt up from the table, dodged a couple of waiters carrying hot coffee pots, and sprinted away through the hedge bordering the adult-only pool, then across the lawns to his room. I was amazed he could run like that with bandages wrapped tight around his rib cage. It just goes to show how Egyptological fever can overcome most things.

He was back almost at once, barely giving Jessica time to dimple cutely at the waiters for more coffee. He dropped back into his chair and propped his iPad on the table amid the breakfast leftovers. We all leaned closer as he Googled Tutankhamun's tomb + Mehet-Weret and selected "images" from the list. The magic search engine did its stuff instantaneously, and suddenly the screen was filled with pictures of a golden couch with the head-end flanked by two gilded cows, each with a huge sun-disc between its upward curving horns, with the blotches of the cowhide represented by closely carved trefoils of opaque blue glass. Like the other pieces in the tomb, it was a golden work of art, and we all stared.

Adam let out a long breath. 'It's one of Tutankhamun's ritual couches. How did we manage to miss it last night?' He clicked a couple of times on the trackpad and started to read. ' "The Mehet-Weret couch is one of three ritual couches found in Tutankhamun's tomb by Howard Carter. The other two have lion and hippopotamus heads respectively. The book of the Divine Cow, a version of which is inscribed upon the interior of the first (outermost) shrine protecting Tutankhamun's sarcophagus, suggests the Mehet-Weret couch was a solar barque, which would speed the king from this world to heaven. The ritual purpose of the other beds is unclear. For Howard Carter, dismantling these couches for their transportation to Cairo Museum was no easy task as after three thousand years the bronze hooks had set tight in the staples and would not budge. It took no fewer than five men to do it."'

He leaned back and I gazed at him. 'You know what this means, don't you?'

His eyes lifted to mine. 'What's that?'

'It means Howard Carter knew the contents of those scrolls. He must have translated them before he bricked them up inside the wall of that tomb. We wondered, remember?'

Adam's eyes went a bit unfocused, though his gaze didn't shift from my face. 'But it was towards the end of his time in Egypt. He didn't get the papyri back from Lord Carnarvon's widow until after the tomb was cleared. The ritual couches were already under lock and key in the Cairo Museum. My God, how frustrating for him!'

'But his deductions led him to the same place we've arrived at. He knew every inch of Hatshepsut's temple. You told me he spent six whole years recording it, when he was first in Egypt as a young man. He must have known the Hathor sanctuary like the back of his hand. We're working on the assumption that Tutankhamun and Ay buried their "precious jewels" somewhere behind the chapel or the shrine. It's the only explanation that fits together the jigsaw pieces of papyri Ay put in Tutankhamun's tomb. Either that, or there's no rhyme or reason to them whatsoever. They're just a random and meaningless assortment of ancient texts stored together for expedience but without any purpose.'

'You don't believe that any more than I do.'

'No, I don't. I believe Ay buried something with Tutankhamun that's a massive clue to whereabouts in the Hathor sanctuary the "precious jewels" are hidden. There can't be an obvious hidden chamber. You said yourself, archaeologists have been crawling all over Hatshepsut's temple for the whole of the last century. They've brought it back from a tumbledown ruin to a quite remarkable state of preservation and restoration. Whatever it is we're looking for, it's gone unobserved by excavators for more than a hundred years. It can't be something obvious. So, what is it about the Mehet-Weret ritual couch that might somehow serve as a key? And, perhaps more importantly, what is there inside the Hathor sanctuary that might pass as a lock?'

'Aten is key,' Adam repeated. 'It has to be the sun disc between the cow horns. Maybe they're detachable. We couldn't find any other Aten-related artefacts in anything we scrolled through last night; although how we missed the couch I don't know. All we found was that golden panel on the throne. Howard Carter knew all the items in that tomb.

He sketched and catalogued each and every one of them. If he's telling us to try Mehet-Weret, I for one am sold. He'd know if there was something else we should try. My God: poor Carter, having to leave it to some unknown future generation to find out what the Aten was the key to unlocking.'

'There must be a kind of slot somewhere in the Hathor shrine. All we need to do is insert the Aten disc into the slot and Bingo!'

Dan had been watching this back-and-forth exchange between Adam and me in a grim silence. 'Before you get completely carried away, do I need to remind the pair of you that the cow-bed thingy is still under lock and key in the Cairo Museum? It's no more accessible to you than it was to Howard Carter. In fact, I should say it was a damn sight more accessible to Carter. I don't suppose anyone would have baulked too much if he'd asked to borrow an item he'd discovered in the tomb for a few days. Somehow, I can't imagine anyone extending the same privilege to you. It seems to me, if ever there was a right time to hand things over to the proper authorities, now's it. You've gone as far with your sleuthing as you can.'

We looked at him in dismay. Even Jessica, who seemed to have a bit of a crush on Dan if I was any judge, looked a bit crestfallen. Ted let out a small sigh but didn't say anything. It was Ahmed who protested.

'No, no; it is still too soon for dat. De police investigations on de body in de Valley of de Kings link him to Mahmoud Said, de one who jumped out of de window in Cairo. Dey know dey were brothers and dat Jessica here was de wife of dis man.' He gave Jessica a respectful nod. 'It has only been a few days since de body was finded. You must let de dust fall.'

'Settle,' Adam corrected him automatically. 'It's let the dust settle.'

'I think dey will release de body soon,' Ahmed told Jessica. 'So, you can have a funeral if you wish.'

Jessica shuddered delicately. 'No thanks. That part of my life is well and truly over. I'm quite happy playing the merry widow, if it's all the same to you.'

Ahmed looked a bit shocked, but let it go.

'The important thing is we need to let a bit more time pass before we introduce the papyri to the world,' I said.

Adam's eyes came to meet mine again. 'So, given that we're at a bit of a loose end, surely, given Ted's credentials, they couldn't object too much to us just taking a look at the Mehet-Weret couch,' he argued, with a note of appeal in his voice.

'We can but ask,' I agreed eagerly.

Dan let out a long, despairing sigh.

'So, who's for a quick trip to Cairo?' Adam asked, oozing boyish charisma.

In the end, it was just Adam and me.

Dan put up a token resistance. He and I had a small, private, mildly heated exchange, walking back from breakfast through the hotel gardens. He said he objected to stepping into the middle of a global trouble spot. While the News reassured us the demonstrations over the results of Hosni Mubarak's trial had died down, Egypt was gearing up for its first democratic presidential race, and the initial round of elections was underway. Support was high for the Muslim Brotherhood, but these things were never predictable and Dan, true to form, wasn't keen for me to plant myself in Tahrir Square, right in the thick of it. We batted it back and forth for a while. In the end he rolled his eyes heavenwards and gave a small philosophical shrug. 'Let's face it Pinkie, at the end of the day you'll do exactly what you want to do. When have I ever been able to stop you from doing anything at all once you've got your heart set on it? Just note, please, as usual, I am giving in under sufferance. Do try not to get locked in anywhere, will you? Just to keep what's left of my sanity intact? My poor, battered body is one thing. But my poor, beleaguered brain needs a bit of respite.'

Jessica's reasons for not coming with us were rather more prosaic. 'I've only just left the damn place, and I have absolutely no desire to return there in the short term, thank you very much.' Her golden curls bounced in consternation and her bottom lip stuck out in a very pretty pout. 'I can't say Cairo holds the happiest of memories for me. Frankly, a day or two chilling out by this hotel's rather lovely swimming pool suits me just fine! Besides, I fancy a ride on Ramses the camel, and there hasn't been a chance until now.'

Ted dithered a bit, and I could see he was torn. But, in the end, I think his older bones protested their weariness. He'd had an exhausting few days, and the mental concentration of hours spent translating papyrus only added to the fatigue. 'You know what? A few hours kicking back by the pool does sound rather wonderful,' he said wistfully. 'I'll put a call in to Shukura and see if I can pull a few strings for you. But you don't need me there to study the Mehet-Weret couch. Adam has all the necessary know-how.'

Ahmed didn't have an option. He was expected back on duty this afternoon.

So, that's how Adam and I came to be the only two checking in for the early afternoon flight from Luxor to Cairo. I couldn't decide if I felt delightedly smug about this, or a little bit forsaken. Adam and I made a great amateur sleuthing partnership, but I'd kind of got used to having the others around. It felt a bit odd for it to be just the two of us again.

'You know, Dan's right,' I said. 'They'll never in a million years let us borrow a sun-disk from between the horns of one of those cow-heads.'

'You're probably right, Merry,' he agreed equably. 'But you never know; something might just turn up.'

I loved his optimism. It was such an intrinsic part of his personality. He'd come out to Egypt pretty much on a whim; chucking in a job he loathed to see if he could find something in this land that he loved so much to see him through. I admired him for it.

We accepted the drink and little packet of pretzels the flight attendant offered us and munched in companionable silence for a while. Adam had indulged me, letting me have the window seat again. I could never grow tired of the sight of the Nile snaking through the barren, tawny landscape below. There's nothing truly green about Egypt. It's not at all like looking down on the verdant patchwork of fields back home in England. Even the narrow strip of cultivated land bordering the Nile on both sides is perpetually covered in dust. It lends a romantic soft-lens-like appearance to the landscape. From twenty thousand feet up, the dusty green strip is largely indistinguishable from the buff-coloured sand and rock stretching on either side of it. Egypt is a desert wasteland, saved only by the miracle of the Nile. Yet it spawned the first real civilisation the world has ever known, and perhaps the most spectacular.

'Do you remember, you talked about us writing a novel together?' I asked musingly.

He smiled, 'Yes, your writing skills and my Egyptological knowledge; we'd be the archetypal dream team.'

'Well, you know, it strikes me there's a novel-in-the-making in the papyrus Pharaoh Ay penned all those thousands of years ago. Who'd have thought that Ay would turn out to be a goodie, and Horemheb would be such a double-dyed villain?'

His smile widened, and his eyes crinkled at the edges in the way I found so irresistible. I've heard it said men reach their prime in their forties. To the best of my knowledge, Adam was just a few months into his. I'd say the "looks" fairy was kind to Adam. If current appearances counted for anything, it promised to be a good decade. 'I don't know if I'd agree he was such an out-and-out rogue,' he said consideringly.

I stared at him. 'But he led a violent coup to overthrow the crown. He murdered Tutankhamun's parents and tried to seize the throne. And when Ay outfoxed him, he forced Ay's daughter into marriage and used threats to bring Ay and Tutankhamun to heel. They're hardly the actions of an honourable man!'

Adam chuckled. 'Maybe you're right.' He was enjoying my outrage. 'But there are usually two sides to a story; so, let's try to see it from Horemheb's point of view…'

I sipped my drink and kept quiet. I felt I'd need a fair bit of convincing to see anything salvageable in Horemheb's character after everything I'd heard.

'... Akhenaten and Nefertiti led a religious revolution the like of which the world had never known. They turned everything topsy-turvy. We may say the worship of one true god is enlightened. But, back then, the common people and, perhaps more importantly, the priests, had worshipped the ancient Egyptian pantheon for centuries. Many argue that Egypt achieved much of its strength on the consistency of that belief.'

'Plus, the annual flood which cultivated the crops, and the natural mines which yielded pure gold,' I pointed out, a trifle cynically.

He grinned at me. 'You're right of course. But don't forget the impact of religion on the hearts and minds of men. More wars have been fought over religion than perhaps anything else. A good analogy here, maybe, would be Henry VIII's dissolution of the Catholic monasteries and Mary Tudor's determination to bring England back to the Papal fold. Countless hundreds of people were willing to die for their faith. Now, I'm not saying things were exactly the same back in the late 18th Dynasty of ancient Egypt. But you have to wonder. This was perhaps the first religious battle ever to be fought, a kind of civil war of the second millennia BCE. Religious convictions run deep, as we can testify, here in the twenty-first century looking back on several centuries of dispute. But so far as we know, Akhenaten's worship of the sun-disc as the one true god was the first time in history this kind of conflict manifested itself.'

I must confess, he had me. His low-pitched voice seemed to throb with a passion as he warmed to his theme. It more than competed with the incessant drone of the engines.

'Perhaps if Akhenaten had been a strong ruler, he might have won the day. But it seems he holed himself up in his new city of Akhet-Aten with his family, priests and ministers; and pretty much ignored everything else. He nearly bankrupted the treasury to build his new capital. And there are records of endless pleas from the rulers of Egypt's vassal states saying their enemies, the Amorites and the Hittites were growing stronger and more aggressive day-by-day. Egypt couldn't hold out indefinitely against their border attacks. But Akhenaten didn't respond. To a man like Horemheb, an army general responsible for protecting Egypt's boundaries; and perhaps a stalwart of the old multi-deity faith, it must have seemed like treason, but perpetrated by the god-king everyone was supposed to look up to and adore.'

I could feel myself being reeled in by his reasoning.

'I think Horemheb toed the line while Akhenaten was on the throne. But when he died and the succession passed to

Akhenaten's younger brother Smenkhkare, my guess is he decided he had to act, and act decisively, or let the rot set in forever.'

'So, he moved to strike,' I said, 'and eliminate the last vestiges of the once glorious 18th Dynasty.'

'Exactly; and Merry, I think you've hit the nail on the head. Because I suspect there was one other factor Horemheb took into account, which was the general weakening of the royal stock through in-breeding. I think the once mighty 18th Dynasty was visibly crumbling. Nobody has been able to prove to anyone's satisfaction whether or not Akhenaten had a genetic malformation. But his artwork would seem to suggest something was a bit amiss. And we know from the deformities in Tutankhamun's mummy that he suffered all manner of ailments as a result of being born of a full brother-and-sister relationship. I can't imagine these ailments weren't discernible to the high-ranking officials, people like Horemheb, who had contact with the royal family.'

'But still,' I said, 'to murder a divinely anointed king and queen...'

'You're right,' he agreed. 'I was just trying to find a motivation for it.'

I daresay I was guilty of romanticising Tutankhamun and his immediate family. Ay was one of them, and we'd heard the story from his perspective. But it still struck me as deplorable that Horemheb hadn't contented himself with regicide during life but felt the need to go after his victims in death too to complete his vitriolic campaign of annihilation. Whilst I might understand what drove him, I didn't like his way of doing business; not one little bit.

So, if Tutankhamun and Ay had succeeded in hiding "their precious jewels" where Horemheb would never find them, it was just fine with me.

Chapter 17

Shukura greeted us joyfully and treated us like honoured guests of the museum. She was wearing a particularly attractive Muslim headscarf in a deep turquoise wrapped around her head and shoulders, framing her face. It lifted the drabness of the navy suit she was squeezed into, and the flat black ballet pumps on her feet. I got a sense that, outside of work, Shukura might be a rather more flamboyant dresser altogether.

'It is lovely to see you both so soon, Merry and Adam. I was not expecting such a nice surprise. Now, Ted informs me you are here to research the influence of Atenism on the reign of Tutankhamun for an article he hopes to write. I am sorry Ted is feeling a little unwell, and not up to making the journey. But he assures me it is nothing serious. And I can perfectly understand him wanting to spend time with his lovely daughter after everything she has been through. To have been held captive by those awful brothers! I shudder to think of it. Do please send her my best wishes when you see her. Now, you wish to study the impact of the Aten on Tutankhamun. How interesting. If course, as a small boy, he must have been brought up in a court that still worshipped the sun-disc. I wonder how he felt about restoring Egypt to the polytheistic pantheon of the old gods.

It might be, of course, that he didn't have very much to do with it. Most people accept Ay was the power behind the throne. I think the theory is that Ay and Horemheb teamed up to bring Egypt back to the old customs.'

I'd forgotten how Shukura loved to talk in her faultless, Oxford-educated English. Seeing as we knew the truth as revealed to us in Ay's papyrus, I listened to her conjectures with only half an ear – just enough to murmur politely in the right places – and let my attention wander. It was late afternoon, and the museum was all but deserted. We'd skirted Tahrir Square, arriving here by taxi from the airport. Plenty of people were milling about, but I'd describe the atmosphere as more party than protest. I was glad we'd come.

I love the dusty disorder of the Cairo Museum. The displays are all a bit ramshackle, some in cabinets that look like they might disintegrate with woodworm at any moment. But somehow this rather shabby and dilapidated air does nothing to detract from the glory of the exhibits. Quite the opposite, in fact; they transcend their surroundings, statues rising in magnificence amid cracked and peeling paintwork, and golden objects glowing with brilliance in their rickety display cases. To walk through the Egyptian Museum is to walk through thousands of years of Pharaonic history. It's jaw dropping.

There's talk of moving the exhibits to a new state-of-the-art museum being built out near the Giza Plateau. I'm sure, if it happens (and I won't hold my breath) it will be amazing. But part of me will forever regret the passing of this relic of late Victorian curiosity.

We climbed the staircase and found ourselves in the vast halls set aside to display Tutankhamun's treasure. Yet again, I was staggered to think how this enormous quantity of items, including chariots, furniture, statues and shrines could possibly have fitted into the four small interconnecting chambers of the tomb. But then, I've seen the famous photographs Harry Burton took just after the tomb's discovery. They show these priceless artefacts piled up in a glorious riot of chaos and confusion. It struck me they probably felt right at home here in the Cairo Museum, where the storeroom vibe was pretty much the same.

I'm being unfair, of course. Many of the items are thoughtfully and beautifully displayed in glass showcases. Shukura led us straight to a raised cabinet in the middle of the main hall where Tutankhamun's golden throne was mounted behind thick glass. It was the same one we'd studied on the Internet last night. Looking now at the real thing I caught my breath. It wasn't the exquisite and colourful workmanship of the piece, or the dull gleam of gold that brought the lump to my throat. It was the tenderness of the interplay between the young pharaoh and his queen that tugged on my heartstrings as she leaned forward to anoint him with perfume. They looked a perfect, beautiful young couple in love. I wanted to imagine a different ending for their story than the reality, which was too sad for words.

'You see the sun-disc here,' Shukura said, pointing. 'It casts its loving rays on the young couple, a few of the sunrays ending in the little hand holding the Ankh, the sign of life. Historians believe the throne may originally have been made for the marriage of the young royal couple, then altered to show their changed names when they reverted to the old ways.'

'As you said,' Adam nodded, 'Tutankhamun and Ankhesenamun wouldn't have known any "old ways". They were both born into the worship of the Aten. I wonder, would it be possible please for us to see the Mehet-Weret couch?'

'Ah yes, Ted told me this was the object you were most interested to study. Follow me.'

She led us to the back end of the vast hall, where it connected with another leading off to the left. At the intersection of the two rooms stood three enormous glass showcases, each one containing one of the ritual couches. Adam and I ignored the lion and hippopotamus-headed beds and made a beeline for the one with the two cow heads.

The bed frame was made in the shape of two almost grotesquely elongated cows. Standing on a rectangular base stand, their long tube-like bodies stretched, dachshund-style, down each of the long sides of the bed. In each corner long legs shaped into cow hooves at the base raised the bed high off the ground. A gilded carved footboard stood at one end between the forward curve of the cows' tails. The actual bed itself was a mesh mattress of red hardwood held together with staples. I daresay it might be possible to get quite a comfortable night's sleep on it. But I'm not sure how I'd feel about laying my head to rest between the two majestic cow-heads, each sporting massive up-curved horns, with the sun-disc prominently displayed between them.

'When is the Aten not the Aten?' Adam breathed, as if he was setting us a puzzle. 'And how do you take it into your tomb with you without causing a stir? Simple. You fall back on thousands of years of religious iconography. The Aten is not strictly the Aten when it's in the form of the sun-disc rising above the heads of one of the ancient goddesses. A nifty bit of disguise, and a great way to hide something in plain sight.'

We stared at the couch in its glass display case for long moments.

'Now, what we need to know,' Adam said at length. 'Is whether those sun-discs are detachable...'

Never underestimate the impact of a handsome man's smile on a woman of a certain age. Or indeed any woman! I daresay I've proved myself susceptible to it on more than one occasion. Adam turned his on Shukura to quite devastating effect.

'Shukura, do you think there's any chance at all the curator here might let us take a look inside the display cabinet? Strictly under his supervision, of course; I wouldn't expect to touch anything.' And he unleashed the smile.

I have no idea if Adam is consciously aware of this weapon, he carries around with him so nonchalantly. All I can say is it worked. Shukura went all fluttery and girly for a moment.

'Well, let me see; I don't see any reason why it shouldn't be possible. It's not as if you're casual tourists. Ted told me you were one of his most brilliant students, Adam. And after everything you've done for this museum, I should think a little return favour might be in order. Yes, wait there; let me go and see what I can do…'

We watched her wiggle off with a vampish swing of ample hips that made me smile. 'Charmer!' I accused, when she was out of sight. 'And they condemn women for using sex-appeal to get what they want!'

He grinned, unabashed. 'We need to take a look at those discs. There's never any harm in asking nicely.'

She returned after a few minutes, trailing a dishevelled little man along behind her. He was wearing a rather dusty white laboratory coat over his clothes. 'Forgive me,' he said, 'I was preserving a great statue of Ramses II.'

Shukura waved away his explanations and got on with the important business of performing introductions. 'Adam, Merry, this is Walid Massri. We are fortunate to have him in charge of our antiquity preservation project here at the museum. Walid, let me introduce Miss Meredith Pink and Mr Adam Tennyson from England.' She gestured to each of us in turn, and we reached forward to shake the curator's hand.

'It's good to meet you, Mr Massri,' Adam said, using his smile to equally powerful effect. 'I'm sorry we've interrupted your work. We're here conducting a research project on behalf of Professor Edward Kincaid.'

'Ah yes,' Walid nodded, 'I have the honour to have met Professor Kincaid, a great philologist, brilliant student of the school of Egyptology, and a very nice gentleman. I was pleased to attend many of his lectures as a younger man. So, tell me, how can I help you with this research?'

Bingo! I thought.

Of course, Adam was right. The Aten discs were detachable, simply slotting into place between the cow horns. We'd never really allowed for any other eventuality. The dead end it would have brought us to simply wasn't in the script, so we never contemplated it. Adam's plan was brilliant in its simplicity. He knew we couldn't walk out of the Egyptian Museum carrying priceless antiquities from Tutankhamun's tomb in a carrier bag. But he wanted to know the sun discs' precise dimensions, their exact weight, and whether there were any carvings, inscriptions or markings on them of any kind. Walid performed all these little experiments in his little office-cum-laboratory in the behind-the-scenes part of the museum. I watched in fascination and Adam took meticulous notes. He was going to have a go at recreating them.

'So, what is this theory Professor Kincaid is working on?' Walid asked at last, having restored the sun-discs to their rightful place between the cow horns on Tutankhamun's ritual couch.

'Ted thinks it's possible Tutankhamun never actually converted back from Atenism. He wonders if the return to the old ways was just political expediency, and, if he hadn't died prematurely, perhaps Tutankhamun would have had another go at raising up the Aten. He thinks these sun discs might be key to unravelling the mystery.'

It was as close to the truth as Adam dared go. I'm not sure how he'd have answered if Walid had asked how the dimensions and weight of the discs could possibly be relevant to the theological debate. But Walid's admiration for the professor knew no bounds, so he seemed quite happy to accept that any outstanding questions would be answered in due course when Ted published his findings.

I felt a bit duplicitous, accepting Shukura and Walid's help without telling them the whole story. But I knew we couldn't take them into our confidence just yet. I contented myself with dreaming about the looks on their faces when the day came to hand the papyri over to them. We weren't deceiving them, I decided; we were just trying to establish the full facts before we let the authorities take over.

Adam and I had been unsure how long our mission to understand Mehet-Weret's secrets would take us. We'd felt it overly ambitious to book onto the night flight back to Luxor, so we'd confirmed our reservations for tomorrow. We'd promised Ted we'd check on his flat and water his pot-plants. He'd said we could stay there overnight, if we wished. But I don't think we felt comfortable with that proposition. So, we decided on a night in a hotel.

Shukura was having none of it. 'I will drive you to Ted's flat on the way home,' she said. 'Yes, you must water his poor plants. But then I insist you come back home with me. I will cook you an Egyptian feast. My children are young adults now – they will not get under your feet. They will be most delighted to meet you. After all, you helped their mother to become famous! I'm sorry; I don't have a double guest room you can share. Merry, you will have my daughter's room tonight; she can share a room with my husband and me. I have plenty of cushions she can sleep on. My two boys already share a room. Adam, you will be alright on the sofa? I will make it perfectly comfortable for you.'

When Shukura was in whirlwind mode there was no stopping her. Adam and I studiously avoided looking at each other at her assumption we were a couple. Neither of us corrected her, I noticed. We simply allowed ourselves to be swept along by the gale of her energetic goodwill.

Adam and I spent as pleasant an evening as I think I have ever spent. Shukura and her family welcomed us to their big, air-conditioned apartment in one of the more salubrious districts of Cairo. Shukura introduced her husband Selim, a dentist. Of course, I thought immediately of Ahmed. I couldn't quite buck up the impertinence to ask Selim what he charged. But judging from the very tasteful and spacious apartment and the self-evident private education of his three children, it was enough to provide a thoroughly acceptable standard of living.

I was right about Shukura's dress sense. She changed out of her tight-fitting navy suit and pumps into a glorious kaftan-type creation in peacock colours. It looked stunning with her turquoise headscarf, and the quantities of chunky gold rings she slipped onto her fingers.

The children, Feisal, Jamal and Rashida were the most engaging trio of teenagers you could hope to meet; politely interested when others were talking, earnest when telling us about their studies, and delightfully spontaneous in their applause when we regaled them with the – highly edited – story of Jessica's release from the captivity of the villainous gang of antiquities thieves.

The meal Shukura prepared us lived up to its billing as an Egyptian feast. I was agog with admiration to watch her throw it together from ingredients she already had in her fridge, and on a work night, too. She served Koshari, a kind of Egyptian-style vegetarian chilli, together with stuffed vine leaves, a tomato and onion tagine; beef koftas, and plenty of pitta bread to mop up the flavoursome juices.

I went to sleep in Rashida's pretty, book-lined bedroom feeling replete and contented, and with only the vaguest half-thought for the evening alone with Adam I'd missed out on.

Selim dropped us at the airport in the morning on his way to work. We thanked him for his amazingly generous hospitality and waved him off to re-join the crazy Cairene traffic.

'Hopefully next time we see his kids we'll be able to regale them with an even more thrilling story,' Adam said.

'You should have told them about rescuing Dan from the clifftop above Deir el Bahri. That would have had their eyes out on stalks.'

He grinned. 'I don't want to be reminded of it. The cuts under these bandages are at the itchy stage.'

I was guilty of forgetting about Adam's injuries a lot of the time. Because the bandages were out of sight under his shirt, and because he carried on as normal, regardless of any discomfort his scraped skin and bruised ribs may be causing him, it was all too easy to succumb to temporary amnesia.

The check-in procedures were smooth and efficient. We spent our time in the departure lounge and on the short flight back to Luxor poring over Adam's iPad, making a minute study of the photographs we'd taken in the Hathor chapel at Hatshepsut's temple. We noted down a number of promising-looking gashes in the walls. These might possibly serve as slots for a giant Aten-shaped penny to be pressed into. We didn't apply ourselves to the conundrum of how we were going to test our theory that we were dealing with an ancient Egyptian prototype for a slot machine. That would come later, when Adam had fashioned something to serve as a penny; no a key, I reminded myself. Aten is key.

'Drop me off in town near the Souk, would you?' Adam asked the taxi driver, as he sped us from the airport back towards the Jolie Ville.

I looked at him in alarm. 'You're not going off on your own,' I objected. 'What about Hussein?'

'Somehow I think it's unlikely he's followed us to Cairo and back, watched us weigh and measure the Aten discs from between Mehet-Weret's cow-horns, and taken a note of which flight we're on,' Adam said blithely. 'Please Merry, go back to the hotel and don't worry about me. I need to do a quick tour of the hardware shops of Luxor, then see if I can remember any of the skills my woodwork teacher worked so hard to hammer into me in my long-ago school days.'

'No pun intended,' I murmured drily. 'I don't like it, but I can see we can't stay holed up in the hotel hiding from Hussein forever. Just watch your back,' I told him.

'I'll be back at the hotel by late afternoon,' Adam promised, and dropped a quick kiss onto the end of my nose.

I decided my first priority on return to the Jolie Ville must really be Dan. I knew I'd neglected him, and not been sufficiently appreciative of his grand romantic gesture in jumping on a flight back to Luxor when he thought I was running headlong into trouble. My only excuse was the riotous confusion of my feelings, and that was really no excuse; not when he'd so nearly plunged to an early death on the jagged rocks in the foothills around Hatshepsut's temple.

A glance at my watch told me it was approaching mid-morning. Adam and I caught an early flight out of Cairo.

There was no sign of Dan lingering over breakfast coffee on the terrace. I strolled around the adults-only pool near the sun terrace, then on through the gardens. I reached the infinity pool with its spectacular views across to the Theban hills lining the horizon on the far banks of the Nile. Dan has always been a sunworshipper. It's how I persuaded him to come to Egypt more than once, certainly not for the history, but for the wall-to-wall sunshine.

I didn't find Dan lounging by the pool, but I did stumble across Ted sitting in the deep shade of a pool parasol, sipping a mango juice and poring over his little notebook. He looked up as I approached. 'Merry, you're back! That was quick! How lovely to see you. So, tell me, any luck?'

I spent a few moments bringing him up to speed on the success of our visit to the Cairo Museum and filling him in on Adam's plan to make a pair of mock-up sun discs. 'We have no idea whether we need just one or both of them to act as the "key" – so we were playing it safe with two.'

'Intriguing,' Ted said. 'That boy has a natural flair for this stuff.'

'You should have seen the way he flirted with Shukura to get what he wanted,' I said darkly. 'I was shocked to the core.'

He smiled. 'Shukura was a rather beautiful woman in her younger days,' he said with a touch of nostalgia. 'We had a very happy season on that dig.' His eyes misted with a far-off look, so I squeezed his shoulder and left him to his reminiscences.

I skirted the pool and ducked behind the little children's playground, then up the pathway leading to the row of hexagonal bungalows set in the gardens beyond. Dan's room – previously my room, of course - was in the next building along from the one I occupied now. I made a short detour to drop off my overnight bag, then walked up the little path to his door and tapped lightly on it.

I was a little bit taken aback when Jessica was the one to open it.

'Oh, hi Merry,' she said brightly, looking perkier than ever in a neat little pink vest and a pair of itsy-bitsy white shorts, with a spectacular pair of ruffle-topped flip-flops on her tiny feet. I noticed she'd given in to the sales pitch of the girls from the on-site beauty salon and had her toenails painted with pretty little daisy designs. This girl would know how to look good in a bin-liner, swollen black eye notwithstanding. I swallowed down the usual unflattering comparison to what I liked to think of as my own brand of shabby chic. Sadly, I suspect this was more shabby than chic. My envy really did me no credit. 'You're back sooner than expected. Come to check on the wounded soldier, have you?'

I made valiant effort to swallow down my sudden suspicious instincts in the same way I'd fought back the envy. 'Yes, how is he?' I said, in my best visiting-the-patient voice.

'Better now,' she said. 'But he started running an awfully high temperature after you left yesterday.' I wondered if I should flatter myself that it was down to stress at my sudden departure for Cairo, but she didn't allow me time for this self-indulgent thought to settle. 'It seems they didn't quite get all the grit out of one of his wounds, and it became infected. They had to perform a mini operation in the end last night, and sort of cauterise it. It was a bit yucky, I have to say, but he seems back to his usual self this morning.'

'Pinkie, is that you?' Dan demanded from the bed.

Jessica swung back the door, and I spotted him lying there under a sheet, looking rumpled but rather fetching with his hair tousled stickily across his forehead, and fresh bandages wrapped around his chest.

'He was a bit feverish,' Jessica said. 'They wanted to keep him in the medical centre overnight, but he was having none of it. He's dreadfully single-minded Merry, isn't he? So, I told the nurse I'd sit with him and let her know if his condition worsened at all. But thankfully I think they got all the yucky stuff out of him, and he drifted off to sleep quite naturally.'

I gaped at her. 'You sat up with him all night?'

'Pretty much,' she shrugged. 'The nurse came to check on him as dawn broke. I went back to my room for a couple of hours of shut eye, and to get showered and dressed.'

She had no right to look as good as she did after a sleepless night, but I had to take my hat off to her. She was a plucky little thing. It seemed my suspicious instincts did me no more credit than my envy.

'Are you coming in? Or are you going to stand wittering on the doorstep all morning?' Dan said irascibly from the bed.

Jessica raised an eyebrow and smiled, 'See? Back to his old self,' she grinned at me.

I stepped into the room. 'I just saw your Dad, Jessica. He doesn't seem to know anything about this?'

'Oh, no; I didn't want to worry him. He had an early night last night, after dinner. Dan and I were sitting out on the terrace having coffee. That's when I noticed he seemed ill. I don't think he'd have said anything. He really is quite stiff-necked, isn't he? But sweat was pouring off him, so…'

'Will you please do me the courtesy of stopping talking about me as if I'm not here?' Dan roared.

She giggled and tossed her curls, and said to me in a stage whisper, 'He thinks he's being masterful!' And she turned and poked her tongue out at him. I observed this pert little gesture of defiance with amazement. Dan rolled his eyes at the ceiling but said nothing. 'Anyway,' Jessica turned back to me and picked up where she left off, 'I forced him along to the medical centre, with him complaining all the way; and the rest you know. I have to say, I think the fact he almost collapsed through the doorway and into the doctor's arms more than justified all the bullying I had to do to get him there!' And she turned, with her hands on her hips, and glared down at Dan as if daring him to contradict her.

'Angel of mercy,' he muttered in a resigned manner, but I had a strong sense he was enjoying the way she stood up to him. She was a tiny elfin-like creature, and he was a great big strapping bloke, but it dawned on me Jessica could have my boyfriend wrapped around her little finger in no time.

'Anyway, I'll leave you to it,' she said lightly. 'I'll go and find my Dad.'

'He's by the infinity pool,' I said, and watched her slip through the door and pull it closed behind her.

I stood rather awkwardly for a moment. All my 'girlfriend' behaviours seemed to have abandoned me. After an undecided pause, I perched on the edge of the bed. 'It was good of her to look after you,' I said, a bit stiltedly.

'Yes, I was feeling decidedly crock over dinner. But I was trying to keep my wits about me in case that devilish Hussein turned up disguised as a waiter or something, ready to slip arsenic into our coffee. Once she started ordering me about it was quite a relief to hoist the white flag and let her bully me into submission.'

A rather uncomfortable silence descended again.

'So, how was Cairo?' he asked at length.

A small sigh of relief escaped me, invited to talk about something straightforward and without any strange undercurrents attached to it. 'Almost ridiculously easy,' I smiled. 'Shukura showed us the Mehet-Weret couch, and her colleague was able to remove the Aten discs from between the cow horns.' I waxed lyrical about all the weighing and measuring and Adam's plans to make replicas; then told him about the wonderful evening we'd spent enjoying the hospitality of Shukura and her family.

Dan watched me throughout with a small, indulgent smile on his face. 'It really agrees with you, all this Lara Croft stuff, doesn't it?' he said softly.

'What do you mean?' I was immediately a bit defensive, wondering if I was about to be treated to the usual lecture about living out a fantasy.

He puffed the pillow underneath his head, and settled back on it, gazing up at me. 'Pinkie, you've come alive since you've been here, any fool can see that. Your eyes sparkle, your skin glows and you talk with the most ridiculous amount of excitement about people who've been dead for centuries, and ancient bits of paper that could disintegrate in a strong puff of wind.'

For once, this brought no stinging retort to my lips. He wasn't haranguing me. Instead, his voice held a kind of soft sadness. I felt my throat tighten.

'I came tearing out here intent on making you see sense and dragging you back home with me; by the hair if necessary.' His smile was a kind of self-deprecating grimace. 'That's the sort of cave man gesture I thought you were looking for; for me to exert my hidden Alpha maleness, so you'd stop looking at me as if I was a cosy pair of slippers with the toes all worn through.'

I started to interrupt him, but he stopped me with a small gesture.

'No, let me finish. I can see that's not what you need. And I can see you're not coming home anytime soon. You belong here in this strange barren land, with its remorseless sunlight, unrelenting heat, and weird history. Let's face it, you love Egypt, and it returns the sentiment with equal ardour. But it's not for me, Pinkie. I'm for the rolling green fields of home and the golf course.'

'But...'

He held up his hand again. 'No "buts". Besides, any idiot can see you and Adam are made for each other. You're like two peas in a pod.'

I stared at him, suddenly feeling as if a lift shaft had opened up underneath me. It took a moment for his meaning to sink in. When it did, I felt myself reverting inexplicably to teenager mode. 'Are you breaking up with me?' I asked in a small voice, feeling sixteen again.

He lifted my hand into his and held it against the bed sheet. 'Yes Pinkie,' he said very gently. 'I am.'

I was taken with an irrational urge to argue. For all that I'd been avoiding squaring up to it, it was impossible not to regret the end now it was staring me in the face. Ours was a long relationship and we'd grown comfortable together. It seemed heartless – a slap in the face to all the good times – to let it go without so much as a token struggle. Stinging tears sprang into my eyes as I looked at his oh-so-familiar face. 'But...'

He raised a finger to my lips. 'I told you, no "buts". You'd have had to do it sooner or later. I hope I've saved you the heartache of when and how.'

And that was his grandest gesture of all.

Chapter 18

I spent the afternoon out on the Nile, under the flapping triangular sail of the hotel's felucca, silently saying goodbye to the last ten years of my life and to the man who'd shared them.

I needed to spend some time away from the others. The company of the other hotel guests who joined me for the trip and in the light lunch the crew served didn't encroach on my quiet grief. I think they sensed my need for solitude and respected it.

I told Ted where I was going so no one would worry about me. Hussein couldn't get to me out on the dark waters of the Nile among holidaymakers and hotel staff.

The ancient river surged beneath the boat and the sun shone hotly from the vaulting blue sky. It bleached the rock and desert stretching beyond the narrow strip of dusty cultivation at the water's edge. The palm trees lining the bank swayed gently in the afternoon breeze, and grubby semi-clad children ran along the riverbank waving sticks and calling to us. It was a scene as old as time. I felt a slow, steady peace settle over me. Dan was right; this mystical land of Egypt was in my blood. I belonged here. I turned my face into the wind and let the tears flow freely.

It was the catharsis I needed. As the felucca turned back down river, and the sun started its fiery descent towards the western horizon, I knew I mourned the loss of my past but could still look forward to my future and know Dan had made the right choice for us both.

Adam was waiting on the little wooden jetty jutting out into the Nile when we moored. As the boat-boy helped me down the narrow plank of wood that served as a gangplank, he ran forward waving two discs in the air. Then he caught sight of my face, and his eyes narrowed as he reached my side. 'Merry, what's up?'

'Dan and I agreed our relationship has run its course. We decided to let it go and just be friends.'

'Oh Merry. Are you alright?'

I felt tears swim in my eyes and blinked them back. 'Just a bit sad,' I admitted. 'We've been together a long time.'

'Would you rather be alone? I can make myself scarce if you'd prefer not to have company...?'

'No, it's fine. That's what the trip out on the felucca was all about. It's for the best, it's just going to take a bit of getting used to, that's all.'

We watched little black-and-white kingfishers dart in and out of the reeds while the Nile lapped around the jetty below our feet. Adam's a sensitive soul, and I knew he wouldn't speak again until I did, letting me lead the conversation in whatever direction I chose.

'I see you made the replica Aten discs,' I said, very clear of my choice.

He brightened visibly and grinned. 'The hardware stores of Luxor came up trumps.' He held them up for my inspection, one in each hand. They were both about the size of a flattened football. 'Can you tell the difference from the ones we saw yesterday?'

'Other than the suspiciously bright gold paint?' I asked. 'It hasn't got the dull gleam of the real thing, has it?'

He looked a bit wounded. 'I wasn't so much worried about what they looked like – although I wanted to make them as realistic as possible. It was more their size and weight that bothered me. I've weighed them on as many sets of scales as I can find and measured them a hundred times. By my reckoning they're as close to the real thing as we're ever going to get.'

'Very impressive,' I agreed, enjoying the way his shoulders straightened at the praise. 'How did you make them?'

'Pretty much the same way the ancient Egyptian workmen did, I think. They used rosewood overlaid with gold leaf. I used rosewood overlaid with gold paint. Et voila!'

I smiled at him. 'You must have spent the afternoon chained to a lathe. Your old woodwork teacher would be proud.'

'I like to think so,' he said modestly.

'So now we've just got to figure out if there's a way we can try them out without getting ourselves hurled into jail.'

'I thought perhaps we could all talk about that over dinner.'

I gave a small sigh. 'I'm not sure I feel in the mood for dinner with everyone else tonight. I thought I might just order from room service and see if there's anything worth watching on TV.'

He looked at me in dismay, and then a thought struck him, and his expression brightened. 'I've got a better idea. How about dinner in town, just the two of us? We can reassure the others we'll get a taxi to the door, and then get another one straight back again; just in case Hussein is prowling around and up to no good.'

'Yes,' I said. 'I'd like that. Tell them not to wait up.'

We went to the Bua Khao Asian fusion restaurant in the Nile Palace Hotel, deciding it was best to stick to the populace tourist spots, rather than stray into the back streets to one of the local restaurants, which would have been our preference.

We sat at a secluded table out on the open terrace at the back of the hotel overlooking the clover-shaped pool and the inky Nile, which reflected the hotel lights in dancing yellow stripes. The Thai chef rustled up oriental delicacies to delight the palate. I'm not sure my appetite was all it might have been to fully appreciate the effort he went to. I don't suppose I was the most scintillating of company either.

'Guess where we were this time last week?' Adam prompted, making a brave attempt to cheer me up.

He looked at me expectantly as I gazed into his deep blue eyes. They were glinting darkly in the soft light cast by the tealight in its pretty dish on the table between us. He had me. 'Where?'

He smiled and looked a bit nostalgic. 'We were staking out a spot in the Valley of the Kings ready to creep into the tomb to see if we could find what Howard Carter hid there.'

'Really? That was a week ago? It seems longer.'

'Time flies when you're having fun,' he parroted the old cliché.

'That's one way of putting it,' I muttered.

'Sorry,' he apologised quickly. 'That was horribly insensitive of me. I was forgetting…'

'No, no,' I waved my fork in the air to butt away his apology. 'I was thinking of some of our more traumatic moments over the last few days…'

'Like when you had to smash you and Jessica through the roof of a cowshed with a water bottle,' he chuckled, interrupting me.

'Or when you rendezvoused with Hussein in the holy of holies at Luxor Temple with a hundred grand in your rucksack,' I shot back.

He grinned at me. 'It seems our spirit of adventure is alive and kicking.'

'I'll drink to that,' I said, and reached across the table to clink my wineglass against his.

His eyes rested on mine for a long moment, and I felt a warm glow spread through me. 'Merry, perhaps I shouldn't ask you this right now, but how do you feel about a bit of an adventure tonight; while it's just the two of us?'

I tilted my head to look at him. Coming from anyone but Adam I might have taken that for a really dodgy pick-up line. 'What do you mean?'

He reached into his trouser pocket and pulled something out, brandishing it on a small chain in front of me.

'It's a key,' I said stupidly.

'Guess what to…'

'Oh my God Adam – it's the key to the Hathor Chapel. How the hell did you get your hands on that?'

'I asked Ahmed to pay a quick visit to our friend Mustafa Mushhawrar to see what the chances were of him getting himself stationed there on night patrol. He's managed to wangle night duty there for the next three nights, since one of their regulars has gone sick – a happy coincidence I believe; although it's fair to say Ahmed's eyes were suspiciously bright when he told me. It wouldn't surprise me to discover they're related. Ahmed's probably arranged a bit of a job swap. I gather while he was there, he asked if he could have a copy of the key to help him in the performance of his duties.'

I felt my eyes widen in disbelief. 'Adam – he gave you a police key?'

'No, I merely have it on loan,' he corrected. 'He wasn't sure if he could be on hand at the critical moment. He's asked me to let him know when we decide to check it out. He'll do his best to keep the coast clear.'

'You're going to be guilty of losing that poor man his job one of these days,' I muttered. 'As Dan once had cause to remark, it really is no way for an officer of the law to behave.'

He grinned at me. 'And as I seem to recall you saying once, Merry; "I have no plans to rob anything, I just want to discover it." Does that ring any bells?'

I had to admit, it did. I seemed to recall saying those exact words when we'd solved the last of Carter's conundrums and realised that he'd hidden something inside the tomb wall. 'But Adam, don't you think it's horribly risky?

If we get caught, they'll lock us up and throw away the key for sure.'

'The same can be said about that night a week ago,' he reminded me. 'And it didn't stop you then.'

I couldn't counter this. I'd been fiercely determined to recover Carter's mysterious item from its hiding place. So, I bit my lip instead.

'Look, Merry, I've been thinking. It's just fleetingly, remotely, crazily possible there's an undiscovered 18th Dynasty tomb from the Amarna period hidden behind the Hathor chapel in Hatshepsut's temple. You'll think me hopelessly romantic; and maybe you'd be right, and it's just my tragic Indiana Jones fantasies coming to the fore again... but, Merry, wouldn't you love us to be the ones to share the moment of discovery? I know the others have been a big part of things over the last few days, but it feels right to me that we should do this together; just the two of us. Just say we find it ... suspend all your disbelief and let yourself dream... Can you imagine, stepping inside and knowing we're the first in more than three- thousand years to do so?'

His eyes were shining with a dark fire, his expression intent and passionate as he gazed back at me. When he was like this, I wasn't sure I could deny him anything. Discovery of a lost tomb; it was after all what every self-respecting Egyptologist – even "thwarted" ones like Adam, and strictly amateur ones like me – dreamed of. I could feel all my nerve endings start to shiver and hum.

'And another thing,' he went on before I could decide how to respond. 'I think we owe it to Howard Carter. If he'd wanted those papyrus scrolls handed over to the authorities, he'd have done so himself. But we know he was trying to protect his good name, and that of his benefactor Lord Carnarvon. If anyone had a spirit of adventure it was Carter. Look at the trail of clues he laid us. So, it struck me we could perhaps take the papyri with us. If we're lucky enough to find the tomb, my thinking is we could put the papyri inside, and seal it up again. That way, no one would ever be the wiser.'

'You'd do that?' I gaped at him. 'Discover perhaps the most sought after ancient Egyptian tomb of all, have a quick look around, stick Carter's – well Tutankhamun's – papyrus scrolls inside, then seal it up again and walk away?'

He shrugged.

'Adam, you'd drive yourself mad with it.'

'I'm not so sure,' he said. 'Carter always said the moment of discovery was the high point with Tutankhamun. I don't get the impression he much enjoyed all the stuff that came after it.'

I stared at him, not sure if I dared take him seriously. 'Well, I suppose it would save me the trouble of coming up with a story to tell the world. I've been racking my brains trying to think up a plausible tale to explain how we came into possession of the papyri. I was rather hoping to avoid admitting I walked out of Howard Carter's house on the fateful night of my lock-in with his coded hieroglyphics in my pocket. And I'd prefer to keep schtum about our misadventures with the Queen Ahmes portrait in the Winter Palace Hotel, if at all possible.' These were all shenanigans we'd been involved in leading to the momentous discovery of the scrolls. 'Not to mention breaking and entering that locked tomb last week!' I finished.

'You make us sound like a pair of out-and-out crooks,' he chuckled.

'Hmm, well maybe I'm starting to feel like one. All this treasure hunting does seem to demand its share of law-bending, if not exactly law-breaking. I'd say we're definitely testing the limits.'

'It's great fun though, don't you think?'

'Well, it beats copy-editing charity newsletters,' I said wryly. 'Given the choice between a bit of mild Egyptological felony and a return to the day job, it's a no-brainer. I've gone over to the dark side, and there's no looking back.'

He grinned at me. 'Now that sounds more like the Meredith Pink I know and love.'

I ignored the little thrill this gave me. 'And there's only one other thing I can think of to avoid handing the papyri over to the authorities with a full confession,' I said.

'Oh?' He put his fork down and looked at me expectantly.

'Well, I was thinking maybe we could take a leaf out of the barbarous Hussein's book and sell it on the black market, like he was planning to do with the antiquities he and his brothers stole. You never know, someone might be prepared to pay us enough to spend the rest of our lives floating on the Nile on a private yacht, drinking cocktails.'

He let out a shout of laughter, 'More likely spend it chained to a rock at the bottom, providing a feast for the fishies.'

I cast him an indignant look, 'I'm just trying to consider all options.'

He took a sip of his wine, watching me over the rim with amusement dancing in his eyes. 'Purely out of interest, Merry; do you have any contacts with anyone operating on the black market?'

I took a last bite of tempura prawn and laid my fork down alongside my plate. 'Not one,' I said regretfully.

I could see he was trying not to laugh. 'And, again, purely theoretically you understand, how do you plan to manage the business of advertising the papyri on the black market without calling the wrath of the authorities down on your head?'

I was quite enjoying the banter. I hadn't given the black market a moment's thought before now, but it was good fun to conjecture on it. I've always prided myself on my ability to think on my feet. 'Well, it occurs to me now, considering the matter, that we do in actual fact have a contact. We could always ask the wicked Hussein to act as our front man.'

Adam laughed out loud, 'Merry, you are a joy and a wonder. Please don't ever change. I am nuts about you.'

It occurred to me he'd said something similar a week or so ago, before Dan appeared back on the scene. It also couldn't fail to escape my attention that I was feeling a whole lot better; was positively enjoying myself, in fact. I let go of the little, guilty frisson this sent up my spine. I didn't need to feel guilty anymore. 'Thank you,' I said modestly.

'So, do we have a plan?' he asked.

I looked down at my newly hotel-laundered white trousers and my pretty top. I'm not sure it was exactly the get-up I'd choose for a visit to Hatshepsut's temple in the dead of night to search for a hidden tomb. But who was I to be fussy, given the opportunity to perhaps discover something the world didn't know existed?

Discover it, I reminded myself, mentally underlining the word. Nothing more, or less – just so we could say we'd followed Howard Carter's quest all the way to the end. Perhaps Adam was right, and it would be better to let the "precious jewels" rest undisturbed for all eternity. But I was dying to know if they were there. I didn't know if I was capable of taking a peek and walking away, back into my ordinary little life; but it seemed a better prospect than any alternative I could think of. Besides, disappointment was the most likely outcome. Still, a night spent in Adam's company unlawfully checking out the Hathor chapel, even if only for its own sake, did hold a rather magnetic appeal.

'Let's do it!' I agreed.

Ahmed came onto his night shift at 10 pm, which was fortuitously not long after we finished our coffee at the restaurant. Adam called him on the mobile and arranged for him to pick up the suitcase from the police station en-route to collecting us from outside the Nile Palace Hotel. He drove us out of town, across Luxor Bridge, along the west bank cultivation and then turned towards the Theban foothills and Hatshepsut's temple.

The temple is floodlit until late evening – and pretty impressive it looks, too, its terraces and porticoes bathed in a soft amber glow. But they don't keep the lights on overnight, so we knew we could skirt the wide open plain in front of the façade and approach the temple forecourt without being seen, provided Ahmed could keep the other guards distracted. He reassured us there was no CCTV, and no other technological wizardry to concern us. It was just the threat to being caught, plain and simple.

'We are de tree musketeers, yes?' he beamed. 'I will keep watch for you, and I will look out for dis Hussein. He will not bother you tonight.'

It was a very hot, very still night, of the type I've only known in Egypt. The heat was like a cloak, or being wrapped in a blanket just removed from a toasty airing cupboard. There was definitely something physical about it. Looking up, the stars were out in force, twinkling dots of diamond-bright light against the velvety black sky. There was no moon.

I felt a powerful rush of adrenaline as we crept towards the temple forecourt through the darkness. Adam was a couple of paces in front of me. He had a rucksack slung over his right shoulder. It held the two replica sun-discs, some water and a couple of flashlights. (The water and the flashlights were courtesy of the Luxor police department store, thoughtfully provided by Ahmed). Howard Carter's suitcase swung lightly from his left hand. If we were caught now, I doubted all the story-telling skills in the world would be enough to keep us from a long spell in jail. I'd never felt more alive. All my senses thrummed with energy, excitement and naked fear.

We avoided the causeway leading across the open plain to the temple snugly embraced by the curving arm of the cliffs behind it. But there was nothing for it but to use the central ramp leading from the temple forecourt up onto the first terrace. We took the shallow stone steps at full pelt, and didn't stop running when we reached the top. The temple was in darkness, but the stars cast a pale silvery light, and our shadowy, darting forms were in full view should anyone happen to be looking. We sprinted across the courtyard in front of the southern colonnade and threw ourselves through the stone entranceway into the pillared Hathor shrine.

Panting and sweating, we hunkered down behind the first column and waited.

There were no angry shouts; no beams of light trained on us... nothing. 'Well Merry, we've done the hardest part,' Adam gasped, gulping down a deep lungful of air. I could hear the elation in his voice. 'We've made it this far undetected. Now for the fun bit...'

It took a while for our breathing to get back to normal, and before we dared to move. We were in almost total darkness. The silvery light from the stars was no match for the rising, densely packed pillars all around us, topped with their Hathor capitals, complete with sticky-out cow-ears. Adam tugged the key out of his pocket, and we tiptoed through the pillars to the stable door. I'm not sure quite why we tiptoed when nobody was within earshot. But there was something creepy and clandestine about the temple at night, all the shapes dark and distorted. It discouraged normal movement and noise.

The two separate parts of the stable door were bolted together. The single key was all we needed to unlock them. It was a breathless moment as Adam pushed the door open so we could enter the chapel carved into the cliffside behind the temple.

'Ready?' he whispered.

Speechless with the thrill of adventure, I nodded.

He reached for my hand, and we stepped over the threshold.

Total darkness enveloped us as he pushed the door closed behind us. It was hot too. I've never quite got used to the increase in temperature in rock-cut spaces in Egypt. It's not the belting heat of the mid-day sun; more a kind of oppressive, suffocating dryness that catches in your throat and sucks the life out of you. Pretty fit for purpose, I suppose.

I could hear Adam scrabbling about in his rucksack. 'Here, you'll need this.' He thrust a bottle of water into my hand. A moment later the beam from his flashlight flooded the small space with yellow light and lit up his face.

I took a deep glug of the water and accepted the second flashlight. I swung it in a slow sweep over the walls. We were in a small rectangular room with two central pillars supporting the ceiling. At the back of the room, two smaller chambers penetrated into the rock. The cheeky little self-portrait of Senenmut, Hatshepsut's architect, was behind the doorway.

I took a moment to settle my senses, watching the way the beam of torchlight seemed to add movement to the life-size images of Hatshepsut carved into the walls. As always in ancient Egyptian temple reliefs, the images were shown in profile, making offerings to the gods. But in the torchlight, they were eerily realistic, as if they might somehow step down from the walls to join us.

'Nervous?' Adam asked.

'Petrified,' I admitted. 'It feels like she's watching us; almost as if she knows exactly why we're here.'

He grinned at me. 'Well, if that's the case, she watched Tutankhamun and Ay in exactly the same way. These carvings would have been a bit fresher then; a mere century or two old, but they were definitely here.'

I gazed about me, trying to get my imagination to grapple with it. I wasn't sure I was supple enough to perform the mental gymnastics necessary to leap across nearly three-and-a-half-thousand years. I tried to visualise the shadowy pharaoh-to-be who'd spoken to us from the papyrus, and his young predecessor Tutankhamun here in this same space, possibly on a stifling night such as this. Did they feel the same thrill, the fear of capture, and the risk of failure? Their mission, if we'd interpreted Ay's scroll correctly, was to hide their "precious jewels"; ours was to see if we could find them. I felt the eyes of eternity upon us and shivered despite the sweltering heat. 'Do you really think there's a hidden tomb behind these walls?' I asked in a strangled sort of voice.

Adam's face behind the flashlight was in shadows, but I could feel the raw energy radiating off him. 'Yes Merry, I do. And I think we're going to find it.'

Chapter 19

My head was full of Howard Carter. He'd searched for Tutankhamun's tomb for years, slowly and methodically; certain in his belief the boy-king's tomb lay somewhere undisturbed in the Valley of the Kings.

Then, on 4 November 1922, he found the first steps. A day later he uncovered the doorway and found the Pharaoh's seals intact. I wondered if he felt then rather like I felt now, the same fevered brow, sweating palms and dry throat. It seemed to me, perhaps fancifully, that our discovery of the papyri was like finding the first steps. Understanding what it said was like finding the intact seals.

Howard Carter had to wait three weeks for Lord Carnarvon to arrive from England before he could proceed further. But then he was able to knock his famous hole in the wall, shine his candle through and see the glint of gold; everywhere the glint of gold, and make his famous "wonderful things" comment. We'd had only a week from discovering the papyri to this moment. It was impossible not to wonder if the glint of gold awaited us.

Can there be a more exhilarating moment for an excavator?

Officially, Carter and Lord Carnarvon were then required to wait until the next day before entering the tomb. Protocol demanded an official from the Egyptian Antiquities Service must be present when the tomb was opened.

But Carter and Carnarvon were only human.

The story didn't come out until years later – long after both men were dead. It told how Carter and Carnarvon made a clandestine visit to the tomb in the dead of night. They knocked a small hole into the wall of the burial chamber (subsequently covered up with reed baskets) and squeezed through. They simply couldn't wait. They had to know what they'd found; whether the boy king lay enshrined in his sarcophagus, or whether all they'd discovered was a fabulous royal cache.

Such is the intoxication of discovery. I've never taken drugs, but I doubt the strongest narcotic in the world could provide the same hit.

I could understand why Adam wanted to do this immediately. Now. Tonight. And so did I. Neither one of us could possibly sleep, not now the replica Aten discs were made. We had to know; and the discovery had to be ours. It wasn't about treasure hunting, or tomb robbery, or personal glory; or even a simple thirst for knowledge, the chance to write a new chapter in the world's history. It was the sheer adrenaline rush of discovery.

'Where do we start?' I asked.

'Well, I've been studying the photographs we took when Mustafa first showed us around. Working on the theory the best place to hide something is in plain view; I reckon we should start with the biggest, boldest, most impressive image of the Aten disc on these walls. By my reckoning it's this one over here.' He led the way across the chapel and pointed up at the reliefs. 'See the disc between the cow horns?' Hatshepsut was shown seated between the god Amun and a huge image of Hathor, depicted as a cow with long up-curved horns. 'And look, see this gash beside it? Doesn't it look big enough and deep enough to you to accommodate one of the Aten discs from the Mehet-Weret ritual couch?'

'Oh my God Adam – try it!' My heart was pounding loud enough to bring an avalanche of rock crashing about our ears.

Adam took one of his homemade Aten discs from his rucksack and fitted it into the deep gash in the stone. The action was very much like pressing a very large penny into a slot. Nothing happened. Adam stared at me, and I could see the disappointment writ large all over his features. 'I was so sure it was this one,' he said in a low, defeated voice.

'Press harder,' I urged. 'It's still sitting proud of the wall.'

'But if I push it all the way in, how will I ever get it back out again?'

I shrugged. I wished there were some insight or inspiration I could offer him, but all I had was instinct.

He looked into my eyes and leaned all his weight against the disc jutting from the wall. For a moment it seemed stuck fast, wedged into the stone gash. Then it was literally like a penny dropping into a slot. It disappeared inside the wall. There was a moment of stillness and silence. We held our breath in a kind of agony of anticipation and dread. Maybe there was just a hollow space behind the wall, and he'd pushed the disc through to simply drop onto the floor on the other side.

'It didn't work...' I started despondently, but a small sound cut me off as if my windpipe had been abruptly severed. It was a rasping sort of sound as ancient stone scraped against ancient stone.

I was still staring into Adam's eyes, so saw them widen with shock. Mine felt like they were bulging out of my head. We both turned in a parody of slow motion towards the sound. A small square panel ground open in the wall, just big enough to crawl through.

The breath caught painfully in my throat, and I choked. For some crazy reason my eyes were brimming with tears, and I felt a ridiculous bubble of hysterical laughter about to burst. I bit it back as the enormity of what had just happened crashed over me. Quite how my legs didn't buckle underneath me, I'll never know. I stared at that small opening in the wall as if the jaws of death had just opened to swallow me. I didn't much like this unbidden analogy, so quashed it in favour of voicing the obvious question.

'Adam, on the basis the Aten disc has just disappeared inside the wall, do you think we have to leave this hole open for Mustafa to find tomorrow? You see, it never occurred to me we might not be able to lock up again after ourselves when it's time to go.'

I could see he was trying to speak, but it took a couple of attempts for anything intelligible to emerge. On the third, he cleared his throat and managed to get a complete sentence out. 'We've still got the other disc. Maybe there were two of them on that ritual couch for a reason. Or maybe the one I've just used has dropped through on the other side and we can collect it again.'

'I'm wondering if you should try the other one to see if it locks it?'

'But if I use it and the opening closes over again, then we're left here on the outside with no way of getting in.'

This was irrefutable. 'You could always make another pair, and we could come back tomorrow?' I suggested. 'The alterative is one or both of us has got to crawl through that gap and risk getting trapped on the other side.'

I could see the agony of indecision raging on his face. 'What if I just shine the torch through and see if it's there and whether I can reach it?'

'But what if it's booby-trapped? What am I supposed to do if you stick your head through and a guillotine falls on you?'

He started to laugh. 'I can see we haven't thought this thing through. What are you suggesting? That whatever's through there is likely to be packed with snares, dusted with ancient poisons or filled with writhing snakes?'

'Well, all those stories about the pharaoh's curse must have come from somewhere. And I'm not just talking Indiana Jones.'

He grinned at me, ' *"Death shall come on swift wings to him who disturbs the peace of the King*", is that what you're saying?'

'You're quoting the curse they found on the lintel above Tutankhamun's tomb,' I accused, suddenly feeling the vice-like grip of a real terror take hold of me. Indiana Jones and all joking aside, the death of Lord Carnarvon from an infected mosquito bite was all too real.

He chuckled, 'Merry, don't believe a word if it. Some enterprising newspaper hound dreamed the whole thing up to sell more copy about the opening of the tomb.'

'But what about Lord Carnarvon?' I said querulously. 'All the lights went out all over Cairo when he died, and his dog back home in Highclere Castle howled, rolled over and died at the precise moment his master breathed his last. Doesn't that have a ring of the supernatural about it?'

His eyes, glowing in the flashlight, seemed very large as they came to meet mine. I could see the amusement in them. 'You've read too much fiction if you believe that. If the lights went out in Cairo, it's because the national grid in Egypt was notoriously unpredictable in the early 1920s. And I suspect the story of the dog was just more media frenzy concocted to sell newspapers.'

'But not all pharaohs' curses were made up just to sensationalise archaeological discoveries, surely!'

'No, that's true. It seems they were pretty keen on them in the Old Kingdom. I think one of the favourites was *"Cursed be those who disturb the rest of a Pharaoh. They that shall break the seal of this tomb shall meet death by a disease no doctor can diagnose."*'

I was starting to feel a bit sick, but I could tell he was teasing me. I'm not usually so superstitious. But then this was the first time I'd been presented with a situation where one or both of us might come up against all the magic and mystery of ancient Egypt. It was pitch dark (save for the flashlight), it was past midnight, and we were in a rock-cut chamber in a more than three-thousand-year-old temple, treading in the footsteps of some of the most iconic names to emerge from antiquity. I won't apologise for my fit of the jitters.

'Merry, we are potentially about to make the most momentous discovery on Egyptological record, and we're holding an academic debate about the veracity of ancient curses. Doesn't that strike you as a bit ridiculous?'

'Not if one of us is about to meet a grisly end,' I said with feeling.

His expression softened, and he smiled. 'Ok, we need to watch out for pit shafts. That's a given. We should probably tie handkerchiefs over our faces in case of bacteria or radiation, given the number of centuries the air has had to grow stale in there. It's potentially a breeding ground for all sorts of nasties.'

'I don't have a handkerchief,' I pointed out.

'No, neither do I,' he admitted. 'They're so last century, don't you think? I'll bet Howard Carter never left home without one.'

'I wonder what he'd have done,' I mused.

He smiled again. 'Something tells me he wouldn't be standing out here debating about it back and forth the way we are. We're talking about the man who once lowered himself on a rope alone and unarmed into a pit filled with a gang of tomb robbers remember? He'd have been through that hole faster than you could say "buried treasure".'

'Hmm, well, call me a coward, but I still want to know we can get out again in one piece.'

Adam dropped down on his hands and knees and shone the torch through the opening. 'It's a corridor,' he said, an unmistakeable thread of excitement ringing from his words. 'It looks like it opens out into a chamber at the other end. And guess what? I'm sure I just saw the glint of gold reflected back at me.'

I was down on all fours before you could say "buried treasure", heedless of my white trousers. Together we peered through the opening. He was right. There was a narrow passageway, perhaps twenty feet long, then, beyond it, a wider opening. The dull gleam of gold was indeed reflected back from the groping torchlight. I caught my breath. I could feel that distant metal exerting a hypnotic and magnetic pull. What is it about gold that's quite so breathlessly mesmerising?

'Why don't you roll the water bottle through?' I suggested. 'Just to see if any spikes thrust up from the floor, or a great big boulder comes tumbling along the corridor, or a snake rears up at it.'

He turned his head to look at me, his eyes a few inches from mine, glinting with humour. 'When was the last time you watched *Raiders of the Lost Ark*?'

'Probably at least twenty years ago.'

'Hmm, it obviously left a lasting impression.'

'Just do it,' I muttered testily.

What he did took me completely by surprise. He rolled sideways and caught me in his arms, knocking us both lengthways, pressed against each other on the hard stone floor of the chapel. His mouth found mine, and just temporarily I forgot about curses and booby traps, snakes and ancient poison. I'd read books that talked about getting lost in a kiss, but I'd never had the experience myself, or even thought it possible. Adam's kiss changed all that. I was conscious of nothing but the feel of his mouth on mine. That and the soaring elation coursing through me.

He broke off to murmur against my lips, 'I'm sorry if it's too soon, but you know how long I've wanted to do that. And if one of us is about to meet a grisly end it seems there's not another moment to lose. Can I do it again before I roll the water bottle?'

'Oh, alright then,' I said, suddenly becoming one with all the heroines in all the films I'd ever watched. There was something about being kissed by the right man that took kissing to a whole new level. I thought if they called "cut" on the movie of my life right now, even without seeing the ending, I could die happy. I'd been kissed the way the girl was supposed to be kissed, and I had the extra thrill of knowing it wasn't acting. The only director staging this particular love scene was the one who orchestrated all our lives, and I wasn't sure I dared name Him, not here in this temple dedicated so conspicuously to the ancient deity Amun, yet with the Aten shining brightly through the ages

'I love you Meredith Pink, and don't you ever forget it,' Adam murmured throatily. 'If I happen to fall into an ancient tomb shaft, or inhale a deadly poison, or step on a snare that rips my body in two, I will still die a happy man because I've lived the last few weeks in glorious Technicolor. And I wonder how many people go through their whole lives and can never truly say that. You're my Technicolor girl, now and always.'

It's a strange thing about Adam, but almost from the moment I met him he could read my thoughts and repeat them aloud like the spookiest psychic imaginable. But he's much more poetic than I am and finds a way of expressing them that sends little shivers of delight through me.

He kissed me again, deeply, thoroughly and entirely satisfactorily. I joined in with equal enthusiasm.

'When we're somewhere a little more comfortable, will you please remind me to pick up where we've just left off?' he asked with a small, soft groan as he lifted his head.

'Yes,' I said. 'I will.'

He grinned at me; his eyes very dark in the pooled glow of the flashlight on the floor behind him. He rolled back a little. 'Ok, we don't want to waste the water. It's infernally hot in here. Can you tip what's left from your bottle into mine? Then we can use the empty one to test for traps.'

A little bit breathlessly I fitted his words to the action. I only spilled a tiny bit. It was his fault for leaving me so molten and loose-limbed.

He dropped a swift kiss onto the end of my nose. It was becoming a little habit of his, and I can't say I minded it in the least. Then he squared up against the opening, positioned the flashlight on the floor between us so it was shining into the corridor, and lined up the water bottle so it was horizontal and ready to roll, so to speak.

'Ok?' he asked.

'Ok,' I confirmed.

He took hold of the water bottle and rolled it firmly into the opening with the light trained on it all the way. There was a very slight downhill incline. All the tombs I'm aware of burrow downwards on a gradient of some sort or other. It rolled about five feet then dropped suddenly out of sight. Adam and I caught our breath as one.

'There's a pit,' he said unnecessarily.

'But nothing immediately on the other side of the doorway.' My relief at this was palpable. Perhaps irrationally, I just wanted to see if we could get the other Aten disc back – if it wasn't trapped somewhere inside the wall.

We performed a couple more experiments. First, we shoved Adam's rucksack through the gap, empty now of all its contents. No spikes speared it from below and no blades severed it from above. It just sat there, on the other side of the opening, looking like a rucksack in a dark corridor. Then we took the papyri out of Howard Carter's suitcase and pushed the case though too. It butted up against the rucksack and pushed it further into the torch-lit space.

There were no disastrous repercussions; nothing at all, in fact.

Reassured, Adam reached his arm through and scrabbled about with his hand on the other side of the opening. 'Yes!' he announced. 'It's here.' He poked his head and shoulders through the gap while I held my breath and waited for the sword of Damacles to fall. Yes, I know Damacles had nothing whatsoever to do with ancient Egypt, but it was the thought that popped into my head in the extremity of the moment.

Thankfully nothing at all fell, and Adam eased his top half back through the opening with the Aten disc clasped triumphantly in his hands.

He looked enquiringly at me. 'So, what's the plan? We want to test if it closes as well as opens the passageway, is that it?'

I nodded. 'Neither one of us is entering that corridor without knowing how to get back out again.' For all that crazy talk about dying happy, I was suddenly strongly aware I had a very good reason to want us to make it out of here without damage to life or limb.

'Fair enough. Up you get then.'

We both clambered up from the floor, careless of the dust clinging to our clothes. He slotted the second Aten disc into the gash in the wall and leaned against it. 'We might as well know if they both fit,' he explained.

Again, there was that same long, breathless pause while nothing happened. Then the strange rasping sound as the ancient stone responded to the hidden mechanism that worked it. A slab of stone ground back into place, covering the gap. Once more we found ourselves staring at a carved wall.

'You'd never know it was there, would you?' I breathed.

'Their engineering skills were unbelievable,' Adam agreed. 'And to think back home in Bronze Age Britain we were living in wattle and daub huts and trying to figure out how to shape metal into something useful.'

He pressed the first disc back into the gash and pushed against it. The slab shifted aside again, protesting the movement with a great sigh of exertion after all these centuries of inaction.

'Ok, now what I want to know is whether the same mechanism works in reverse,' I said. 'One of us needs to go through the opening and see if there's a way of getting out from the inside.'

'You're not taking any chances, are you?'

I beamed at him. 'I've suddenly found I'm quite attached to my life. I'd prefer it not to be cut short, if it can be avoided.'

He opted to be our guinea pig. He ducked down and crawled through the narrow gap, taking an Aten disc with him, leaving me the other one.

'Now what?' he said when he was on the other side, his voice echoing through the gap in the stone. 'There is a gash here. But it strikes me if I push mine through, then you've got both discs on the other side, and I'm trapped here without one – so I'll need you to let me out again. Do you think Ay and Tutankhamun planned it that way, so they always had to be here together?'

'I couldn't begin to speculate,' I said. 'But I think we have to give it a go.'

'Ok, here goes then; I'm about to push the disc into the slot.'

There was a tense moment of nothingness. I held my breath. One moment; then two... and the slab of stone scraped back into place across the gap. I waited for Adam's disc to fall at my feet, my heartbeat ringing in my ears. I wasn't sure it was the end of the world if we were left with only one disc, since we knew it worked from my side of the wall to both open and close the doorway, but I felt a whole lot happier with two. I nearly cried with relief when it dropped onto the floor beside me from a gash in the wall I hadn't even noticed. The hidden mechanism inside was conceived by a genius.

Back in possession of both discs, I immediately fitted the one I was holding back into the wall, pressed down on it with all my strength, counted heartbeats, and watched the stone crunch aside again.

Adam's grinning face peered out at me from the shadows. 'Well, I won't pretend it wasn't a bit spooky being in here on my own, but are you happy now, Merry? Can we please go exploring?'

We checked both flashlights were working, picked up the water and the papyri, leaving the rucksack and Howard Carter's suitcase just inside the corridor. 'Let's leave the Aten discs here so there's no way we can lose them or drop them once we're inside,' Adam suggested. 'Ok, let's go and investigate that pit.'

I crawled through the opening and joined him in the corridor. It was just high enough to stand up in. We edged forward, with our flashlights trained on the floor where the water bottle had disappeared.

The tomb shaft was deadly; a sheer drop into what looked like a bottomless pit. We dropped onto all fours at the edge and shone both flashlights down into it.

'Do those look like spikes to you?' I asked, training my torch on the lethal, upward pointed staves I could see staked into the ground far below.

'There's no need to sound so gleeful about it,' he muttered, pressed close alongside me in the narrow corridor. 'Let's just say I wouldn't want to come tripping along here in the dark and take a sudden tumble. You were right to urge caution, Merry.'

'So, how do we get across? It's got to be at least six feet to the other side. A long-jumper might make it, but I don't fancy our chances. There's not enough space for a run-up.'

He set his mind to the problem for a moment. 'What about those scaffolding planks back outside?'

'What scaffolding planks?' I asked blankly.

'Didn't you notice them the other day when Mustafa was giving us his little tour of the wall reliefs in the southern colonnade? They're doing some restoration work on the upper wall carvings. We might be able to borrow one.'

Even as he said it, he was backing up the corridor. I sat in the tunnel, mopping perspiration from my face with the back of my hand and taking small sips of water, waiting for him to return. I swung my flashlight in alternate sweeps back towards the opening, down into the pit shaft, and then further along the corridor. There was definitely the glint of gold down there.

A scant couple of minutes ticked off on my watch before Adam re-joined me. He was an enterprising individual, and an observant one. 'Here, take the end of this,' he said, feeding the plank into the corridor. 'It should hopefully do the trick.'

I helped him push it across the pit. It was more than long enough, protruding by a good arm's length on both sides. But I wasn't sure I liked the look of how narrow it was. The plank was just short of body-width wide, but only about three inches deep.

'We'll have to body surf along it,' Adam said. 'To keep our weight evenly distributed. It's too dangerous to walk across.'

I baulked even at that, but there was no other option available if we wanted to proceed further. It was take our chances with the plank and the spikes, or forget the whole thing and go back to the hotel.

With the amount of adrenaline we both had surging through our veins, I don't think the giving up option was ever seriously on the cards. But still, my heart was in my mouth and my whole body felt clammy with terror as I watched Adam ease himself onto the plank. He reached both hands out in front of him and pulled himself along it. I kept hold of his ankles until it was no longer safe to do so. There was a horrible breathless moment while his whole body was stretched along the plank, his fingertips still inches away from the other side, and his toes just beyond my reach. Adam's about six feet tall, so I'd underestimated the distance across the pit by a good twelve inches.

He eased himself forward, and the air left my lungs in a great big whoosh of relief when he made it to the other side.

He got to his feet and turned to grin a bit shakily at me. 'I suspect that might be easier without bruised ribs and scraped skin. Ok Merry, you need to throw the flashlights, the water and the papyri across to me. You'd better put the papyri back in the case to give it some weight.'

All actions successfully accomplished, he looked back across the pit at me, training the flashlight on the wall between us so it wasn't shining in my eyes. 'Right Merry, your turn.'

I quailed. 'I'll tell you what...' I said, '...before I come crawling across this plank, do you want to just take a sneak peak into that chamber at the end there and let me know if there's anything worth risking life and limb for.'

He chuckled. 'Meredith Pink, ever the pragmatist.' But he turned to do my bidding. I'm not sure he was any keener than me to have me suspended over those pit spikes.

I watched him tread cautiously along the rest of the corridor. He kept his right arm outstretched holding the flashlight before him, just in case of more hidden terrors, but reached the end without mishap.

I watched him shine his flashlight into the chamber in one slow sweep. Time stood still. It was a curious frozen moment as I saw him stiffen and grope at the wall alongside him, as if to steady himself. Suddenly he dropped down on one knee, almost as though his legs had buckled beneath him.

My heart felt like it was being slowly and painfully crushed in my chest. 'Can you see anything?' I croaked.

There was a long, breathless pause. Finally, his voice echoed back along the corridor, cracked and choked and a bit spectral. 'Yes,' he said. 'Wonderful things.'

Chapter 20

I made it across the plank with no great consciousness of the deadly spikes rearing up from the depths below me. Adam came back to hold it firmly in place while I shuffled across. He reached out a strong arm to haul me the last few inches. My whole being was centred not on the narrow wooden board beneath me, but on what I was about to see in that shadowy chamber before me. Egyptological fever had me firmly in its grip and held me fast.

The first thing to hit me as I followed Adam along this deeper part of the corridor was the noticeable change in the air quality. It was hot, musty and bone-dry; so dry it caught in my throat, a choking mix of dust and dead air that made it difficult to inhale. I breathed slowly and shallowly through my nostrils, trying to acclimatise to the lack of oxygen and the strange stale smell.

But I snatched in my breath in a sharp, involuntary gasp as we reached the end of the corridor, and the chamber opened up in front of us. 'Oh my God Adam, this is beyond wonderful.' I was almost frightened to blink, as if I might somehow blink away the miracle of treasures before my eyes. I swung my flashlight wildly, trying to take it all in at once.

Everywhere my erratic torch beam fell reflected the dazzling gleam of gold back at me. I understood why Adam's knees buckled beneath him in that first moment. I felt myself sway, and his arm came to support me. Leaning against each other, we stood and stared in a kind of speechless, spellbound awe, drinking in the magnificence of the treasures crowding the space before us. This wasn't the haphazard jumble of artefacts crammed into Tutankhamun's tomb. Everything seemed carefully and lovingly positioned to show it off to best effect. But the quantity of items was staggering.

'Dear Lord, if this stuff ever finds its way into the outside world, they won't need just one new museum at Giza to display it – they'll need a whole city of new museums,' I murmured.

My gaze fell on a fully assembled golden chariot, carved with images of the sun-disc and inlaid with the fabulous glitter of carnelian, lapis lazuli, jasper and coloured glass. The gilded throne alongside it made the one we'd been studying in the Cairo Museum with such admiration seem a rather amateurish imitation. I found myself revising every definition I'd ever known of the word exquisite. Not one was adequate for the purpose. This stuff was the epitome of perfection ... flawlessly painted and inlaid ornamental caskets; translucent alabaster vases, intricately carved white ivory chests; finely wrought chairs; a golden inlaid couch with a row of sun-discs serving as the headboard; jewelled stools of all shapes and design; and solid gold statues with obsidian eyes gleaming in the torchlight.

'It makes Tutankhamun's tomb look like a prop room for a theatrical production, full of replicas and fakes,' Adam whispered alongside me.

I knew immediately what he meant. 'It's almost as if he wanted to bury all the most spectacular items here – the most precious jewels with his most "precious jewels" and was quite content with the cast-offs for his own tomb.' Like Adam my voice was pitched at a whisper. I don't think we could have spoken in everyday tones had the rotation of the planets depended on it. It was as if we'd trespassed into a deeply holy place and whispering was the only way to preserve its sanctity.

'I've always felt a bit sorry for Tutankhamun,' Adam murmured. 'His seemed such a tragic little life, especially with what we've discovered from the papyri. But if this was his achievement, the legacy of his short reign, it's nothing short of a triumph.'

'But how on earth did he manage it?' I gaped, looking at the stunning array of treasures spread before us. The vast chamber was rectangular, perhaps thirty feet long by twenty feet wide. It was carved from the living rock of the cliffs behind and underneath the upper terrace of Hatshepsut's temple. Every inch of space contained a priceless relic from the Amarnan court. It was positively stuffed with them. Unlike in Tutankhamun's tomb, nothing was left in pieces. Every item had been reassembled, including the golden chariot, the ritual couch, a huge solar boat longer than a modern canoe, and a scale model of a city complete with palaces and temples, wrought entirely in gold. This must surely be Akhenaten's virgin city of Akhet-Aten immortalised in the precious metal. My poor fevered brain was still struggling to take in what I was seeing. These were riches beyond belief.

'I think Ay gave us a clue to that in his testimonial,' Adam whispered. 'If he could hire a workforce in secret to literally change the shape of the Valley floor to hide Tutankhamun and Ankhesenamun's tombs from discovery by Horemheb, then I imagine he and Tutankhamun did similar here. Perhaps the workmen were blindfolded on their way to and from the temple, so they could never be sure where they were. They may have imagined they were in the Valley. And, when their task was complete, no doubt they were dispatched to the granite quarries of Aswan or the salt mines up north near the Dead Sea.'

I shook my head in wonder, despite the casual disregard for human labour Adam had speculated. Tutankhamun and Ay had pulled off a miracle. Their "precious jewels" had rested here, hidden and undisturbed, for close on thirty-three centuries.

Something about this thought knocked the stuffing out of me. My legs gave way, and I dropped heavily onto the stone floor beneath me, feeling flushed and feverish and out of breath.

'Merry, are you ok?' Adam's concerned face swam in and out of focus in front of my bleary eyes. He uncapped the water bottle and shoved it into my shaky hands. 'Here, drink some of this.'

Obediently I took a sip; but it wasn't the airless, bone-dry atmosphere of the chamber that got to me. I suddenly appreciated it for what it was: a tomb. 'Adam, do you think they're here?' I rasped.

His eyes were huge and luminous in the torchlight as they rested on mine. 'Yes,' he said quietly. 'They're here. I'm sure of it.'

All at once it dawned on me what a tomb was. I'd trooped in and out of several on my visits to the Valley of the Kings, gawping at the painted reliefs, agog at the size and depth of some of them. But I'm not sure I'd ever fully seen or appreciated them for what they were. Even inside Tutankhamun's, where, uniquely, his body still rests, it was more like visiting a tourist site than a ... well a ... 'Adam, we're inside a grave,' I said chokingly. 'Somewhere beyond this chamber are the mummified remains of perhaps the most beautiful woman in history and one of its most controversial men. We're standing on the threshold of their crypt.'

I've never been a great believer in the supernatural or the occult. But suddenly it seemed to me a whole gallery of ghosts was peering down at us. I fancied I could feel the eyes of Hatshepsut, whose temple this was we'd broken into. Then came Ay and Tutankhamun, who'd somehow led us here. Or was it Howard Carter who'd done that? Was he looking over our shoulder too? Did he know this discovery had the potential to forever cast his into the shade? He'd known this place existed from his own translation of the papyrus, and he'd helped us find the Mehet-Weret key. But could he have had any idea about the immensity of what was here?

Whatever; his wasn't the ghost bothering me right now. Two more were making their presence felt; and quite right too, considering we were intruding on their everlasting rest. 'Perhaps we shouldn't go in,' I said softly. 'They've lain here for eternity. Who are we to disturb them?'

'They're dead, Merry' Adam murmured, cupping my face in his hands and peering deep into my eyes. 'They're not in a position to argue.'

'So why do I feel like they're watching us?'

Something of my trepidation transmitted itself to him. We hovered in the doorway like two startled rabbits who'd bounced in front of the farmer's double-barrelled shot gun and didn't know which way to turn.

'Think of it this way,' Adam said after a while. '…If Howard Carter and Lord Carnarvon hadn't taken the papyri from Tutankhamun's tomb on their unauthorised nocturnal visit back in 1922, this sepulchre would have been discovered ninety years ago. Do you think the excavators back then would have shared your qualms?'

'Maybe not,' I admitted. 'But it doesn't feel right. I feel like an intruder, trespassing on a sacred burial place. We've read Ay's scroll. We know how important it was to him and Tutankhamun for all this to remain hidden and undisturbed.'

Adam shifted from his crouching position to sit on the hard stone floor beside me. He draped one arm across my shoulder. 'You've hit upon the most profound ethical dilemma facing all archaeologists,' he smiled. 'Can it still be classed as grave robbery when more than three thousand years have passed, or is it the search for historical knowledge, and does that somehow justify the sacrilege?'

My eyes seemed drawn to the golden throne standing on the stone floor a few feet away. Tutankhamun's version was a pale imitation. In the work of art before me the royal couple were etched onto its backrest with such skill it looked more like a photograph than a carving. The sun-disc illuminated them from above and they seemed luminous with life, glowing with power, radiant with religious conviction, and resplendent with love. Nefertiti and Akhenaten in their prime, despite the somewhat distended and elongated bodily proportions favoured in the Amarnan iconography. It took me long moments to drag my gaze away from that shining image and back to Adam's face. When I managed it, I found I was looking at him though a sheen of tears. 'Part of me thinks these beautiful objects should be on show to the whole world – protected in a museum as an everlasting tribute to this most remarkable age and the larger-than-life people who populated it,' I said. 'But a bigger part of me thinks they deserve peace and enduring escape from the indignities of DNA testing, CAT-scanning and the mawkish gaze of the masses.'

Adam's arm tightened around my shoulders. 'I adore you, Merry,' he whispered. 'And I don't think I could have put it better. You and I are of one mind, as usual. So, I suggest we stick to Plan A. I reckon we should treat this visit as having one purpose in mind, which is to return to its rightful place the papyri our friend Carter took from Tutankhamun's tomb. Perhaps, in the great scheme of things, our unauthorised nocturnal visit here can somehow atone for his all those years ago. Let's see it as coming full circle. We'll leave the papyri here, lock up behind us and leave.'

I gazed at his handsome face, shadowed in the torchlight. 'Do you think we're strong enough to carry this secret with us our whole lives?'

He grinned at me. 'Well, I haven't given up on the idea of the co-written novel. Perhaps we could write it from Tutankhamun's point of view and call it Tutankhamun's Triumph …? If some enterprising archaeologist is minded to wonder where we got the inspiration, we can leave all the investigations to him or her.'

The weight lifted. This was a plan I could live with. It somehow released me of the awesome feeling of responsibility so I could enjoy the here and now. 'Ok, let's have a little look around,' I said, feeling happier.

But still the first few steps into that relic-packed chamber were choked with emotion and uncertainty. The immensity of history crashed over me, leaving me weak and quivering. My whole being was alive to the possibility the last footfalls in this place were Tutankhamun's; the last lungs to breathe this dead air his. The sensation of time collapsing like a concertina was overwhelming and made me feel a bit drunk. How was it possible for thirty-two-or-three centuries to feel but a heartbeat? It was as if Tutankhamun had locked this place up yesterday, and we'd returned today. My brain couldn't conceive of the passage of time in between. I felt I ought to be able to reach out and touch him. I was breathing the same air, treading on the same excavated rock, looking at the same priceless objects, positioned exactly where he'd left them. I could touch the things he'd touched, my fingerprints merging with his. It seemed somehow our lives were inextricably linked, yet we lived in different worlds, different ages. Here, in this timeless, eternal place, I felt I could retrace my steps up the corridor, out into the Hathor Shrine and somehow find myself in 18th Dynasty Egypt. The modern 21st century seemed a far-off place viewed from the shadowy depths of this ancient sepulchre. Tutankhamun couldn't have conceived it. But it was my reality; yet now, somehow, impossibly, so was this.

The last time anyone breathed the air in this place, its occupants had been dead maybe a handful of years. They'd walked and talked and ruled the world within living memory. The number of centuries since then was almost inconceivable. Yet here I was among priceless objects that were theirs. Akhenaten rode in this chariot, his hands clinging to the golden frame. Nefertiti sat on this couch and selected rings and necklaces from this casket with its solid gold Aten-shaped clasp. They'd lived among these objects. Each was a silent witness to their everyday lives. It brought them close. Time was an irrelevance.

A strange euphoria took hold of me. I felt myself immortal, transcendental, eternal. Did Howard Carter feel this way? He'd shared the experience of stepping across the threshold of time. How many people can claim they've crossed more than thirty-two centuries with a single footstep and entered a place with ancient life still clinging to it?

With such thoughts to occupy me, I moved through the chamber, swinging my flashlight hither and thither; each artefact seeming more remarkable than the last. I was beyond words now – there simply weren't superlatives worthy of the objects illuminated by my torch. My eyes weren't equal to it either. It felt more like I was absorbing it all through my pores.

At the end of the chamber was a narrow opening in the far wall. 'I reckon this is it,' Adam murmured, taking my hand. 'The burial chamber.'

Hardly daring to breathe, we squeezed through the gap. It was a much smaller rock-cut room. The immediate difference was the plastered and painted walls. The vaulted ceiling was a deep cobalt blue intricately patterned with neat yellow stars. But it was the walls that immediately caught my attention. Instead of the conventional rows of mortuary deities drawn from the ancient Egyptian Pantheon of gods and goddesses so typical of the tombs I knew, the walls were filled with images of the pharaoh and his queen. The colours were fresh and bright, as if the ancient artisans had laid down their paint-pots just yesterday. An enormous yellow sun-disc filled a huge upper-section of one wall, casting its life-giving rays on the royal couple lifting their hands towards it in worship.

But the walls didn't distract my eyes for long. Two huge sarcophagi filled the space in front of us.

'They're here,' Adam breathed. 'I'd thought they might be in separate chambers. But they're both here – literally alongside each other.'

Both granite coffins shone with the patina of polished rock as we trained our flashlights on them.

'This one's smaller,' I said, running my hand in a soft caress over the smooth surface of the fashioned rock that stood as high as I did.

There was just a single line of text around the upper rim. 'Well, I'm no great reader of hieroglyphics,' Adam said. 'But even I can recognise the titles of Nefertiti.'

I tried to imagine her, the most beautiful woman in history, desiccated and decayed within her mummy wrappings inside this stone sarcophagus and any golden coffins it may contain. Was it possible any of her renowned beauty had been preserved by the ancient mummy-maker's skill – or was she as grotesque as some of the ghoulishly pickled forms I'd gawped at in the Cairo Museum? It was another of those unanswerable dilemmas. The skill of the ancient morticians was beyond question. Yet to gaze on an unwrapped mummy was to look at an ancient relic from which all vestige of humanity was long gone – impossible to imagine the living, breathing, thinking, feeling being who once occupied those brown and parched remains.

I wasn't sure whether it was a blessing or a curse that the most beautiful woman in the ancient world had been preserved thus.

Adam was tracing the hieroglyphs with one hand, *"'Here is the Heiress, Great in the Palace, Fair of Face, Adorned with the Double Plumes, Mistress of Happiness, Endowed with Favours, at hearing whose voice the King rejoices, the Chief Wife of the King, his beloved, the Lady of the Two Lands, Neferneferuaten-Nefertiti, May she live for ever and always.'"*

A shiver went through me.

'You know, there's debate among scholars about whether she died before or after her husband,' Adam said softly. 'Some even suggest she ruled briefly in her own right. Whatever, my bet is that Akhenaten himself ordered those words for her sarcophagus before his death, and before Tutankhamun conceived of the idea of moving them here away from the destructive hands of their enemies.'

'And his?' I asked, moving sideways so I could shine my flashlight on the gleaming stone of the heretic pharaoh's final resting place. 'What does his say?'

Adam shone his flashlight this way and that, illuminating the huge granite sarcophagus that stood inches taller than he did. 'Nothing,' he said at length. 'There aren't any inscriptions at all. But look at this …' He shone the beam of light at the two corners of the huge granite box visible from where we were standing. 'These carved images at each corner are of Nefertiti. She's shown with her arms outstretched providing protection to his mummy in the roles traditionally played by the female deities Isis, Nephthys, Selket and Neith. It must mean he already saw her as a divinity by the time of his death.'

We stood there in a humble silence, heads bowed, paying our respects.

Then I heard a sound that made my blood run cold.

'Adam, what was that noise?'

I couldn't have been more terrified if I'd heard the sound of breathing coming from inside the coffins. But the noise was behind us, beyond the outer chamber. Someone was moving along the corridor.

Adam clutched at my hand. 'Oh my God Merry, unless that's Ahmed, I think we've been caught.'

We turned and stumbled back through the gap into the outer chamber. My heart was thumping and my stomach churning. I was dizzy and nauseous with fear. I clung to Adam's hand as if it were a lifeline and followed him across the chamber, dreading to see Mustafa Mushhawrar shining his torch into our guilty eyes.

It was almost a relief when Hussein Said's pot-marked face leered at us out of the shadows in the corridor. Let's be honest; his turning up here was almost predictable. There was a hideous inevitability about it. He seemed to be able to sniff out our whereabouts with the deadly accuracy of a heat-seeking missile.

'This man is turning into a bloody nuisance and a bad penny all rolled into one,' Adam muttered. 'How the hell did he get past Ahmed?'

Hussein was standing on the other side of the pit shaft, his bulky frame blocking the corridor. He was wearing trousers and a filthy T-shirt. One hand waved a torch and the obligatory knife at us. My body temperature dropped by a few degrees when I saw what he was holding aloft from the other. It was one of Adam's replica Aten discs.

'Please tell me he doesn't know what to do with that,' I pleaded.

He barked something at us in Arabic.

'What did he say?'

Adam had been taking language lessons from Ahmed. He wasn't fluent like Ted or Jessica, but he could make a pretty good fist of it.

'He wants to know what we've found. He said he's been staking this place out since we were here the other day. He knew we'd be back, so he's been waiting and watching. He's asking if it's a tomb.'

I was starting to wonder if he was telepathic. He certainly had all the villainous instincts of a tomb robber, with an unswerving ability to pick up the scent of buried treasure. 'So, what do we do now?'

'We've got to work on the principle he doesn't want to be caught here any more than we do. He's a wanted man with a price on his head. We've got to hope it means he won't blow the whistle on us.'

'Ask him what he wants.' I said.

Adam said something in careful Arabic and listened to the growled response.

'He says he wants us dead and rotting like sheep carcasses.'

'Charming,' I muttered.

'And he wants gold.'

'Well, he can't have it!' I said stoutly. 'Tell him Ahmed knows we're here and will swoop down to arrest him in a heartbeat.'

'He said he plans to be long gone before any of our friends some looking for us, leaving our bodies for them to find.' Adam translated a moment later.

We stared at Hussein and Hussein stared at us across the deadly pit shaft in a tense, glaring standoff. We were the guardians of the tomb behind us. But he had our freedom at his back.

I don't know how long it could have gone on like that, but after a few minutes it became obvious someone had to make a move. If he had a gun he could've shot us, but the knife wasn't quite so effective being waved at us from more than eight feet away.

I hadn't allowed for quite how enterprising our despicable opponent could be. He grinned menacingly at us in the torchlight and backed down the corridor towards the entrance into the Hathor Chapel.

'What's he doing?' I asked. But it soon became obvious.

Brandishing Adam's Aten disc at us, he crawled backwards through the narrow gap.

'I think he's decided to lock us in,' Adam deduced. 'He must have figured he can wait us out. We're low on water and don't have any food. He can leave us here to die of thirst and hunger, and let himself back in at his leisure, without the inconvenience of us getting in his way.'

'But Ahmed knows we're here,' I objected.

'Yes, but not how to find us! Not trapped behind the rock. Luckily our friend doesn't appear to have remembered the second Aten disc. Look, it's still there...' Adam shone his flashlight beam up the corridor. The sun-disc was sitting on the floor inside the entrance where we'd left it. 'So, we can give it a few minutes, crawl across the plank and let ourselves out, then find Ahmed and see about getting this bastard arrested.'

But we'd underestimated our intrepid nemesis. Adam was right about him locking us in. We heard the scraping sound echo down the corridor as he pressed the disc into the gash on the other side of the wall. But in the couple of heartbeats before the stone door rasped into place, Hussein flung himself through the opening, joining us in the tomb as the stone doorway closed behind him.

'I wasn't expecting that,' Adam murmured.

The Aten disc dropped onto the floor at Hussein's feet. He stooped to pick it up, and the other one, and let out a triumphant volley of guttural Arabic.

'He says he has both discs, and the knife. It gives him the upper hand. We must do what he says.'

'I accept the odds have swung somewhat in his favour,' I muttered. 'So, what does he want us to do?'

'Bring him anything gold and portable.'

'Do you have any bright ideas about how we might extricate ourselves from this situation?'

'I think our best bet might be to play along for the time being. We need to find a way to get those discs off him. Let's see if we can distract him with the glint of gold.'

Adam left me to shine my flashlight into Hussein's distant face while he retraced his steps into the tomb. He returned a moment later holding out a breathtaking golden statue. It was of Nefertiti. I could tell it was heavy by the way he was gripping it. It must be solid gold. It was an exquisite piece; a standing statue about twelve inches high. It showed the queen in her distinctive flat-topped crown, with the folds of her sheer linen kilt etched into the precious metal.

Adam held it up in the torchlight. 'Is this the kind of thing you want?' he said in English.

Hussein moved forward along the corridor until he was standing on the edge of the other side of the pit shaft. I could see the avaricious gleam in his eyes. He barked out a command.

'He wants us to throw it across to him,' Adam said. Slowly he shook his head. 'If you want it, buddy, you have to come and get it.'

Hussein raised his voice and repeated his order, waving the Aten discs threateningly.

'You know, he could still cotton onto the idea of waiting us out,' I said.

'Perhaps; so, for now our only hope is to get him this side of the pit shaft. We might be able to catch him unawares and get the discs back. Let's see if we can entice him with more of the same.' He disappeared back into the chamber and returned with another magnificent golden statue, this time of Akhenaten with his arms raised in worship. He placed both statues carefully at our feet and shone his flashlight down on them. Golden prisms of light dazzled our eyes.

Hussein was getting quite agitated if the volume and incessant flow of his words were anything to judge by.

Adam sat down and leaned up against the wall, making himself comfortable. He started to whistle. I stared at him; then dropped down onto the floor to join him. I leaned my head against his shoulder and started to hum along to the same tune. It was *Ten Green Bottles*.

Hussein was thoroughly unnerved. He waved his arms and yelled, then fell silent. There was another long standoff. We went on with our tune. I was pretty sure we were down to only three or four green bottles by now. I watched Hussein from the corner of my eye, and feigned nonchalance I was a long way from feeling.

It was a game of nerve, and we won.

Hussein switched off his torch and levered it into his pocket. But there was no way he was letting go of the sun-discs or the knife. He stepped onto the plank. We'd both crossed it so he had no reason to doubt its strength.

Adam and I both turned our heads to watch him as he put one foot in front of the other and started to cross the plank towards us.

'I'm not quite sure how we're going to manage this Merry,' Adam murmured, breaking off from his whistling. 'I think one of us might need to clunk him over the head with one of these statues. But don't make any sudden moves and make sure he's fully on this side of the pit before you take any sort of action. We're going to have to play it by ear.'

Hussein waved his knife at us in an unmistakeable "stand back" gesture.

Adam moved the statues back into the corridor behind us, and we both stood a couple of paces back from the pit shaft. All I could think of was how to grapple the sun discs off him. Perhaps we could shine our torches full in his eyes and momentarily blind him.

Hussein seemed to think of this tactic at the same moment I did. He stopped halfway along the plank and let out another stream of Arabic.

'He wants you to put your flashlight down at the edge and stand back from it.' Adam interpreted. 'Switch it off first.'

With the two Aten discs held aloft over the pit shaft, I didn't see I had any choice, so I did as instructed.

Hussein ordered Adam to shine his flashlight at the plank so he could watch his step as he shuffled along it.

We all watched him steadily placing one foot in front of the other. He was about three paces away from us when a loud crack rent the air. It sounded like a gunshot. Adam's torch beam swung wildly as he jumped violently and dropped it. Hussein's expression registered shock, then panic. The plank broke in two beneath his feet. Adam was right; it needed the weight more evenly distributed across it. I clutched at the wall behind me as Hussein screamed, threw up his hands and started to fall.

'The discs!' I yelled, watching frozen and helpless as he let them go.

Adam acted on instinct, diving across the space as if to catch a rugby ball. He missed the discs. I watched in a horror of slow motion as they bounced into the void. But he didn't miss Hussein's clutching hand. It stopped his fall but left him swinging over the shaft.

For the second time in days Adam lay stretched out at the edge of a precipice with a man dangling precariously from his grip. This time I'd quite happily have watched him let go. I may even have cheered. But sadly, I'm not sure it's in Adam's nature to stand by and let someone fall to his death.

'This is turning into a bad habit,' he grunted. 'Merry, I need you to secure my legs to prevent him pulling me over.'

I grabbed hold of Adam's legs, pressing my back against the wall for purchase, trying to lock myself in place. 'If he starts to struggle, let him go,' I muttered. 'I, for one, won't miss him.'

Adam started to heave backwards. His efforts weren't helped in the slightest by the screams our murderous friend was emitting. 'Can't you tell him to shut up?' I groaned.

Slowly, painstakingly and with an agony of strain on already pulled muscles, Adam hauled him up over the edge.

I'm not sure quite what I expected Hussein to do once he knew he'd been saved, but it wasn't to lunge at his saviour. Adam didn't see him coming. Winded, and with all his energy spent, I doubt he could have fended off the vicious assault even if he had.

I screamed a warning, scrabbling up from the floor, but it was too late.

There was a sickening thud as Hussein sent Adam reeling against the wall with one mighty stroke of his fist. Adam's head crashed against the rock, and he dropped like a felled tree, smashing his flashlight beneath him and plunging us into darkness.

Chapter 21

I was too sickened and terrified to scream. Adam's inert form laid limply on my left, Hussein somewhere just in front of him. I took three running steps to my right, towards the treasure chamber, and ran smack into the wall. I'd misjudged it. My only thought was to get away from Hussein before he rescued his torch from his pocket and came after me. My little yelp was drowned out by the sound of Hussein flinging something to the floor, where it smashed with a shatter of broken glass. His torch, I guessed. It must have broken, wedged into his pocket, when Adam hauled him over the pit ledge. He let out a vicious string of Arabic profanities, judging by his tone of voice. Using his invective as a cover, I moved again, edging along the wall, keeping my hand in contact with it to guide me. This time I nearly tripped. My foot connected with something solid, stubbing my toe. I sucked in the pain, desperate not to make a sound that would help him locate me. I bent forward at the waist, keeping one hand flat against the wall, and groped for the object I'd almost fallen over: the Nefertiti statue. I lifted it, feeling the reassuring weight in my hand, and scooped around in the blackness for its mate. I needed all the weapons I could lay my hands on. I was equally keen not to leave a handy bludgeon lying around for Hussein to stumble across.

With both statues in my hands, I edged forward along the wall, using my shoulder as a guide against the living rock until I felt the opening where it joined the chamber beyond.

Stygian blackness pushed in on me from all sides. I tried desperately to remember the layout of the vast room; where all the larger items were positioned; where, in short, I might hide.

I could hear heavy breathing closing the gap behind me. He was closer than I thought, and he didn't have the same need to keep quiet that I did. His reaching hand brushed the nape of my neck. I let out an involuntary scream and leapt forward, crashing against an object that splintered as I collided with it. One of the exquisite wooden inlaid caskets; I registered regretfully. I didn't have time to mourn the damage. Luckily Hussein's sense of direction in the darkness was no better than mine. I felt him pass me, so closely his shirtsleeve brushed my arm, sending goose bumps leaping across my flesh.

I stood stock still, holding my breath, but shaking uncontrollably. I could smell stale garlic on his breath, or permeating from his skin, or both. He was close. I daren't step forward or backwards, knowing my feet would connect with splintered wood and crunch it against the stone floor.

With senses sharpened by the loss of sight I felt the air shift close to my arm. I understood at once what he was doing. He was reaching his arms in circles, almost like a breaststroke swimmer. The blood froze in my veins. A couple of inches more and he'd find me. I had no doubt he'd throttle the life out of me when he did.

I knew I had one chance and one chance only. Still holding my breath, I raised both hands above my head. My arms shook with the weight of the golden statues held aloft. I counted silently to three, then brought them crashing down into the space where I judged Hussein to be.

Only one statue connected. The other one spun me sideways. I heard the crack as maybe a hundredweight of solid gold smashed into Hussein's skull. We fell together. I lost my balance through the force of my swing. He succumbed to the strength of my blow. Every bone in my body jarred as I crashed onto the stone floor; only to have all the breath knocked out of me in a great heaving gasp as the dead weight of Hussein's body landed on top of me. I lay like a corpse, unbreathing, pinned to the floor for long moments before my shocked brain fired into action. With a cry I started scrabbling desperately to release myself from his stinking frame pinioning me against the rock-cut floor.

It took a concerted effort to shove his unconscious body off me. Maybe I'd killed him, I wondered wildly. I've never perpetrated violence on another human being in my life. But the choice was stark and simple: him or me. I doubted he'd suffer a single, solitary stab of conscience if our roles were reversed.

Gagging with fear and repulsion and the desperate need to get back to Adam, I found the strength to wriggle out from underneath him. I groped about wildly in the dark. I'd lost all sense of direction. I had no idea where the corridor opening was. I crashed against another irreplaceable object and heard the heart-wrenching crack of another breakage. 'I'm sorry,' I whimpered, feeling about me on the floor for something I could identify to help me locate my position. 'I'm so sorry. Adam?' I wailed, hearing the terror on my voice. 'Can you hear me?'

Oppressive silence greeted my plea. Real panic descended. I was too frightened to cry; but great rasping gasps tore from my throat – somewhere between sobs and screams. 'Get a grip Merry,' I schooled myself between aching gulps that threatened to burst my chest cavity. 'You're no good to Adam in this state.'

I lay on the floor in the darkness for a moment, panting and sweating, and trying to bring myself under control. After long moments I felt myself grow calmer. I reached out in the darkness and felt my fingertips connect with a narrow curving shape. I crawled closer and explored it with both hands. It was a wheel; and the only wheels I remembered were on Akhenaten's golden chariot. I closed my eyes and concentrated. The closed eyes were unnecessary – the texture of the enveloping blackness didn't change. The chariot was positioned sideways on to the corridor if I remembered rightly. The harness was at the front, to the right of the chamber entrance. I felt my way feverishly along the wheel arch, and lifted my hands to explore the treadwell and the raised bar above it where the pharaoh would have clung for balance. Yes, I was at the back. That meant the corridor was behind me.

I retraced a couple of steps, so I was level with the wheel again. Then I dropped down on all fours and started crawling forward. My beleaguered brain told me it was only a few paces from the corridor to the chariot, yet I felt I crawled for miles. Did that mean I was in the corridor? No. At last, my groping hands connected with the wall in front of me. But I had no idea whether I'd veered left or right. I felt my way to the left, and didn't take too long to stumble into another Amarnan treasure. This time, thankfully, I was going slowly enough not to send it sprawling. Crazy, to still be so mindful of the priceless, irreplaceable nature of these relics. I reached out and made a slow searching study of the object. It was Nefertiti's jewel case. I recognised the Aten-shaped clasp on the front. It meant I'd veered right, and the corridor was behind me.

I turned around, still on my knees, and felt my way back the way I'd come, never once breaking the contact of my open palm with the living rock of the chamber wall. Finally, after a seeming eternity, I felt it disappear at right angles around a corner.

'Thank God,' I breathed and crawled into the corridor. Adam would be on my left, I knew. I'd placed my flashlight – a million years ago – on the floor at the edge of the pit-shaft. I edged forward with slug-like slowness. I had no desire to misjudge the distance and send myself hurtling forward onto those up-pointed spikes.

After an age my forward-feeling fingers disappeared over the edge into the gaping hole of the shaft. I drew in a sharp breath and stopped, motionless and rigid. The flashlight was here somewhere. I groped carefully left and right, desperate not to inadvertently knock it and send it tumbling into the abyss. It seemed a lifetime until my minutely reaching fingers connected with the smooth plastic casing. I nearly fainted with relief when they did.

Trembling and with strangely nerveless fingers I reached out and snatched it up. I was shaking so badly it took me three attempts to switch it on. When, finally, I managed it, I rolled backwards onto the hard stone floor and admired the light, thinking the pale yellowish torch beam the most beautiful sight I'd ever seen.

A moment later urgency gripped me, and I sat up abruptly, clutching the flashlight in both hands and swinging it sharply to locate Adam's inert form. He was only a couple of paces away, crumpled in an ungainly heap on the corridor floor.

'Adam?' I shuffled across to him. I didn't dare lift his head. I'd heard the sickening crunch of his skull connecting with the stone wall. And I could see the small spreading stain of blood on the rock underneath his hair. I knew better than to move him if a clot was forming. But I needed to know he was breathing. I leaned close against his face and nearly prostrated myself with thanks to all the deities of all the ages when I felt the warmth of his breath against my cheek. 'Darling, just hang in there,' I murmured, touching his beloved face and leaning forward to pepper his face with desperate kisses. 'I'm going to check on our nemesis.'

I prised myself up from the stone floor and staggered back along the corridor, dreading to see the mess I'd made of Hussein. It was fair to say the blood spreading from Adam's head wound was nothing compared to the little pool spilling across the rock from the gash in Hussein's head. But the villain had the temerity to groan even so. 'He's down, but he's not out,' I murmured to myself. I could see he was coming round, and I knew I had to immobilise him once and for all. My eyes fell to the Nefertiti statue prostrate on the ground beside me. I reached for her, but my hand froze mid-way. I couldn't do it in cold blood.

I hovered uncertainly for a while. But Hussein's next groan galvanised me into action. My eyes darted everywhere, searching for something to tie him up with. The trouble was this stuff was more than three thousand years old. It could dissolve into dust at the slightest touch. I needed something sturdy and unyielding.

I was backing up the corridor before the thought really registered.

'Adam? Can you hear me?'

The sound of the little grunt that escaped his lips was the most joyous music to my ears.

'Adam, how many fingers am I holding up?'

His eyelids fluttered open, long lashed against his pale cheeks. 'Three,' he murmured.

'And now?'

'Five,' he said. 'Merry, you know I learned to count when I was about three years old. Why are you giving me lessons now?'

I leaned forward and pressed my lips against his. I thought it might distract us both from the tears tumbling freely down my cheeks, but embarrassingly they just messed up the kiss with a load of salt water.

I took a firm hold of myself, swiped away the giveaway tears and said, 'Adam, I need your bandages. Can I move you?'

His answer was to push himself, groaning, into a sitting position. 'Bloody hell, my head's pounding fit to burst,' he grimaced. He reached his hand up against the back of his skull and stared at his open palm as it came away coated in blood. 'I should have let him fall into that spiked hole and be done with him!'

'Amen to that,' I said with feeling; 'but he's not out of our hair yet.'

Adam manoeuvred himself out of his shirt among grunts and gasps of pain. 'Ok, unwind me,' he invited.

It took time and effort to peel two lengths of bandages from his torso. But I couldn't think of an alternative. The groan echoing down the corridor from the chamber behind me lent dexterity to my fingers. Finally, Adam's scraped and bruised chest was revealed in all its purple glory; but I didn't have time to pause and admire it.

I grabbed the yards of bandages and darted back down the corridor with them, leaving Adam in darkness. Hussein's eyes were open as I approached him. His watchfulness unnerved me and gave me the strength I needed to kick him. It wasn't a very powerful kick, and it connected with his shoulder, not his head; but it was enough to immobilise him, and that was all I needed.

I sucked in a deep, nauseous breath and rolled him sideways. The vast quantities of blood were from the gash above his left eyebrow. Nefertiti had landed on his forehead, not his skull, and he'd bled like a stuck pig.

I made a great job of tying him up in the bandages, though I do say so myself. I was leaving nothing to chance.

I wound the first length around his elbows, pinning his arms behind him in the way I'd seen the enemies of Egypt tied up in the carvings on temple walls. I secured the second roll around his ankles, pulling it tight and threading it in a devilish knot no man could break free from.

He came to just as I was finishing. I stood back, well out of kicking range, and stared down at him. 'If I had a gag, I'd stick it across your stinking mouth,' I advised him, looking into his evil dark eyes. 'Why Adam saved you I will never know. You didn't deserve it then, and you don't deserve it now – so I suggest you sit quietly and reflect on your actions.'

I was aware I sounded like a prim and priggish schoolteacher, but I didn't care. He didn't understand me anyway. If he'd had the good grace to acknowledge defeat when we took the stolen papyri and the ransom money back, I could perhaps have forgiven him. But I'd never forgive him his attempt to push Dan off the cliffs above Deir el-Bahri, or for the shiner he'd landed on Jessica or, most of all, for the blood-curdling swing he'd taken at Adam tonight.

'You sit there and stew in your own juices,' I instructed him. 'At this point, I couldn't care less whether you live or die.'

I staggered back down the corridor and sank onto the stone floor alongside Adam.

'That told him,' he grinned.

'Adam, are you alright?' I asked urgently. 'That was one almighty clunk on the head he gave you.'

'Well, let's see,' Adam said, straightening. 'I'm locked in an 18th Dynasty royal tomb, bleeding copiously from a gash in the head, and with my bruised and bloodied torso on display. But these are not the full extent of my ills. It strikes me we might be entombed here forever, our only means of escape languishing among spikes at the bottom of a deadly pit shaft more than a hundred feet deep. We have a few mouthfuls of water left at best and no way of letting anyone know we're here. All things considered; I'd say I'm feeling remarkably chipper.'

I pondered this for a moment. It was a pretty accurate summing up of the situation. But somehow the horrors of a few moments ago had gone. With Adam compos mentis again, I felt downright cheerful.

'I'm wondering if we should bandage up your head,' I remarked. 'I don't like the way it's oozing blood. I should have thought of the before I used all the bandages tying up our filthy friend over there.'

'There's still the one tied around my arm from Youssef's knife wound,' Adam said helpfully.

'Hmm,' I said, unwinding it. 'Your run-ins with the dreaded Said brothers have left you a bit the worse for wear. This dressing's been so much a part of you over the last few days I've stopped noticing it.' The knife wound, being a week old, was healing nicely. I wish I could've said the same about the gashes on his chest, which were revealed in all their livid glory. How he'd hauled Hussein up from the depths with bruises and abrasions like this across his skin I will never know. I kissed him with all the passion the sight of his battered body aroused in me, then turned the bandage over and wound it around his head. The gash was on the back of his cranium, above the nape of his neck. He was lucky; a crack on the head like that could have killed him. I secured the bandages on his forehead, neatly tucking in the ends like every good nurse should. 'Ok?'

He grinned broadly up at me. 'If we get out of here alive, please will you remind me to get into another life-threatening scrape with all possible haste. It definitely brings out the best in you, Merry. I could sit back and enjoy your tender ministrations all day!'

I leaned forward and kissed him again, then settled myself on the floor alongside him. The beam from our single remaining flashlight penetrated the shadows all around us. The parched heat of the corridor was really quite cosy. 'How long do you think the torch will last before the battery goes flat?' I asked.

'Perhaps twenty-four hours,' he replied with a small shrug. 'I think we'll find the thirst will set in before the darkness does.'

For some time, we didn't speak.

'We can die in each other's arms, Merry,' he said at length. 'It's an oddly consoling thought. And, you know, we're in pretty good company. I mean, forget the hideous Hussein. He's a bit of a blot on the landscape, admittedly. But if we must pass into eternity in a hidden rock-cut tomb, I can think of worse people we could share it with than Akhenaten and Nefertiti.'

'That bump on the head was worse than I thought,' I murmured. 'Adam, you're delirious.' I found the water bottle and uncapped it. There were less than a few sips left. 'Here, have some of this; and then perhaps we can put some energy into figuring a way out of here.'

He took a tiny sip and passed it back to me. 'We need to try and make it last.' He moved to get up, reeled and sat heavily back on the hard stone floor. The colour drained from his face.

I stared at him in alarm. 'Adam?'

'Dizzy,' he muttered, closing his eyes.

It was the jolt I needed, spurring me into action. 'Are you ok if I leave you here in darkness and take the torch?'

'I'll be fine,' he murmured. 'Just give me a moment to get my strength back and I'll join you.'

One look at his ashen face told me that wouldn't be happening any time soon. What I needed was a rope. Something I could secure around one of the heavy solid gold items in the treasure chamber so I could lower myself into the pit shaft and recover one of the Aten discs. Then I needed to find something to replace the plank, so I could go for help. Adam was in no fit state to start bodysurfing across whatever makeshift bridge I could fashion. Ahmed was out there in the guard post near the car park. I glanced at my watch. It was approaching dawn outside. He must be starting to wonder what was taking us so long. Never had the saying *"so near and yet so far away"* held such poignancy.

I was past the point of seeing the treasures as sacred and untouchable. The damage I'd done already made me feel sick at the sacrilege, but in that moment, looking down at Adam's white face, I knew all the fabulous objects in the tomb put together were worth less than his life. If I had to tear the place apart, I'd do it if it meant I could get him out of here.

I staggered back into the treasure chamber at a half-run. Giving the inert form of Hussein a wide berth, I jerked the flashlight in all directions, looking for anything that might help me. Behind the golden throne the torchlight illuminated a wooden box that had split open, perhaps from centuries in this stultifying dry atmosphere. I caught sight of what looked like a fragment of cloth, sewn with golden spangles that glittered in the light of my torch beam. I knew swathes of linen were found in Tutankhamun's tomb. Hope surged, and I darted forward and prised the split wooden casket apart. But no sooner did my fingertips reach for the fabulous cloth than it dissolved in a shower of soft, powdery dust. The little sequins scattered across the floor in a shower of glitter, as if Tinkerbell had appeared, waved her wand and let loose a cloud of tinkling fairy dust.

I gasped in horror and jumped back. Dust caught in my throat, and I choked. I was parched and thirsty, but I'd left the water with Adam. In any event, he needed it more than I did.

I flashed the torch beam wildly this way and that again. This stuff was fabulous, remarkable, but no bloody use to me at all.

Hours later I stood back with the dead air of centuries clogging my throat and gave in to the defeated tears spilling from my gritty eyes and making tracks down my dusty cheeks. I'd searched through every casket, box and basket in the place. I knew I'd done damage, despite my desperate attempts to be careful. I'd come across jewellery too exquisite for words; unearthed games boards and writing palettes; little alabaster pots with the musky odour of ancient perfume still rising from the carved stoppers, and eye-popping ceremonial daggers encrusted with semi-precious stones. But no rope. And nothing light enough to lift or long enough to stretch across the perilous pit shaft.

I stumbled back into the corridor. Adam was lying pretty much in the same position I'd left him. He hadn't touched the water. I knelt down, lifted his head onto my lap and unscrewed the cap. His eyelashes fluttered open. 'You need to drink,' I said softly.

He stared at me for a long moment. 'Am I dead?' he asked at last.

'Not yet,' I murmured, feeling tears well up again.

'Oh,' he said. 'It's just you're shining like an angel Merry, all golden and glowing.'

I looked down at the coating of dust clinging to me. Small particles of gold dust shone from my clothes and bare arms.

'I had a small mishap with a ceremonial robe,' I admitted.

'You look beautiful,' he murmured. 'My golden angel.' And he closed his eyes again.

This time my throat clogged with more than dead air.

'Please Adam,' I pleaded. 'Stay with me and drink some water.' I lifted the bottle to his mouth and forced some between his dry lips. I watched him swallow and let out a heartfelt sigh of relief. I wondered how many more minutes that thimbleful of liquid had bought him. I took an equally miniscule sip myself. It was barely enough to moisten the inside of my parched mouth, but I closed my eyes and gave myself up to the sheer pleasure of the wetness on my tongue.

'Maybe we should switch the torch off to preserve the light a bit,' Adam suggested after a while.

I was reluctant, but I knew he was right. I needed to rest in the hope I'd get a fresh burst of energy and think of another way of getting the Aten discs out of the pit. I'd need light for that. I stretched out flat alongside Adam and put my arms around him. He let out a little sigh of pleasure.

'Mm, you know of all the ways of departing this mortal coil, there are worse ones I can think of,' he murmured.

I gazed at his pale face in the torchlight for a long moment, imprinting every feature on my memory; then snapped off the flashlight switch, plunging us onto darkness. I kept the torch in my hand, a sort of talisman. For a long time, I lay still and listened to the regular pattern of Adam's breathing. There was no better sound on earth.

I must have slept, for when I opened my eyes again it was with the cramped, stiff feeling of muscles protesting too long spent in one position on the hard stone floor. The darkness was thick and absolute. The air remained hot, close and musty. I imagined being entombed here, without the benefit of a sarcophagus to wither up in. In this dryness our bodies would desiccate not rot. It was small consolation. I wasn't ready to die – not here, not anywhere.

Adam's breathing was regular but sounded shallow to my emotionally attuned ears. My numbed fingers closed over the flashlight and, pointing it away from us, I switched on the beam. It was definitely not as bright as before.

I eased my aching arms from around Adam's body. He murmured a small protest and opened his eyes. 'Good morning beautiful,' he whispered.

I glanced at my watch. 'It's not morning, it's late afternoon,' I said. 'Come on, we need another sip of water. After this there's only enough for one more each.'

He pushed himself into a semblance of a sitting position and groaned.

'How's your head?'

'Just about ready to explode,' he muttered. 'I'm seeing stars; put it that way.'

He accepted the water bottle and took a tiny sip, then handed it to me and I did the same. The few hours of oblivion had done me good. With a renewed sense of purpose, I kissed Adam's dry lips and left him alone in the dark again. I wasn't prepared to just sit there and wait for death to come on swift wings to take us. If there was a way of getting at those Aten discs, I was determined to find it or die trying.

Hussein's eyes opened when I shone the flashlight on him. He watched me as I entered the treasure chamber. 'If we perish down here, it will be all your fault, you stupid imbecile,' I croaked at him. But after that I ignored him.

He'd die first; and that was fine by me. I wasn't wasting a drop of our precious water on him; that was for sure.

This time I headed for the burial chamber. I knew there was nothing in the treasury to help me. Despite the dire straits we were in, it was still a curiously awe-filled experience to squeeze through the narrow gap and join the controversial pharaoh and his famous queen in their final resting place.

'I'm sorry to disturb you, but I'm searching for some way of setting us free,' I murmured. It struck me thirst might be sending me barmy. I was holding a one-sided conversation with a pair of ancient corpses. But the running patter of my mumbled monologue somehow settled my nerves and made me feel better. 'It's just I vaguely remember seeing something else in this chamber, besides your two huge stone sarcophagi. But, as you may recall, your royal highnesses, Adam and I were interrupted in our exploration by the unwanted arrival of our deadly enemy. He's pursued us with the same sort of malicious intent I imagine Horemheb had when he made it his mission to destroy you and your immediate successors.'

I squeezed around the edge of Akhenaten's larger sarcophagus and my waving torchlight caught on the glitter of reflected gold I thought I'd noticed earlier. It was some sort of shrine, if I was any judge. If Adam were with me, he'd know immediately. I had no idea of its significance, or why it merited its special place in this inner chamber alongside the earthly remains of the "precious jewels". All I cared about was that it was covered in a thick, tightly woven cloth, tightly sewn with glittering sequins. The fabric had something of the appearance of golden-threaded hessian.

I reached out and brushed my hand against it, holding my breath and expecting it to disintegrate in a puff of shimmering dust like the ceremonial robe. The fabric shifted and glittered under my touch, much as a sequined ball gown might, but it didn't shatter or dissolve. It simply swung back in heavy folds over the shrine as I pulled my hand away.

I could have shouted with triumph. But some last vestige of brainpower reminded me I was in a sepulchre and shouting was probably inappropriate. Besides which, I needed to conserve my energy.

Gasping at the weight, I dragged the folds of draping cloth off the shrine, bundled it under my arm and trailed it back through the gap in the wall and across the treasure chamber.

Adam opened his eyes in the bouncing torchlight as I approached him. 'That beam is definitely getting dimmer,' he said matter-of-factly. 'My God, what's that?'

'I need to make a rope,' I grunted, weighed down by the gold-sequinned bolt of cloth. 'I'm hoping this will be long enough.'

He stared at me, immediately divining my purpose. 'If you think I'm going to let you lower yourself into that pit shaft dangling from a three-thousand-year-old shroud, you've got another think coming.'

I blinked at him, feeling hysteria bubbling up in my throat. 'But I have to get the discs or we're never going to get out of here.'

Something of my agitation transmitted itself to him. 'Ok, bring it over here. Let's see how strong it is.' He pulled at it, with his fists clamped into the fabric. 'Wow, remarkable!'

'I was kind of thinking we could tear it into strips and knot the strips together to make a rope,' I explained.

'I don't think this stuff's for tearing,' he said. 'It's like woven chain mail.'

I remembered the jewel-encrusted knife. 'Wait there!' I ordered and set off into the treasury again. It took me a few minutes of frantic searching to relocate it among the boxes and caskets of jewellery, pectorals and precious unguents. But finally, the glittering object was in my hand. I wondered briefly whose fingerprints had had left their mark on this golden handle before mine but didn't pause to speculate for long. We had work to do.

The woven gold thread of the ancient fabric was almost impossible to cut. Adam tried sharpening the knife blade against the stone floor, but it became obvious very quickly we had a long and tedious task ahead of us. The dribble of water left in the bottom of the plastic bottle tempted and mocked us. But we didn't dare drink it. Once it was gone, it was gone. But all the time there was a small quantity remaining we could kid ourselves we weren't going to die anytime soon.

We took turns, working the blade of the dagger through a few inches of the spangled cloth at a time. I think we both knew it was hopeless. But it gave us a desperate kind of focus.

I could see Adam's strength failing. I had no idea how much blood he'd lost from the gash in his head. His hands were trembling, but he tried hard to keep them clenched so I wouldn't notice.

I decided there was a grim irony in that the only bit of ancient cloth we'd found didn't dissolve into a puff of smoke at the slightest touch, instead being strong enough to withstand the blade of a knife. 'Perhaps it's the pharaoh's curse,' I muttered darkly.

Adam smiled at me in the fading torchlight. 'Well, we'd already decided we wanted to keep this place a secret. There's no better way of achieving it I can think of than getting entombed in it. Let's face it, we were in some doubt about whether we were strong enough to lock up behind us, walk away and never breathe a word to anyone. Getting stuck here kind of guarantees it. The papyri are safe now.'

A heavy weariness descended over me, and I felt my eyelids droop. 'I wonder if we'll just go to sleep and not wake up,' I mused.

'So long as you're in my arms at the time, it's fine by me,' he murmured.

'Do you wish I'd never got locked up in Howard Carter's house and found those hieroglyphics,' I asked softly.

'No Merry, I don't – because then I'd never have met you. I told you I could die happy after these last few weeks with you, and I meant it. I wasn't aware I was tempting fate quite so recklessly, but it doesn't make it any less true.'

There didn't seem to be much left to say after that.

I tucked myself alongside him and we fell into a kind of waking stupor.

I don't know how much later it was that a small sound brought me sitting bolt upright. 'Adam, did you hear that?'

He muttered something unintelligible and took a bit longer to ease up into a sitting position.

I strained my ears listening and started to think my fevered imagination was playing ghoulish tricks on me. It was Hussein, I decided. He must have rolled over and brushed against something. But I could have sworn the noise came from the opposite direction, on the other side of the pit shaft.

I was just about to subside back against Adam in an agony of despair when I heard it again. It was a scraping sound. In fact, it was a scraping sound I recognised; that of something grinding against rock. It sounded just like an Aten disc being pressed into a gash in the stone wall. But I knew that was impossible since both Aten discs were languishing in the depths of the pit shaft.

My poor overwrought brain was incapable of making sense of it, but I counted the seconds none the less. It took about five of them before the ancient mechanism ground into action, I recalled.

Adam and I were clinging to each other in the dying torchlight, our eyes trained on the darkness of the corridor on the other far-off side of the pit shaft where we knew the opening to be. I heard the rasping sound first; quickly followed by a vertical strip of light that slowly opened up into a square radiant with the blinding light of what seemed a hundred flashlights.

One of those flashlights sent its beam along the corridor and smack into our eyes. But I didn't need to be able to see to know whose light it was blinding me. 'Meredith,' a familiar voice barked impatiently, 'this whole getting locked-in malarkey is turning into a disturbingly bad habit of yours. It's really becoming quite a chore having to ride to the rescue every five minutes.'

Second only to the sound of Adam's breathing, I don't imagine the heavenly choir of angels could have sounded sweeter to my ears than Dan's voice did in that moment.

'What on earth are you doing decked out in a gold lamé bedspread?' he enquired after a moment's pause as the flashlight ran all over us.

I could imagine we must look rather fantastical. The huge bolt of sequinned cloth was draped all around us, and back along the corridor. It glittered and shone quite spectacularly in the torchlight.

'I knew he'd find us,' Adam murmured happily alongside me.

'Liar,' I croaked.

'Not at all,' he said. 'He owed me one for rescuing him from the clifftop. And let's face it, you mean more to him than most. I'll bet he's been turning the place upside down. Ahmed must have raised the alarm ages ago. I'm just surprised it's taken them so long.'

Dan crawled through the opening and stood shining the torch along the corridor at us. Then he bent down and scooped something up from the floor. As other bodies squeezed through the space behind him waving their beams of light wildly, it illuminated the glowing disc in his hand. I was well enough acquainted with pure gold by now to know the genuine article when I saw it.

'My God Adam, he's got the Aten discs from the Mehet-Weret couch!' I gasped. 'The real ones!'

'What else was I supposed to do, woman?' Dan growled, hearing me. 'It occurred to me you might not have the simple sense to check your exit route before you succumbed to archaeological fever. So I figured I didn't have time to ponce about with a load of woodwork tools to create new ones.'

I let the outrageously insulting inaccuracy of his accusation go in the gaping wonder of his achievement. 'But how did you…?

I got my answer when the glowing bands of torchlight illuminated the faces all now huddled around in a little crowd on the other side of the pit shaft.

Ted and Jessica were there, of course; staring across at us in a kind of stupefied amazement, no doubt taking in the spectacle of the sequinned shroud and the jewel encrusted dagger we'd been using to tear rents in the priceless relic. Ahmed was even now trying to squeeze his bulk through the narrow opening.

'Our friend Hussein is tied up in here,' Adam called to him encouragingly.

Ahmed popped through the gap like a cork exploding from a bottle. 'I'm going to arrest dat man!' he shouted delightedly.

But it was the three other faces that made it clear exactly what Dan had been up to for the last twenty-four hours or so; and the powers of persuasion he'd put into force. I stared in turn as the torchlight illuminated the gaping faces of Mustafa Mushhawrar who'd brought us here

403

so trustingly; and then, from the Egyptian Museum of Antiquities in Cairo no less, Shukura al-Busir, who'd shown us such generous hospitality, and Walid Massri; who'd so innocently partaken in the weighing and measuring of the Aten discs.

'Well Merry,' Adam whispered. 'If ever there was a time to put your thinking cap on and your vivid imagination and story-telling skills to good use, it's now. By my reckoning you've got about fifteen seconds to come up with something convincing.'

'You know what?' I murmured. 'I might just have a go at telling the truth and see where it leaves us.'

THE END

Author's Note

Researchers have long speculated that Howard Carter and Lord Carnarvon did indeed find papyrus in Tutankhamun's tomb. Apparently, a small statement claiming that 'important papyri' had been found in the tomb was made in a dispatch in The Times after the tomb's official opening. It's possible this was a misunderstanding or even an error on the part of the copywriter; but it was not the only time the scrolls were referred to.

When the tomb was first opened, Carter and Carnarvon approached a number of experts for help in the clearance process. One of the people they turned to was Professor James Breasted, the American founder and director of the Oriental Institute of the University of Chicago. Breasted was an expert in deciphering hieroglyphs and translating the ancient Egyptian hieratic, cursive form of writing used in everyday texts. Carter is said to have summoned him to Luxor in order to study 'important papyri'.

On his arrival however, Breasted was told a mistake had been made and the items that had been taken for papyri were, in fact, simply folded bed linens and garments belonging to the king. This explanation is, of course, entirely possible. But part of me wonders…

Another suggestive anecdote about the existence of some mysterious papyri came in a letter Carnarvon wrote to the Curator of the British Museum, Wallis Budge. Announcing the tomb's discovery, Carnarvon said they had found papers that would change the thinking of the world.

If papyri were indeed found in the tomb, they have never come to light.

The looting of items from the Egyptian Museum in Cairo in early 2011 took place as described. In March 2011 the Ministry of State for Antiquities, previously known as the Supreme Council for Antiquities, published a long list of stolen items on its website. Each item I have described was on that list. To my knowledge, these stolen items have not been recovered.

The final years of Akhenaten's reign remain shrouded in mystery. Most believe he reigned for 17 years. Nefertiti disappears from the historical record in Year 14. Many theories have been put forward about what happened to her, including one that she actually achieved the status of pharaoh in her own right, co-ruling with Akhenaten and perhaps even succeeding him. Whether or not this is the case, she had to have been dead for Tutankhamun to succeed to the throne, so it remains conceivable that her mummy could have been moved along with others being shifted from The Royal Tomb in Akhet-Aten to The Valley of the Kings. Fragments of Shabti figures inscribed for Nefertiti are now on display in the Louvre and Brooklyn museums. Shabti figures were small figurines placed among grave goods, intended to act as servants of the deceased in the afterlife.

No tomb or mummy of Nefertiti has ever been found. She remains one of Egypt's most elusive and enigmatic queens.

The mysteries surrounding the tomb of KV55 in the Valley of the Kings are as Adam describes them. It does seem likely that this tomb was a royal re-burial of Amarnan family members taken from Akhet-Aten on the orders of Tutankhamun, since a fragment of his necropolis seal was found on the original door block.

Speculation and dispute have raged for over a century, since discovery of the tomb in 1907, about the identity of the body (a skeleton) found there. The tomb was clearly vandalised in antiquity. Inscriptional evidence in the tomb seems to point to Akhenaten. The results of genetic tests published in February 2010 in the Journal of the American Medical Association (JAMA) show the body to be the biological son of Amenhotep III and the father of Tutankhamun. The genetic research team, led by Zahi Hawass, former Minister of State for Antiquities Affairs in Egypt, concluded the body was "probably" Akhenaten.

But other scholars have hotly contested this conclusion. They argue the STR analysis (a method on molecular biology for comparing specific loci on DNA from two or more samples) shows the KV55 mummy is highly unlikely to be Akhenaten. They suggest an alternative family tree that is arguably a better fit to the genetic findings of the Hawass study. Enter Smenkhkare, who seems likely to have been another son of Amenhotep III and Queen Tiye, Akhenaten's younger brother.

The Hawass theory requires us to accept that both Akhenaten and Tutankhamun had secondary wives who somehow escaped the historical record. In Akhenaten's case, this wife would have been his full sister and the mother of a succeeding king. In Tutankhamun's case, a different wife would have been mother to the foetuses found in his tomb – not Ankhesenamun. This is the only way it is genetically possible for Akhenaten and Tutankhamun to have been father and son on the DNA evidence. To me, the invisibility of not one but two royal wives stretches incredulity too far.

If the KV55 mummy is Smenkhkare, as many believe, this problem goes away. The fact Smenkhkare (not Tutankhamun) succeeded Akhenaten to the throne seems to me further proof Tutankhamun was not Akhenaten's son.

If the KV55 mummy is Smenkhkare, then Akhenaten and Nefertiti have never been found.

Most historians believe Akhenaten died and was originally buried, as he intended, in his rock-cut tomb in

Akhet-Aten. His empty sarcophagus was found there, smashed to pieces. It has since been reconstructed, and now resides outside the Egyptian Museum in Cairo.

What's certain is the Aten cult Akhenaten founded fell out of favour after his death. Later kings referred to him as "the heretic" or the "great criminal". Akhenaten, Smenkhkare, Tutankhamun and Ay (the four 'Amarnan' pharaohs) were excised from the official lists of pharaohs. Instead, Horemheb was shown as the immediate successor of Amenhotep III, with their regnal years added to his. This is thought to be part of an attempt to erase all trace of Atenism and the pharaohs associated with it from the historical record.

It is not proven that Ay was Nefertiti's father, although it seems likely he was Queen Tiye's brother. What seems more certain is that he had a daughter called Mutnodjmet. The historical record also suggests a sister of Nefertiti by the same name. It is known that General Horemheb married a woman called Mutnodjmet before he took the throne. Her tomb has been discovered in Saqqara. While we can't be sure this is the same lady, it seems highly likely and would certainly tie the relationships together.

Horemheb's attempts to obliterate the Amarna period proved remarkably successful. Akhenaten was lost to history until the late 19th century when archaeologists unearthed the surviving traces of his reign.

So, where are Akhenaten and Nefertiti now?

Whilst it's possible their bodies were destroyed in antiquity, as Ay's seems to have been, isn't it far more appealing to think there may be an undiscovered tomb out there somewhere…?

I hope you've enjoyed this second book in the series following Meredith Pink's Adventures in Egypt. If so, please leave me a review on Amazon. It's always an exciting moment for an author to read a new review. I also read and respond to all comments on my website https://www.fionadeal.com

Fiona Deal, September 2012.

If you enjoyed Tutankhamun's Triumph, you may wish to continue Merry's adventures in Hatshepsut's Hideaway.

To download Hatshepsut's Hideaway from Amazon.com:
http://www.amazon.com/Hatshepsuts-Hideaway-Meredith-Pinks-Adventures-ebook/dp/B00B7PUP5M/ref=sr_1_1?ie=UTF8&qid=1435479908&sr=8-1&keywords=hatshepsut%27s+hideaway

Or Amazon.co.uk: http://www.amazon.co.uk/Hatshepsuts-Hideaway-Meredith-Pinks-Adventures-ebook/dp/B00B7PUP5M/ref=sr_1_6?s=digital-text&ie=UTF8&qid=1435481174&sr=1-6&keywords=fiona+deal

Here is the first chapter …

Hatshepsut's Hideaway

Chapter 1

Summertime 2012

The ancient Egyptian tomb felt ridiculously crowded with nine of us inside it. Actually, it was ten if you included the unconscious Hussein. To be fair, we weren't exactly crammed in. The rock-cut chamber was big enough to hold us all comfortably. The trouble was it was jam-packed with treasure. Every one of the priceless artefacts dated back to the golden age of the pharaohs. We were all edging around these inestimable treasures with as much care as if we were tightrope walking, desperate not to stumble or trip and cause even the slightest bit more damage than I had already disastrously – but unavoidably - inflicted.

Shukura, our friend from the Cairo Museum, had tears streaming down her plump face and was gulping in the stale air in a quite alarming fashion. It seemed to be stuck fast in her windpipe, blocked from making its passage to her lungs. The erratically darting beams from everyone's torches flashed wildly this way and that, trying to take it all in at once. The wonders before us eclipsed any superlative you could possibly dream up confronted with so much gold. Take the word spectacular, for example. It didn't come close. Each and every item was unique, exquisite, and loaded with a historical significance that was quite simply unsurpassable.

Walid Massri, wispy-haired and perpetually dusty-looking curator of the Egyptian Museum of Antiquities, was opening and closing his mouth in a fair imitation of a goldfish. It took him three attempts to speak. When he eventually managed it, his words came out in a kind of strangulated wheeze. 'And you say this tomb belongs to Akhenaten and Nefertiti?' he rasped at me. But he didn't wait for a response. There was no need. He had all the proof he could ever wish for right before his staring eyes. Let's face it; he'd studied Egyptology his whole life. The distinctively distorted statuary of the ancient world's most controversial pharaoh, and the fabled beauty of its most enigmatic queen must be as familiar to him as his own reflection. Both were beamed back at him in the jerking torchlight just about everywhere our flashlights penetrated the darkness. Immortalised in statues, carvings and shrines, Nefertiti and Akhenaten were everywhere. 'It's too incredible for words!' He shook his head as if expecting his vision to clear. When it didn't, he blinked a couple of times. But it was all still there, glittering provocatively back at him. 'Unbelievable!' he whispered faintly.

I brought the fading glow of my own flashlight to rest on a gilded throne with a lifelike image of the royal couple carved onto the backrest. The skill of the ancient artisan who'd created it positively radiated from the piece. Made of wood overlaid with pure beaten gold, with small details like Nefertiti's crown and Akhenaten's pectoral picked out in jasper, carnelian and turquoise, it was more like a portrait than an item of furniture. Impossible to believe it was more than three thousand years old.

I felt an explanation of some sort was in order. 'Their mummies were brought from Ahket-Aten by Tutankhamun for reburial here,' I said. I daresay I had no right to sound as normal as I did, uttering such a mind-blowing statement. But I'd had quite a bit longer than the others to come to terms with it. I had, after all, spent the last couple of days trapped in here.

'You'll find them next door in the burial chamber,' Adam supplied helpfully. 'They're lying next to each other in two huge granite sarcophagi.'

Like me, Adam had a head start on absorbing the wonder and magnitude of it all. Until a few minutes ago, we'd believed ourselves to be entombed in here together for all eternity - and without the benefit of our own pair of sarcophagi to quietly desiccate in.

Walid's throat worked convulsively. Like his colleague Shukura, it looked for a moment as if he was about to be overcome with emotion. But he kept a hold on himself and managed to bring the fishlike opening and closing of his mouth back under control after another moment or two. 'They're here?' he croaked at last. 'By all that's holy, this is beyond imagining.'

Alongside him, Mustafa Mushhawrar, of the ministry for the preservation of ancient monuments here in Luxor, settled the beam of his torch rather shakily on the gleaming model of the city of Akhet-Aten. Rendered in solid gold and about the size of a table-tennis top, it was a stunning replica of Akhenaten's virgin city, known as the Horizon of the Sun. Complete with temples, palaces, a garrison, and the dwellings of the nobles and peasants alike, it gleamed with the patina of burnished gold. 'This is incredible,' he breathed. 'Look, they've even crafted the Window of Appearances into the model. It's where Akhenaten and Nefertiti dispensed the golden collars of valour and other tokens of their appreciation to loyal subjects. Forget everything else in here, this piece alone is worth a king's ransom.'

I thought it a peculiarly British expression for a thoroughbred Egyptian to come out with. But the awed wonder in his voice transcended all subtleties of language and nationality. Impeccably attired as always in a crisp white shirt, smart coffee-coloured trousers with a razor-edged crease down the front, and crocodile skin shoes polished to a mirror-like shine, and smelling of citrus-fresh cologne, his gaping expression was distinctly at odds with his debonair appearance. Even his narrow moustache was quivering. The fastidiousness I'd sensed about him at first meeting was still there in the pristine white cotton handkerchief he was squeezing between his clasped hands. But in all other ways he was engagingly abandoned in his reaction to the staggering Pharaonic riches laid out before us.

Another voice cut into the breathless disbelief holding everyone spellbound. 'Personally, the chariot's what I'd bid for, should this crazy assortment of antique bling ever come up for auction and I happened to have a spare several million quid lying around.' This was said in a deadpan tone from the dark shadows behind the waving flashlight beams.

I couldn't help but smile. Dan Fletcher, until approximately two, or maybe it was three, days ago my other half … partner … boyfriend … whatever you may choose to call him, and now my ex, has always had a quite remarkable ability to be unfazed by life's unlikeliest scenarios. It was hard to think of one unlikelier than being hemmed in on all sides by vast quantities of treasure in an undiscovered ancient Egyptian tomb. His torch beam shone on the object of his desire with almost as much brightness as the ironical glint in his eyes.

Akhenaten's golden chariot was indeed a marvel of ancient Egyptian transportation. Fully assembled (unlike the dis-assembled jumble of jigsaw chariot pieces found by Howard Carter in Tutankhamun's tomb), it showed the wear and tear of use but gleamed with a quite excessively vulgar quantity of pure gold; inscribed with the titles of the king, and inlaid with semi-precious stones. It managed to look both sturdy and spindly all at once; strong enough to traverse rough and rocky desert terrain, whilst decorative enough to rate as an exquisite work of art in its own right.

Dan's bone-dry sense of humour is an often endearing, occasionally infuriating but fundamental part of his personality. It has the ability to cut through most things. But it made no impression at all on the gaping stupefaction of the others. Even the lovely Jessica, who seemed to me to have developed a rather serious crush on Dan over the last week or so, appeared not to notice his droll turn-of-phrase. Instead, she added the object of her own desire to his imaginary auction.

'I'd go for the jewels,' she murmured breathlessly, gazing at the golden adornments spilling from Nefertiti's ivory casket with covetous ardour. The delicate box had split apart at some point during its thirty-odd centuries in this arid atmosphere, littering the living rock of the tomb floor with exquisite pieces once worn by Egypt's most famous queen. Under the trembling beam of Jessica's flashlight, the ancient jewellery glittered with a dull fire, bursting with occasional explosions of brilliant colour where the light caught on semi-precious stones set into the gold. 'Look at that necklace…' she said. 'It's magnificent; turquoise, amethyst, carnelian and lapis lazuli, onyx and jasper set in pure gold.'

I had to hand it to her; she knew her Egyptian semi-precious stones. And I had some sympathy with her choice. Really, what woman in her right mind can resist the allure of jewellery?

Jessica lacked the regal beauty of Nefertiti as captured in the famous bust now on display in the Berlin State Museum. Cute, elfin and pixie-like are the words that spring more readily to mind looking at Jessica. But jewellery is jewellery. And I daresay some of those ear-hoops; bangles, collars and cuffs would look equally good on a pretty girl with blonde curls, a heart-shaped face and dancing blue eyes as on the stunningly beautiful black-eyed queen they'd been made for. I couldn't help but wonder briefly if they might also look rather fetching on the grubby, lank-haired, sweat-stained individual that was me. I decided a shower and change of clothes might make all the difference.

The shame of it, I suppose, was that in reality Nefertiti's fabulous jewels would spend the rest of their days under bright white lights inside the reinforced plate glass cabinets of a museum. Never handled, never worn, never warmed by the flesh of a living, breathing woman.

I shivered. One woman and one woman alone in the whole of history could lay claim to those dazzling jewels. And, as Adam had just said, she was lying in her stone sarcophagus a short distance away in the burial chamber. It was impossible to imagine how much of her renowned beauty the ancient mummy-maker had succeeded in preserving. But whatever his skill, her skin was no more capable of warming the ancient jewels than the harsh lights of a museum display case. Even so, the jewellery was hers, intended to remain with her through all eternity. I shivered again, reminded of whose silent, immortal company we were keeping.

'So, this is what Pharaoh Ay was banging on about in that crumbling papyrus scroll you found,' Dan said sagely, swinging his flashlight in wide sweeps across the treasure chamber. 'Well, he promised you "precious jewels", and he wasn't kidding around, was he? There's enough bullion in here to resolve the global debt crisis about five times over.'

Under normal circumstances, Dan's refusal to take things seriously is prone to get under my skin. He's always pooh-poohed all things Egyptological to a quite aggravating degree; possibly just to annoy me. He labelled me an Egypt-freak years ago, perhaps with some justification. I may be an Egyptologist of the strictly amateur variety, courtesy of the Internet, Discovery Channel and National Geographic, but I'm no less ardent for it. Yet despite his wry tone, I could tell he wasn't as unmoved as he pretended to be. There was a definite tremor in his torch-beam arcing back and forth.

Besides, I was feeling particularly kindly disposed towards Dan. If it weren't for him, Adam and I would still be languishing here in the stultifying dead heat of the tomb, without water, in possession of one fading flashlight with almost-spent batteries, and with the lifeblood draining out of us. In Adam's case, the lifeblood was draining out of him quite literally, thanks to the vicious clunk on the head the hideous Hussein had landed on him.

I glanced across at Adam through the shadows. The bandage I'd wrapped lovingly around his head gave him the appearance of a walking mummy bereft of most of his wrappings. He was pale, dust-coated and dishevelled. But, thanks to Dan, he was breathing and walking upright on his own two feet. Whether his renewed vigour was due to the unexpected appearance of our little band of rescuers – all seven of them – or the bottle of water Jessica had thoughtfully thrust at him and which he'd downed in one, I couldn't say. But my relief at seeing him upright again was truly heartfelt. It struck me I must rather like the bruised and battered look. To my eyes, he'd never looked more appealing or more handsome. His blue eyes were shining in his wan and blood-stained face, and his ripped shirt exposed the livid purple bruises on his chest.

I tore my gaze away with a supreme effort and refocused on my erstwhile boyfriend.

I could just about imagine the lengths Dan had gone to in the last few days to launch his rescue mission. When he realised Adam and I were missing he must have hazarded a pretty shrewd guess we'd gone tomb hunting. We'd all come to the conclusion there might be an intact royal tomb lying undiscovered in the cliffs behind Hatshepsut's temple. This was thanks to an ancient papyrus we'd found. But Adam and I had been the ones to go off searching for it in the dead of night two … or it might be three … nights ago.

We'd failed to anticipate that our nemesis, the deadly Hussein, an antiquities thief and double-dyed villain, would follow us with murderous intent. Thankfully, he'd failed to rob us of any treasure we found, leaving us rotting like sheep carcasses. I think that was the charming turn of phrase he used. But he succeeded quite spectacularly in entombing us – himself included – in among all the gold and royal regalia he'd intended to steal.

How much of this Dan had worked out I had yet to discover. But his appearance a few minutes ago, along with senior members of staff from the Cairo Museum and brandishing a couple of priceless relics originally from Tutankhamun's tomb, spoke volumes. The priceless relics – a pair of solid gold discs – worked a hidden mechanism in the temple wall. This in turn opened a stone entrance passage to reveal the tomb hidden beyond. Adam had fashioned replica discs in our quest to discover the royal burial. But Dan had somehow, unbelievably, persuaded senior antiquities officials from Cairo to fly to Luxor with the real thing stowed in their luggage.

It revealed a side to Dan I'd never even suspected was there. If things turned out as I was beginning to feel they might, then Jessica was a very lucky girl.

It was Jessica's father who responded to Dan's reference to the "precious jewels" Pharaoh Ay had promised us in the crumbling parchment. Ted Kincaid was a professor of Egyptology, retired from the Oriental Institute at Oxford University, where he'd specialised in philology. He'd moved out to Cairo a few years back, and Adam and I had enlisted his help to translate the ancient papyrus scroll we'd found.

'The "precious jewels" Pharaoh Ay referred to were Akhenaten and Nefertiti themselves,' he said hoarsely. 'Good Heavens! I dared to hope we might find a reburial. But I never dared imagine anything like this. It's a discovery beyond words. All this puts Tutankhamun's tomb in the shade.' He indicated the bewildering quantities of golden artefacts with a vague wave of one hand.

The gulp alongside him betrayed Shukura's attempts to bring her overwrought emotions under control. Ted stepped forward and put a comforting arm around her. They looked faintly incongruous standing together like that. Ted was a dapper silver-haired gentleman in his seventies, with wire-framed glasses precariously perched on the end of his nose; small and slightly built. Shukura was a pleasantly plump woman in her mid-fifties; squeezed into a too-small navy suit, with black ballet pumps on her feet and patterned headscarf wound around her head and shoulders. She wore several chunky gold rings on every finger of both hands. I knew she and Ted had enjoyed a romantic dalliance once, briefly, many years ago on an archaeological dig in Syria after Ted's wife died and before

Shukura met her husband. The bond of affection was still strong between them.

We'd made a friend of Shukura (a professor specialising in the study of ancient coins at the Cairo Museum), and an enemy of the villainous Hussein, in one fell swoop. We'd helped her to expose his gang of antiquities thieves, and to seize back priceless artefacts he'd stolen from the museum during the revolution in early 2011.

So, here we all were: a rather unlikely little band of people to be breathing the stale air of this ancient sepulchre for the first time in more than three thousand years. Shukura, Walid and Mustafa, native and professional Egyptians whom Dan had somehow persuaded to help him save Adam and me from a slow and tortuous death among this mind-numbing collection of grave goods. And Ted, Jessica and Dan; our friends, who'd shared the translation of Pharaoh Ay's papyrus scroll with Adam and me, and guessed at a hidden tomb, but never dared to imagine a find like this.

The only person showing no reaction whatsoever to the startling collection of golden objects glinting darkly at us was Ahmed, our chum from the local tourist police here in Luxor. Considering he's descended from the most notorious family of tomb robbers in the area, this was quite possibly deeply suspicious. In his defence, he was gleefully occupied resting his impressive bulk on the supine form of our nemesis, the dastardly Hussein; a man he'd been yearning to arrest for almost as long as we'd been on this incredible treasure hunt.

'And you say Tutankhamun himself brought these treasures here from Ahket-Aten?' Walid asked, still struggling to come to terms with the evidence of his eyes.

'Yes,' Adam nodded, tucking an end of his bandage that had come loose securely back into place behind his ear. 'General Horemheb was leading a campaign to topple Akhenaten's Atenist religious cult. Tutankhamun took drastic action to prevent Horemheb desecrating the original tomb Akhenaten had prepared for himself and his great royal wife Nefertiti, and where they were originally buried. He moved their bodies here in secret. It was Tutankhamun's great triumph.'

Walid continued to shake his head as if trying to clear it of tomb dust. 'Astonishing,' he said. 'Everything seems so carefully positioned, almost as if it's on display. Not at all like the jumbled assortment of grave goods in Tutankhamun's tomb. His treasures were piled higgledy-piggledy and with a quite shocking disregard for their fragility.'

I was somewhat heartened to hear him say this. It was the self-same thing that had struck me, gazing into this treasure chamber for the first time. Everything was carefully and lovingly positioned to show it off to best effect. The trouble was, now I wasn't in imminent danger of perishing in here, all I could see as I looked about in the torchlight was the damage I'd wrought. It brought me out in a cold sweat and made me feel quite sick. A casket containing once glorious ceremonial robes was hopelessly smashed, its contents reduced to a pile of glittering powder. I'd knocked over a golden shrine, now lying with one panel unhinged on the floor. And a wooden game box, beautifully carved and inlaid with exquisite hunting scenes was in bits where I'd tripped and fallen on it. My only excuse for this unforgivable sacrilege was that I'd been trying to save Adam's life at the time. He'd been unconscious for a frightening number of our hours trapped in here. Whilst I'd tried to be careful, I'd searched through baskets, caskets and boxes, growing ever more desperate in my search for something I might use to fashion a rope. I needed this to lower myself into the pit where the evil Hussein had dropped the Aten discs that would free us. I couldn't just sit about in the hope of being rescued. I had to take some action while there was still breath left in my body and enough spirit to fight the helplessness of our situation. I'd failed of course; hence my eternal gratitude to Dan for setting us free. But the wanton destruction that seemed so justifiable when our lives were hanging in the balance didn't seem half so forgivable now that we were fairly certain of seeing another sunrise.

Thankfully, the others seemed to accept these breakages as the inevitable consequence of the artefacts' thirty-odd-centuries of storage in this stagnant-aired sepulchre. Nobody seemed to be looking for a more recent explanation for the less than perfect state of preservation of some of the priceless relics from ancient Egypt's glorious 18th Dynasty.

I decided I could breathe again and allowed the awesome solemnity of the tomb to cast its spell on me once more.

'To think the last person who breathed this air might be Tutankhamun himself,' Ted said in a sanctified tone of voice.

'Along with Pharaoh Ay, who succeeded him to the throne, and helped him conceive of this hideaway,' Adam said, in no less awe-filled tones. Now he'd recovered from his frightening bout of dizziness, he seemed as boyishly determined as ever to enjoy the moment.

'I've got this strange sensation of time collapsing,' Shukura murmured alongside him, pressing a tissue against her damp cheeks. 'It doesn't seem possible that more than three thousand years have passed since someone was last in here. I keep thinking I might turn around and see Tutankhamun himself standing there.'

'I feel quite giddy,' Walid admitted. 'I've spent years of my life at the museum preserving antiquities. But some of these artefacts look as if they were used only yesterday. It brings the past crashing against us in a quite shockingly immediate way.'

'I know exactly what you mean,' Jessica breathed. 'It makes time seem so insubstantial, doesn't it? As if more than three thousand years is just the blink of an eye.'

'Does anyone else have the feeling we're being watched?' Mustafa asked a bit chillingly.

'Oh please! Let's not start imagining ghosts,' Dan said, hanging onto his dry asperity for all he was worth.

But I knew what the fastidious Egyptian meant. I, too, had experienced the unnerving sensation of ancient eyes watching and judging our trespass on their eternal rest. And there was a distinct moment about halfway through our entrapment when I'd started to believe in the pharaoh's curse. Perhaps it was more than just a load of superstitious baloney designed to scare off tomb robbers. It had seemed all too terrifyingly possible that death would come on swift wings to claim us for daring to disturb the peace of the king and his queen. Always having prided myself on being free of superstitious dogma this was a definite low point.

'It's easy to get carried away with all the treasure and forget we're standing inside a grave, complete with dead bodies,' Jessica shuddered.

Adam and I exchanged a look. We'd come perilously close to doubling the number of corpses this tomb was designed to hold.

'We're intruding on a sacred burial place,' Shukura whispered. 'I wonder if we should make an offering to pacify their spirits.'

I rushed into speech before Dan could make the comment that I knew must be scalding his tongue. 'I think it might be a bit late for that now. But Adam and I were sort of paying our respects when our heinous friend over there turned up and started throwing his weight around.'

'I've got to see the burial chamber,' Walid murmured.

'And me,' Mustafa agreed, lifting his flashlight to the far wall where a narrow opening betrayed the entrance to Akhenaten and Nefertiti's final resting place. 'I can't believe we're inside the living rock behind Hatshepsut's temple. I've worked at this site for years. In all that time I never imagined something like this! I keep thinking I'm going to wake up and find I've been dreaming.'

Adam fingered the bandage covering the wound on the back of his head. 'It's real alright.'

Leaving Ahmed on police duty guarding the still-unconscious Hussein, we edged through the close-packed chamber in single file. The dead air of centuries clogged our throats as we held our collective breath. We skirted around priceless relics from Egypt's ancient past as if they might be trip wired. None of us dared brush against anything for fear of sending one of these irreplaceable artefacts sprawling. I might add I was especially careful. Our flashlights illuminated ornate tables, ritual couches and ivory game boxes. There were carved wooden linen caskets, chests of writing implements, clay jars filled with oils and unguents, decorative cosmetic boxes, tightly woven reed baskets, and almost translucent alabaster vases. Each was an item drawn from daily life in the royal court intended to serve in the afterlife. These day-to-day pieces held an intimacy somehow more poignant than the glittering golden objects like the throne and chariot. They spoke of private moments away from the rituals of royalty and religion.

Reaching the narrow opening carved into the rock at the back of the chamber, we squeezed through one-by-one. It was a tight fit for us all inside the burial chamber as the two huge granite sarcophagi filled the small room.

'My word! Look at the wall relief!' Ted gaped.

'Unbelievable!' Walid shone his flashlight in a slow sweep on the portion of the walls visible above our heads. Bug-eyed, he stared unblinking at the exquisitely carved and painted relief. Unlike the treasure chamber, whose walls were simply chipped away from the living rock, still bearing the marks of the ancient workmen's tools, here in the burial chamber the walls were plastered and decorated; the ceiling painted with multitudes of yellow stars against a cobalt blue background.

The upper section of the wall was completely filled with a huge golden sun disc. It seemed to glow, radiating with life-giving energy, light and heat. This was Aten; the one true God elevated by Akhenaten. The traditional mortuary deities drawn from the ancient Egyptian pantheon of gods and goddesses were notable by their absence. Instead, the sun disc cast its loving rays on images of the pharaoh and his great royal wife carved into the walls. Akhenaten and Nefertiti were depicted with their arms raised in worship, hands outstretched, palms upwards, towards the reaching rays of the sun. Each sunray ended in a little hand, some holding the ancient symbol of life the Ankh. These reached down to bless the royal couple, whose upraised palms seemed designed to channel the radiance of the sun. It looked uncannily as if the ancient sun god and his representatives on earth were reaching out to touch each other.

'The colours are incredible,' Shukura said. 'So fresh and bright one might easily believe the ancient artisans laid down their paint pots just yesterday.'

This same thought had struck me, entering this sacred sepulchre for the first time. It brought the past crashing into the present again in a quite head-spinning way.

'So, here they lie.' Mustafa said solemnly, gazing at the polished granite surface of the sarcophagus he was squeezed up against. It stood taller than he did, an immense chunk of crafted stone with a thick granite lid. 'Akhenaten and Nefertiti, preserved for all eternity.'

I'd swear the same chill passed through us all at his words. We stared sombrely at the pair of great granite sarcophagi containing the earthly remains of ancient Egypt's most notorious pharaoh and his queen. I felt the full weight of history pressing down on me. Goose bumps prickled along my flesh, and I shivered despite the dense suffocating heat.

'What's this?' Dan asked, edging around the smaller sarcophagus with Nefertiti's throne names carved around its upper rim.

Adam and I followed him until we were all three of us pressed against the back wall of the burial chamber. Jessica squeezed in behind us. But there wasn't enough room for her to see the long niche carved into the living rock. It formed a kind of raised platform along the back wall. I knew exactly what we'd find resting on that chiselled dais. I'd divested it of its golden coverlet during the long hours of Adam's and my entombment. My plan had been to rip it into strips to knot together into a rope.

This hope had proved frustratingly futile. The ancient blanket was made of pure gold thread. It had been woven into a fine chainmail-like fabric; impervious to the knife I'd taken to it. It was huge, originally draped all the way across the long rectangular box it covered. I'd left it back in the entrance corridor where Adam and I had been using it a bit like a duvet in the long hours after we'd given up trying to rip it apart and before we'd been rescued.

The truth is that it wasn't a blanket. It was a shroud.

'This,' Adam said with a distinct thrill in his voice,' 'is an anthropoid coffin. See this rectangular box? Well, if you look inside, you can see a human-shaped coffin resting inside a bit like a Russian doll. See? Look, it's painted with a face and headdress, and these gold bands are meant to represent mummy wrappings.'

Dan frowned at the box illuminated in the darkness. 'So, you're telling me there are three corpses buried in here, not just the mummified king and queen we've been whispering about?' He didn't sound particularly happy about it.

'It certainly looks like it. Although I don't think we're looking at another re-burial from Akhet-Aten. This style of coffin dates from further back. I'd say the early part of the 18th Dynasty at the latest. This was probably made somewhere between one and two hundred years before Akhenaten and Nefertiti's time. How intriguing. If I could just get my head to stop pounding, I might be able to lean over and see if there are any inscriptions.'

'We need my Dad,' Jessica piped up from behind me. 'He'll be able to decipher any texts or hieroglyphs it may contain.'

'What have you found?' Ted was already shining his flashlight around the corner of the massive sarcophagus behind us.

Jessica and Dan performed a little acrobatic number, making space for the professor to come and join us by twisting around each other. I noticed she didn't let go of his hand once their contortionist manoeuvres were finished. I'd thought I might mind, but I didn't. I was much more concerned to notice the way Adam was wiping perspiration from his brow with his shirtsleeve. His eyes looked over-bright and feverish in the reflected beam of the flashlight. This could be down to archaeological fervour or a return of the dizziness that had afflicted him earlier. It was difficult to tell with Adam. His passion for all things Egyptological often put that strange hypnotic glow in his eyes.

'Good Lord!' Ted exclaimed as the beam of his flashlight further lit up the anthropoid coffin. 'What a strange thing to find in a tomb of the Amarnan period.'

'It makes me wonder if this wasn't here first,' Adam said in a hushed undertone, rubbing his eyes as if his vision was blurred. 'Maybe Tutankhamun and Ay simply remodelled this sepulchre for their own purposes, rather than go to all the effort of carving it out from scratch.'

'You know what, my boy? I think you may be right.' Ted leaned forward, peering closely at the ancient coffin with his flashlight held about an inch away from the surface. His glasses slipped in their habitual fashion to the tip of his nose and perched there precariously. I was quite distracted, waiting to see if they'd fall off. He was very quiet for a long moment, his brow wrinkled in concentration. Then he straightened and gazed back at the coffin. He highlighted a small, inscribed section with his torch. 'See here, it says, *'Neferure, everlasting beauty of Re; may she be justified; beloved of Maatkare Hatshepsut and Akheperenre Thutmosis.'*" He looked around at our staring faces. 'We're in a hidden chamber carved into the mountainside behind Hatshepsut's mortuary temple. And if I'm not very much mistaken, this is the anthropoid coffin of her daughter.'

It was at this point that Adam passed out.

To read on please download Hatshepsut's Hideaway from Amazon.com: http://www.amazon.com/Hatshepsuts-Hideaway-Meredith-Pinks-Adventures-ebook/dp/B00B7PUP5M/ref=sr_1_1?ie=UTF8&qid=1435479908&sr=8-1&keywords=hatshepsut%27s+hideaway

Or Amazon.co.uk: http://www.amazon.co.uk/Hatshepsuts-Hideaway-Meredith-Pinks-Adventures-ebook/dp/B00B7PUP5M/ref=sr_1_6?s=digital-text&ie=UTF8&qid=1435481174&sr=1-6&keywords=fiona+deal

About the Author

Fiona Deal fell in love with Egypt as a teenager, and has travelled extensively up and down the Nile, spending time in both Cairo and Luxor in particular. She lives in Kent, England with her two Burmese cats. Her professional life has been spent in human resources and organisational development for various companies. Writing is her passion and an absorbing hobby. Other books in the series following Meredith Pink's adventures in Egypt are available, with more planned. You can find out more about Fiona, the books and her love of Egypt by checking out her website, following her blog and subscribing to her email list at www.fionadeal.com.

Other books by this author

Please visit your favourite ebook retailer to discover other books by Fiona Deal.

Meredith Pink's Adventures in Egypt

Carter's Conundrums – Book 1
Tutankhamun's Triumph – Book 2
Hatshepsut's Hideaway – Book 3
Farouk's Fancies – Book 4
Akhenaten's Alibi – Book 5
Seti's Secret – Book 6

More in the series planned in 2015.

Also available: Shades of Gray, a romantic family saga, written under the name Fiona Wilson.

Connect with me

Thank you for reading my book. Here are my social media coordinates:

Visit my website: http://www.fionadeal.com
Friend me on Facebook: http://facebook.com/fjdeal
Like my author page: http://facebook.com/fionadealauthor
Follow me on Twitter: http://twitter.com/dealfiona
Subscribe to my blog: http://www.fionadeal.com